CLOSURE

ACKNOWLEDGEMENTS

This anthology would simply not exist had it not been for the administrative and coordinating work of Kadija Sesay, Inscribe Series Editor, and the meticulous editorial overview and support of Managing Editor, Jeremy Poynting. And of course Hannah Bannister, Operations Manager – the very paradigm of efficiency and sanity.

Thanks also to the placements and volunteers and staff whose assistance throughout was critical in bringing *Closure* together: Dorothea Smartt for her encouragement and support of the Inscribe writers included in the anthology, Grace Allen, (internship with University of Leicester), Jade Neilson, Matthew Bourton and Rebecca Patenton.

CLOSURE

EDITED BY JACOB ROSS

SERIES EDITOR KADIJA SESAY

PEEPAL TREE

First published in Great Britain in 2015
by Inscribe an imprint of
Peepal Tree Press Ltd
17 King's Avenue
Leeds LS6 1QS
UK

ISBN 13: 9781845232887

CONTENTS

Remembering Kahlil 'Kahls' Lewis.
Walk good, young fella. You were loved.

A NOTE FROM THE EDITOR

Make up a story... tell us what the world has been to you in the dark places and in the light. Don't tell us what to believe... show us belief's wide skirt and the stitch that unravels fear...
— Toni Morrison, The Nobel Lecture, 1993

The two-year process of selecting and editing submissions for *Closure* presented an opportunity to give some thought to the modern short story, the way it is evolving and the tendency towards increasingly rigid (some may say constricting) definitions placed on the form. It seems to me that over the past few decades much effort has been dedicated to taking the short story from the domain of being a basic human reflex and need for narrative, and relocating it somewhere that is increasingly esoteric. Writers themselves – in interviews and discussions about their art – have at times contributed to this idea of the short story as a kind of visitation experienced only by the lucky or the anointed, whilst contemporary "narratologists" have devoted serious intellectual effort to come up with authoritative taxonomies of the different types of short stories – of which I've counted seven so far.

I contend that the short story is simply the *de facto* narrative mode across human cultures and time: from the oral "folktale", myths of origin, parables designed to caution, instruct or merely stimulate insight, through to the contemporary written narratives of encounter, trauma, self-exploration and discovery that we find in an anthology such as this. I dare say that, notwithstanding

Vladimir Propp's meticulous contribution to our awareness of the universal mechanics of "story" in *Morphology of the Folktale* (1928), humans have always understood and valued its role as a way of making sense of the world, and their place in it. *Closure* is essentially about human striving.

The last anthology that featured short stories by Black British writers appeared fifteen years ago. At the time, *IC3: The Penguin Book of New Black Writing in Britain* highlighted what *Closure* still confirms: that there is no shortage of Black and minority ethnic writers engaged with the short story – writers capable of bringing a distinctive and striking fluency to the form. The current spate of short story competitions, prizes and online publishing opportunities is uncovering an undeniably rich seam of short stories by Black British writers. In fact, several of our contributors have been winners of, or shortlisted for, major international, national and regional short story prizes. Interestingly, many of these writers refer to themselves more readily as novelists, poets or playwrights, partly due, one suspects, to the fact that the short story is still perceived as not offering the same career-enhancing opportunities as the other forms of fictional output, in particular the novel.

But perhaps, with dedicated and notable collections of short stories emerging in Africa and the Caribbean by writers such as A. Igoni Barrett, Mohammed Naseehu Ali, Sefi Atta and Doreen Baingana (Africa) Barbara Jenkins and Sharon Millar (Caribbean), the same will begin to happen here.

What stood out during the selection process and the editing of *Closure* was its richness: of form and voice and tone; of stylistic and thematic range; of the diversity of subject matter, and the varying stances of the writers – ranging from the fantastical, the other-worldly, the speculative and oblique, through to the raw representation of reality.

I was interested in selecting narratives that offered something additional to good writing. I was on the lookout for pieces which, while offering the concentrated intensity expected of the short story, also gave a sense of writers setting themselves challenging places to get to, and wrestling with language or the very form of the short story in order to do it, so that the writing became an adventure. I think there are a good few stories in the anthology that fit this description, but I will leave it to the reader to decide which ones they are.

The writing has moved on from the *IC3* anthology, which appeared in 2000. There is less of an attempt by writers – overtly or through their characters – to self-define. "Black Britishness" is what it is – a lived reality that is like air or breath or blood: important, but hardly at the forefront of one's consciousness except in moments of confrontation or self-assertion, and even then, it is not always recognised as such, as we see in several of the stories.

Here, like the music instructor deciding who she wants to be, are characters more concerned with the treacherous business of confronting their own demons in 21st century Britain than in the injustices levelled against their forebears. They are recognisably contemporary: a successful female stockbroker who finds herself at an abortion clinic with a pop star and an avid churchgoer, each handling her personal crisis; a young Londoner – accosted by a local abductor and potential rapist after a late night rave – attempting to save herself by "stylin" her way out of the danger, Ananse-fashion; a male cleaner collecting abandoned hymens and through this activity learning to empathise with the many oppressions of women; a narcissistic young man who refuses to accept that the time has arrived in his life when the partying must stop and his true self be examined; ghosts who are themselves haunted by their memories of the awful tyranny they suffered in the house they occupy; a young man who cannot find the strength to break from the woman who abuses him.

And there is more – a great deal more – all intensely wrought narratives about humans engaged with the fractious business of life, some of whom are marginally better equipped than others to deal with it. None of them is completely at ease in the world.

Why the title, *Closure*? We chose it precisely because it undermines itself. Literary fiction is rarely – if ever – about closure. Rather, it is concerned with the opening up of possibilities. At best we are taken to a point of rest rather than a neatly tied-up ending. So, we were interested in the prospect of subversion that a theme/title such as "closure" might trigger in the more rebellious contributor who, we hoped, might say "To hell with all this closure bizness" and dare to offer something different and quite startling. And yes, in this anthology we have stories that were submitted in that spirit!

Good stories are unforgettable precisely because their meanings are not fixed; the pleasures, even the lessons we derive from them gain fresh significance over time. We'd like to believe that the short stories in *Closure* possess this quality. We hope you think so too.

Jacob Ross

FRED D'AGUIAR

A BAD DAY FOR A GOOD MAN IN A HARD JOB

Are not the sane and the insane equal at night as the sane
lie a dreaming? Are not all of us outside this hospital, who
dream, more or less in the condition of those inside it,
every night of our lives?
— Charles Dickens, *Selected Journalism* (1850–1870).

My 250cc Yamaha zigzags through bumper-to-bumper traffic for
three city miles of two-finger signs, horns and indecipherable
shouts from taxis and buses – the sonic equivalent of a scalpel
applied without anaesthetic. Close shave at one junction as a few
of us bikers edge to the front of the queue at the lights and
accelerate from the pack on the change to green, nearly encoun-
tering a car crossing our path. All of it caught on the speed camera.
Spooked by this I go slow all the rest of the way to my hospital
shift for a 7:30AM start at 7:40AM.

I find Ward Three and try to blend into its routine – well
underway without me. Sorry, traffic. Sorry, bike played up. Sorry,
accident delay. The nurses from the night shift hand over to the
day shift in the stuffy little office. The report comprises mostly of
who slept and who did not and who required an extra dose of
some cognitive muffler or other to invite sleep, and no news of
any new arrivals in the night. The usual routine.

I suppress a yawn. I hear from the night nurses that James slept
fine; Cheryl slept fine. That's it for them. My two charges for my
shift both off to a good start after a good night's sleep. Keep that
good luck bouncing my way for the rest of my day. Only hiccup
that the night nurses report concerns another ward. One of their

patients has gone awol and when the police find him they will bring him kicking, back to where he does not want to be – my ward, since he left the hospital without permission and must upon his return be retained on a locked ward. Maybe the police will take the seven hours of my shift to locate him and by the time they appear with him I'll be biking out of the hospital parking lot. Keep that good luck bouncing, please.

I walk with another nurse, Katie, as she checks off a name and we dispense, making sure the tablets or liquid match the name and the dose matches the doctor's prescription. Each patient takes the small plastic cup, throws his or her head back with a thank you or nod or nothing, until we make small talk to hear them talk back – a way of making sure they swallowed. James is perky today. Wants to go and play tennis, asks me if I could accompany him the short walk through the park and across the bridge over the train tracks to the tennis courts. I tell him I will find out from the doctor if that is an okay thing to do. He knows and I know that he cannot leave the locked ward and the constant supervision of nursing staff, because he was assessed as an acute danger to himself after a botched overdose. (He took a bunch of pills and made a call that was traced so that he was found in time to have his stomach pumped and get compulsorily committed to psychiatric treatment.) He took a shine to me; told me as much – that my forehead shone with my keenness as a nurse, which I took as a compliment. He has an ironic charm for a broken human, glimpses of which suggest a will to live rather than give up or opt out or whatever it was Timothy Leary advocated.

James stood there as if I should call the doctor that second. "It'll have to wait until the doctor does his rounds, James."

"Okey-dokey," he says.

Cheryl wears her dressing gown. She knows that when the day shift arrives she should rise and dress and be ready for breakfast. I will have to put that down in her notes and it will be read as a minor setback in her day. In nursing parlance, for a patient to get out of bed and get dressed means a declaration to engage with routine, however humdrum. What seems like one small step for a patient leads to one giant assumption on the part of us nurses, who are on the lookout for any such signs.

"How are you today, Cheryl?"

She says she is fine and opens her mouth lion-yawn-wide to show me that she swallowed the pills.

"I'll be back for a chat as soon as I finish with the trolley."

"Suit yourself," she quips. Oh-oh, what is up with her, I wonder, but I say nothing.

It is always best to say nothing in a profession where words can never be taken back. I look at Cheryl quizzically and glance at her feet and hands for any sign of a disruption in her composure, any dishevelled look to denote a struggle waged against herself in the form of an excessively repeated act, such as washing her hands or doing-up and undoing a cuff button until she tears her sleeve in frustration.

Katie, who stands on the other side of the drugs cart, raises her eyebrow at me and we press on with dispensing. We make small talk between the double checks of names and doses.

"Didn't I see you at the bar last night?" she asks.

"Maybe."

"It was you with the Redhead, wasn't it?"

"Maybe."

"Did you score then?"

"None of your business, Katie Murphy."

"You scored, didn't you?"

"Maybe."

Another fifteen minutes slips by before I get back to the office with the trolley, and Katie and I secure it in the drugs room. We head off to find our respective charges for a chat, which we will both record.

The nurse in charge heads me off in the corridor and steers me into the stuffy main office.

"Zack, you have to do something about your lateness. Last warning."

"Yes, Zoe. Promise. You doing okay?"

"I'm fine, except for you being late on my ward all the time."

"You want me to make up the time?"

"No, I want you to be on time."

"Will do."

"Hope so. Keep your ears open and your eyes peeled. We don't want anyone escaping like that chap from the other ward. I don't need to remind you that your patients are on suicide watch."

"No, you don't."

"And more details in your notes, please. You're still too elliptical. I know you've just qualified. You almost need to be boring in what you report to get it right. Got it?"

"Yes, Commandant. No, seriously, thanks. I appreciate it."

"Okay, now get lost."

"Yes, Commandant."

"Zoe, wiseass! Unless you prefer Nurse Ratchet."

She means the totally old school nurse who runs Ward Two just across the corridor (the one from which the patient escaped last night). That nurse would have hauled my ass on report long ago. Old school is jackboots nursing care by numbers, bingo healthcare, fog of drugs; new school is all talk-therapy and a delicate cocktail of pharmaceuticals.

A bell rings. I walk fast to the main office. Zoe answers the phone and orders me – her moon-eyes urgent and clear – to make my way to Emergency Admissions. I run, I walk – like in the Olympics. What is the nature of the emergency this time? They ask for a male nurse to be sent from each of the three open wards. I am not the most senior male nurse on duty on my ward, but Zoe specifically sends me. That can only mean one thing. But I quell my suspicion. Before I reach Emergency Admissions I hear a lone voice shouting what to the untrained ear might sound like unadulterated aggravation, but to my culturally attuned tympanic membrane is none other than that unique mix of adrenaline and scattergun unreason identified with a full blown psychotic episode. A Jamaican accent.

The banging might be feet kicking out or someone falling against corrugated zinc.

I rush into a room whose doors to the street are blocked by a police van, parking lights flashing.

The van's back doors fling open; a policeman holds them in place as it spills its contents. A black man with a goatee and a tight tangle of waist-length dreads speckled grey, curses very loudly. His cockney herders in uniform shout at him to stop hitting and kicking and they pin him to a wall. He is a big man and solid with it. He pushes from the wall and they all move like a giant spider into a table, and chairs scatter.

He is shouting as he struggles. "I-an-I man free to walk earth as I-man please and nobody can stop I-an-I dread from wandering through Jah creation. For I born free. No chains can hold I-man. I-an-I man walk in peace and wisdom flow from I-an-I pores and Jah power behind everything I-man do. Jah-Jah protection cover I-man back and walk before I-an-I."

Two other male nurses arrive at the same time as me. I know one, Rollins; the other I've seen enough times to nod to him. His name is Smyth. He tells me that this is the patient who escaped last night.

"Does he have a name?"

"Rodney Samuels."

"There goes my luck."

The police try to hold the man still across the top of a table and he sputters against a forearm that pins his neck. Remarkably, the man wears handcuffs. With his arms behind his back he still presents a huge problem. The police look at us. Rollins and Smyth look at me. I step forward.

"Mr Rodney Samuels, I'm Staff Nurse Zack Prior."

I pause to allow for an answer, for a general air of calm to prevail. Nothing.

"Call me Zack. You're safe now. Do you know where you are?"

I pause again, taking in the man. "Mr Samuels, may I call you Rodney? I will ask the police to release you but you must sit and talk to me or this won't work. Do you understand?"

He nods. The police ease their grip. They straighten their clothes and remove his handcuffs. One of them stipulates that they will go straight back on if he shows any misconduct. Mr Samuels shakes his arms and massages each wrist. He twists his neck as if righting an untidy stack of vertebrae. He stares at me, his eyes bloodshot and rheumy.

Just as the doctor walks into the room, Mr Samuels shakes his dreads, inhales deeply and resumes, "I walk without fear and only my enemy should be afraid as I-an-I bring down the walls of Jericho and Babylon fall before I-an-I. See the lamb flock to I-an-I. And when I call, my sheep hear my voice and they come to I-an-I. I-man walk in righteousness. I-an-I come to Babylon and I chant with the power of Jah in I-an-I and Babylon fall. So I will reach the kingdom of the most high and rest in His chambers."

The four police officers suppress smiles and keep their hands on truncheons, pepper spray, handcuffs. They chat among themselves, and with the doctor and nurses as we stand around waiting for the doctor to tell us what the next move should be.

The doctor decides on a course of action that is astonishingly conciliatory towards a man the size and hostility of Mr Samuels. The doctor's approach piques the nurses' interest, mine included. We glance at each other and they must wonder, like me, how this will turn out. The doctor is earnest and clear.

"Thank you for everything, Officers. Mr Samuels, my name is Dr Woolicotts. You've met Nurse Prior. And you know Nurse Smyth and Nurse Rollins. They're here for your safety. Do you remember leaving the hospital last night?"

Nothing. Rodney Samuels resumes his invective. "Any man who stand in I-an-I way must fall before my sword and eat the chaff of a whirlwind harvest for I-an-I wield the mighty sword of Zion."

The doc speaks over him.

"You're in an agitated state, Mr Samuels. I could prescribe something to help calm you down. Would you be agreeable to that? As you're aware, you must stay here for 72 hours under our observation. If you try to leave, the police will arrest you and throw you in jail and bring you before a magistrate. You heard the officer. Your best option is to cooperate with us, and together we can get to the bottom of what troubles you. Does that sound good to you, Mr Samuels?"

Perhaps, I, or one of the other nurses, or all of us, should have moved in earlier. The signs were obvious to us, but the teaching hospital we're in gets these trainee doctors from the world-renowned Institute next door. They turn up and behave like walking textbooks. We chat about it in the pub all the time – the way you can almost see the cogs of their latest untried and untested theory turning as they respond to a crisis.

Rodney Samuels appears to listen to Doctor Woolicotts but he makes a fist. He stares at the doctor but remains worryingly silent. Dr Woolicotts stands with a bit of a smile etched on his face, while he poses questions, pausing between each for a possible answer. For a while the two of them look like they're in a transaction. The doctor seems not to notice the closeness of his body to that of the agitated man in front of him. My colleagues and I take a small step forward. Mr Samuels glances over at us and the doctor follows his gaze. The doctor actually waves us away. Rollins, Smyth and I take two steps back. I glance at them and they both shrug.

Mr Samuels opens his hands in slow motion and the sight of his bright palms makes Dr Woolicotts, Smyth, Rollins and I relax a little. Mr Samuels raises his arms to chest-level and Rollins, Smyth and I are tense again. Dr Woolicotts maintains his smile and even begins to offer his right hand in a handshake of agreement of some sort.

He's light years from here, I think. Why should he want to shake your hand?

Mr Samuels leaps high in the air and, with a growl, lands on Dr Woolicotts. The two of them swing and fall and we lunge at them. Mr Samuels lowers his face to Dr Woolicotts and closes his teeth on his right ear. The doctor screams for us to help him. He struggles to shake off Mr Samuels. I hold Samuels' head in place and the doctor is smart enough, even in his distress, not to pull his head away from the vice of Samuels' teeth.

Smyth and Rollins each grab one of Samuels' arms and peel them off the head and neck of Dr Woolicotts. I push my face close to Samuels' and I shout at him in my most trained voice to let go. I repeat myself. His red eyes meet mine but do not seem to register my presence. This time I add, please. My fingers brush against a steel trap of teeth and saliva. Smyth hugs Samuels' arm, which brings him up against Samuels' body and he starts hammering his fist on Samuels' face while shouting at him to fucking release the doctor. Rollins attaches himself to the other of Samuels' arms while he uses his free fist to pound the ribs of Samuels. I pull my hand away and a lot of blood spurts from the head of the screaming doctor. I make a fist and am about to land it on Samuels' mouth when he pulls away from Dr Woolicotts, turns his head to one side and spits a small bloody mass to the floor. Dr Woolicotts rolls away from Samuels, clasps his left ear, stumbles to his feet and slumps to the ground. More nurses pour in and all of us pile on Samuels, holding his limbs and head and sitting on his midriff. He is a strong man. He tries to speak but Rollins punches him in the mouth and he falls silent. A nurse brandishes a restraining jacket and we hitch Samuels into it. Smyth injects the sedative and antipsychotic drug straight into the man's thigh, I mean right through his trouser leg. Samuels jolts but says nothing. We hoist him onto a gurney, strap him in and two nurses wheel him to the locked ward.

Dr Woolicotts' colleagues rush in and they administer rudimentary first aid and inject the remains of his ear with a painkiller and antibiotic. One of them gingerly retrieves the bloody piece of ear. They escort Dr Woolicotts to an ambulance that's always on standby, and with a flurry of sirens it ferries Woolicotts to the general hospital just across the road.

James meets me at the door the moment I unlock it and step into the locked ward. My hands are shaking. I should have joined Rollins and Smyth outside for a smoke.

James looks at me a little puzzled.

"Don't ask," I say.

"Okey-dokey. What did the doc say about my game of tennis?"

"James, you'll have to forgive me but something came up. I'll get to it now. Where can I find you?"

"Ah, here?"

"Silly question. Catch you later."

Back in the office I sit with unsteady hands around a coffee cup. Zoe, the charge nurse, pulls a chair up so close to me our knees are almost touching. She stares into my face with her big clear blue saucers. I know that professional look. We're all trained to do it to optimise empathy and leave the subject in no doubt about the caring nature of our enquiry. But turned on me like this, by Zoe, in such textbook fashion, it fills me with an urge to flick my hands with the coffee cup at her face. Yet I feel compelled, even pleased to tell her the story.

I turn away both James and Cheryl from the office as I write my report of the incident as if it were part of a choreographed scene: strictly motor activity, and the exact words I heard. No impressions, no conjecture.

In keeping with procedure, I meet Rollins and Smyth for a

thirty minute session mediated by a psychotherapy nurse. Smyth says he panicked when he injected Samuels through his trousers. He wonders why he did not wait just one more minute while he accessed Samuels' bare arms by rolling up a sleeve. Says he feels weak for panicking.

Rollins chimes in about his anger while restraining Samuels from doing more damage to the doctor. That he viewed any means at his disposal as necessary to stop what he saw as a grave danger to the doctor. Was he a bad nurse for using maximum force against a fellow human being who was not in control of his normal human faculties? The psychotherapist looks at me. I smile and say everything happened so fast, I felt shock and fear from head to toe and I felt close to everyone in the room except the person who most needed my empathy, but for whom I felt not the slightest affinity at that moment.

They all look at me. I quickly add that I know I share cultural, gender and racial affinities with Samuels, but at that moment I hated him to my core. I even felt shame at his behaviour, I say, that he somehow let the race down by his aggression towards his helpers in the midst of his despair. The nurse looks at me with eyes that suggest there's nothing they cannot and will not contain.

She nods and says my anger is appropriate and clearly I understand it and own it and Mr Samuels was lucky to have me in his corner.

Rollins and Smyth concur. We sign off and thank the psychotherapy nurse then return to our respective wards. Rollins walks with me a part of the way. He says I should not blame myself; it's the system that should be blamed for always putting me at the front of the queue whenever a black man was brought in.

"But my presence is supposed to help calm him down."

"Not in this instance, Zack. The guy was some place where we couldn't reach him."

"Yeah, I suppose so."

"Hey, I hear from Katie that you scored with the Redhead last night."

"Christ, news travels fast round here."

"How was the Redhead?"

"None of your business. She has a name, you know."

"Which is?"

"I can't remember. See you later for a quick pint?"

"Sure. Will the unnamed Redhead be there?"

"Course not. I mean, I've no idea."

"Later then."

"Oh, any word on Woolicotts?"

"They've stitched it back on. He'll be fine. Might even start to listen to a lowly nurse as a result."

Cheryl meets me at the entrance to the ward. She asks about my contacts. I say I woke up late and had no time to put them in. She says I look as if I had no sleep.

"I look that bad?"

She always starts our talks with some personal observation before launching into her feelings of despair modulated by our magic combination of antidepressants, one-on-one talks and therapy.

"Can I talk a little later?"

"But I've waited all morning to chat with you."

"We will talk, I promise, but I need to catch James first."

"He left the ward a while ago to play tennis."

"What? Excuse me a minute."

I run to the main office and find Zoe. I ask her if she knows anything about James leaving the ward.

"He left about fifteen minutes ago to play tennis. He told me you spoke to his doctor, Dr Arbutnot and Arbutnot said it was okay. He showed me a note."

"No, Zoe, what note? I didn't speak to Arbutnot. Why would James say that? We've got to find him."

Zoe calls the front desk of the hospital and they say James passed there with a permission slip from his doctor. Her eyes saucer and pool. She grabs her hair and her tone of alarm heightens.

She hangs up, throws the mobile on the desk instead of back into its charging station, snatches it up again and dials the 3-digit hospital emergency number which throws the entire site into emergency mode and alerts the police to be on the look out for a missing patient.

"Zack, find James. Hurry."

I dash out of the hospital without my leather jacket and regret it the moment I step into the cool autumn air. I shiver and realise it's not from the cold, but adrenaline. I jog up the street, cut into the park. As I run I look left and right for James. Pigeons scatter from my approach. I take the north exit and bound up the stairs of the footbridge that arches over the railway line. As I cross the old splintered planks of the bridge, I glance at the station platforms, trip and recover awkwardly. On the semi-crowded platforms I pick out a figure in white tennis clothes, standing a hundred yards away. He looks squarely in my direction, lifts his arms and waves. I grab the diamond-patterned wire fence that encases the bridge.

"James! James!"

The train rumbles under the bridge and blocks my view. As it enters the station, its brakes fill the air with a high-pitched whine. A handful of pigeons swoop from the station.

"Zack! Zack!"

I peer towards the other side of the bridge and there is James in white tennis gear, tennis rackets under his arm and a tube of tennis balls held high in the air with the other hand. He looks at me and at the train. He shakes his head and raises his eyebrows to show his surprise.

I run up to him and squash an impulse to hug him and punch him all at once.

"What are you doing off the ward?"

"I secured Dr Arbutnot's permission myself but I told a little white lie to cover your ass. I told Zoe that you called him for me. You've been busy."

He digs into his pocket and pulls out a green slip. I grab it from him. The date is today's and the signature resembles Arbutnot's indecipherable scrawl.

The train pulls away with a hum that rises in pitch as it picks up speed.

"Why would you think it was helpful to me for you to tell others that I said it was okay for you to leave the ward?"

"I like you, Zack, but you are new to the nursing game; you just qualified for God's sake. By the way, I told Cheryl to cut you some slack. She's been chasing you all morning. I'm feeling like my old self, even if you can't see it."

"I'm glad you're okay, but I'm mad at you for lying. Let's walk back."

"Okey-dokey. The tennis courts are being cleaned so I can't play anyway."

"Who were you going to play with?"

"My friend, Mr Charles."

"Not Mr Charles again, James. I thought you got over him."

"I tried but he came back for a game of tennis."

"You and I know full well that there is no Mr Charles."

"Just a minute ago, on the platform, you saw him wave at me."

"That was Mr Charles?"

"The one and only. My confidant and tennis partner."

"We can talk this one through when we get back to the ward."

"Okey-dokey."

I dial the ward. Zoe picks up. I tell her to stand down the emergency code, James is fine and we're on our way.

Zoe meets us at the entrance to the ward. A broad smile makes two slivers of her eyes. She pats me on the back and leads James by the arm to a room for a consultation. He winks at me as he follows her in. I pour myself a coffee and drop into a chair in the office to make a few notes about the incident with James. I call the locked ward to ask about Rodney Samuels. The nurse reports that he's sleeping; the sedatives have taken a hold on him and he'll be out of it for days, revived for meals and the toilet, but kept under a strict and heavy drugs regimen. That protocol for aggressive sick people ensures no more violence or break-outs, and amazingly, when patients surface from it, they behave with zest and a keen regard for life.

A rap of knuckles on the translucent plastic pane of the office door makes me look up from my scribbling. A purse-lipped Cheryl with an exaggerated hangdog look stares in at me. I jump up and pull the door open. She waits for me to say something. It's only a moment's hesitation but enough for her to turn on her heels and storm off.

"Cheryl, let's talk, now."

She spins around and her face lights up. "Really?"

"Yes, right now."

I walk with Cheryl to a quiet part of the ward, near a set of windows that look out on a patient-maintained garden. Cheryl says she feels better already and asks me how my eyes are doing.

"Fine. How about yours?"

"Not so good. I cried all day and I lost a lens. Washed it clean away."

"Why the tears?"

"I don't know; I just feel bad. An overwhelming sadness. Just want to crawl into a hole and curl up in there and never look at the world or anyone again."

"You woke up feeling that way?"

"No. It just welled up in me when James said he was going to play tennis and I realised I did not want to do anything, and I mean nothing."

"You are doing a lot, Cheryl. You're here working very hard, everyday, to get better."

"But I don't feel better."

"It comes slowly. I've seen a big improvement. Remember how you arrived curled up like a bean and wouldn't respond to all my entreaties to you to take your medicine?"

"Nope."

"You were catatonic. Didn't blink. Your contacts dried on your eyes."

"Oh, yes. You used a pipette to drop saline in my eyes with your shaky hands."

"Yep, and when the lens fell out of my glasses you helped me to look for the tiny screw and you told me about where to get cheap contacts."

"I remember we never found that screw. Didn't you use sellotape to hold the lens in place?"

"Aha. Shall we look for that lost contact of yours?"

"Don't bother. I change them daily."

"Of course. Did you go to the art room?"

"No, but I will now if you'd just shut up."

"Right, then. See you later."

"Thanks, Zack."

"No sweat."

I zip back to the office. Katie clasps my coffee in one hand as she huddles over her notes, in a pool directed from the angle-poise lamp. She looks up and says she did not want my coffee to go to waste. I thank her for her consideration. She offers to make a fresh pot and refill my cup. But I tell her to forget it. I let her know that it's late in the day and I'll need more than coffee to get over the shift. She gives me a hug, hands my cup to me and exits. I tip my head back and drain the dregs and smack my lips like I've just knocked back a shot. I resume my notes on James, with those to be made for Cheryl politely waiting in line.

I turn left from the ward into the main corridor with its six lanes of foot traffic and twin fluorescent strips evenly spaced overhead and unerringly the same lustre, night and day. I tear along at a rapid pace, weaving left and right around more casual folk. Actually, no one who works here is casual; all of us have some-where to get to by yesterday, but I'm the rabbit with the fob watch able to hop at twice their rate. A drop of water falls off my chin and lands on my shirtfront. I reach into my back pocket for my handkerchief and wipe my face.

I smell the canteen before I see it. The food and the central heating conspire to produce a witch's cauldron. Yet my mouth waters. I walk in, scan the place for a familiar face, see none and feel glad for the isolation. I join a short queue with my tray and post-9/11 plastic cutlery.

But one look at the congealed rectangular trays of rice and pasta baked under the heat lamp puts me off. I advance to the refriger-ated section, choose a triple BLT in shrink-wrap, a banana, a single oatmeal cookie, a small bottle of apple juice and cup of coffee and still the woman at the till says "anything else?" I take my seat in a corner with a view of the exit. I stretch my legs under the table, lean back in the plastic chair and pull out my mobile from my front pocket of my jeans. I dial Katie back on the ward.

"Katie, do me a favour. Have you seen Cheryl?"

"Not at the moment, but I'm at the dispensary. What about her?"

"She's on the ward, right?"

"I couldn't tell you. What is it? Should I find her?"

26

"No, I'll head back. Thanks Katie."

"Not sure what I did, but you're welcome, Zack."

I gulp my food. I drink the entire 300 mls of apple juice in one tilt. I inhale the banana – I mean divide it into three parts and each third I crush and swallow. I break the cookie into two and wash the halves down with my coffee cup.

Cheryl cries for half the day and in just a few minutes she perks up as if she'd grazed her knee in a playground. That's too much of a 180° turn even for my nursing skills. Or am I just so plugged into this place I'm unable to take a thing at face value?

Cheryl has never thanked me for anything. She takes all that I have to offer and I leave her and never fail to feel like I could have done more for her, listened better, coined a more inviting observation to engender further disclosure from her. But she thanks me. That can't be right.

I drop the tray off at the counter section for dirty utensils, recycle my apple-juice plastic bottle, and toss my napkin, free-throw-style, into the wide dustbin beside the exit. I make a quick pit stop at the gents. Wash my hands and rejoin the corridor. It's about a dozen sets of overhead lights from the canteen to Ward Three. I make two steps to cover each set of pairs and another two steps to close the gap between lights. I know this because Cheryl told me a while back that that was how she made it from the ward to occupational therapy. If she did not count her way along she would feel too much panic to make the short trip. The same mathematical logic powered her life around the ward. At the collapse of that system she took to her bed and her bones locked in foetal pose. She moved so well with her counting system, as I walked with her and talked, that I forgot that she could hold a conversation and still count her way along. I had been so keen to make up for not seeing her all day that I forgot to think about the fact that where we went to sit and talk must have been measured by her, and that as we talked she must have counted out those steps without variation. To break up her code we sometimes practised walking up and down and deliberately taking an extra step after she arrived, and rather than having to start the whole thing all over again I'd get her to talk to me about something – anything long enough for the anxiety to quell, hence our detailed and repetitive discussions about contact lenses.

I take a right into the ward and Katie tells me she looked for but could not find Cheryl and she wonders if Cheryl might have gone to art, psychotherapy, or some other appointment. She is still saying something to me but I turn and run to the front desk at the hospital entrance. I jump to the front of the queue of three people, announce that it is an emergency and ask the porter if a patient fitting Cheryl's 5' 5", shoulder-length frizzy brown hair, thin with a prominent nose and slightly red blue eyes left here in the last quarter-hour or so. The porter scratches his head.

"Was she wearing a red cardigan?" I ask.

He nods.

"Are you sure?"

"Of course I'm sure."

I run to the station for the second time that day, but this time I hear sirens. I turn into the park. Pigeons flare up around my feet. I bolt for the north exit and meet people coming from the station. I listen for the sound of a train, thinking I might hear the wheels on the track as it pulls away, but the traffic from the nearby road drowns everything but the sirens. Passers-by talk excitedly; some cover their mouths or wipe their eyes. I stop an old man in a hat and long raincoat. I ask him what's wrong. He pulls his arm away from my grip, lifts his hat and runs his hand through a mop of silver. He gestures with his hat at the station.

"A young lady…" But he doesn't say anymore. He tugs his hat forward on his head and leaves me on the spot.

KAREN ONOJAIFE

HERE BE MONSTERS

Arike's Daily Plan of Action:
1. Drink herbal tea
2. Ten minutes of each of the following, **every** morning:
   a) meditation
   b) yoga
   c) writing positive thoughts in journal
   d) looking in mirror while repeating positive affirmations
   e) listening to life-affirming songs
3. Treat others as you would like to be treated
4. Surround yourself with positive things and people
5. Engage in a spiritual practice
6. Exercise!

2 likes, 0 comments

★

It's the summer. You start to think about your chakras.

You are committed to becoming your best self. You are not going to care that everyone else is getting married or getting promoted, or having babies or buying houses. When friends tell you their good news, you will simply smile and then send them gift baskets of baked goods because your heart is a lighthouse, as opposed to say, a black dwarf star, colder than Alaska.

You make an action plan and you post it on this blog, for the sake of accountability. You have precisely ten followers, so if you mess it all up, hardly anyone will know.

You pick a Monday morning to start. By the time you've had your tea, meditated, yoga'd, journaled, affirmed yourself and listened to upbeat songs, you're late for work. You dash into the office, stressed as fuck and you imagine your chakras curling like week-old lettuce.

"What would Oprah do?" you ask Tieu Ly when you call her later that day.

"She would write a cheque to her hurt feelings, dreams and aspirations," Tieu Ly says.

This is an example of why you don't tell Tieu Ly everything and why you most certainly will not be sharing the details of your action plan. Your best friend can be an emotional terrorist.

★

Things Arike is scared of:
1. Dying
2. Dying alone
3. Dying before having the chance to clear browser history

5 likes, 2 comments

★

It's still summer. One of your teeth just crumbles in your mouth while you are eating a Toblerone. You are forced to go to the dentist for the first time in years and he tells you that the tooth has to be extracted. You are consternated because:
   a) who wants to hear that kind of thing and
   b) your dentist is very good looking.
It seems cruel that the one time that you have a legitimate reason to be close to someone like this, he is charged with the task of looking into your decaying mouth.

"Let's talk about your diet," he says.

You don't feel like talking about the cakes, sweets and chocolate that you eat and eat every day, but only when you are by yourself. That you eat until your stomach is a tight, anxious drum and your mind is a flat, sleepy haze. Besides, you never throw up. That would mean you have a problem.

"I like the odd sweet every now and then," you say.

He swivels away in his chair, in an attempt to disguise his eye roll, while you wonder when you developed a taste for wildly pointless lies.

He listens to Shostakovich while he works. As he creates a

30

temporary filling, you are already thinking what to tell your friends. You know you will make something up, because to explain that your teeth are rotting out of your head because of something that you did is too forthright and truthful.

★

Arike's online dictionary
"Leap and the net will appear" – an utterly meaningless phrase. Speakers of sentences such as this should be bestowed a swift chop to the throat.

7 likes, 0 comments

★

Your chakras will not realign themselves and so you turn to self-help books, but these tend to make your chest grow tight with rage. The books all seem to have been written by and for those with no concept of real life. It's easy to have an epiphany concerning one's spiritual purpose while residing at an ashram, herding goats on an Italian hillside or building wells in a West African village. You are yet to ascertain how any of the "lessons" these authors impart can be applied to your existence in a poky flat in Haringey that you can barely afford.

It seems to involve a lot of magical thinking and the last time that worked for you was when you were six years old. You happened to say out loud that you were hungry and your father, who was passing by, agreed to make you a cheese sandwich.

"It's not you," Tieu Ly says later that evening, when she calls you from LA. "The people who write these books don't come from immigrant families."

You think of your own parents, whose thirst for risk was exhausted five decades ago when they crossed an ocean to come to live in this cold place. The stuff they went through they barely ever talk about. But if you were to tell them now that you wanted to resign from work so that you could write? Fiction, of all things? All your aunts and uncles in Nigeria would agree that you had murdered your parents.

Like you, Tieu Ly did what she was told (in her case be a doctor, in your case, an accountant), as opposed to what she wanted. Still, she consoled herself by moving overseas to practice medicine.

That way, she can tell herself that their victory (and by implication, her defeat) was only partial.

As old as you are, you still don't like to disappoint your parents and they are happy not to be disappointed. See? It all works like it's supposed to.

★

Arike is: not in love with the modern world

4 likes, 0 comments

★

There are so many things that you love about having a job, save for the actual job itself. The office is That Place and your life outside it is Everything Else. You spend between 8 to 11 hours a day at That Place and a lot of the time you think you manage it pretty well. By manage you mean that you are able to maintain a reasonable façade despite the fact that you feel you are on the verge of fucking up on an epic scale at any given moment.

This is what you are thinking about as you make your way to work this morning, and so you almost walk past the two kids squalling on the pavement, a worried woman standing next to them. They are two little black kids and the woman, white, is in her early twenties. She asks them questions in a soft voice but this just makes them cry even louder. You're tempted to keep walking because you're already late, but you imagine your nephew and niece standing there and you come to a halt.

They are brother and sister, both under ten. You work out that they got off at the wrong bus stop and so have no idea how to get to school. They don't know their address, they don't know anyone's phone number; all they have in their satchels are sandwiches and colouring books. They are holding hands like something out of a fairytale, except there are no breadcrumbs in a forest, just dog shit on asphalt and the relentless scream of traffic along the main road.

Eventually, you and the woman decide to call the police. The kids have stopped crying now, but the older one, the boy, has a look on his face that says he knows he's going to catch a world of trouble for getting lost. You want to fold him into you until he stops worrying, but are aware this would be alarming. So, instead, you tell him about the time you got lost when you were a kid and how you thought you'd get in trouble too, but that your mum was so happy to see you, it's like she forgot to be angry.

He doesn't look reassured, so you tell him not to worry, but then you don't know his life. You reflect that it's adults coming on like they know everything that leaves kids fucked up. The amount of lies kids must hear before they're ten years old, just so an adult can have the satisfaction of making them feel better! Or for the adult to make themselves feel better. Because, maybe, that's what you wanted more than anything else. Not to have to think about what might happen to that kid when he got home.

The police finally arrive – two white men, one old and one young, in a squad car with tinted windows. They are nice enough but it makes you wince when they make jokes about putting the kids in the back of the car. The little girl smiles the way kids smile when adults say funny stuff that they don't understand, and the boy just looks up at the clouds out of the corner of his eye.

The officers make more jokes about the kids being excited to go for a ride, and perhaps they are, though maybe these kids have heard bad things about the police and maybe ten years from now the boy will be stopped and searched every other time he steps out of the house. You think that maybe you're the crazy one for thinking these things, seeing that the three other adults in this situation are just standing around and laughing because problem solved, job done.

Back at your desk you get a client call. You give out your e-mail address, which includes your first name. You spell it out for what must be the thousandth time this year.

"Oh, that's a nice name!" the client says. He asks you where it's from and you tell him. When he asks you how long you've been here, you're confused.

"At this firm?" you ask.

"No, no, in the country?'

You laugh as you tell him "all your life" because he's just an old man being curious, a man who is always sweet to you on the phone but there's something about the exchange that leaves you sour.

You end up snapping at Seth, the new guy, because he takes far too long at the colour photocopier. You bore eyes into the back of his head as he hums and jingles change in his pockets and you know he is trying to piss you off now because he just started work today and so there is no way he can legitimately require a run of 100 copies of anything, let alone double sided paginated prints in laminate.

Prick.

★

Arike's daily plan of action (autumn edition)
1. Get out of bed
2. Anything thereafter is a bonus

   12 likes, 3 comments

★

Seth is OK, you guess. By that you mean he is ridiculously attractive. You don't know why you didn't see it before. The worst thing? You are not sure if he actually is that good looking, or if it is the fact that Seth is the only man in an office full of women. After a while, you don't care either way.

When Seth talks, everyone draws near him like flowers turning their heads to the sun. He has the sense to be embarrassed about it so you don't hold it against him too much. Besides, he was the only one to laugh when you made that joke about ThunderCats in the team meeting, plus he smells really nice and yes, sometimes your bar really is set that low.

★

Arike is: too lazy to hate herself but is well versed in malign neglect.

   7 likes, 0 comments

★

You go to a presentation on domestic violence after work which, okay, you knew was not going to be any kind of stand-up comedy show, but still. It takes about ten minutes before you want to start crying, but you have a rule about not doing that in front of strangers unless you are on public transport.

It makes you think of stuff you hadn't thought about in years. The things that made you want to live small and quietly, so that you could pass unnoticed. The times you heard the thumps through the wall or the sound of her screaming. The way you got that pounding in your chest before you walked into the front room, trying to conjure the right words to make him stop.

He could walk into a room and the air would be sucked out for several seconds – the time it took to gauge his mood. You loved him then and you love him now, but it's easier these days – old age has softened him. He talks about his childhood and you think of that stupid phrase "hurt people hurt people" but back then, you didn't see the hurting, he was just a hurricane.

You remember the afternoon you went to her in tears and asked her to stop fighting with him – as if she had chosen their worst moments. She said yes, anyway, and it wasn't until years later that you realised what you had asked. For her to bite her tongue and step on her heart. She did it, for you, despite the hurt.

Now you're older, you want to take it back. You want to tell her to save herself because you would love her through anything, but you don't have the words. Instead, you try extra hard to make her happy. So you really mean it when you say you'll lose weight.

★

"How I learned to stop worrying and to love the complete waste of time that is the annual performance review" – a memoir by Arike A. Douglas.

10 likes, 4 comments.

★

You and Seth have been hanging out. He's funnier and kinder than you expect. He catches you near hyperventilating in the stairwell as you try to prepare for your work appraisal, but he doesn't say anything stupid, just sits down next to you.

"Tell me something," he says, knocking his knees gently against yours.

"Years ago, I read about a woman who smelled oranges every time she was about to have a *grand mal* seizure. Now, although I don't have a history of seizures, I can get very stressed if I smell citrus fruits without any easily identifiable source for the aroma."

Seth looks askance at you, before moving the conversation onto the appraisals.

"You nervous?" he asks.

"Nope."

"So you're ready?"

"Well, hold on."

"Maybe this'll help," he says, bringing out his MP3 player. You watch him as he slips a pair of headphones over your ears and the world is muffled for a few moments while he cues the song.

Part of you is worried he might start playing gospel music as a prelude to asking if you've accepted Jesus as your personal saviour, so you're pleased when you hear M.O.P's 'Ante Up'.

He grabs your hands and pulls you up with him so you're both standing. He takes a step back, rocks his head from side to side and bobs his shoulders up and down. You shake your head when he beckons for you to do the same.

"Sorry… this is what, exactly?"

"This is you, getting ready to kill it when you walk into that room. I'm serious; it's an all-rounder. Need to prep for a difficult meeting at work? Ante Up. Need to tell your boy that his girlfriend's been stepping out on him? Ante Up. You're in Sainsbury's near closing time, there's one last lamb rogan josh on the shelf and the only other person with their eye on it is the guy with a crap trolley. You going to let him steal from you?"

"Don't eat meat," you shrug.

"You're being obtuse, but that's cool," Seth says, feinting a few jabs. "I'm just going ante up. You going to let trolley guy steal that vegetable biriyani from right under your nose? Or are you going to…?"

"Kidnap that fool!" you say, gun-hands blazing. Your exclamation coincides with the appearance of Martin from Accounts in the stairwell. Martin looks disturbed, but he is the kind of person who feels that two black people in conversation is the equivalent of a riot, so you can't feel too bad. Seth does not help matters by giving you a conspiratorial grin and a thumbs up, but you can't stop yourself from giving an obvious wink in return as you make your way up the stairs. Martin's gaze shifts between the two of you while he grips several A4 ring binders to his chest.

"Hey, Ari," Seth says. He waits for you to turn round before he continues. "Sweep the leg."

You turn back, shaking your head but only because you don't want him to see the smile on your face. You sing the lyrics under your breath all the way to the meeting room and it's only about five seconds before you open the door that you remember to take off the headphones.

★

So the Thanatos urge is a real, scientific thing. Who knew?

3 likes, 2 comments.

★

It's not that you want to kill yourself but sometimes you imagine doing something like jumping off a building, for no reason whatsoever. A friend tells you that there is a name for this – the Thanatos urge. It's a little hard to take seriously – it sounds like it should be the name of some indie band, or a disaster movie from the seventies.

Still, in a way, it makes you feel better – that there is most likely a name for every thought and feeling a human has ever experienced. No matter how reckless or dark your thoughts get, someone else has been there first.

Yet this does not help much on the days when you cannot get out of bed, or when you cannot stop crying, or when you cannot stop eating, when so many ugly thoughts are roiling through your mind and you can't touch anything or anyone because then you would make these things stupid, ugly and worthless too. At these times, you get scared because you feel yourself getting worse and you wonder what your rock bottom will look like, or if you will know when you get there. At these times, you imagine your mind is like one of those old fashioned maps from when the world was meant to be flat and people would designate the unknown territories with the legend "Here be monsters".

★

You know how sometimes you force yourself to get all dressed up and go out and it turns out to be amazing and you think, "Wow, I should make the effort more often!"? Yeah, me neither.

12 likes, 4 comments

37

★

You are invited to a hen party. It's at a club in Wood Green called Vibez and it is as terrible as you expected. You have been glittered. The elastic cord of angel wings cuts into your back. A pink plastic Stetson sits uneasily atop your Afro.

After some dancing, the drinking games start. You can time the precise moment the mood slides from aggressive hilarity into maudlin regret.

Ireti talks about how she thinks she made a mistake in marrying Ben. Anna talks about how sometimes Fergus hits her – just little slaps – when she doesn't want to have sex. Nailah talks about her Dad's dementia and how hard it is to keep him safe at home. Farzana worries that her girlfriend will leave her for the colleague who just got a PhD. Abiola talks about – well, by now you have stopped listening because you have never understood this part – why women always have to break themselves into little pieces before they can find one another palatable. They look at you expectantly but then "Candy" comes on and you lead the charge back onto the dance floor so that you can fail spectacularly at executing the perfect Electric Slide.

★

Arike's thought for the day: a penis is not penicillin.

24 likes, 15 comments

★

You are at another domestic violence seminar, held in some hall near work, when you realise that Seth is also in the audience. When he starts to speak you hold your breath, worrying that he's going to be one of those "let's play devil's advocate" men but instead he talks, in a shaky voice, about when he was younger, moving from safe house to safe house with his mum and kid sister, because of his Dad.

It's hard to imagine Seth, with the long stretch of his body, big hands and easy smiles, as a little boy. Scared silent. Wetting the bed.

You bump into each other on the way out and he starts a little at the sight of you. You just nod at him because you are not sure what to say about what you have just heard.

He doesn't seem to want to talk about it either, suggesting

instead that the pair of you buy tickets for the fireworks display at Alexandra Palace that evening.

"Buy tickets?" You look at him sideways. Why pay when you could watch it from your bedroom for free? And so this is what the two of you do, your windows thrown wide open so that your room fills up with the scent of November.

Someone in your block is playing The Eagles and you both surprise each other by knowing all of the words to "One of These Nights". Seth goes for the big finish and you have to say that he matches Don Henley's falsetto in enthusiasm at least, although perhaps not flair.

You don't know if it's that or the fireworks that makes you kiss him. It's a good few moments before he kisses you back but then he is everywhere and for once you are not thinking about what your body looks like because it is too busy moving; under him, above him and alongside him in a dark room with the whisper of your skins outpacing all other noise.

He stops in the middle of things, puts a hand on your thighs and looks up at you.

"What?" you ask him.

He's completely still aside from his thumbs which swipe warm semicircles, sweeping higher and higher until he is tickling the place where your thighs join your pelvis.

So you stare back although you should have known he wouldn't mind that. You think he wants you to look at him when he is like this, sprawled out on his back with you on top of him and a half smile on his face. You move to get off of him but he tightens his grip on your legs.

"Stay a minute," he says.

"Just don't do that."

"Look at you?" he asks.

It feels silly to explain how you find it hard to hold anyone's gaze or how you're not used to anyone observing you for more than a few moments at a time. You worry that if he looks at you long enough he'll sense all the mess that is inside and he will either flee or try to fix things, when really all you want to do right now is come.

So you lean forward and you kiss him. He tries to say something at first but your mouth swallows the sound and it's the sweetest thing you've ever tasted. This is when you realise you're in trouble. Well, more so than usual, anyway.

JENNIFER NANSUBUGA MAKUMBI

MALIK'S DOOR

Katula was in the corridor staring at Malik's bedroom door when she felt her heart curl in anger. But then, just as quickly, the desire to leave him went. It was replaced by guilt. *After all he has done for you*, and her heart palpitated and she perspired all over her neck and shoulders.

"I am leaving," she said, glaring at the closed door. "I am."

She turned away and walked towards the end of the corridor where their warm clothing hung. She sat down on the chair and started to pull on her winter boots. For the past four years she had swung with indecision like a bell around a cow's neck: *nkdi* – I am leaving, *nkdo* – how can I leave? *Nkdi* – this time I am going, *nkdo* – which going?

The problem was that Malik had outfoxed her. But it was not the clear-cut, cutthroat outsmarting of certain marriages she knew back home. There was immeasurable kindness blended with concealment, immense generosity mixed with touches of arrogance. Her biggest problem was her empathy with Malik's reasons for outfoxing her. In his position, she suspected she would have done the same. All these things haunted her every time she decided to be strong and leave him. Strength, in these circumstances, felt like ruthlessness.

Even then, as Katula pulled on her gloves, the words of her mother – a perpetual cynic whose children each had a different father – came back to her. "All things we humans do are selfish."

"Even love?" Katula had asked.

"*Kdto!*" her mother had clicked her tongue, "Especially love! It hides its selfishness behind selflessness. I got tired of pretending."

Katula clicked her tongue because, in the beginning, her own love for Malik had been selfish. She needed to be convinced that Malik's selfishness was bigger than hers.

Her glance fell on his door again. All the doors in the house were closed but his door seemed barricaded against her. Katula stood up, wrapped a scarf around her neck and called out, "I am going out to post the postal ballots."

A brusque "Yeah," came from behind the door.

Yeah? Perhaps he had not heard what she said. Sometimes, because of her Ugandan accent, Malik did not catch her words and said *yeah* to save her from repeating herself. She was about to rephrase the statement when the door opened a crack.

"Kat," his voice floated down the corridor, "I might be gone by the time you return. I am going to spend the weekend in Sheffield with my mother." His eyes were the marbles Katula used to roll on the ground as a child. He blinked, looked away, then looked at her again.

"Okay," she said, not *You're lying. You think I am dumb? I know you're going to him.* "Say hello to her for me."

Katula was sure that Malik was going to see his friend, Chedi. Chedi had been to see them two days earlier. There was a pattern: Chedi came, then, soon after, Malik visited his mother for a few days.

Malik withdrew his head and the door closed. It opened again and his head popped out.

"I'll leave the money for the plumber on the table." His smile spread slowly, folding back his cheeks. It flowed into his eyes, lifting his brows and creasing his forehead. Somehow, it loosened the tension in Katula's jaws.

"Thanks."

"I'll leave an extra fifty pounds in case you want to go out with the girls to the movies or for a meal."

Katula dropped her gaze to the floor and ground her teeth. Her resolve returned. But when she lifted her head, she smiled. "You don't have to."

"I am your husband; I take care of you."

The smile still on his face, his head withdrew and the door clicked shut.

Katula picked up the house keys, sucking her teeth in contempt at her weakness. Outside, she was met by the whiteness of winter. The snow in her garden was fresh, crystalline and untrodden. The layer on top of Malik's Citroen-Picasso was pillow-thick. It felt still outside, in the way only winter stills the world. She heard footsteps crunching and looked up. A woman and a child in Eskimo coats walked past. Across the road, a double-decker bus pulled up hissing and sneezing. Steam burst from its backside like a farting elephant. The bus pulled away and the air became still again.

I am leaving him this time.

Katula had met Malik back in summer 2001 when she was still being hunted by Immigration. It was like duka-duka – being on the run during war back in Uganda. While there were no bullets to dodge or jungle set alight to flush you out, it was war nevertheless, because when Immigration captured you it did not matter whether you were in pyjamas or a vest, they took you as you were. In Britain, Ugandans would sell each other to Immigration for a fee – the way neighbours sold supporters of the opposition back home. There came a time when Katula envied the homeless derelicts she saw on the streets – the sheer waste of a British passport.

She was a student nurse when her visa expired. To renew it one needed to show a minimum of six hundred pounds in one's account. Katula earned twelve hundred pounds a month. She had thought this steady income would suffice. As a precaution, she sent her renewal forms to Immigration by post because a Ugandan friend had warned, "These days Immigration keeps a van ready and running: any failed applicants, *toop*, into the van and *shoooop* to the airport, there and then!"

After a month, UK Border wrote back to say that at one time in the past six months her account had dipped below six hundred pounds. This demonstrated she did not have sufficient funds for her maintenance in Britain; she should leave the country imme-diately. Instead of moving back to Uganda, Katula moved house and changed her job. Friends advised her to hook a British husband as soon as possible. To buy time, she sent her passport back to Immigration to appeal, using a friend's address.

Malik fell like manna from heaven. Katula was at the bus-stop

43

outside the University of Manchester Students' Union, when she saw him across the road standing near Kro Bar. He stood out because he was exceedingly tall and held his head as though the clouds belonged to him. Aware that she was less than pretty, very good-looking men made Katula uncomfortable. He was young and handsome and therefore not a potential husband. Katula targeted white pensioners who, she had been told, had a penchant for young African women.

She was scanning the horizon for a 53 bus when she realised he was standing at the stop, smiling down at her. Katula looked at him, thinking irritably that God must be in an extravagant mood.

"I think I know you: are you Ghanaian?" he asked shyly.

"No, Ugandan," Katula smiled back.

"You remind me of someone from Ghana."

"A lot of people mistake me for a Ghanaian."

Now that Katula looked at him properly the man was odd. His jeans were not cropped as she had thought: they were shortened rather shabbily above his ankles and he wore a long shapeless shirt. Was he trying to hide his good looks? His thick beard and clean-shaven head made Katula realise that he could be Muslim.

She asked, "Are you Tabliq?"

"What is that?"

"A sect of devout Muslims."

"I am Muslim, my name is Malik; how did you know I was Muslim?"

Katula explained that in Uganda, Muslims who wore their trousers above the ankles and had a beard were Tabliq. Tabliqs were devout and no nonsense.

Malik's interest was piqued. Was Uganda a Muslim country?

"They are a minority."

He asked her name, and when she told him he said, "African names have a meaning, don't they – what does Katula mean?"

Katula loved the way he said her name, Kat-u-la, as if it rhymed with spatula. She laughed but it came out as a cough. How do you tell a man you want to ensnare that your name is a warning? She decided that the truth – however absurd – was the best option.

"Katula is a tiny green berry which on the outside looks innocuous but bite into it and it will unleash the most savage bitterness you'll ever taste."

Malik threw back his head and laughed. "Who would call their child that?"

"To be fair…" Katula felt she needed to defend her parents, "the katula berry is very good for heart problems. My name is a warning against underestimating people because of their size." Now she too laughed. "You know Africans – we don't dress things up."

"Did you know that man, Idi Amin?"

Katula was fed up with people in Britain dredging up Amin. Every time she mentioned that she was Ugandan, Amin was thrown at her, as if he was her country's chief cultural export. She smiled and said that she was born just after Amin was deposed. She started to hope. You could hook this man, she told herself. On top of the visa, he could give you two gorgeous daughters – one Sumin, one Sumaia – and a son, Sulait. But first you need to hint that you don't eat pork, drink alcohol and that there are Muslims in your family.

"When I saw you across the road," Malik was saying, "I knew you were African."

A number 53 bus drove past.

"You are so dark-dark. I wish I was as dark as you." He looked at her as if being dark-dark could actually be beautiful in Britain. Before Katula responded, he added, "Only you Africans have that real dark, almost navy-blue skin. Look at me…" he showed Katula his inner arms. "Look at this skin; see how pale I am."

Katula did not know what to say. No one had ever envied the darkness of her skin. Pale people tended to be proud of theirs. In Britain, people with skin as dark as hers were not allowed to be "black" together with mixed-race people, Asians or other non-whites.

Another 53 bus came along but Katula could not tear herself away. When the third bus arrived, Malik offered to travel with her. She was not believing her not-so-pretty self anymore! Perhaps he really was attracted to her. By the time they got to Manchester North General Hospital, Katula knew that Malik was not seven foot tall as she had thought but a mere six foot five. His mother was mixed race, with a father who had come from Liberia, and a mother who was Irish. His mother still lived in Sheffield, but his father had returned home to Tobago. "My big brother is dark because our dad is 'dark-dark', but I turned out pale. The only time I get dark is when I go to the Caribbean." Malik walked Katula to the entrance of the hospital and they exchanged telephone numbers. That night, as she worked, Malik's name, his soft voice, perfect face and Britishness kept coming to her and her heart spread out in her chest.

Now Katula walked along the walkway until she came to the end of the last block of the Victorian semi-detached houses and crossed the road. She came to the local pub, The Vulcan, with its Tudor façade. The blacksmith god, the pub's insignia, swung on the sign. Men and women stood outside smoking, despite the cold. From there she could see the red postbox across the road from the local primary school. Just as she prepared to cross Manchester Road, a gritting truck rolled past, dropping grains of sand – or maybe it was salt – on the road. The grains disappeared in the snow slush without effect. Katula made a mental note to pick up salt from the corner shop on her way back. There had been no salt in Tesco the previous weekend because of panic buying – people were using it on the snow on their driveways.

As a devout Muslim, Malik could not be alone with a woman without a third person in the room. Hence, they met in halal restaurants in Rusholme. Even then, Malik never sat too close to her. As their relationship grew, he told Katula that he was not born a Muslim. His name had been Malachi until, sometime in his twenties, he went astray. "I got into some bad-bad, real crazy stuff," he said, without going into details.

To keep away from the bad stuff, he turned to God. However, he had found the Christian God too lazy and laid back. "I went to all sorts of churches but nothing worked for me. I needed a God with a strong grip to put me straight." Then he found Islam and changed his name from Malachi to Malik. Apparently, Islam's God had a tight grip: the five prayers a day kept a rein on him.

They talked about the future: could Katula commit to wearing the hijab? Sure. Could she take a Muslim name? Of course, Hadija. Could she embrace Islam? She took a deep breath but then visualised the British passport. Yes of course! To demonstrate her commitment, Katula's dresses started to grow longer and wider, even though Malik had not pressed her to dress differently. Eventually, he found a third person to be with them and invited Katula to his house.

That day Katula wore kitenge wrappers, including one on her head, because Malik liked it when she dressed "African". Malik's house was a two-bedroomed semi-detached in Oldham. It had a very high ceiling and the rooms were spacious. But it was slummy. Malik had covered the floorboards with cardboard. He had hung bed sheets against the windows. The kitchen was rotting; the house was dark and cold.

Katula surveyed the squalor with satisfaction. Here was a job for a proper wife. Three months in this place and all would be transformed. Malik would not miss his bachelor days.

The living room doubled as Malik's bedroom, even though the house had two other bedrooms. As she walked in, she saw an African youth, not older than twenty-one, sitting on a settee close to the door. He was so good looking that Katula hesitated – when African men chose to be beautiful they overdid it! The lad wore a white Arabic gown with a white patterned taqiyah on his head. The whiteness of his gown stood out in the grubby surroundings. He looked up as she entered and quickly looked away. Then he remembered to say hello and flung the word over his shoulder. Katula dismissed his rudeness. From his accent, he was evidently one of those "my-parents-are-originally-from-Africa-but-I-was-born-in-Britain" types who tended to keep away from "home grown" Africans, as if they would catch being native African again. Katula wrinkled her nose at the youth. His name was Chedi.

She walked past him and sat on another settee; Malik sat on his bed facing Chedi. Apart from the few times Malik asked Katula whether she wanted a drink, the two men were engrossed in conversation. Katula noted that Malik's eyes shone as he listened to Chedi, even though he was only talking about a certain sheikh's views on food, especially meats, from supermarkets. Apparently, for a proper Muslim, not even tomatoes were safe to eat because they were genetically tampered with. Chedi promised to lend Malik the sheikh's CD. Even though she had grown up in a culture where men, in the company of other men, ignored their wives, Katula was uneasy about the way she was not invited into their conversation. They probably did so because she was non-Muslim; maybe Islam did not allow women to join in men's conversation. Katula decided it was best to play dumb; she was on a mission.

The next time Malik invited her over to his house, she was surprised to find him on his own, but she did not ask why. She sat on the sofa; he sat next to her and held her hand as they talked. She was tempted to kiss him. When she stood up to leave, he hugged her and Katula held on. Malik went rigid. She relaxed and let her body melt slowly in his arms to encourage him a little. Malik could have been hugging his mother. When Katula reached up to kiss him on the neck, he tore away.

"In Islam," he said breathlessly, "a man must guard his neck at all times. It is at the neck you lose your life."

Katula crept out of Malik's house, shrinking with shame. On the way home, she chastised herself for pushing too hard. *Slow down! Malik falling in love with you and giving you children are just the toppings – focus on the passport.* She had never dated a British man before; maybe that was the way they were. *You know what they say about Africans – oversexed. The British are no doubt restrained.* Katula's stomach chewed itself all the way home.

The following day, Malik came to see her at the hospital. He was waiting outside the gate when she finished her shift. Pleasant surprise broke through her mortification, and her hope rekindled. He seemed worried and invited her to come to his house the following weekend. She overcame her embarrassment and smiled.

Malik wore a towel when she arrived. Katula stared. If she had thought that Malik was good looking before, undressed he was magnificent. This time he had even made an effort to clean the house. He had the air of an expectant lover about him. He told her to make herself a cup of tea while he took a bath. As she had tea, Malik came out of the bathroom grinning.

"You know, the other day a man followed me all the way from Asda," he said as he dried his hair with a towel. "The man said I have the cutest legs, no?" He turned his legs to her.

Apart from the hairs, Katula wished Malik's legs were hers. "As far as I am concerned, everything on you is close to perfect."

Malik turned around. His eyes shone. He walked towards her and held her. Then he kissed her on the lips but Katula was not sure that she liked it.

"Do you like my body?" He smiled into her eyes.

"You're stunning."

"Then I am all yours if you'll marry me."

The earnestness in his eyes prompted Katula to tell him that she could not marry him because of her visa troubles. But instead of getting suspicious, Malik got angry. "They make my blood boil."

To protect her, and to help her save on rent, Malik asked Katula to move in with him. However, he said, they could not share a bedroom until they were married. She moved in the following day. To make herself useful, Katula started to clean the house. The nagging fear that things were moving too quickly, that Malik would change his mind, that it was all too good to be true, was dispelled when he said that he wanted to fix the wedding date as soon as possible.

First, he gave her money to return to Uganda to renew her student visa. She returned to Britain a month later, and applied for a Certificate of Approval, the first step in obtaining permission to marry and live in the UK. When it was granted, Malik asked for her shift roster.

The day they got married, Katula was due to work the nightshift. Malik had suddenly informed her that they were getting married because a couple had cancelled at the last minute and the imam had slotted them in.

"But I am working tonight. Should I call in sick?"

"No, you don't have to. We're getting married at midday."

There was no time to dwell on the fact that Malik evidently expected her to work on their wedding night and must have already notified the registrar in advance.

Also unknown to Katula, Malik had already bought the clothes she would wear for the nikah. "I got them yesterday," he said, as he handed her an Indian gown, similar to those she had seen in Asian boutiques in Rusholme. Turquoise, it had glittering sequins and beads. It had a scarf that she wore on her head. The gown fitted.

At the wedding, Katula did not know any of the guests, not even her witness. Chedi, Malik's friend, did not turn up; Katula had expected him to be their witness. Malik's mother was not at the wedding either; she could not make it at such short notice. Afterwards, they went to a Lebanese restaurant for lunch. When they returned home, Malik offered to drop her off at work. As she stepped out of the car at the hospital, he leaned over and kissed her on the lips. "See you tomorrow, wifie."

Malik did not come to pick her up in the morning. Somehow, she had expected him to, even though he had not promised. When she arrived home he was in his bedroom but the door was locked. His greeting from behind the door was curt. When he stepped out of his room, his expression said, "Don't you dare come near me!" He rushed about the house as if worried that Katula would pounce on him. He ate in his bedroom and left money for the house on the kitchen table.

That first week after the wedding, silence spread throughout the house like ivy. Katula cried. This had nothing to do with British reserve, or with Islam; this was rejection.

She spent the early months of their marriage in her bedroom. She did not watch TV. She did not go into any other room other than the kitchen and bathroom. She did a lot of overtime. Two years lay ahead of her before she could change her visa to permanent residence, then another year to get her citizenship. She would do it. In the meantime, she continued to refurbish and cook. After cooking she would call out, "Food is ready," at Malik's door. Then she would leave the kitchen so that he could come and get his food.

One day Katula came home from work and found Malik waiting in the corridor. He told her that they were eating out because it was their six months' anniversary. She went along with the plans suspiciously. When they came back home from the restaurant, Malik told her about mahr. He said it was a dowry normally in gold, given to a bride in Islam. He gave her a satchel.

Inside were a three-colour herringbone gold necklace with gold earrings, an engagement ring, a wedding ring and a gold watch with a matching bracelet. He had also bought himself a similar wedding band and a watch like hers, only his were larger.

"They are twenty-one carats; I bought them at a His & Hers promotion."

Katula blinked, then sighed. When she accepted the dowry, Malik held her tight for a long time. Then he buried his head in her shoulder and his body started to shake.

"I am not a bad person, Kat," he wept. "I am not."

"I know."

"I'll look after you, Kat. You trust me, don't you?"

"Of course I do."

He let go of her suddenly, walked to his bedroom and locked the door. Katula went to her bedroom and she too cried. She knew. Of course she now knew. But she could not think of a way to say, *I understand*, or, *Let's talk about it*.

She wasn't trapped, Malik was. And if sometimes she felt she was, at least the door to her cell was open; she could walk out of the marriage. He could not walk out of himself.

One day, out of the blue, Malik told Katula that they should start sending money to her mother, that he knew how hard life was in the Third World. She knew Malik had never sent money to his dad in Tobago. In fact, his face clamped shut whenever Katula asked about his dad.

"My father is a brute. He thinks that to be a man everyone must be like him," he once said.

When Katula rang home and told her mother about Malik's generosity, she said, "God has remembered us." The last time Katula rang, her mother had begged, "If doctors over there have failed, come home and see a traditional healer. Sometimes, it is something small that hinders conception, Katula. You can't risk losing him: he is such a good man."

"Malik is British, mother; they don't leave their wives just because they are barren."

"Listen child, a man is a man; sooner or later he'll want a child."

To get rid of her mother's nagging, Katula said that she would discuss it with Malik and she would let her know.

On pay days, Malik transferred half his salary into Katula's account for their upkeep. Katula wanted to contribute but he said, "In Islam, a man must meet all his wife's needs. Your earnings are your own." Sometimes, however, Katula was overcome by irrational fury, especially when Malik gave her money and said, "Why don't you go and buy yourself some shoes or handbags? Women love shopping." In such moments she wanted to scream, *Stop apologising!*

Sometimes Malik's strict adherence to the five prayers a day seemed slavish to her, as if he was begging God to change him. She would clench her fists to stop herself from screaming, "How could God create you the way you are and then say, *Hmm*, if you pray hard to me and I feel like it I can change you?" Instead she would glower, avoid him and bang her bedroom door. At such times, silence came to the house for days, but Malik would coax her out of her dark moods with generosity. She knew that a lot of women in Uganda would consider her extremely lucky.

As she reached to slip the envelopes into the letter box, she looked up. Near the school gate, a lollipop lady was walking to the middle of the road. She stopped, planted the lollipop on the road, blew her whistle and held her hand out. The cars stopped. Parents with little ones crossed the road. Katula looked beyond them at the barren park covered in snow.

This time, when he gets back home, she promised herself, I'm going to say, *How do you propose we're going to have children?* Or maybe I'll be direct and say, *When do we go for artificial insemination?* Kdto, they call it IVF in Britain.

She let the envelopes fall through the mouth of the post box and turned to walk back to the house she shared with a husband who played at marriage the way children play at having tea.

TARIQ MEHMOOD

THE HOUSE

I was waiting for a fare close to the Marriot Hotel in Islamabad, watching a couple of bored policemen sitting under the shade of a tree, twiddling with the barrels of their guns, when a bellboy from the hotel, followed by a tall thin woman, came towards me. The woman stopped, looked around at something and then followed the boy who was already by my car.

"Your lucky day, sir," the boy said to me.

I handed him a fifty rupee note. He brushed it away saying, "It's a big booking. Hundred."

"She's a Pakistani madam," I said, pushing the note back towards him.

"Foreigner," he said quickly, snatching the note whilst insisting with the index finger of his other hand that I give him more money. I swore at him under my breath and handed him another fifty. He turned to the woman and opened the back door.

"Yes, madam." I said in Urdu, "Where would you like to go?"

She took a deep breath and replied in Pothohari. "There is so much I would like to see, but can't."

I touched the key, my lucky charm, which dangled off the rear view mirror and looked at her face in the mirror. She had long grey hair, with streaks of silver that fell over her shoulders. The way she held her head was just like the madams of Islamabad. By the way she talked and looked she could have been someone from my village, but the black kameez jacket, her top, with its embroidery of gold running down her front and the edges of the arms meant she was not short of money.

I cursed the bellboy inside my head, *You son of a donkey. I waited for over two hours for a fare and you dump me with this one.*

53

"Where can I take you?" I asked in Urdu.

"Do you not speak Pothohari?" she asked, looking for something in her handbag.

"Yes. Yes, madamjee," I said in Urdu with a taxi-driver laugh. "It just doesn't feel right talking in that language with a madam, especially someone from round here."

"I'm Indian," she said. "Talk to me in Pothohari."

Thank you, Allah, I thought inside my head.

"As you would wish, madam," I said in Pothohari. "I can take you anywhere. And get you whatever it is you desire," I added quickly.

She flicked her eyebrows disapprovingly and repeated, "There is so much I would like to see but I can't."

Oh yes, I thought, I know what your type wants.

I was just getting ready for the long game that would eventually mean me getting her what someone like her was really after but was finding difficult to say, when she took a cigarette from her bag and lit it.

"Do you mind if I smoke in your car?" she asked, blowing smoke out of the window.

"This car is at your service, madam," I said, thinking over what sort of a boy she was likely to be after.

"Do you smoke?" she asked, offering me a cigarette.

"Which taxi driver doesn't?" I looked at her pack. It was one of the expensive foreign ones.

"Keep it," she said. "I have more."

I took it from her. As I did this, she said, "Drive."

"Where to, madam?"

"Just drive."

I put the cigarettes in the glove compartment, touched the dangling key and started the car. As I drove past the policemen, they looked at me and then chuckled to themselves, nodding towards the woman in the back of my car.

I turned left on the road and decided that she was the sort who would like to go to Taxila. Indians loved that and they were good tippers. If I was lucky she might want to go to the ancient ruins of Katas. Then I thought, maybe she is a Sikh. She would no doubt want to see Panja Sahib in Hasan Abdal.

I had only gone a short distance when she asked, "Why did you touch that key?"

"Just one of those things we drivers do, madam."

"Just one of those things we drivers do," she mimicked, and then said, "I was born in Gujarkhan and have dreamt of one day visiting the house of my birth."

I detected great pain in her voice.

A traffic policeman, who was standing in the middle of the road directing traffic, flagged me to stop. I tried to sneak past him but he blew his whistle a few times. I stopped and snatched a look at the woman. She didn't look like the madams of Islamabad anymore but almost like a mother who was searching for a lost child.

"Majee," I said thinking of my own dead mother, "you can go to Gujarkhan right now. It's not far; I can take you."

She smiled a sad smile and said, "I'm Indian; not allowed. And besides everyone in India warned me not to go to Pakistan; it's not safe, especially for Sikhs."

"This is Pakistan. No one is safe and Allah decides," I said, hoping she would want to go to Gujarkhan.

I prayed inside my head, *Ya rabbah, oh God, make this my lucky day. I've never had one of these returning Sikhs. Especially someone as rich as this one. Oh Lord let this day be my eid.*

She went silent for a while and then her eyes lit up. "I have dreamt a thousand dreams, to see where I was born."

As I turned onto the Islamabad Highway, going south towards Gujarkhan, she asked, "Are you married? Do you have children?"

I glanced at her in the mirror, trying to work out what she would most likely want to hear. She looked the motherly type. She could have grandchildren, and then she might feel sorry for me if she thought I should be married but had not managed to save enough money.

"Well, is it that difficult a question to answer?"

"No, madam…"

She turned towards me. "Either call me Majee or auntiejee, but not madam." Before I could answer, she added, "Majee."

"Jee, Majee." I stroked the dashboard next to the steering wheel, pointed to the black ribbons I had tied to the side mirrors and said, "This is my wife and my mother."

She laughed and then sat silently with her hand up to her mouth. Every now and again, when she saw a child or an animal, she would let out a deep sigh.

When we crossed Mandra, just as we went past a village, she asked me to stop. She pointed her thin finger at a house where a woman was rolling dung in her hands and then putting it on the side of the wall of a house.

"People here still dry dung and use it for fuel to cook with," I said.

"The little girl near the tandoor, the oven. When I was young, I used to light our tandoor just like her. See those twigs sticking out from the top of the tandoor, just above the flames? I can hear them crackling, even from here and I can smell the wood burning just like that little girl. I would stand close to my tandoor, especially at night and watch the flames going up and the twigs falling down and the sparks flying about. Maybe they are still the same last sparks I saw, when they told us to leave."

How could those be the same sparks? I thought and said, "Maybe, Majee, maybe." Then I asked her, "Why did you come to Pakistan?"

"I am a poet. I came to recite."

A poet, I thought. At least she is not like all the ones I know. Broke.

She started humming to the tune of Saif-al-Maluk. She stopped, let out a strange little laugh and said, without taking her eyes off the little girl by the tandoor, "It was the middle of the day in that year; 1947. I had lit our tandoor and then went to hang the washing on the walls. Mother had made the flour into dough and I went and sat next to her and helped her make paeras from the dough. Mine were always either too small or too big, but Mother never once told me off. She would just pick them up, smile and roll them again into the right size. My father was out somewhere, doing whatever he did, always turning up just as the rotis came out of the tandoor.

"A few other women, four neighbours, came with their dough. They always did. Ours was a big tandoor. Mother placed our flour, all neatly rolled into perfect balls, on a silver tray and put it on my head, then she went to greet the women. I followed her and we all went to the tandoor. She began chatting with the women about how bad the times were getting. All the Sikhs in Choha Khalsa were dead, they said. Sukho was in flames. No one knows who is alive and who is dead. All the Sikhs from Domeli had left. Ours was a big tandoor." She looked at me and asked, "Did I tell you that already?"

I nodded.

"Mother had built our tandoor with her own hands. It was big enough for lots of rotis to cook in. She usually let the other women make theirs first, but today, for some reason, she started on ours. She had just put four or five rotis into the tandoor when our door smashed open and soldiers with guns burst in. There were so many of them. The women screamed. I ran behind mother.

" 'You are leaving for India, right now,' they said.

"Mother held my hand tightly. Her hand was hot and she was trembling.

"Before anyone could say anything, the soldiers pushed us out of our house. Mother kept looking back at the tandoor saying, 'My roti will burn. My roti will burn.' But the soldiers just pushed us out of the house. Outside, there were more soldiers and so many terrified people. I called out to father, but how could he hear me, amongst all those others who were calling out names?

"We walked to the railway station; mother never let go of my hand. I kept calling out for father all the way. Even as they made us get onto a train, I kept calling him. I had been on a train before, but this was not like any other. It was so full of people; some bleeding, others crying. I remember the eyes! The eyes – they were all bloodshot. As the train pulled away, I heard a raging river of screams, screams I have never stopped hearing.

"Mother never talked much after that and when she did, she would say, 'My roti will burn.' "

"And what happened to your father?" I asked.

"I never did see him again."

She didn't say anything else all the way to Gujarkhan. When we got there, I parked my car behind the courts. She remembered the banyan tree and she led the way as if she had never left. We walked around some narrow streets for a while.

She would suddenly stop and say, "My house was here," and then shake her head, walk this way and that and then stop again and say the same thing.

After a little while of doing this she said, "It's been too long."

We headed back to my car. She walked slowly now, lost in thought.

Just as we got into the bazaar she said, "When I was young, there was a Christian called Khaled, who used to sell little sweets on a raeree, a little wooden cart which had a broken wheel."

"Maybe someone remembers him," I said.

She shook her head, "After all this time!"

I looked around till I saw an old shopkeeper. He was a big fat man who was looking at us whilst picking up fistfuls of daal from a sack close to him and letting it fall through his fingers. I went up to him and asked, "Uncle, do you remember a Christian who sold sweets around here, before the partition?"

He looked at me for a while, then looked the woman up and down and said, "The Christian is still here, still selling things on a raeree." He then told his son – a round little spitting image of himself – "Take them to Khaled Masih."

We followed the boy through the bazaar up towards the GT road. After a short while he stopped and pointed, "That's Khalid Masih," and disappeared into the bazaar

As soon as she saw Khalid Masih, she cried, "Ya rabbah, oh God."

Khalid Masih was a small, dark man, with a deeply wrinkled face. On his raeree he had combs, socks, locks, mirrors and other small things.

She walked up to him ever so slowly. When she got close, she asked, "Are you Khalid Masih?"

He looked up at her and nodded.

"Do you remember Karamjit Singh, son of Harjit Singh Kataria?"

Khalid Masih's small eyes became even smaller. A sad smile flashed across his toothless mouth. "Kamli Kaur. You? Here?"

She hugged him and cried, "Babajee, you are still alive and still have your raeree!"

"I died a long time ago, daughter," he replied.

Pulling away from him she examined the raeree. "At least this one doesn't have a broken wheel."

He shook his head.

"Do you remember my house?"

He nodded, wiping his eyes with the back of his hand.

"We have searched everywhere for my house. Nothing looks like what I remember. Is my house still here?"

He nodded.

He left the raeree and we followed him. He had taken only a few steps when she asked, "What about your raeree?"

He turned around and pointed at the bazaar and smiled. Everyone was looking at us.

For an old man he walked fast. We went through countless narrow streets, until we came to a big house. "That is where you were born." He turned to leave.

"Come with me," she said to the old man.

He stepped away from us. "I am still an untouchable. They will think I have contaminated you."

She watched Khalid Masih until he went out of sight and then said to me, "This is not my house; maybe he is mistaken."

"We've come all this way. Let's knock."

"Maybe if they find out I am a Sikh…"

I interrupted her, "I'm with you and the Almighty is my witness, I will let nothing happen to you."

She knocked on the door.

After a little while, a woman's voice from inside the house called, "Who?"

"I've come from India and I am looking for the house where I was born," Kamli Kaur replied hesitantly.

There was a little pause and then the door opened. A young woman with a child on her hip stood in front of us. Kamli Kaur's face turned white. She pointed to the veranda. It was an old wooden one, with carved curving arches. It was painted blue. With tears streaming down her eyes Kamli Kaur pointed inside saying, "My name is Kamli Kaur. This is the house where I was born. And the veranda is still blue."

Beckoning us in, the young woman said, "It is still your house, Majee, and the veranda has always been blue."

As we stepped inside, the young woman handed her baby to Kamli Kaur and ran towards a tandoor, saying, "My roti is burning."

Whilst the young woman retrieved her rotis, Kamli Kaur walked around the veranda, holding the child close to her. I stood where I was.

A few moments later a frail old woman, much older then Kamli Kaur came out. "Kamli!" she cried.

I went outside, stood by the door and lit a cigarette. A short while later, a door close to me opened and a young man asked me to come inside. He pointed to a tray of food on a small table and said, "Eat, Ustad," and walked back into the house.

On the way back to Islamabad, Kamli Kaur sat in the front passenger seat. She looked much younger now.

"What's your name?" she asked, lighting a cigarette.

"Iqbal. Raja Iqbal." I replied. "We are refugees from India."

"Do you know where from?" Then she added quickly, "How could you, you were not born then."

"No Majee, I wasn't born then," I said, "But my mother, may the Almighty grant her a place in heaven, never stopped talking about her house. She said we had a great big peepal tree in the middle of our yard. We had the biggest well in the whole area, which never went dry and from which everyone filled their pitchers. It was close to the Pir-I-Dastgir shrine."

Kamli Kaur threw her cigarette out of the window, touched my lucky key and went silent for the rest of the journey.

It was late at night and there was not much traffic so we made good time.

I pulled up outside the Marriot and said, "Majee, I want no fare from you. I will never forget this journey."

She held my hand tightly in her trembling hands and left the car. As I withdrew my hand I noticed there was a key in it, and there was a small pile of one thousand rupee notes on the passenger seat. I picked up the money and drove off, the key in my hand. I stopped a short distance from the hotel, put the light on inside and stared at the key.

A chill ran down my back. I held it next to my lucky key.

They were exactly the same.

CHANTAL OAKES

THE WEIGHT OF FOUR TIGERS

Neon Banks had been working on the piece of performance art for so long, he had begun to wonder if it was actually possible that some sort of butter might be made from tigers. How pungent would that substance be, how feline? Would it be too rich for the human palate?

George Mbewe, on the other hand, one of the cleaners at Chatsworth Villa, with its museum, park and zoo, where the performance was to take place, felt lucky to have the job as it was so much easier than the succession of short-term contracts involving hard manual work he had been employed in before.

He now cleaned beautiful wooden floors and hand-woven carpets and rugs in what seemed to him the epitome of peace and quiet. Neither guests nor staff raised their voices as he cleaned the gilt door handles and light switches. He made sure the grand front step was always spotless in case the owners ever visited, and all around him it was as hushed as a shrine.

As he cleaned he listened to his small radio tucked in his shirt pocket, switched on low. He didn't like the feeling of dislocation when he plugged headphones into his ears, and he didn't want to be taken unawares. He listened to talk programmes mostly; today there was to be a live radio broadcast from his place of work. He would listen from his small side room, grateful to whoever the artist was for the extra shifts.

From the west wing windows of the grand house – modestly labelled a villa – beyond the corridor and the small storeroom where he kept his cleaning materials, he could see the radio station van topped with a large aerial. And there was Harry Cook, the radio presenter, getting out of his mobile changing room, ready to start his broadcast.

Harry Cook always sounded very jolly on the radio and looked jolly too, even though he wore a suit and didn't sport a beard as George had always imagined.

Five minutes later, at 11 o'clock precisely, Harry Cook told his listeners, "Good morning to you all." George replied, "And good morning to you," half expecting to hear his voice relayed back to him through his radio. He listened to Harry Cook most work days, and now here he was on the other side of the corridor wall.

"We are delighted to bring you this live broadcast from Chatsworth Villa with its Zoo and Country Park. The sun is shining," Harry Cook told his listeners, "but today, I am inside, standing by a purpose-built glass room, manufactured in Germany and constructed on-site in the Great Hall of this palatial house, for a groundbreaking performance featuring the famous American scientist, Charles Draper, and four of the park's tigers. Here in the room are assembled a large group of interested individuals, many of whom have travelled a great distance to be here. I'm with Neon Banks, who instigated this piece of performance art, and the curator of Chatsworth's Museum, Susan Jones. Good morning to you both."

George only half-listened to the artist talking about re-examining the connections between words, African peoples and global culture. It was time for a sit-down. He had been working hard all morning, mainly keeping the caterers from dropping food on the 17th century rugs.

In his storeroom, resting on a small 200-year-old wooden chair with a beautifully embroidered pad, George waited for the kettle to boil. Harry Cook was still talking to Neon Banks about being a black artist living in the UK and Banks was interrupting to protest that he was actually born in England, but the kettle drowned out the rest of his words.

Harry Cook began speaking to the curator, Susan Jones. She was always very nice to George and so he paused to hear what she had to say.

"The timing was perfect. The breeding programme at the Zoo was very successful and as Neon wanted to work with tigers it was a fantastic opportunity for us to collaborate with this up-and-coming artist. It has taken us many weeks to rearrange the Great Hall collection for his work, but we are happy to be part of a groundbreaking project of international stature."

At seven that morning, George had been inside the Great Hall to sort out the chairs. Three of the huge white statues of naked men were now painted brown. The effect had been unsettling because they looked real in the shadowy early morning light.

As if to explain this, Susan Jones continued: "…Even though my specialised research area is in classical art history it was Neon who informed me that the statues, so faithfully reproduced from the Greek and Roman period by the Victorian and Edwardian artists, were, in fact, originally painted in bright colours. Since both the Greek and the Roman forces throughout the world were what we would today call multicultural, having raised large armies in northern Africa, for instance, the artist is being factual, but the effect is very interesting. We invite visitors to come and see them when the gallery reopens to the general public."

For some reason, this information annoyed George. He sipped at his tea distractedly and scalded his lips. He put down the cup and took out his mobile phone to play Tetris.

When Harry Cook told the listeners that Devon Derbyshire, his co-presenter, was with some protesters at the perimeter fence, George lost his concentration and then a life in the game.

For a moment his mind flashed back to the mob that had scaled his compound wall, and driven his family into exile – after he had pleaded for their lives – over several days of looting and general mayhem.

He checked outside the storeroom but all was quiet. He put away his phone and drank his tea, now it had cooled. He didn't want to think about the past.

"Morning, Harry," Devon said. "I am here with a group of protesters at the gates of this lovely estate. They have come here to make their feelings known about the performance taking place inside. Oliver French is with me now. He has travelled all the way from Sheffield to be here. Sir, can you tell us why you are protesting today?"

Oliver French was trying hard not to shout. "We do not think it's right that animals are being used in this way; in this day and age it's disgusting," he said. "This so-called work of art is cruelty. We're not protesting at the use of animals by humans, but we say that non-human animals must be given respect."

The crowd cheered him on. "We don't think a black man should even be considering using animals in this way. How can anyone think this is art?" The crowd murmured their agreement again.

"Why does the artist's colour make a difference?" Devon Derbyshire asked.

George was wondering the same.

"Africa is being stripped of its natural wealth of wildlife and resources," French stated, and then asked: "Should Neon Banks really be considering more of the same?"

George tried to forget the taste of some of the wild animals he'd been forced to eat as a young boy, during the colonial wars. He had been seven and wondered how he had not died from diarrhoea.

When he returned to the present, he found that Devon Derbyshire, unsure who had carried out the asset-stripping in Africa, had signed off and returned the broadcast to Harry Cook.

Harry Cook started to describe the apparatus involved in the art event as he moved past the rows of seating George had put out around the glass room. He entered the main glass chamber where Professor Draper stood with his assistant, an intensely composed and small woman called Helen Preston.

They had taken two days to set up a complicated arrangement of measuring instruments, attached to a clump of elephant grass that circled a mature tree, itself held upright by a series of strong wires secured to the floor and ceiling. They had changed the atmosphere in the chamber, reproducing the heat and humidity of the tropics. Harry Cook was impressed. He marvelled at the technology of a hydraulically powered platform from where they would record the data, and a five-foot high secondary glass wall enclosure with an electronic door that circled the tree and the elephant grass. Both structures would contain the tigers when they arrived.

Harry Cook commented, in passing, on the condensation on the glass enclosure, and so George Mbewe picked up the window-cleaning tools and let himself out of the store room, closing the door softly. He would be needed in the Great Hall after all. He left his little radio behind in case of feedback. Now, he would be able to see and hear everything first-hand.

He entered the room through the small door behind the great tapestry. Harry Cook was talking to the professor. George discreetly watched the interview from behind the assembly of dignitaries and the radio station technicians.

Professor Draper, now as relaxed and avuncular as a scientist could be, described what his instruments would be measuring.

The specific tests were divided into three sections, he said. Firstly "friction", where he and his assistant would be examining paw-to-dry-grass contact ratios i.e how much friction could four tigers create on the amount of grass it was possible to grow within such a localised area, considering they each weighed approximately 500 pounds. The second set of instruments would consider "spontaneous combustion", i.e. would the heightened emotions of the tigers along with their hot breath and the reproduced heat of their habitat contribute to a conflagration; and finally, "liquidisation".

Just as the professor was about to describe the conditions required for liquidisation, George dropped his squeegee and the metal handle clattered on the granite floor. He had been trying to signal to Susan, the curator, to ask if he should clean the main glass enclosure of condensation when it slipped out of his hand. Harry Cook gave him a sharp look but the moment was saved when Tom Wright, the head keeper from the Zoo, radioed the Great Hall, informing everyone that the tigers were ready and waiting in the wire corridor, specially constructed to get them through to the glass enclosure, now dripping with moisture.

Professor Draper and his assistant took their positions and Harry Cook left the enclosure, continuing to talk to his listeners. The process of getting the tigers into the Hall would take a few minutes and because the glass was soundproof they would not hear the felines approach. Harry Cook continued to enthuse about the workmanship of the construction, and George, patiently standing in a corner, found himself fixated on a slow but steady drop of water meandering down the thick glass.

As a side panel in the main enclosure rose, Harry Cook

informed his listeners in a voice that was louder than usual: "The tigers are here!"

They were magnificent beasts, standing at least four feet at the shoulder and over eight feet in length. They prowled into the space, wary and watchful, sniffing out the environment and circling under the professor's specially built platform, now raised eight feet off the ground. One of the tigers defecated and Harry Cook wondered aloud if that would change the outcome of the experiment in any way.

That was Harry Cook at his best, George thought, displaying the tongue-in-cheek humour that had made him so popular with listeners. George had tried out Cook's technique on his wife a few times, but it had failed to lift her depression.

"We have radio contact with the Professor inside the enclosure," Harry Cook said. "Professor, can you tell us? How do you intend to get the tigers into the second, smaller enclosure in order for them to circle the tree?"

The Professor did not reply. He and his assistant were completely focused on their experiments. Both Harry Cook and George looked up and saw several large cuts of meat being lowered down through the tree branches.

The tigers were interested; three were already walking under the tree in the second, smaller glass enclosure. Everyone in the Great Hall held their breath waiting for the fourth tiger to do the same. When at last it sniffed its way in, the professor with a flamboyant flourish of the hand, directed his assistant to close the glass gate.

The tigers did not circle or begin to race each other around the tree. Bunched together, their tails began switching, and first one tiger, then another, jumped out of the tight enclosure and began to prowl again under the platform and around the perimeter of the main glass enclosure, their tails lashing at the air with concern.

The professor signalled his assistant to raise the meat and as it slid out of view the movement attracted one tiger's attention. It stretched up the tree trunk, extending its claws to grip the bark then leapt with no effort at all, onto the lower branches. The tree began to lean.

Finding its quarry among the limp foliage, the tiger wrestled it from the wire that held it. The wire snapped causing the tree to lean even more dangerously. Harry Cook, amazed by the prowess of the animal and noticing one of the tigers eye-balling him, fell silent.

The animal that had retrieved the meat jumped to the ground with it, and a tussle began, each tearing at it with their mouths while trying to bat away the others with heavy swipes of their paws. The soundproofing was very effective. It was like watching a silent movie.

One of the animals retreated from the fight and approached the platform sniffing. The assistant opened her mouth and presumably screamed as the tiger leapt up towards her but fell short.

"Oh gosh…" Harry Cook said – all his usual jollity vanished. "I can see one of the tigers is making ready to leap up at the platform again. Oh look! Professor Draper has raised a gun. He is pointing it at the tiger."

The entrance gate rose and George saw chunks of meat had been laid to entice the tigers away. Distracted by the rising door the animals moved off, except for the one that continued to explore the potential for a fresh meal on the platform. Everyone watched it as it prepared to spring again. They did not hear the gunshot; it was the shattering of the huge outer enclosure of glass that alerted them to what the professor had done. It seemed, however, that the shot had missed the tiger. It bit through the glass and continued across the room until it found the arm of one of the statues. Harry Cook dropped his microphone and ran with the rest of the assembled audience as the arm crashed to the floor. A second shot sounded as they stumbled through the main door and slammed it shut, leaving the professor and his assistant inside.

George ran under the tapestry towards the small secondary door. Neon Banks followed him, his eyes on the tiger which, though injured, was still on its feet. As they scrambled through the exit into the west wing corridor, quickly closing the door behind them, four more shots rang out, accompanied by the screams of the professor's assistant. The screams went on and on.

At last the Hall became silent. George and Neon Banks quietly opened the small door and re-entered, peeping around the giant tapestry.

The room, now strewn with glass and upturned chairs, presented a very modern display. The tiger on the floor was motionless. Professor Draper held his now quiet assistant against him.

What George said next was transmitted to Harry Cook's listeners.

"Look at this beautiful creature – I wish I had the words to describe how regal the animal remains even in death. I have not seen anything like it before – and it is still warm." He sat next to the animal and ran his hand along part of its back.

"The fur… each hair is as thick as a fine needle… that huge jaw and those eyes, big enough to engulf a person. I wonder what it would have been like to have tigers in Africa," George said, but Neon Banks was too busy sorting out his camera equipment and packing up the excellent footage to answer.

George wondered if he might have the pelt, but in the distance, the swirling sound of emergency vehicles broke his reverie.

MICHELLE INNISS

WHATEVER LOLA WANTS

Jason Truman sat at the back of the café, at the same table they'd been sharing almost every day for the past six months. The same waitress, with the false blonde hair and too much make up, took his order. Double espresso. He'd thought about ordering for Lola but decided against it. She hardly ever arrived on time. She'd stroll in late and heads would turn. At least the men's would; the women would shoot her dead with their looks.

It was a shame but he had to end it. He had told her from the start: work and home, him and her were separate. But she had started to text him at work and now she had rung him at home. Luckily Katie had been in the bath when she'd called. Next time he mightn't be so lucky. No, this madness had to stop. He had to bring it to an end, but it wasn't going to be easy.

In his office he was known as the level-headed one. If you were looking for calm appraisal and integrity, then Truman was your man. None of that applied to her. She had slithered beneath his skin. He remembered the first time they kissed. "Your lips," he whispered. "They're so nice, so big."

"What you tryna say?" she asked. "How are my lips so big?"

He felt his face redden. *Well they aren't anything like Katie's.*

"It's nothing," he said, pulling her closer. "You just taste so good."

Driving home later he found himself thinking that it was the first time he had ever kissed a black woman. When he was younger you just didn't see white guys with black women; it just didn't happen. It wasn't that he hadn't found some black women attractive, but he wouldn't have made a play for one… not back then. But wasn't everyone "in the mix" now?

He'd asked her if they could meet up for lunch the following day. But she couldn't do days. She was studying. Jason knew then that he was probably twice her age, but if he could hit on an eighteen year old woman who looked like her and pull it off, then even at fifty, he must still have it. Most married men his age had let themselves go – too much wine and rich food. He swam every morning in the pond on Hampstead Heath and the colder the water the more energised he felt.

The next time they met, to his surprise, he began to blabber. "I want to kiss you all night."

She had smiled and said, "Shuuut up! No-one's ever said nothin' like that to me before."

He couldn't help thinking: *God, this woman is so beautiful but when she opens her mouth she sounds so… rough.*

He soon got used to her deep London accent. It became a part of her charm. Some of the things that fell from her mouth really did make him laugh, though. He couldn't ever imagine Katie calling him "Babe", or "J", or "Sweet Pea".

Jason looked around the café. He slid his hand through the growth of silver that lit up the sides of his hair. He pulled down the sleeves of his silk suit despite the heat.

He was just about to ask for a glass of water when the door opened and Lola came in. As she sauntered towards him, his eyes clung to the rise and fall of her short skirt as it hugged her hips and slim legs. The conversations around him trailed away. He saw the heads turn in Lola's direction. He couldn't stop himself smiling.

All these men can only imagine what they'd like to do to her. I'm actually doing it.

There was only one word he could use to describe Lola… 'Hot'. It was a cliché and he should have done better, especially since he was in advertising and original thought was his trade-mark, but there was no other word for her. Lola was hot. He'd tried once to persuade her to ditch studying and go into model-ling; her type was in real demand.

"An' what exactly do you mean by my type?" she asked looking puzzled.

The red had risen to his cheeks again. They were the words he used at work. There were types. There was the size 0 – flat-chested, cropped hair, pass-for-a-boy type. Then there was the collagen enhanced, tall, long-haired type and there was her type. Curly hair, naturally thin, with lips that all those collagen-induced women longed for. Her colour, how would he describe it? Coffee – no, too dark; coffee with cream, but how much cream? Cappuccino? Latte? Halfway between a cappuccino and a latte? Shit! How could he tell her she looked like coffee with a lot of cream in it.

"Come on, Lola, chill. You're my type, beautiful and sexy."

He'd slid his hand along her inner thigh and she'd laughed.

"Oh, I get you, that type."

Jason observed her now. She looked a little thinner. Her skin had broken out in spots. He hadn't meant to, but he found his hand stretching over the table to take her hand.

"You look like shit," he said.

"Feel like shit," she said, staring down at her chewed nails. "I've been tryna contact you, J. How come you never texted me back?"

He tried not to look at her. His eyes hovered over the silver rope bracelet twisted round her wrist like a sleeping snake. The waitress came to take her order. She asked for a glass of milk.

Milk? It was usually a diet coke.

He ordered another double espresso. They sat in silence until the waitress returned with their drinks. Jason watched Lola drink her milk with a pink straw. He wanted to reach over and kiss her; she looked so young. She looked up at him.

"You know, don't you, J? That's how come you didn't text me back."

"Know what?" he asked.

"About... about the baby."

Jason felt the cup slip from his fingers.

She's phoned home again. She's spoken to Katie. Oh shit! How else could she know about the baby?

71

The cup bounced off the saucer, tumbling onto the table. Jason's eyes fell on the waitress, who was staring at him. He tried to smile. He looked away and put the cup back onto the saucer, ignoring the dark stain seeping into the white table cloth.

"What are you talking about, Lola?" he said. "What baby?"

"Our baby, J." Lola was stirring the rest of the milk with her straw. "I'm gunna have our baby. I'm pregnant, J."

They had been using an apartment that belonged to a friend of his who was working in America. Jason would meet up with her after work and they would go back to the apartment, spend two or three hours there, then he would shower and drop her home. It was the perfect set up. Her mother was a midwife and worked nights at the Royal Free Hospital and her father had gone AWOL when she was a baby, so she was never missed. They had started going to the apartment twice a week, but two nights soon became five. Jason knew then that he was losing control but he couldn't stop.

It must have been that last time.

He'd forgotten all about that evening. They hadn't even made it to the bedroom. He lay on top of her, on the floor in the living room. He was just about to come.

"Shit!" he said.

"What is it?" Lola asked, opening her eyes.

"I don't have any condoms. I left them in my other bag at work."

"Don't worry," she said, giggling. "There's always the pill."

He beamed down at her.

"In that I case I won't."

Afterwards, he'd led Lola to the bedroom where they fell asleep. When he awoke, he hauled himself out of bed and dragged Lola to the bathroom and they had sex again in the shower.

It was close to 5:00am when Jason finally got home, the latest he'd ever been. He slipped into bed next to Katie, who he thought was sound asleep. The next morning Katie told him that she'd waited up for him. He told her that the company was involved in a big contract, so coming home early just wasn't an option. It seemed as though had Katie believed him because she didn't dig too deep. Jason tried to get out of the house as soon as possible saying he'd grab breakfast on the way to work, but Katie said she had something important to tell him.

She was going to have a baby.

He'd almost asked her how. He hardly slept with her. He had tried to have sex with her in the same way he had sex with Lola, but, afterwards, she just lay there next to him in silence. He knew that she hadn't enjoyed it. But none of that mattered now. Maybe the baby would bring them closer. Maybe he could start to feel the way he used to feel about her. He didn't have a choice; he had to return to reality. From that day he stopped ringing Lola.

He had wanted to tell Lola that it was over between them but he just couldn't face her. If he met up with her, if he gazed into her dark, fuck-me eyes, it would start all over again. The smell of her perfume on another woman had brought back the sensation of his mouth buried in her flesh. Three weeks had passed and Lola continued to text him at work. Yesterday she'd rung him at home.

Jason eyed her now, studying her dark eyes.

What the fuck is she playing at? She's set me up. He felt like slapping her.

"You're a liar," he said, raising his voice.

The pink straw Lola was chewing slipped from her lips. "What?"

"You heard. Lola, you're a liar."

She leant forwards and tried to grab hold of Jason's hand.

"I'm not, J." She began to cry. "Please J, don't shout at me."

Jason looked away and realised the waitress was looking at them. He lowered his voice.

"You said that you were on the pill."

"No, I didn't, J."

"You did, I remember you saying it."

"What I said, J, was… was there's always the pill."

"What the fuck does that mean, Lola? Stop fucking me around."

"I'm not fuckin' you around J, honest I'm not. What I meant was, I could go to the clinic, y'know, an' get the mornin' after pill."

"Jesus Christ, I can't believe this shit. I thought you said you were on the pill."

Lola shook her head. Her hands trembled as she picked up a serviette to wipe her eyes.

"So what happened, Lola? Are you trying to say that the fucking pill didn't work?"

"No," she said, looking down. "I told my friend, cuz I know her older sister done it."

"Done what?"

"Gone to a clinic, you know, for the mornin' after pill… But then…"

"But what, Lola?"

"She asked me if it was for me. Of course I said, no. Then she said somethin' about how you had to be like, sixteen or the clinic would want your parent's consent."

"But what the fuck has that got to do with you? You don't need your mum's consent." Jason stared into Lola's eyes. "Do you?"

"I'm sorry J, honest I am," she sobbed. "I'm gunna be sixteen in two weeks. I just couldn't do it, J. I couldn't tell my mum. I'm so sorry, J, I just thought I'd be alright, d'you know what I mean?"

He had met her in a night club. She was the only woman he saw as he descended the stairs. Lola was standing next to the bar, her head thrown back, laughing. She was wearing the shortest of shorts and a skimpy top. He had crossed the dance floor and offered to buy her a drink. She was wearing too much make up but the suppleness of her body couldn't be hidden. He had danced with her. He remembered feeling fantastic, every nerve-ending in his body buzzing. It was a long time since he'd felt so alive.

Jason watched Lola now as she wiped her nose with the back of her hand. He observed how she drained the rest of the milk in the bottom of the glass with her pink straw, slurping as she reached the bottom. He felt he was seeing Lola for the first time. *Does eighteen year old skin and fifteen year old skin look that different? Does it feel that different?*

He considered the womanly way in which she moved when they were together but acknowledged that even though her body moved like a woman's she lacked a certain… *sophistication*. He recalled the tantrums she sometimes had, which he thought a bit odd to begin with, but had decided were kind of cute, something particular to her. She thought of herself as a bit of a princess and he had indulged her. He had even turned it into a sexual game: if

I give you what you want, then what will you give me in return? She would pout, move closer and run her hand along his trouser leg until she reached his zip. He felt his cheeks burn as he thought of the times she had gone down on him whilst he was still at the wheel of the car. He'd had sex with her one night in an alleyway. Katie would only have sex with him in the bedroom, on the bed. Once, when he had tried to pull her down onto the floor, she'd been horrified.

"Jason! Not on the floor! The carpet can burn, you know."

It was not all Katie had withheld from him. But everything he had wanted to do with Lola, she had allowed. She'd done things to him no other woman had ever done.

Woman, but Lola's not a woman is she? My God. She's fifteen!

Jason felt as though the table had moved away from him.

I could lose everything, my job, my home, my baby. Everything! He felt a surge in his stomach. *I could even go to prison.*

He was going to vomit. He needed to think. Having sex with a minor and, as if that wasn't bad enough she was… he threw his hand up to his mouth. His chair fell backwards as he pushed his body upwards, using the table to steady his shaking legs.

In the bathroom Jason bent his head over the sink and threw cold water onto his face. The urge to vomit subsided. He stared at himself in the mirror.

"Think, Truman!" he muttered at his reflection. "Think!"

The door to the bathroom opened. Lola stood behind him crying.

"What is it, J? What's the matta?"

Jason turned round to face her. *She was a mess. She'll be sixteen in two weeks' time. Two weeks. Surely I could ride it out.*

"Does anyone know about the baby?" he asked.

Lola shook her head.

"Well, you mustn't tell anyone, okay?"

"Why not?"

He took hold of her hands. "Do you love me?"

"Course I do, J, you know that."

"I don't think you really do love me, Lola."

"I do, J, honest I do. I'd do anythin' for you."

He stared into her eyes.

75

"Anything?"

"Yeah, J, anything." She was resting her hand on her stomach. "Don't leave us, J. Please don't say you don't want me no more."

"But you know that we've got a problem, don't you?"

"What problem, J, what you talkin' about?"

"The baby, Lola."

"The baby?" she said, stepping backwards. "But how's that a problem? I'd be a good mum, J, I promise. I could go back to school after the baby's born. I can do this, J, I know I can. Other girls in my school have done it."

"Don't be stupid, Lola, you are only fifteen for fuck's sake."

"I'll be sixteen soon."

The urge to slap her returned. He stepped forward and caught hold of her hands.

"What about me, Lola? What about us? Listen. You know I still want to be with you. Trust me, Lola. You do trust me, don't you?"

Lola nodded.

He pulled Lola towards him as he stepped backwards into the toilet. He stopped when he felt the toilet bowl touch the back of his legs.

"If you love me, Lola, you'll do what I ask."

He started to close the door with his right hand and with his left hand he pushed Lola up against the door. Then he locked it.

"It's for the best; you know that, don't you?" He stroked back the curls that had fallen onto her face. "You have to do it Lola, so we can still be together."

Lola opened her mouth to speak.

"Shush." He rested a finger on her lips. "Who knows best?"

"You do," she said, lowering her head.

"Will you do what I ask, Lola, will you?" His hand glided upwards along the inside of her thigh. "Do you love me enough to do it?"

"Yes, J," she said, as the tears collected at the tips of her eyelashes. "Whatever you say, J, I'll do it."

"Good girl," he whispered.

Ten minutes later Jason pulled up his zip. He stared at Lola and grinned.

"Now fix yourself up and smile; don't start that pouting game with me." He looked at his watch. "If we go to the apartment now, I could be back at home for eight."

Jason opened the toilet door and walked to the sink where he washed his hands and face. He looked at himself in the mirror. His reflection winked back at him.

Ask Truman. He ran his fingers through his silver highlights. *He's your man.*

He left the bathroom with Lola trailing behind him. He pulled out his wallet and threw £20 on the table.

A nice tip for the false blonde.

He walked slowly across the room, deliberately looking into the eyes of the people at the tables.

"Oh, thank you," said a voice from behind him.

So she's found the tip.

When Jason reached the door and turned, his eyes met the steady gaze of an older woman in an apron. Her face was serious, her lips taut. She had a heavy-handed dose of blusher on her cheeks. He was about to call out, *No problem*, but the woman cut him off before he could speak. The café had fallen silent and the other patrons had their eyes fixed on him. The woman's harsh tone bounced over their heads.

"Are you alright, love?" Then pointing at Truman she said, "Has your dad here been giving you a hard time?"

LYNNE E. BLACKWOOD

CLICKETY-CLICK

The carriage clock continues its muffled clickety-click as it has done for generations. It was The Mother's pride and joy. The carcass of the brass mechanism is an ugly towering beast of veined marble and gilt. It has sat on the mantelpiece for as long as Marge can remember. No one knows why it made that noise. It just did, even though carriage clocks were supposed to be silent. It murmured like the sick heart of a ghost – the brass balls turning in uneven rhythms to a silent sarabande.

"Balls…" Uttering the word sent The Mother into an indignant rage. "You are a dreadful, vulgar child. I forbid you to say that. Spheres, brass spheres, that's what they are."

As a grown woman, she still confuses spheres with fears and cringes at the admonishing whiplash of The Mother's voice. "Discipline, discipline, that's what you need."

Discipline was as regular as the clickety-click of the circling brass: the heavily-perfumed hand on a child's cheek filling the mouth with copper-tasting blood. Dusky bruises on the skin while the gleaming clock on the mantelpiece measured out The Mother's moods.

Marge turns in her seat to face the empty armchair opposite. No breath disturbs the air, no pulse of flaccid flesh, but she continues to feel The Mother's presence. The Mother is a shadow against the stained and faded chintz of the armchair. Marge sits further back into her seat, fingers twitching. The dense smell of rotting foliage rises with dancing blackflies from a neglected houseplant hidden somewhere in the darkened room.

"A penny for them, Marge," Violet says.

Her aunt is perched on the sofa – a tiny bird unbalanced on a wire. A battered black hat sits askew on her head. Strands of spun gossamer escape the hat in misty wisps. The Mother's younger sister, the runt of the family, is always dishevelled, as if she's run out of time to dress. Small and – like herself – submissive towards The Mother, Marge has never called Violet "aunt", because as a child she had sensed their shared suffering.

"You'd have to give me ten pounds for my thoughts, Violet," Marge says.

Lightness, she thinks, we need lightness in this room.

"Oh, I can't afford that on my pension," the aunt laughs nervously. "She is still here, isn't she?"

The quiet hangs between them, broken only by the clickety-click on the mantelpiece.

There is a tiny glint from where Violet sits, as she slides the silver spoon around the porcelain cup of tea. A faint whiff of camphor wafts from the shapeless black outfit on Violet's bony frame. A childhood memory returns to Marge: a decomposing blackbird with scattered feathers lying on the ground.

Violet always looked so frail, while The Mother's rolls of fat and goitred throat betrayed her eating excesses up to the moment of her death.

Marge stares again at the stained chintz armrest. She is uneasy. There, where The Mother's paralysed hand had lain, where sweaty palms had soaked the fabric over the days, months and years, is a semi-invisible imprint. She makes out what could be the blurred outline of fingers and again, pushes her body farther back into her seat.

Move away, escape, slip between furniture, hide in corners was the quickened sarabande she had danced from the time she was a child. No more hiding now.

The Mother had gone quickly, unexpectedly.

Old fears creep back and Marge's fingers grip the armrest. The touch of the fabric is reassuring and she gently scratches it with her nails, feeling the chintz's roughness against fingertips.

Clickety-click fills the darkened room.

The furniture will be thrown out, she thinks. She looks down at the carpet where, in front of the armchair, The Mother's slippered feet had lain. No stain, but the pile is worn.

"She certainly stamped her feet a lot, didn't she?" Violet's tiny voice drifts with the smell of tea and camphor across to Marge.

"Yes, she did, Violet. And the kicks, trying to trip us up all the time. Do you remember? A full tray or cup of hot tea and she'd do her best to make us fall. She couldn't get up, but knew how to swing those fat legs right up to the day she died."

The two women fall quiet.

"She's still here, you know," Violet whispers. "I can feel her."

"Me too, Violet, but she can't harm us anymore," Marge says, but doubts her words.

"She always was a wicked one. The way she treated you was terrible." Violet shifts on her perch and attempts a smile with faded lips.

"Yes," Marge says.

It is all she can say. The Mother's death has cleansed the hurt and ended the wait – the years of counting the hours and days till she could be free from her.

Marge now floats in a calm emptiness and welcomes the relief. She looks intently at the clock. Clickety-click.

"Not long, now, Violet. It will soon be finished. Then we can go." The brass spheres, dulled by dust and grime, continue their slow sarabande. "She will never be able to make you afraid again."

"You won't leave me again, here with… her, Marge, will you?"

"I won't abandon you, I promise," she says, sending Violet a reassuring smile. Violet's fear is palpable across the camphor and tea-scented air.

It is night behind the drawn drapes. A sliver of lamplight enters from the street. Clickety-click. There is a porcelain clink as another lump of sugar dissolves in the hot whirl of tea and milk.

"Do you think she remembers, like us?"

"I hope so, Violet." Marge continues, gazing at the carriage clock.

"What she did to you was…"

"I know. Unspeakable. So let's not talk about it. It won't be long, now. Be patient, and remember what she did to you as well."

Clickety-click.

The women wait, Marge held safely within the cushion feathers, fingers scratching the chintz fabric, Violet still teetering on the sofa's edge, picking at invisible threads sprouting from her black clothes.

Clickety, clickety. Then silence.

The spheres cease their slow sarabande. Marge smiles. The darkness has swallowed the faint shadow on the armchair.

"She's gone, Violet. We can leave."

Violet's pale features light up. "Now?" The word tumbles out as she rises, holding out her hands to the younger woman.

"No goodbyes will be said, Violet. It is time to leave for better things." Marge cocks her head and listens. "I can hear them coming. We should go now."

The two women take a last glance at the front room. The sound of muffled voices coming from the hallway grows nearer. They lock hands, hover and listen.

"Blimey, James, find that bloody light switch, will you?"

"Alright, I've got it. Don't tell me you're afraid of the dark, Steve? A big man like you!"

"Not anywhere else, mate, but this house… people talk, you know. Things happened here. You're a young'un, you won't remember."

"Bloody hell, look at all this! Couldn't the old biddy get a cleaner in from time to time, with all the money she had?"

"Mean witch, that's what she was. I lived down the road, you know. I knew the girl, the old witch's daughter and the aunt. They all lived here together. Then the girl died. An accident, they said. She fell over in the front room and hit her head on the fireplace. Pretty girl too, only thirty or so. Aunt died about fifteen years later and the old biddy lived alone after that. We all thought she killed them. My word – who's been – looks like somebody's been having a cuppa in here."

A porcelain cup containing mouldy tea-dregs lies on the table beside an empty sugar bowl. Blackfly dance a slow sarabande above a stained chintz armchair. An odour of camphor lingers as the blood-red marble carriage clock on the mantelpiece ceases to tick. Clickety-click, click… click…

PETE KALU

GETTING HOME: A BLACK URBAN MYTH
(THE PROOFREADER'S SIGH)

Strange things happen after midnight. Three weeks ago, a Friday,
I was coming back from London. Earlier trains had been cancelled and I was in this crowded last train. We were all crammed
in, my mouth was dry as feathers, my stomach twisted with
hunger. I got out at Manchester Piccadilly, uncreased myself, and
headed to the city centre bus stop on Oldham Rd[1] to get back to
Oldham where I live.

OK, nobody rushes to get back to Oldham. There are no
flowing cornfields, no marble terrazza[2] leading to sublime water-
falls in which bronze demigods frolic, no sumptuous hot sand
beaches up which fishermen haul their boats, land and fry their
catch to the praise songs of waiting villagers. Nevertheless, it is
home; there is a lockable door there for me and, behind that, a
decent mattress.

I must have dozed on the train like a horse[3], sleeping on my
feet. The train must have been further delayed en route because
it was later than I'd thought – the battery on my phone had no-
barred me somewhere between Stoke-on-Trent and Crewe[4] so I
couldn't check the time.

Waves of cleaners were slipping in and out of office blocks.
McDonalds[5] had placed a security guard on their door. I get

---

1. Sic. Fact check: actually Oldham Street.
2. Sic. Cannot mean *terrazza* as in balcony. Probably means *passaggio*
   (walkway) though these are never marble.
3. Sic. Generally, horses are not found dozing on trains.
4. Sic. No London trains call at both Stoke-on-Trent and Crewe.
   Probably means Stafford and Crewe.
5. Sic. Fact check: there is no McDonalds between Manchester
   Piccadilly and Oldham Street.

knocked into "no offence like" by some burly bloke. A girl – a buttery mix of cigarette, alcohol and Chanel No. 5 – ran up and kissed me, no doubt for a dare and I didn't fight it. Someone was dry-heaving by the Spar All Night Kiosk.[6] It was that kind of late.

The air was some strange miasma[7] – a balmy cocktail of pepperoni pizza fumes and the convecting heat of a long, hot day was infusing the night with good vibes. Mancunians are not used to this – heat – and they're all a bit thrown. I drag my weary ass through it all, clutching my flight bag of poetry publisher's proofs. As I walk, I reel off a couple of Inshallaahs, God Willings[8] and pluck the entrails of a sacrificial chicken in my sleep-addled mind, before stepping up to the podium, face oiled, every one of my twisted dreads in immaculate place as I ask, please, no more applause, I am not worthy, my poems are not worthy...[9]

It was only when I got to the bus stop I realised that the regular buses had stopped. I looked around. There were six of us at the bus stop, or spread about, waiting; only one of us, me, was sober. There is no greater hell than being the only sober person at a bus stop after Friday night's pub and club chuck-out time. Everyone's heaving or bawling or boasting. Nobody but you can read the bus timetable.

I could feel a long line of zeds waiting to rush my brain; I could feel my consciousness slipping off like petals from a fading flower; I could feel the God of Sleep arriving in her spray-gold Chariot.[10] A not unpleasant numbness was just beginning to settle over me when the bus shelter frame shook and the glass I was leaning on shuddered.

This tattooed knucklehead, at least forty, staggers up to me – big chops, red face, rubber legs. He has this wary, I'm-a-hard-man-just-finished-my-prison-sentence-for-gbh look. He sways

---

6. Sic. See Note 5. No Spar All Night Kiosk either.
7. Sic. Miasma is an unpleasant smell. Prob. means ether.
8. Repetition: Inshallah means God willing.
9. I am not paid enough to untangle the confusion of tenses in this paragraph.
10. Sic. Perhaps a reference to the Greek God Hypnos (male). No reference in antiquity to him ever arriving in a gold chariot, whether sprayed, dipped or painted.

past me and he's in front of the timetable board at the bus stop, squinting.

He turns to me. "When's the next bus?"

It's a bark, a command. Maybe he's ex-military, I muse; there were many around now – damaged in mind and body – after all the illegal British wars.

"According to the timetable it's at half past twelve – half past midnight," I say, smiling at him.

"What time is it now?" he snaps back, swaying – which is a hard trick to pull off.

"Yeah, when's it comin?" someone else calls out.

I'm wearing jeans and a black jacket. I don't have a clip board or walkie-talkie or anything, but everyone seems to think I work for the bus company. Maybe it's my rahtid[11] flight bag.[12] My mouth opens to tell them all to go fuck themselves, then closes again. I shrug off my zeds. The Windrushers[13] arrived in Britain and became bus conductors. Although my roots are African – not West Indian – this subtlety is for another time. I bow to my role. This is honouring our predecessors. We are born to conduct buses.

"It's half past," I say, "bus should be along any minute."

There's a row of three young women, not past twenty, on the doorway steps behind the bus stop. Standing by them are two lads[14] – the boyfriends I presume – both swaggering drunk, giving mouth[15] to whoever passes by. One of them, the slightly heavier one, has a long stick by his side, like a cue stick. A Pakistani-looking bloke my age, still in kitchen whites under his coat, comes along. He pauses at the stop, takes in the scene and, wisely perhaps, carries on walking. So I'm still the only sober guy here.

---

11. Jamaican patois. Yet later narrator says he is of African heritage?
12. If he slept like a horse, perhaps saddlebag is better here than a flight bag? He has after all stepped off a train, not a plane.
13. Only reference I can find to Windrushers is to a UK gliding club. Were they blown off course? I suggest cut or rephrase.
14. Maths is not this writer's strong point I suspect. So far seven people "at or around" bus stop including himself, not six, as stated earlier.
15. Is this a Northern expression? It reads as slightly sexual, or is that just me? Suggest rephrase or omit.

And I'm the only one who's not white, not that anybody's mentioned this so far. I've been around the world; I can handle the situation.

The two boyfriends get a quarrel going with a couple of bouncers standing outside the King's Head just four doorways down. I thought bouncers were trained to be calm and negotiate a situation without violence. These must have been on holiday when they ran that course. The boyfriend with the cue stick that isn't a cue stick starts doing these Bruce Lee kung fu moves, goading the bouncers. His mate is bopping about like the old style boxers used to. The bouncers are huge. The two lads are puny. Do I intervene? Are you crazy? I decide I can do without the bus, it's only ten miles.[16]

As I walk on there are various yelps, expletives, splintering and ejaculations coming from the vicinity of the nightclub doors. I'm about to turn round but… nah, still not worth it. If people's sense of fun extends to rushing at bouncers to get their heads busted, so be it.

I look down the road to Oldham. It's a vast, bleak, empty landscape, known locally as Miles Platting. And now rain.

I suppose in this situation, for some, a hotel becomes a viable option. In my eyes I am a promising young black poet with several publications under his belt, on the cusp of literary and financial greatness. In the mean eyes of the grasping telephone loan arrangers, I am no more than a 37-year-old Lancastrian with 15 years of sporadic missed payments who, *if I may speak off the record, sir, would be best advised to change career. The poetry obviously does not pay; after 15 years even you can do the maths on that one, with respect, sir.*

Yeah, right. Expensive loans but free careers advice.[17]

So, I'm walking home out of the city centre along Oldham Rd. It's 2 a.m-ish, dark, light rain – par for the course for Manchester. The street is deserted. I walk on and on. The rain keeps it up. A white woman comes into view on the same side of the street.

The navigation of public space by a lone black male in the night

---

16. The tenses are all over the place in this paragraph. Again.
17. Good advice for this writer. Every so often someone at a call centre speaks sense.

is problematic with or without hoodies, with or without "stand-your-ground" laws, with or without a Neighbourhood Watch committee in place – or whether or not that space is "gated", should we say? Likewise, the ability (as opposed to the right) of a lone woman to move unmolested through the night in whatever kit she's decided to don. I nudge my zeds[18] aside and try to process the information provided by my eyes. From this distance she could be a very light-skinned black woman, in which case she might give me a short nod of recognition as we glide past each other, our black solidarity thing boosted. She is in a party dress. (I would like to provide more information on the dress: e.g. an A-line bolero effect with diamante detail and a flounced flapper hemline, scrunched at the midriff, clutched at the waist, and single shoulder strap. But a man's got to know his limitations. It was a dress. A party dress.)[19]

You can speculate why she is walking late at night:

a.   A party just finished and no taxi money?

b.   A lover's tiff?

c.   She's her auntie's main carer and needs to get back to help her auntie dress in the morning?

d.   Kids to get to school?

The gap between us is closing and I can see now she is alabaster white. Her body language – a stiffening of the back, a slight drop in the head, a faltering in her footwork – tells me we two are not about to duet to the soundtrack of *Fame*. Her increasing hesitation makes me decide that out of consideration for her, conscious of her vulnerability, and to make it easy for us both, I'll cross to the other side of the street. But she must have had the same idea. Just as I cross, she crosses too. She's convinced now I'm after her. We're on the same side of the street again and closing. She crosses the road again and starts walking back in the direction she has just come – slowly at first, then faster till she's running. Running away from me along the deserted London Rd.[20] Ah well, I did my best.

---

18. Infelicitous?

19. Should either describe the dress or not. Brackets become annoying. Dress as described is a logical impossibility.

20. Sic. It was Oldham Rd a couple of paragraphs earlier. Fact check: no London Rd in Manchester leads to or from Oldham.

It's 2 something a.m. The light rain has lightened into almost a mist.

Beauty is everywhere, even on the road to Oldham. I come across a scene that slides my eyebrows up my forehead and bunches my cheeks. Rabbits. Like a scene out of *Watership Down*, a hundred rabbits are bobbing up and down, nibbling grass on the wide roadside verge where the Italian Restaurant used to be before they flattened it for lack of custom. By day, this arterial road roars with lorries, commuters, bankers, fish vans, prison vans, car-parts couriers, mobile hairdressers. And lo, by night, there appear jug-eared, white, bob-tailed, jerky-up-and-down, fluffy, cuddly-toyable, cookable rabbits. I've stopped. They look at me. I look at them. They dart, then sit. Dart, then sit. Like my career, or Jockey Wilson[21] (Prince of the Flighted Arrow).

Misty rain is the long distance walker's dream. This is the mist rain of my high school's feeble showers, the mist rain of a dog's sneeze, the mist rain of a girlfriend's errant hair spray. It soothes the soul and coats my glasses so I have to keep taking them off and wiping them. It's while doing this that I turn the corner and there's a man, a white man, lying on the edge of the pavement. He's shouting, "Help me! Help me!"

He looks in a bad way. Maybe a car has swiped him. It's wet, late. I'm tired, but you can't walk by. Did not that great Roman thinker, Thucydides[22] say it is the duty of every citizen to come to the aid of his brother? This is the very essence of our civilisation, the foundation stone of citizenship itself, without which the Barbarians will soon be clambering over our city walls, our temples to destroy, and we will all be hastened to hell in a handcart? Something like that.

He's seen me coming, and he's been trying, uselessly, to get up. All he needs is a helping hand. I shuffle my flight bag from one shoulder to the other, sweep my dreads off my face, bend down

---

21. Darts player. Died 2012. Fact check: his nickname was "Jocky". Can find no reference to him being "the prince of the flighted arrow".
22. Sic. Thucydides was Greek; need I say more? The entire reference is a load of cobblers, containing as many errors as you can shake a stick at.

and offer my hand. He sees me close up and a mask of horror has installed itself on his face.

"Somebody else help me! Somebody else help me!" he shouts.

I pull back my hand and straighten up. Some civilisations deserve Barbarians inside their city walls.

This walking home business is not so simple, I decide. Maybe I should try hailing a cab. Three empty taxis have gone past in the last half hour of my walking, all of them heading back to the city centre. Surely they would want to make a little more money before calling it quits for the night? But I've got no cash. There's a Post Office close by with a cash machine in its wall. No one around. No one to panic. I put my card in the machine. A police car screams round the corner.

"Stay right there! Hands where I can see them!"

It's three something a.m., light rain, dark. I'm tired. "OK."

I'm too wet to run anyway.

While they're questioning me – who I am, where I live – a car with no headlights comes screaming round the corner and smacks into a bus stop, concertinas it, then catapults into a lamp post that crashes into the road.[23]

"You going to see to that?" I ask the cops. "You could do me later?"

They hate advice.

"We're doing fine here," they say. "Now, how long have you lived at this address and what is your mother's maiden name?"

They continue frisking me. There's blood oozing from the wrecked car, groans, but they display a complete insouciance to that. Once they've crawled all over me so they can recognise me in the dark by the shape of my frozen genitals, they let me go and proceed to the RTA23.

I turn to continue my transaction with the global capitalist system but my card has disappeared. Yeah. Still, the cops who frisked me found a tenner in my back pocket and handed it to me, though they kept my little bag of herbs.

I walk on, watching to hail a cab. For the same reason – known

---

23. No local newspaper articles cover this accident and I can find no official crime report on it.

only to God – that buses do this – several come at once. The first has an "I Heart Pakistan" sticker. It flies right past me – en route to Lahore I suppose. The second cab's driven by a huge Rasta. He appears to be pulling over, then speeds up and off. "Heh, heh, heh!" Yes, Rasta, you can laugh. The third cab has this bald-headed, olive-skinned guy at the wheel. He veers towards me, only to speed through this mother of a puddle, drenching me. In the back of that third cab I distinctly see the woman who fled back on London Road and the guy who'd been knocked over. The woman is waving my plastic cash card at me. And the guy's waving my little bag of herbs. As I'm taking all this in, the late night bus, all its lights off, flies past me, empty.[24]

---

24. Finished? Thank God!

LEONE ROSS

THE MÜLLERIAN EMINENCE

The Müllerian ducts end in an epithelial [membranous tissue] elevation, [called] the Müllerian eminence... in the male [foetus] the Müllerian ducts atrophy, but traces ... are represented by the testes... In the female [foetus] the Müllerian ducts... undergo further development. The portions which lie in the genital core fuse to form the uterus and vagina... The hymen represents the remains of the Müllerian eminence.

In adult women, the Müllerian eminence has no function.

—*Anatomy of the Human Body*, Henry Gray, 1918

Charu Deol lived in the large cold city for five months and four days before he found the hymen, wedged between a wall and a filing cabinet in the small law office where he cleaned on Thursday nights. The building was an old government-protected church, but the local people only worshipped on the weekend, so the rector rented the empty rooms. If Charu Deol had been a half-inch to the right, he might have missed the hymen, but the sunshine coming through the stained glass window in streams of red, blue and green illuminated the corner where it lay.

Charu Deol thought it strange that a building could be protected. There were people playing music on the trains for money, and two nights ago, he'd seen a man wailing for cold in the street. He thought the government of such a fine, big city might make sure people were protected first.

Still, he'd known several buildings that acted like people, including his father's summer house, with its white walls and sweating ceiling and its tendency to dance and creak when his parents argued. They'd argued a great deal, mostly because his mother worked there as a maid and complained that the walls were conspiring with his father's wife. Charu Deol was also aware of a certain nihilism in the character of the room where he now lived – the eaves and floor crumbling at an ever-increasing and truculent rate. When he ate the reheated fish and chips with curry sauce that his landlady left him in the evenings before work, he could hear the room complaining loudly.

The hymen didn't look anything like the small and fleshy curtain he might have imagined, not that he'd ever thought about such a thing. At first it didn't occur to him that he'd found a sample of that much-prized remnant of gestational development, the existence – or lack thereof – which had caused so much pain and misery for millennia. He hardly knew what a hymen was, having only ever laid down with one woman in his life: the supple fifty-something maid who worked for his mother.

Away from his father's summer house, his mother had her own maid, because what else did you work for, after all? She had offered warm and sausagey arms, the sweet breath of a much younger woman, and a kind of delighted amusement at his nakedness. After he'd expelled himself inside her – something that took longer than he'd foreseen, distracted as he was by the impending return of his mother – she'd not let him up, but gripped his buttocks in her hands, pressing her entire pelvis into him and pistoning her hips with great purpose and breathlessness.

He was left quite sore and with the discouraging suspicion that she'd used him as one might a firm cushion, the curved end of a table, the water jetting out of a spigot, or any other thing that facilitated frottage. Afterwards, she treated him exactly as before: as if he was a vase she had to clean under and never quite found a place for.

He used the side of his broom to pull the soft, tiny crescent-shaped thing toward him; then, bent double, he touched the hymen with his forefinger.

First, he realised it was a hymen. Next, that the hymen had lived inside a twenty-seven-year old woman, for twenty-seven years. When she was twenty-four, her boyfriend returned home, bad tempered from a quarrel with his boss. When she asked him what was wrong one time too many, the boyfriend – who prior to that moment had washed dishes and protected her from the rain and gone with her to see band concerts and helped her home when she was drunk, and collapsed laughing with her on the sofa – grabbed her arm and squeezed it as tight as he could, causing a sharp pain in her shoulder and her heart. When she said, "You're hurting me," like the women in movies and books, he squeezed all the tighter and looked happy doing it, and the little flesh crescent inside her slid through her labia and down the leg of her jeans and onto their kitchen floor. The boyfriend swept it up the next day. The bin bag burst in the apartment rubbish dispenser; the hymen got stuck to the edge of someone's yellow skirts and this little pink crescent was pulled along the cold and windy city streets.

Now it was gently pulsating in Charu Deol's horrified hand.

The knowledge inside the hymen did not manifest in good and tidy order, like a narrative on a TV screen. It was more, thought Charu Deol, like being a djinn or a soul snake, slipping inside the twenty-seven-year-old woman's skin and looking out through her eyes. He had the discomforting feeling that her body was a bad fit, and stifling, like a hot-water bottle around his thinner, browner self, baggy at the elbows and around the nose. He knew the woman was still with her boyfriend and that she had thought about what she'd do if he ever squeezed her arm again. Charu Deol knew they pretended that the arm-squeeze and the not-stopping was a nothing, or a small thing, instead of the cruel thing it was, and that the hair on her arm where the boyfriend gripped her was like a singed patch of grass that never grew again.

Charu Deol sat down on the floor of the law-office church and saw that his hands were shaking. The hymen felt like thin silk between his fingers. What was he to *do* with it? To discard it was like throwing out a prayer book or a sacred chalice. Before he knew what he was doing, he took a new dusting cloth from his cart, carefully wrapped it around the hymen and placed it in his pocket.

When he got home, he stole a small, plastic bag from his landlady's kitchen – the kind she packed with naan and Worcestershire sauce – and tied it up with a plastic-covered piece of wire for work. She would be angry when she discovered his theft, so he left a pound coin on the floor, to the left of the refrigerator, as if he'd dropped it.

She'd put the coin in her pocket without asking if it belonged to him.

Alone in his room, he unwrapped the tiny, silken, throbbing thing and rubbed it between his thumb and forefinger. He was assaulted with the woman's story again: the squeeze, the disbelief, the lurking, tiny fear. This was why, when the boyfriend slapped the backs of friends or laughed too loud, a small part of the twenty-seven-year-old woman winced and moved away.

Charu Deol placed the hymen inside the plastic bag and sealed it, setting it on the nightstand where he could see it.

He was a witness, and that was important.

He couldn't sleep, conscious of the lumpy mattress, the large cupboard that took up most of his boxroom, the smell of the thin blue blankets his landlady stole from the old people's home where she worked. No one wants them, she said, no one has any use for them. He didn't know why she stole them; all she did was stack them in the cupboard.

He thought of his father, a man who had never held him or, as far as he knew, been proud of him at all.

He got up and slipped the plastic bag in between the ninth and tenth blue blanket. Before he did so, he examined it one more time. In the dim light, the hymen looked like a beautiful eye: brown and dark and soft and wet, its worn edges like eyelashes, an expression he couldn't fathom at its centre.

Charu Deol took long walks. That was what big-city people did. He went to a small and well-manicured park during the hours he should have been sleeping. He bent his head near the small park pond and dipped his long cracked toes in the water until someone stared and he realised he was up to his ankles at the cold, dank lip. He watched a man teach his two girls cricket with a tennis racket. He watched an orange-helmeted man run down the path, holding his son's scooter, laughing and calling, *Use your brakes!* He thought about city people soaking in baths and whether they noticed the scum floating to the surface like bad tea, and about the landlady asking him if he'd like her bath water after she got out and how he'd stammered, No thank you. That's the way you do it here, she said, and her face reminded him of his mother's when his father's wife went out to get sweet biscuits at the end of a meal – his mother's long, dignified neck.

A woman walked past with a shrill voice and a plaid shirt and a friend eating grapes, while he dried his cold feet on the grass. When they were gone, he saw the small, iridescent thing by his big toe and wanted to ignore it, or to decide it was a lost earring. He closed his eyes. But he could not leave it there, forsaking his new knowledge, as if he had no responsibility.

Charu Deol lay on the grass, curled around the hymen, and played nudge-chase with it, like a cat with half-dead prey, snatching at the air above it, using his thin sleeve to push it around under the soft edges of the setting sun. This shrill-voiced woman's hymen was not as soft or simple as the brown eye that lay between the ninth and tenth blue blankets in his room. This one was round, with seven holes in its centre, reminding him of the way thin, raw bread dough broke when you dragged it across a hot stove; but he'd never seen dough encrusted with stars. This hymen glittered so ferociously against the wet grass, he thought it might leave him and soar into the sky where it belonged.

He touched it, expecting it to burn him.

The woman with the shrill voice had been raped twice before her tenth birthday, each time by her father, who smelled expensive then, and still did now. It was not the pain the woman remembered, but the shuddering of her father's body and the way he closed his eyes, as if he could see the burning face of God. She had never had an orgasm because she couldn't bear that same shuddering inside of her; if it broke free, it might kill all the flowers that ever were. Charu Deol knew all this and also that the shrill-voiced woman sometimes wondered why no more than twice? Was it because her father had stopped loving her?

Charu Deol shivered on the grass. After a while, he picked up the silver-star hymen and put it into the plastic bag in his coat pocket because part of him had known another would come. He watched the geese until a park attendant nudged him with a broom. What's up, chappie, he said. He was an older man, with the dark chin of an uncle.

What do you do when evil comes, asked Charu Deol.

The attendant took out a pack of mentholated cigarettes. He sat down next to Charu Deol and smoked two while watching the geese. I don't know, said the park attendant. But I think you have to be rational and careful about these things.

Charu Deol took the plastic bag out of his coat pocket and showed it to him.

I think you're very emotional, said the park attendant, and bared his teeth. He didn't seem to see the bag. Chin up, laddie, he said.

Charu Deol sat on his lumpy bed that night and examined the bagged and beautiful hymens. Surely, he thought, they belonged to virgins. But neither of these violated women were pure. Was this a strange sickness of city women that no one had thought to tell him? Certainly he hadn't known city women before, with so many ideas and so many of them about him. More than once, he'd found himself feeling sorry for them, even the ones who looked at him strangely on the 453 bus and moved their purses to the left when they saw him.

His Tuesday job was for a company that made industrial bleach. He liked it best there. Despite the smell of ammonia, his cart shone and the teeth of his lady boss also shone and she looked into his face, not through the back of his head – and laughed loudly when he told her about the cracks in every one of his landlady's china cups.

Is your country very beautiful, Charu?

He thought it very familiar of her to address him so. He could see she was made of the same stuff as his mother's maid, very different from the finer skin of his father. She lifted the hair off her neck, which was something he thought she should only do with a man she knew well. Nevertheless, he nodded politely and the boss lady left and he went to the large unisex toilet and scrubbed yellow and brown stains out of the bowls, his rubber gloves rolled all the way up his wrists and forearms.

When he backed out of the stall and turned around, there were three hymens on the floor. One of them was like a piece of thunder singing a dark song and rolling back and forth – the hymen of a woman in her fifties who got something called a good backhander when she talked too much, and a pinch on the waist when her opinions sounded more clever than her husband's. The second reminded him of a teardrop. When he lifted it to his face, it filled him with memories of a woman whose husband once ironed the inside of her left thigh like a shirt. The third one slipped him inside the skin of a woman who had a happy life except for the time she'd walked home from school and a stranger crept up behind her, put his hand up her skirt and clutched her vulva.

Charu Deol was so startled by the sudden feeling of invasion that he dropped the hymen in the soap dish and had to fish it out again. Two more hung from the rolling towels, like wind chimes, twins: one raped, one not, but he knew the untouched sister stayed with the violated twin because she wished it had been her instead. He clutched the sink; he couldn't see his reflection because there was a spray of crystalline hymens across the mirror, each smaller than the last. He bent closer and realised it was only one after all, exploded across the glass like a sneeze. The woman it belonged to had clouted her best friend's fiancée when he'd tried to hold her down. He hit her so hard in return he made her deaf in one ear. She had never told her best friend, but she didn't go to her house anymore and that had caused problems between them. The blood from her ear had tinged the hymen spray a shy blush-pink.

Charu Deol set about gathering them all.

He thought them safe, slipped between the blue blankets, until Friday. Friday was his landlady's cleaning day; till then he was expected to keep his own room clean, and did so. But he came home to find her shining his floors with a coconut husk and changing the sheets on his bed, her fat, brown back unexpectedly familiar. The blue blankets were stacked on the floor, one plastic bag peeping out from a crevice. He was so frightened she might have thrown them away, or hurt them, that before he knew it he was speaking in his father's baritone, demanding she respect his privacy, please and thank you, and if she couldn't, she could find someone *else* to pay her every Sunday for this shithole. It was a city word and he felt powerful saying it to her.

The landlady stared at him as if he was a new and rare object. Please yourself, she said, and shuffled away from the half-polished room. Do someone a favour, he heard her muttering, as he scooped up the plastic bags. Look what you get.

He bought himself a long coat from a charity shop. The coat had many pockets and, after his Sunday job, he sat on his bed and sewed more into the lining. His Sunday job was at a university, where he cleaned staff offices and found thirty-eight hymens. Some were like bright cherry-red fingernails; one was s-shaped, glimmering wrought iron; he tapped it and heard a ting-ting sound like his mother's bracelet on her kitchen pots. One re-minded him of a cat's paw; another smelled like a fresh sea urchin; another like a wet leaf. It didn't surprise him to find that eleven were from women abused by scholarly, well-respected men.

As the numbers increased, anxiety overtook him: the risk of forgetting even one precious story. To forget would be sacrilege. He stole two reams of recycled typing paper from his Sunday job and wrote down the stories of the women and read them at night, trying to commit them to memory. On Wednesday, he was fired from his Wednesday job when he refused to take off his suspi-ciously bulging coat for the security guard. On Thursday, the landlady left a note from his Sunday job, to say he must not come back – their cameras had recorded his theft of paper.

At his Tuesday job, the boss who was overly familiar left her hymen on the edge of her computer desk.

It was so pretty he mistook it for a small, white daisy. When he touched it, his head reeled with alcohol: cranberry vodka and alcopops. The previous Friday she'd gone around the back of the pub with two men who seemed quite nice; she was sexually aroused but also frightened and when one of them said some-thing lewd and dark, she wanted to run back into the pub but the second one had a hand on her hip and she decided she might as well bite her lip because making a fuss might. Might. Might just.

Hurt.

She found Charu Deol weeping for her, his cheek hard against

97

her computer screen and fired him for the way he looked at her, his face broken open. She said if he told anybody about unfair dismissal, she would say he tried to rape her.

Don't look at me, she said. You don't know.

Charu Deol's head is light and empty as he walks through the early morning sunshine. The coat full of hymens rubs his ankles; the satchel on his back is stuffed with scribbled paper. He is concerned about himself. He has taken to muttering in public places, to stopping men on the road to tell them about women. He needs help. He cannot witness these stories alone. If he could just explain; if he could just ask them, politely, not to hurt anyone; if he could just talk to enough of them, it might stem the tide. Most thrust him away, mistaking him for drunk.

It's not true, say the few who listen when he tells them that it's one in every three women he sees. It's complicated, say the men. What can I do, they say.

He doesn't know.

His skin hurt. He feared it was transparent, exposing his internal organs. This was not a job for one man, not for a man who needed to pay rent, although he found himself less concerned with such banalities. He didn't speak to women at all; he didn't want to hurt or offend them. He found himself respectful with his landlady, since his last harsh words, cleaning not just his own room, but the entire house, including her roof, and digging her backyard until she yelled at him. He was relieved that she was among the unscathed, and marvelled at women on the streets for their luck or stoicism.

One tall lady left a trail of hymen strands behind her like golden cobwebs, a story so long, fractured and dark that he bent over in the busy street and cried out his mother's name. He wondered if he would ever see his mother again; if he could bear to take the risk, now that he was witness. He watched the golden cobweb woman laughing with a friend, swinging her bag, her heels clicking. How was she standing upright? How did they restrain themselves from screaming through the world, cleaving heads asunder, raking eyeballs? How did the universe not break into small pieces?

He became convinced that the hymens in his coat were rotting. Despite their beauty they were pieces of flesh, after all. At other times, he imagined them glass; feared he would trip and fall and shatter them, piercing his veins and tendons. Still, he walked every day and gathered more. They littered his room, piled under the bed and towards the ceiling.

He bought a lock for his door.

On Monday, or perhaps it was Thursday, he took himself to the church that was a law office. The gravestones ached with the weight of early Spring daffodils. The rector found him bent over one of the graves, inserting his fingers into the damp earth, hands going from coat pocket to soil. When he said, Son, can I help you, Charu Deol asked if this was blessed earth, and would it protect blessed things. He clutched the area around his heart, then the area around his neck, and whined like a dog when the rector tried to soothe him.

Can you not see them, Charu Deol said.

What, my son, asked the rector.

Charu Deol grasped the man's lapels and dragged himself upright. He was weeping, and frightening a holy man, but the hymens were thick on the ground like blossom, and the task was suddenly, ferociously beyond him. He released the rector and ran through the graveyard, past clinking, bleeding, surging, mumbling pieces of women.

The hymens were a sea in his landlady's front yard. He crushed them underfoot, howling and spitting and weeping, feeling them splinter, break, snap, squelch under his heels, like pieces of liver. He tried his key, once, twice, again, wrenched it to the left, and pushed inside. The place was quiet, the dull, lugubrious walls mercifully blank, his bed cool against his face.

The landlady knocked and entered. Lawks lad, she said. I'm worried about you. It can't be all that bad, now. She sat on the edge of the bed and looked at him.

He remembered a son she'd once mentioned; he'd never taken the time to listen. Tell me of your son, he said.

She did, saying that she knew young men. All they needed was a firm hand and a loving heart. The two of them, they'd got off to a bad start, but now she saw he was in need of help. Would he like a cup of tea? He was too handsome a lad to get on so. Charu Deol sniffed, tried to smile, inched forward, put his head on her soft knee. She patted him awkwardly, and he felt a mother's touch in the fingers, and a fatigued kind of hope. He crawled further up her knee, put his face into her hipbone. She smelled familiar. His teeth felt sharp, his fingers sweaty. He could hear flesh outside, beating on the door, crawling up the windowpanes.

He didn't see the hymen inching down her thigh, like a rubied snail, like torn underwear.

GAYLENE GOULD

CHOCOLATE TEA

Dollo can't remember how to make the Chocolate Tea. With an unsteady hand, she pours the viscous condensed milk into the pan and then shakes a carpet of cocoa powder on top. She wonders whether the sweetness might kick off his diabetes. Once they receive the results, she'll be rid of him. But if his disease progresses he'll have to stay. She stops pouring and snaps the lid back onto the cocoa tub.

In the week leading up to his arrival, she'd trawled the one shop that sold the kinds of goods she'd spent the last forty years trying to forget. She dusted tins and packets of carcinogenic items: condensed milk, hard-dough bread and heavily salted fish. She checked their sell-by dates before slipping them into a basket lined with a soiled local newspaper. After his arrival, she'd risen early every morning to fix his breakfast but, of course, he never had a good word to say. The porridge wasn't cornmeal and there was no plantain with his eggs. She explained that too much fried food wasn't good for his condition. He said she'd become too English, which was why she has trouble keeping a man.

She was shocked when she caught sight of Dick at the Arrivals. The breadth in his shoulders was gone and his thin, birdlike neck strained out of an overly large shirt collar. Even his gait, once long and graceful, snapped awkwardly like a rooster's.

When his eyes caught hers, her heart jump-started. His smile suggested he was pleased to see her. She'd gathered up her shopping from between her feet, and pushed her way to the end of the barrier.

By the time she stood in front of him, his smile had slipped into the bitter twist that she remembered well.

"Dollo, you get fat," he said, his eyes travelling from her face to her feet. She looked down at her widening ankles and soft black shoes deformed by bunions.

"I hope you not going to feed me up so I get fat like you."

He passed her the handle of his old-fashioned, army-green suitcase. His hands, free now, rested on the space where his firm belly used to be. "You see I like to keep myself fit and trim for the ladies and I don't want you messing with that."

He laughed briefly before stalking off, clicking his way through the airport. She watched him walk confidently in the wrong direction, noting that his body was, in fact, eating itself up from the inside. She glanced down at her own fleshy bosom.

★

"It ain't ready yet?"

She jumps, turns to find him standing behind her by the kitchen table.

"Almost," she says, turning back to the stove.

"This here England making you dotish. It's already 8.30. If you'd stayed back home you'd be getting up with the cock. But I forget. Ain't no cock here to wake you."

She waits for him to finish chuckling over his own joke.

★

The hunger and the heat had left her weak and listless that day. She'd been hiding under the house from the sun, throwing stones at the chickens and watching them dash about, hoping to find grain only to peck at hard grit. Just then his shiny shoes and sharp-seamed trousers (pressed by her sister Jackie, no doubt) appeared. He bent over until his head was upside down, and smiled. It was like the sun had come to rest under the house.

"Want some mauby and rock cake?"

Her body twitched with the promise of sweet raisins wrapped around dense dough, washed down by the bittersweet drink.

"Go fetch me some and I'll give you a piece."

★

"What time the doctor calling?"

He is sitting straight-backed at the table, his hands worrying the handles of the knife and fork in front of him. Earlier this week, when she pretended her back was turned, she noticed him repeat this gesture a few times – a shaky worrying of the hands. She had learned to never completely turn her back on Dick even though she made it appear as if she did. She had perfected this as a child, along with a quick surreptitious glance that, in a split second, registered all pertinent facts and potential dangers. Both came in handy when keeping a secret watch on her ex-husband, Eric. That's how she first noticed Dick's shaking hands as he picked up the graduation photo of her son, George, from the cabinet shelf.

"He look like his father."

She had paused, the heels of her palms sunk into the soft dough, which was refusing to firm up despite her aching triceps.

"A good looking boy."

He sighed happily before slipping into a satisfied laugh and replacing the frame back in the wrong spot. He stretched and sauntered toward the living room door.

"He didn't get any of you, did he?"

She lifted the dough and slammed it hard on the tabletop as the door closed behind him. She marched the breath through her nose until the rise and fall of her chest evened out and her head swam with air. Slowly she pivoted forward, until her forehead rested on the floury tabletop.

★

She holds the little brown nutmeg to her nose, smelling the musky fertileness of the Caribbean, before grating soft flakes from the aromatic seed into the pan.

"This morning they said…"

"I bet you hoping they give me the all-clear so you can send me home."

She turns sharply to find him watching her with amusement. Slowly, she carries on her stirring.

★

The rich brown earth whirred beneath her bare feet as she hurried down the sunbaked path to Miss Molly's. She'd speeded up, imagining the first mouthful of rock cake and mauby filling her mouth. She'd take a bite and then swill any leftover space with the ice-cool drink. She'd hold onto each mouthful for as long as she could, chewing thirty-three times like Mother instructed, until the sweet and bitter mixture ran down her throat all by itself.

Hands on hips, Miss Molly smiled as she panted up the yard.

"You a mad dog or an Englishman or what?"

It was the first time she had heard that phrase. She'd seen a mad dog once before, down by Barraouallie Beach. It was spinning on itself, white froth spurting from its mouth but she couldn't imagine a red-cheeked Santa look-a-like behaving that way.

In the shadow of the doorway overhang, sweat ran down her face and the front and back of her dress. She waited a second so the words wouldn't pile into each other.

"I come for Dick mauby and rock cake, Miss Molly."

Miss Molly raised her eyebrows and pushed up her bottom lip at the same time.

"Eh henh," she said, shuffling into the shadows of her kitchen. "He must be pleased with himself to treat himself so."

She returned with the pitcher of mauby and a large paper bag in her hands. Dollo had to clench and unclench her fists to stop from grabbing them from Miss Molly's soft, dimpled fingers. Miss Molly held the bag and the jug toward her but, as the girl reached forward, she pulled back half an inch.

"He going give you some for coming all this way?" Miss Molly gave her a suspicious look.

"Of course."

How dare Miss Molly doubt her brother so – he being a policeman-in-training and as tall and graceful as he was? Dollo folded her arms in a gesture of solidarity with her brother and raised her chin defiantly at Miss Molly.

"Well, that all right then," she said and handed over the treats. The girl could hardly remember dropping the money into Miss Molly's hand before she was at the bottom of the lane, her eyes fixed on the mauby in the pitcher.

★

"You going to stir that chocolate tea to death?"

The chocolate tea is thick and stewy. Her stomach churns at

the thought of so rich a taste so early in the morning. She can no longer smell the citrus from her own cup of Earl Grey turned cold on the sideboard.

★

Dick was sitting on the veranda when she returned. He looked like an ice pop, his crisp white shirt perfectly ironed and his hem hovering above his ankles. His face was not even shiny, the shelter of the veranda keeping him cool. By the time she reached the bottom step, the heat was making her tremble.

He held out his hands without leaning forward so she had to walk right up to him and place the sweating pitcher and the bag in his hands. He took them with a tug.

She had imagined it in such detail that, as he took that first bite of cake and swig of mauby, she closed her eyes. She opened them to see crumbs escape his mouth and a stray raisin roll under his seat.

His jaw worked as he broke the cake up in his mouth and she watched the first few gulps of mauby bullet down his throat. She shivered as a damp itch crawled over her skin, and the empty hole in her stomach threatened to swallow her up.

The bites he took were large. Two, and already half the cake was gone. His Adam's apple rose and fell underneath the pitcher bottom – one, two, three, four, five, six times. When the pitcher came down, it was almost empty.

Her chest was tightening, so she had to breathe quickly around it. He didn't even look at her as he took the third bite, the last piece of cake crumbling into his hand. With the other, he picked up the pitcher and, before tipping it back, smiled at her. More crumbs fell to the floor and the panic rose to her throat. Before she could stop herself she'd said it.

"Dick, give me some, nah?"

★

The cup of chocolate tea is on the placemat in front of him. But still she stands there holding the hot pan. It is heavy. She can feel the warmth of the handle through the tea towel.

She looks down on him just like that other time. This time his hands aren't smooth and long but gnarled and twisted, the top of his fingers bending away from the inflamed knuckles. She notices the black hair dye spilling into his bald patch as he brings the shaking cup to his lips. He takes a long, slow slurp. There's a second of quiet and then half a gulp before the rest is sprayed out onto the plastic tablecloth she'd bought especially for his visit.

"Jesus Lord! You trying to poison me?"

He looks up at her, but the challenge in his eyes has gone and all that's left is the urge in her fingertips. She bounces the heavy, steaming pan in her hand twice.

★

He was looking deep into the pitcher as if whatever he had to consider lay in the bottom. There were wet smiley mauby marks on either side of his lips. His long pink tongue slowly wiped them away. It was while she was imagining the taste of mauby on skin that, without looking up, he slowly held out the pitcher toward her. She hesitated for a moment then reached out.

Before she could touch the cool sweating sides of the pitcher he jerked his elbow, launching the remainder of the juice into her face. The splash took away her breath and blinded her, leaving her gasping. Long after he had gone and the mauby had dripped and dried on her chin, she remained on that spot, trying to put a name to the part of her that had dribbled away beneath the floorboards.

★

The telephone is vibrating, it's face lighting up with each ring.

They stare at it for five rings before looking at each other. She keeps her eyes on his as she places the hot pot on the table and answers the phone. As she listens to the doctor's even voice, she continues to stare into Dick's pleading eyes while breathing in the pungent smell of burning plastic.

In the taxi, on the way to the airport, they sit next to each other on the back seat, their eyes trained out of opposite windows. Only for a moment does she look down into his lap. With shaky hands, he is threading the warm scarf that she bought him.

"When Mother was sick, she was in a lot of pain you know," he says, his head turned away from her. "We sat with her all through the night and she cried out. One piece of bawling. Like she was coming into the world not going out."

The car jolts as it turns into the airport, jostling into the right lane for the terminal.

"It make you realise."

She looks at his hands threading and rethreading the scarf.

"What did it make you realise?"

"That, in the end, all dem things that we hold onto just disappear. Gone. It's like we are born again."

★

They wait silently in the check-in queue. She can see over the top of his head. At the desk he can't hear the agent properly so she makes sure he has an aisle seat not far from the toilet and that his diabetic meal has been ordered.

At the departure gates she hangs back.

"You ain't coming?"

She shakes her head. "No. I can't go no further."

He looks confused, his eyes not focusing on anything in particular. His arms hang awkwardly by his side. Around him excited holidaymakers with their newly highlighted hair and Day-Glo clothes grab goodbye hugs and blow kisses.

She places her bag on the floor and walks toward him. She holds out her arms and there is an involuntary spasm of his shoulders, an extraordinary passing of electricity that lights his eyes. She bends forward, drops her hands on his shoulders and slides them slowly down his back. The tiny wings of his shoulder blades and the marbles of his spine feel fragile and she imagines them skinless – bleached and bare. She feels him stiffen beneath her fingers and then, with a tiny crack like the splitting of a wishbone, a minuscule part of him lets go. She holds him like this for a while, like he is her son and she is leaving him at the school gates.

VALDA JACKSON

AN AGE OF REASON (COMING HERE)

The Father

It's not really money you know, weh make me come here. No, I didn't come here just for that. It's the baby body buried in your granny's yard. I couldn' live there with it. And I didn't have anywhere else to take you all.

You don't remember Michael. No, you couldn't remember him. You was just baby yourself when he die. You didn't even have your second birthday yet.

I couldn't stay there. I just couldn't stay. But your mother never want to leave her mother's yard – they were real close – and if it wasn't for the baby grave, I could stay there as well, for her mother was a lovely lovely woman. And she was real real good to us.

You know, I move all over Jamaica before I end up in St Thomas. Although is St Ann where I born, and I live in a whole heap of other places as well, I feel St Thomas is my real home because nowhere else did I feel as welcome and as happy as I did there.

And it's there I meet your mother.

When I first meet her… I tell you, Julie, I couldn' believe my luck.

From the first time we meet, I know I have to marry her.

She was going to market for her mother. Another time after that she was coming back from town.

We talk for just a little while and I tell her that I really like her ways, and I would like to see her again. She tell me that if I want to see her, I have to come to her house and meet her mother and the rest of the family as well.

You know, your mother never really walk up and down.

She never go a dance, nor walk and chat. Mm mm.
She always stay at home and help her mother.
Your mother was a serious Christian. I could see that.
She was just eighteen when we meet.

She take me to her mother. And I tell you, that woman, Mistress Catherine, you couldn' find any better than she. She was so lovely.

It was just few weeks after May and I meet that I talk to her mother. I say, "Mistress Catherine, I'm real serious about your daughter, and if I have your blessing, and if she will have me, I going to ask her to marry me."

It's not that I really asking permission of her, you know, for I believed that she would give it. But I wanted to have her full blessing.

And also… I never want her to think that I would take advantage of her as a widow-woman, having no man there to protect her and her daughters. Because nuff-nuff man was ready in them times to mash up young girls and then walk away. And she was a good good mother to me as well.

You know I was orphaned when I was a small boy; I never know anyone to call mother. But you see, Julie, when I meet your mother, it's not just wife I find. I find a mother as well. *Her* mother was a real mother for me.

So you see, I was happy at your granny's yard. She was good to us… but I know we couldn't live there forever. We did have a plan that when we save enough money we would buy piece a land down a Yallahs and build a little house and plant it up. But you know something? With that little grave in Mama's yard… I really couldn't stay there any longer.

I just couldn't stay.

They have advertisement all over, telling people to come to England to work.

So… I tell your mother I want to go there and work. And you know, we believed we could save even quicker to get that piece of land. I tell her it would be better if we leave you girls with Mama and go together but she say she can't leave you and your sisters them. I beg her come with me.

Even her mother pleading with her. Even Mama say we must go together and leave you all with her because she can take care of the three of you.

And I would trust her. I would trust that woman with my life. I know that she would do her very best for unnu girls.

But May, she say no... she not leaving you all. She wouldn't come.

She never want to leave her children.

She wouldn' come.

So, I leave St Thomas on my own.

Just as I come.

I used to write your mother. And you know my writing not so good, for when my mother die I have to stop going to school. But I write anyway, for I miss her. I miss all of you.

I feel it, yu see.

I really feel it.

I tell you Julie, it wasn't easy leaving you all behind... and without your mother as well.

It was hard... them times... I really want her with me.

Chu... them times were tough.

Tough tough.

Sarah, First Born

I don't remember having a childhood after Mummy left. When she left, that was the end of being a child for me.

I never played. I was too busy looking out for us.

It was after Michael died.

I bet you don't remember when Michael died, do you?

But I do.

It was awful.

I think I was five.

I just remember. Mummy suddenly calling out to her mother: "Mama. Mama. The baby dead." Mama came running in from the kitchen.

I can still see Mama trying to hold Mummy up… and the crying, I still hear it sometimes. You've forgotten, haven't you?

Wish *I* could forget.

It wasn't long after that Daddy left.

And then when *she* left to join him that was it for me.

The end of freedom.

The end of play.

I mean – we weren't protected, Julia.

There was no one really looking after us.

At that time, remember, Mama still had three of her own teenage children living at home. Of course Aunty G was supposed to be helping with us, but I don't think she was even fourteen then.

Then there were other cousins living with us as well because two of Mummy's older sisters had already gone to England, and Mama was looking after their children as well. So she had the three of us – you, Elaine and me – and our cousins Maureen and Collette and there was Sherrie and Millicent, and Aunty Enid's boys, and Aunty Evelyn's as well. There must have been more than eight or nine of us grandchildren all below the age of eight. I'm not even counting those older boys. She couldn't manage so many; no matter how much she loved us. It's not possible.

I could see that, and I was five.

Elaine was just four and you were only two. I felt I had to look after the two of you… and you, you weren't easy. They had to tear you off me every morning so I could go to school, and then I'd come home and find you damp and tetchy, just rocking and banging your head against Mama's kitchen wall. It's a miracle you have any sense left… though sometimes, Julia, I do wonder.

I remember when Elaine was ill soon after Mummy left and Mama had to get her to the doctor. She had the three of us with her and I think two or three of our cousins as well.

It was a long walk and Elaine couldn't manage it. Mama had to carry her most of the way. I think that was the time she had a sore on her leg that just wouldn't heal. It was probably due to the sickle cell. But Mama wouldn't have known.

111

No one knew then.

To get to the clinic we had to cross the river and it was flood time.

The only way Mama could get us across was on her back.

And that's what she did.

One at a time.

She tied up her skirt – carried one over, and came back for another till we were all on the other side.

You must remember the passport, Julia.

When we came, the three of us came on one passport – and it was mine.

Bet you don't even remember what it said, do you?

It said: "Miss Sarah Andrea Jenkins aged 8 accompanied by two small children." Miss Jenkins, that was me. Accompanied by Elaine and you; the small children. Hah.

It didn't even have your names on it.

You lost your glove on the plane.

All three of us had these little white gloves when we left. Mummy sent them in a parcel from England. D'you remember? Probably the prettiest things we'd ever owned. All lacy. One of yours disappeared down the toilet on the plane and you wouldn't stop crying for it.

I didn't know what to do so I went and told the stewardess thinking she could get it back. But of course she couldn't. We had no idea then, I mean, we'd never seen a flush toilet before. And anyway, that stewardess was supposed to be looking after us. But she didn't really pay any attention to us. Nobody did. They just made sure that we got on the plane and saw to it that we got off again. Then someone else took us to Immigration where we had to wait for Mummy to pick us up.

She was really late.

You were miserable and cried all the time.

I couldn't stop worrying. I thought she wasn't going to come.

And when she did come, even *I* didn't recognise her at first. She'd put on so much weight. Elaine didn't recognise her either, and *you*… I had to drag you over. You wouldn't go near her. Then you refused to talk to her. Kept on saying you didn't know her, and you wanted to go back to Aunty G.

Honestly, Julia, you were so contrary. When she left us in Jamaica you wouldn't let Mama or anyone else touch you. Just hung on to me crying for your mummy. We come to her and you're still grabbing on to me and pleading to go back to Aunty. Then you refused to say, "Mummy", calling her Sister May... as if we were still back home at Mama's!

But that's what our cousins and everyone else called her.

Even her own mother used to call her Sister May because she was a Christian. But *we* shouldn't have.

Anyone would think you really wanted her to send us back. Weren't you worried?

I was always fearful that she might. She seemed so powerful. Even when she'd left Jamaica she had power. She still managed to keep us safe. I mean, those big boys messing with our cousins; even they knew that they mustn't mess with you, me or Elaine. They knew who our mother was and that she was going to send for us. Everyone knew that *we* weren't going to be left forever like the others. And if she couldn't get us to England with her, then she would come back. I knew it because she told us. Everyone knew. Except you. *You* forgot before she even left. But *those boys* knew she'd be back; and there wasn't one of them brave enough to touch us and then face our mother.

You don't remember any of this, do you?

I had to keep on telling you, "She *is* our mother, Julia, and she sent for us, and now that we're here you *have* to call her Mummy."

The Mother

You know, I was never really meant to come here.

I never wanted to leave my children. And it was never part of our plan.

I never wanted to come.

It's your daddy want to come. And we agreed that he would

come and work so we could save more. I wasn't meant to come. It was never part of our plan.

And then, after the baby die… You couldn' remember him, for you were just small… your daddy say he couldn't carry on living at my mother's yard. He couldn't live there anymore with the little baby body buried there.

We did plant some Joseph's coats around it.

You wouldn't believe how quick they grow up and spread across the little plot.

And even before they start to show, your daddy was already gone.

But I never want to come here; for although the baby die, we still have you three girls.

And I couldn't leave you. I just couldn' do that.

You must know I never want to leave you.

I really never wanted to leave you to come here.

It's not what we planned.

Those first letters that your daddy write, I know he wasn't happy. He try to make them sound good, but I could feel how he was struggling. He write and say how he's missing us, and I must come join him because with two of us working we would manage better, and we could save more money to buy the piece of land. But I reply and say I couldn't leave my children.

I remember one letter in particular. He was almost saying his "good bye" because he couldn't see how he was going to support himself in England and send enough money back home for us as well with just one wage packet, and he begging me to come and help him.

But I didn't want to leave unnu.

It was Mama persuade me to come.

When I read the "good bye" letter, she see how upset I was and she say, "You know, Sister May, perhaps you really should go."

Is she make me leave.

I tell her, "No. I can't leave my children."

I wasn't going to come here. And if it weren't for Mama, I would never have come.

I ask her, "How I must leave my children and go so far?"

114

Mama get vex and tell me that it's because I don't trust her with my children. For if I have trust in her, then I would do what my sisters did and leave the three of you there with her and join my husband in England.

But it wasn't that.

No. It wasn't that. It's just that I couldn' bear to not have you all with me.

It's really Mama make me come.

And then when I come here, I couldn't rest.

I could not rest until I had you all with me.

I couldn't rest.

And you know, the day I book your tickets, your daddy never know.

Even though he and I share a bed the night, in the morning I leave the house after he already gone to work… and I book the flight.

I tell him when he come home that evening.

When I tell him, he throw his hands up and say, "Lord! Woman yu mad? Where yu goin put them?"

Yu see, is just one room we have. And by that time we already have George, and Rosie was baby… and all four of us living in one little room in Sparkbrook.

I was off shift next morning and I leave the house early and start looking. I tell you that day I walk, I walk, I walk so till…

English people not letting to me. And finding two rooms instead of one… I could find nothing. And I tell you, is when my foot swell up and I ready to drop, I walking back home I bump into Brother Wilkins on the Stratford Road.

You remember Brother Wilkins? He did have a daughter name Jacqueline. You must remember her from Sunday school. Well anyway, he say that he have two rooms in his house and it wasn't far, so I walk with him round there. I ask him how the rooms come to be empty and he say that the family that had the rooms before had children, and their children and his daughter didn't get on. He show me around and it was really a nice house. It had three floors. The two rooms were on the first floor. Nice big rooms. My heart glad that I see him that day.

But then I meet the daughter… Oh… she was a brat.

115

I could see why the other family had to move.

I couldn't bring you all up here to that house.

I just wanted a place where my children could live and not be teased.

I did see an advertisement for a house for sale on Goldney Road. But we never have money to buy house. I never really give it any mind. Remember your daddy only come to save up to buy land in Jamaica so we were not thinking of buying house in England. I have to beg to persuade him to come look at this house with me.

We had to scrimp to find the deposit. But by the Grace of God we manage it. And we have somewhere to put you.

It was almost three years yu know since I leave you girls in Jamaica with Mama.

On the Sunday night I soak up my pillow with tears and I decide I'm not going to cry any more nights for unnu. I just going to have my children with me.

I book your tickets on the Monday morning and you all were coming on the Saturday. So… we didn't have much time.

Not even a full week we have.

But we found Goldney Road.

And we managed to find the deposit.

God is good.

Elaine, Second Born

Ooh Julia, I like this. It's like one of those tinted photos of us from the sixties.

Hang on a minute… I need my glasses for this.

Oh my life… it's… it's us. That is us. It is us, isn't it?

There we are, me, you…

How come Sarah's not there?

We were a threesome then. In those days.

Where are we though…?

Oh I know… I do know. It's the dining room at the old house in Goldney Road.

116

I really loved those curtains.

And the wallpaper with the apples and the grapes. D'you remember when Daddy hung that paper? I remember that. And he had no idea how wallpaper should be hung. None of us knew that he should match up the pictures at the edges, did we? …That the fruit should be matched so you don't see the separate strips across the wall like that.

It stayed up for years that wallpaper.

Can't believe you remember all this… How much time did you spend painting this? Must have taken you ages.

Why?

Why would you want to paint this? I can't believe it.

We're wearing our judging clothes. Did anyone else call them that? I think we must have been the only ones who called them that.

And Daddy singing and swinging the little ones on his leg.

Look how Rosie's holding on.

Wasn't she a lovely? She was a beautiful baby.

And little George waiting his turn – with his hands in his little pockets. Oaoaorh sooo cute… There are some photos some-where of him standing just like this. So lovely.

Shame we never had any baby photos of us…

You've really captured the likeness of everyone.

He used to let them sit on his foot and hold on to his leg.

This is sooo funny. It's really weird… remembering all this stuff.

Why've you painted this? It's odd. Really weird.

Why do you even think about this stuff, Julia?

I don't know why you do it.

You need to forget it! That's what I did.

I never think about those things.

I really don't.

I can't believe you even remember it.

Just look at you standing there. Looking at them.

So like you.

I don't know why it meant so much to you. You really wanted to have a go didn't you? You wanted to join in.

117

I remember… I was pulling on your skirt to make you sit back down but you just stood there… watching.

Waiting.

Hhhuh.

And then you actually asked for a go.

I wouldn't have even asked. I'd never ask them for anything.

I mean, what's the point?

I knew you wouldn't get a turn.

We never got turns at anything.

The trouble is, Julia…

You really wanted to be like them, didn't you?

You wanted to be one of the little ones.

I've always thought that. You wanted to be like them.

Even Sarah used to say that you *should* really be one of them because you were quite young when we came here and you weren't that much older than them. You were really small. Still a baby really. *She* thought you should be treated the same.

You really *did* want to be one of them, didn't you?

But you weren't born here were you?

You were one of us.

One of the bigger ones.

Rosie, One of the Little Ones

Julia, I just peeped my head round the door of your studio. I hope you don't mind… but that painting, I had to go in and take a closer look. I was on my way upstairs to see what the kids were up to, but honestly, Julia… it just drew me in.

Gave me goose bumps it did. Really made the hairs on the back of my neck stand on end.

It's beautiful. All that detail. Tch, you're so clever, you are.

Everything about the old dining room at Goldney Road, you've got it all, to a tee. Even the wallpaper… That wallpaper was up forever.

All these years I never even thought about that time. Then suddenly… Honestly, it jumped me right back to it. I mean, I found myself holding on for dear life to Daddy's leg and felt the great whoop of rising up through the air, head thrown back and looking up at him. Like staring into the eyes of God. He seemed so far away. I used to think I was flying... And the song just poured out of my mouth. Do you remember it...?

Oh my God, after all this time... and that funny little song... there it was in my head... Daddy's song – every word, just came back to me. You probably heard me singing it...

Here on our rock-away horse we go,
Johnny and I, to a land we know,
Far away in the sunset gold,
A lovelier land than can be told.

Where all the flowers go niddlety nod,
Nod, nod, niddlety nod.
Where all the flowers go niddlety nod,
And all the birds sing by-low
Lullaby, lullaby, by-low.

One minute I was singing and then I burst out laughing as though I really was rising through the air. And swinging... Honestly... I was, right in that room, and I was almost hysterical. I really was that tiny child again. It was utter joy. And then before I realised it, I was crying my eyes out... I mean, properly sobbing, Julia.

I had to sit down ... and great idea putting the old sofa there by the way; I dropped into it; and you were right, you can't have too many cushions... So, I'm all cushioned up with the sound of Daddy's voice. Didn't he have a lovely voice, Julia? It was so soft... really gentle. Pure velvet. I could actually hear him, It's as if I was being cradled, like he was rocking me... I felt so warm... and Julia, you're not gonna believe this...

I fell asleep.

EASY ON THE ROSE'S

The first thing Donna noticed about working at The Raven was that the floor stuck to her feet. It became a bedtime ritual to peel off fag-butts and scraps of beer-mat from the soles of her shoes. The next thing she noticed was that punters stuck to her as well.

Fifteen years ago, two weeks after moving back to the old house, she'd stopped by the local pub for a lime and soda and an application form. The owner of a tiepin, which read "Gavin", introduced himself as the man in charge. He was younger than Donna but his Bar and Ents management CV, he told her, was as long as her arm, and he'd looked at her arm as he said it.

The pub, as it stood now, had another six months in it, Gavin said, and then it'd be closed for a refit. The Raven would re-open as an eatery specialising in Valentine's and Christmas menus, and the old regulars, if they hadn't already vanished while the place was closed, would all be gone as soon as the smoking ban kicked in. Now, at the end of each day, Gavin said, they needed a wrecking ball to get rid of them.

When she began work, Donna would prompt one of the regulars into a conversation about something else that had disappeared or was on the way out: mugs of ale, proper music, the welfare state, human rights, smoking next year, this place soon enough, or *us lot* – whichever they got to first.

She carried their voices back to the house where they blended with those on the rolling news channels throughout the night. This was her routine for her first six weeks at The Raven until Sal took occupancy of the stool nearest the cigarette machine.

Sal had appeared in a moulting camel overcoat with a burnout velvet shawl around her narrow shoulders in defiance of the May sunshine outside. On the stool, she looked like a warbler on a reed. Fragile, the coat and shawl seemed to be all that kept her in one piece.

She delved into her coat for her pack of Berkeley's and a lighter. Face powder drifted from her in tiny clouds, smelling of Yardley's April Violet. Donna recognised it as the scent on the folded-up bedclothes in the airing cupboard at her house.

"Who *is* this nut?" Gavin murmured in Donna's ear.

He brushed past, fiddling with the Bluetooth headset attached to his left ear, and arrived in front of the old woman just as she breathed a cloud across the bar. Gavin fanned the air in front of his face. "Yes, love?"

She spoke as she moved, in puffs of vapour. "Well, first of all…" There was a huge drag on the cigarette, from which the crinkle of the paper cylinder could be heard across the pub. "Good afternoon, dear." Another drag. More ash dropped to the floor. "Now, what I would very much like you to do is to fetch me a gimlet, would you?"

Gavin was already at the optics. He placed a single gin on the bar in front of her.

"And what's this, dear?"

Gavin directed his response to the gallery of regulars at the other end of the bar. "That's a gin, my love, just like you asked for."

"I'm perfectly aware that it's a gin, young man, but are you aware that I asked for a *gim*-let?"

"A… gimlet?"

"Yes, dear."

"Not a gin."

"Well, gin is a constituent, yes."

Before he could prolong the conversation, Donna grabbed a bottle of Rose's Lime Cordial and caught the old woman's eye.

"Now, you see," said the woman, "this lovely young lady seems perfectly appraised of the situation. So perhaps she might also be able to locate a second shot of gin to go with the one you were kind enough to bring. Would you, dear?"

Gavin nodded a retreat. Donna took the glass of gin to the Gordon's optic, added a shot, dropped in a wedge of lime and returned to where she'd left the cordial in front of the old woman.

As she poured, a slim, crumpled hand curled around the neck

of the bottle. "Ssh, ssh, ssh!" said the old woman. "*Easy* on the Rose's, dear."

A sip brought a momentary stillness to her hand. The rim, pressed into the circles of rouge on her cheekbones, left grooves in her skin and a faint blush on the glass, now held out to Donna for a refill.

Donna built another gimlet, her every move chaperoned by murmurs of admonishment or approval. The old woman gave the end result a sigh of satisfaction and sat for a moment in weary euphoria before a new fluster came over her.

"I do have the means to honour this…" She let her voice trail away. She delved into her coat pocket and produced a 20p coin and a cloakroom ticket. "If you would care to set up a chit, I could –"

Another 20p and the plastic shell of a Kinder egg. Donna tried to calculate whether her share of the tips would cover the woman's two drinks. She reached over to prevent her from going back to her pocket, but instead found herself catching two £1 coins, some silver, a muslin cloth and a ten pound note.

"Silly of me to monopolise your time without establishing my probity, dear, wasn't it? Now, would you be very sweet and tell me your name, so I don't have to keep calling you 'dear'?"

Donna gathered up the change after taking the price of two gimlets. "It's Donna."

"Yes it is – Donna. How lovely. And you, my dear, must call me Sal. How lovely… how lovely that I can trust you, can't I, to prepare another of your gimlets which really are excellent, dear, they really are."

Donna made gimlets for the rest of her shift.

The next day Sal was back with another pocketful of foreign objects and the correct amount of cash to keep the cocktails pouring. If Donna was in, Sal would be served by no one else. Over the course of a week, this had taken on the status of a sacred ritual. Donna observed how The Raven manufactured its own folklore, how zones of exclusion formed around tables and bar stools, tankards and buttons on the jukebox.

Sal's shawl never left her shoulders; it was held in place by a brooch. Four birds, either completely green or silver-bodied with green wings, sat on a leafy branch, each head facing in a different direction, beaks open in song. Donna would admire the detail, how the different greens reflected various stages of the dawn.

She had mentioned this to Sal one afternoon when the old woman seemed in a particularly jittery state, and the dance of the flame from her lighter to her cigarette threatened to veer out of control before Donna steadied her hand.

"The birds? Ah, the brooch, yes, hmm." Her fingertips traced the edge of the brooch, then gave a dismissive flutter. "Well, honestly, it's only a little something from John Lewis."

The way she said it, John Lewis could have been a former suitor who used to festoon her with love trinkets. She continued to wave away imagined compliments, her eyelashes batting in anticipation of a panorama of appreciative glances. This ended when she took a heavy drag of her Berkeley and puffed out the smoke.

"Thinking of anyone in particular, Sal?"

Sal's lips smacked on her glass. "Oh yes, dear. Yes, it could be anyone. That's really it, you see. It could be anyone."

She sat in silence, staring at the middle distance, occasionally blinking. Only when Donna began making another gimlet, did Sal re-emerge. She now held Donna in her gaze, the scent of Yardley's April Violet hovering between them.

"And what about you, my dear? A young woman like you. Is there anyone in…?"

"In…? Oh, *in particular?*"

"Precisely, dear." Sal's mouth spread into a crimson grin.

Donna shook her head. "No, there's just me."

There was a loose ice cube glinting on the bar. Donna wiped the water around it then gathered it up with a bar towel. She watched the towel absorb the water and the cube. "I've got a great big house all to myself."

"And that's splendid. I'm so glad," Sal said, drifting back to the middle distance, "so very glad… Oh! she's done ever so well for herself, oh yes, a house of her own… But you see, dear…" The lines around her mouth were deeply defined. "Be careful because if you just stop where you are…" Now she was clasping Donna's hand, "if you just stop, you might forget how to start again."

★

Donna was polishing champagne flutes in an area of the bar that provided a chapel of rest from unwanted conversations, when Gavin approached her.

"Can I be real with you, Donna? When the eatery opens it's really not going to be the sort of place where you can spend all day chatting up some auld tramp and plying her with gizmos or whatever… Don't get me wrong! You're rinsing her for the cash so there's no complaints."

"It's almost like she belongs here," Donna said.

"Ex-*actly* – but when we get the place sorted, your dipso mate will be brick dust, and I worry you'll have a problem with that. Just being real."

"I appreciate how real you are, Gavin."

"But! A little bird tells me you don't have to worry about rent or a mortgage on that gaffe you're in down the road. What I'm saying: there'll be a job for you when we reopen – hold that thought." He caressed his Bluetooth headset and left Donna with a thumbs-up.

Sal had a mannerism: with a gimlet in one hand and a Berkeley in the other, the glass and the cigarette would be on either side of her mouth, so that moving her lips to either simply required a grimace in one direction or the other. She'd then use a free ring-finger to scratch away a globule of excess mascara from her lower lashes. The eyes themselves would be lit and flickering at these times, peering, it seemed, over a mindscape of shadows. She held this pose until she needed recharging from one hand or the other. Then she would return to a conversation Donna had forgotten from ten minutes earlier, or the day before.

"And you have no way of knowing if it's the morning or the afternoon?"

"If? Well – it's… two – coming up to twenty to three, Sal."

"My word, dear, no – your appointment, you were saying – the gas board, dear, with the gas board."

"Oh! The new boiler?"

"Hallelujah."

"Yeah, it's on Friday – before four, they reckon."

"And this means what, exactly? You can't possibly work here if you're going to be called away at any –"

"Oh, no – no, I'm taking the day off. Now or never, really. Be getting cold again soon. Where did the summer go, eh, Sal? Time just evaporates."

Sal's face was again in its tobacco-gin cradle. Her eyes disappeared behind the smoke.

"Yes, that's very true. But, you see, sometimes it petrifies… sometimes it petrifies. And you're left with just the rocks to carry around."

Donna unscrewed the cap of the Rose's cordial bottle by way of an invitation for Sal to continue.

The old woman reached out her fag hand, ash spilling along its trajectory, and brushed Donna's right cheek. "As you know, I came to motherhood very late in life."

"I didn't… so… where do your children…?"

"Child." Sal's reply was emphatic, though she still appeared to be addressing a space over Donna's left shoulder. "A daughter." There was a sigh. "Yes – came late, and left early. Another gimlet, Donna, if you would?"

This time, when Sal's finger moved to flick away some loose mascara, it found a speck swelling with liquid already drawing itself down the edge of her nose, leaving a trail of blue-black freckles.

The new boiler came on the Friday, which meant the radiator in the front room could at last perform a function beyond that of a slow clothes drier for underwear. Sal wasn't in The Raven when Donna returned to work the following evening. Her stool remained empty on the Monday, and throughout that week. When Gavin closed the place down for the refit, the stool was one of the first items thrown in the skip.

In the weeks The Raven was closed, Donna stayed up most nights, kept company by news reports of natural disasters and insurmountable social problems. She worked some relief nightshifts in the bar of a hotel on the dock road and she'd go by the market on her way back to the house to stock up on fresh limes. The Raven reopened the week after Valentine's and she settled into a perpetual graveyard shift. Unordered specials incorporating goat's cheese were daily tipped into bins where she used to empty the ashtrays. The cigarette smell hadn't been entirely scrubbed away and, when she lifted the bin lids, she smelt the feather touch of April Violet, a gasp of juniper.

When nights are sleepless, you quarter a lime and squeeze one wedge into a tumbler you've liberated from your workplace. Add ice cubes and give it a rattle round with a swizzle stick. Pour in enough gin to quieten down the ice. Unscrew the cap from a bottle of Rose's Lime Cordial and stop yourself just before you tip the cordial into the glass. Slow down and add just a rumour of Rose's. The lime cordial that makes it out of the bottle should be less an ingredient and more a memo, notifying the glass of the existence of liquids other than gin. Wipe around the rim of your glass with another wedge of lime and toss that in. Carry the gimlet back into the front room and repeat until morning.

One early morning, inspecting a thread of green weaving among the ice cubes, Donna noticed more of an emerald sparkle than usual. The curtains in the front room were rarely opened but a small flap had worked its way loose from its runner and sunlight was reaching through the room and into the drink. Donna set down the glass and switched off the lamp. She crossed the room, turned off the television and pulled the curtains open.

Outside, a man walked his dog back from the shop with the morning paper. Milk bottles sat on a neighbour's doorstep. On Donna's side of the road, a sparrow struck up its part of the dawn chorus on a tree branch whose leaves, inflamed by the sunlight, bounced balls of green light against the bird's feathers. Another sparrow, and then a third, joined the line-up on the branch. Donna waited until, answering a sequence of calls by the other three, a fourth bird emerged through the leaves to perch on the same branch.

She placed two fingers on her lips, kissed them, and tapped them on the window. Behind her fingerprints, the four birds continued their song. Donna turned around, gathered the duvet up from the sofa, carried it upstairs to her room, and went to bed.

PISS PALS

Damo caught a glimpse of himself as he strode past the darkened window of Woolsmiths and stepped up his swagger. *Tschhhhh! Damn fine.* He was late but that didn't matter, he was worth it. Shit yeah, Matty would never be able to compete with £250 faded Marischo Narvadis – originals of course – limited edition with customised ass-rip below left buttock, revealing a purple sliver of £80 Drice Nortons. *Sweet as.*

"Fucking slow down, will ya!" Tameka called from down the street.

Damo slowed outside Rekordz. The window featured posters of some boy band. Although Damo knew he would always have the edge over any manufactured high street wank, he was struck by how much they looked like him. There was a difference though – a big difference – maybe not to the untrained eye. But the people that mattered knew. You couldn't fake real style with no cheap chic.

"What's the fucking rush; we're already late, aren't we?"

Breathing hard, Tameka adjusted her black Asher Pearce handbag from left shoulder to right. Damo set off as she drew up. He still had it, he was still ahead. When the high street caught up with your styles, that was when you needed to worry.

He undid a button on his Sempuriio shirt. *Let the tan breathe – that's cool, that's allowed, not too posy in this weather.* A low cut tee might have been a better option than the Sempuriio, though. A tee would have worked well – especially a Giorgius with sleeves rolled up.

He pulled the layered Morracka gem-beads up from beneath the 3-grade cotton, then carefully laid them back inside. He loved to feel them flop against his waxed pectorals and his ripped rectus abdominis. Erotic.

"Oi! I am in heels, remember!" Tameka click-clacked behind.

Damo stopped to let her catch up. She leaned a delicate hand against Krenco Caffè, careful not to get dirt on her Paschlina wrap. She adjusted the straps on her 3-inch Harpers.

Damo lapped up the show of cleavage. Yeah. Not the biggest but she did make use of what she had. Blinding. A knockout. He flashed Tameka his trademark grin and patted her arse.

"S'okay babes, don't worry." He looked at their reflections. "Fucking gorgeous."

★　★　★

Damo scanned the room as soon as they entered the pub-restaurant. It was no place he'd choose, but this was Matty's home turf. Old locals, a smattering of youngsters, the usual non-clubbing awkward geeks: Goths, Tuck-ins, Eco misfits. The back of Matty's gelled three-quarter scalp (a "style" he had not altered for as long as Damo had known him) was visible in the far corner. Damo pulled Tameka forward by the waist and felt several manicured nails dig into his flesh. Damo regarded her with puzzlement.

"I need… to… pee."

Tameka hurried off; he rubbed his forearm, tensing the flexor carpi muscles. Beneath his tribal dragon tat there might well be a set of crescent-shaped blemishes. He smiled. *Feisty.*

His best mate Matty was still engrossed in banter with his girl, Claire. Not an argument though. All sicky lovey-dovey.

Stay cool, Damo. Cool cool.

He strutted towards the bar pretending not to appreciate the nudges between a group of alco-pop girls. They wouldn't often be blessed with seeing the likes of him in these parts. He could clean up in this town. They probably thought he was some celebrity. He often got that.

★　★　★

Four drinks crashed onto the table. Lager sloshed onto Matty's Fenchcross polo tee. It was an old one; Damo had seen him in it before. Anger flashed across Matty's face. Then he looked up and saw it was Damo.

"Don't even serve Krostburg in this shithole," Damo announced.

"Damo!" Matty pulled his arm from around Claire. He stood up to embrace Damo.

Mindful of the spill on Matty's shirt, Damo pulled back, "Easy pal, Sempuriio, yeah."

Matty raised an eyebrow at Claire. He wiped his tee-shirt dry, held up his hand, then punched Damo in the abs. Damo countered with two swift kidney punches, faked a jab and then pulled Matty into a headlock. Sweet citrus tickled Damo's nostrils. Was that Assati cologne? Subtle musk, hint of menthol. Some Dravidus moisturiser as well perhaps? Well played, Matty. Matty slipped Damo's arm and they wrestled each other into the wall. Claire tutted as they collided with the table.

"Settle down, boys."

They disentangled and smoothed out their shirts.

"Not bad, Matty lad." Damo slapped Matty's abs. He tried not to sound out of breath, "Still going the gym?"

"Nar, not been for ages."

"Yeah, me neither." Damo pulled up a seat and swigged a gulp of lager. "Claire," he nodded.

"Hello Damo, you alright?"

"Good babes, good. You?"

"Yes, very well thanks. We're good." She draped Matty's arm across her shoulder as he sat down next to her. "So, where's… your girlfriend?"

Damo took another swig. He looked over their shoulders and saw Tameka emerge from the lav.

"Tameka? Just coming." He pointed with his pint and enjoyed watching their expressions as they turned their heads.

He stood up when Tameka arrived.

"Y'alright, babes?" He kissed her cheek, let his hand linger on firm arse beneath silk Avanti dress as he sat her opposite Claire. Tameka had taken the opportunity to touch up her make-up. She glowed. *Good girl.*

"Tameka – Matty. Matty – Tameka. And this is Claire. Claire – Tameka."

Damo caught Matty's eye. He translated his mate's arched brows and puckered lips: "Fucking nice one, mate, well done. Fucking babe."

Damo returned the telepathy with a wink: "You don't know the fucking half, mate –absolute filth!" *That would do it. Satisfactory. Best possible entrance under the circumstances.*

★ ★ ★

The meal went better than Damo had expected. He'd been worried about Tameka fitting in and her banter level. They never really talked about much; she didn't often get his jokes. Claire stepped in though and the two seemed to be getting on.

Claire always made an effort to be nice to his girlfriends. He appreciated that as he knew she must feel intimidated. Claire was clever and everything, funny, but with that girl-next-door kind of look. Didn't really make the effort. Decent tits but body-fat ratio leaning towards pudgy.

Matty would have to watch that – Claire's arms showed early signs of turkey wobble. He looked over at Tameka's arms. Tight. Not Madonna-muscled, but just enough cardio to keep every-thing toned. No excess. Claire acted almost as if she didn't care. Damo remembered describing Claire to Tameka, and the time she spilled sticky toffee pudding on her fake M&P top. Custard, the works. When Matty pointed it out, Claire had just laughed and slurped it up, not even bothering to wipe the stain. Damo knew Tameka would never embarrass him like that. Tameka had laughed with him at that story.

While Tameka and Claire bonded, Damo leaned over to Matty.

"So, let's get some toot, yeah?" He tapped his nostril twice. "Tams would be up for it. Go find a club, yeah?"

Matty shook his head and glanced over at Claire. "Aw nar, mate."

"What? C'mon, mate. How long is it since we had a proper blow-out?" He kept his voice down. "She doesn't have to come if she's not up for it."

"Yeah but we've got her folks round tomorrow."

"Shut up. Even more reason. Go on mate, grow a fucking pair.

Must be some decent clubs somewhere round here. I'll get the taxi, soft lad."

"I dunno, mate."

"C'mon fella. I'm only up here one night. Couple rounds triple voddie Red Rag to start us off?"

"Aw, fuck off, I'm not touching that again."

"Yeah, you could never handle your drink." Damo clinked his glass against Matty's.

"Remind me – who was it puking their guts in H-bar that got us kicked out again?"

"I told you." Damo pointed a fork in Matty's face. "Dodgy pizza that was."

They both laughed.

"Good times."

"Good times," Matty echoed.

To be fair, Matty could hold his drink.

They'd finished their burgers and the girls had both been to the lavs, but Damo was not going to break the seal before his mate. He knew Matty could point to the fact that he had been there half hour before him and was one pint ahead. No, he was not letting Matty have that. Matty would break soon. He was starting to look uncomfortable; he was sweating.

Damo saw that Matty was about to get up. Damo placed a hand on his shoulder.

"Mate, remember that time at Sanko's? Tell Tams about us two at Sanko's. Mad it was."

Matty sank back in his seat and recounted the story of when Damo had knocked out some twat who had been hassling Matty. It was good to hear someone else recall the events, even if Matty did miss out a few details. Matty finished the story and rose. Damo was too slow to drag him back.

"What about in the kebab shop as well, Matts?"

Matty's face tightened in a near grimace.

"You tell it mate. I gotta piss." He turned to leave.

"Weak bladder that one," Damo declared downing his pint.

Matty turned back to the table, "Same again all of you?"

"Yup, put it on me ISAX, pal." Damo slapped his platinum

ISAX on the table. Matty made for the toilet and Damo stretched his arms wide. With the contest won he had lost concentration. He felt a dribble in his purple boxers. He crumpled forward and drained his glass.

"So what about this kebab shop?" Tameka asked. Claire had heard this one many times.

"Aw, let Matty tell it when he gets back. He tells it better." This was a lie but it was good to compliment Matty in front of his girl. He started to drum his legs on the floor. "Fuck it, I'll get the drinks, ladies. He'll be ages."

Damo got up from the table. Still cool. He walked to the gents as slow as his bladder would allow.

★   ★   ★

Bursting through the door Damo found Matty waiting for a free urinal. Having to readjust his expectations caused more warmth to trickle into Damo's Nortons. He tried not to let his anguish show.

"Geezer," he nodded at Matty.

"Geezer," Matty replied.

They both turned their attention to the two people in front of them. The cubicle displayed the red engaged sign. If Matty wasn't here Damo would have pissed in the sink. He realised he was humming and stopped himself. Matty's knees crouched together as he shifted his weight from one leg to the next in time to the ancient Perushia remix playing outside.

Damo removed the Niksim 2.0 from his pocket and pretended to check the screen. Matty stared ahead. One of the guys was wagging his right arm with the closing strokes. Damo inched a hand into his free pocket to nip the bulb of his dick between thumb and fingers.

Both twats finished, the one closest to Damo turning first. Although Damo's path was clear he waved Matty forward, managing a tight smile. *Squeeze. Tense.* It would not do to fall at the last hurdle. The second urinal became free and Damo joined his pal.

Matty had just a zip on his Krabin's and was already pissing. Damo's fingers trembled to undo his G-Rope belt. He felt real fear as another little bead released itself in anticipation. If he was not careful the seepage could show through the white denim. He pushed out his backside as much as he dared, body pinched in the middle, squeeze, squeeze, pulling hard at the oversized Narvadi buttons. Care. ful. Not. To. Pull. One. Off…

"Ahhhhhhh," Matty let out a satisfied sigh. Damo freed his cock and had to fight to point it at the porcelain. He exhaled as the amber blast cascaded onto the rubber splash-mat.

"Few cans before I came out." Damo could talk now.

Matty snorted a laugh – he seemed happy just to be relieving himself.

"So, we having it tonight then or what?"

"Mate, let's just have a few bevvies, yeah. I'll whoop you at pool next pub."

"As if. Lame mate, lame."

"You done well there, you know." Matty jerked a chin back towards the pub-restaurant.

"Yeah, she's alright." Damo played the moment down. To brag would be as good as pissing all over his own Doranos. *She's alright* – to be interpreted as *Yeah she's a part-time model but I could still do better, I can pull girls like that all day*.

There was no requirement for Damo to return the compliment. He had told Matty "not bad" when he introduced Claire to him the first time. They'd been engaged for a year, or maybe two now, so to comment again was not necessary. Damo offered his customary question, "So, you set a date then?"

Matty hesitated. *Shit. They're breaking up.* Well, he knew Matty could do better. She was a nice lass, been good for him. Not bad. Nice tits. Damo would sort him out though, get him down London – pissed, pilled, coked. He'd find loads of birds for his old pal. In fact there was that…

"Yeah, we have actually."

"You wot?"

"Yeah. We set a date."

Damo remained silent.

"Next August. The 27th."

Damo squeezed out another stream. Fucking hell. Moving in together was one thing, but fucking married? *The idiot.*

Matty was shaking out his last drops.

"Fuck," Damo offered. "No, I mean good luck. Congrats, mate."

Damo had lost concentration; yellow spots splashed his Doranos. "Shit!" He flicked his feet to disperse the wetness.

Matty laughed, zipping up his jeans.

Damo began to redo his buttons. He joined Matty at the sink. "Bastard! 200 quid these bad boys!"

"We were thinking as well that we'd like you to be best man." Matty looked at Damo; Damo kept his eyes on the mirror. Matty's smile looked genuine.

"Me? Yeah. Cool, yeah 'course. Cool. Cheers mate." Damo wiped a hand on the back of his Narvadis and offered it to Matty. Matty shook it in a firm two-handed grip. Damo clapped his mate on the back. *Way too formal.*

Matty beamed.

Damo recovered some of his composure, "Fuck, well this is going right in me speech – you admitting I'm the best man when we just had our cocks out!"

Matty didn't laugh as much as Damo thought the quip warranted.

"Seriously, though," Matty turned to Damo, "You'll do it, yeah?"

"I just said I would, dickhead. 'Course I fucking will." *Maybe a little too aggressive there.* "I'd be honoured, pal."

"Cool." Matty finished smoothing his three-quarter scalp. Damo ran wet fingers over his trimmed eyebrows.

"So you gonna bring Tameka?" Matty asked.

'Tameka?' Damo could detect no trace of malice in the question. "Yeah – I mean yeah. Depends. Yeah. I'll bring her."

"Nice one." Matty punched Damo on the arm. "See you back in there, pal."

Damo stared at his reflection, not focusing on anything in particular. The flush from the cubicle sounded and some Indie dweeb walked out. He dared the dweeb to brush his Sempuriio. Just to even make eye contact. The dweeb scampered past, head down, without even washing his hands. Yeah, you better run thought Damo, fists clenched. Damo went into the cubicle and sat down.

Matty. Matty. You fucking idiot. He'd carried Matty all through college, all the time he had known him. What the fuck was he doing? It would all be downhill for his best mate now. His own fault. Damo could have offered him the real life, bright lights, fast living. Matty would get bored with all that family shit. He'd cheat on her, he was bound to; then, when Claire left him, he'd be too old and fat to get back in the game. That scalp-cut was not going to hide his baldness for many more years. Matty was done, trapped, finished. Mortgage. Kids. Pussy-whipped. Life over. Loser.

No woman would ever have that power over him. Wouldn't have it any other way – no worries, no responsibilities. He and Matty had agreed on that very thing. People who gave up, settled – that was the saddest thing in the world.

Maybe Claire was pregnant? Silly bastard. That's what you get when you settle for someone who doesn't take it up the arse. Poor Matty.

Damo punched the toilet door. Hard. It rattled against its hinges. He rubbed his knuckles then smacked the door harder. *Fucking fool. Not Matty.*

Damo sniffed, wiping his nose, then his eyes. Annoyed with himself for his show of weakness. He kicked the door.

Fuck it. Fuck 'em all. He would never stop.

Damo creased his eyes against the tears. He fiddled with the toilet roll, pulled some paper to dab his grazed hand, then pulled open the door.

He paused in front of the mirror to adjust his collar, pointed at his reflection. Winked. "Fucking gorgeous."

RAMAN MUNDAIR

DAY TRIPPERS

Parminder didn't like to admit it but she had a type. For as long as she could remember she had an aversion to Asian men. Years of her overbearing Daddyji and chachas had created a distaste for her Asian brotherhood. No. She preferred her men pale and interesting.

She had met David at a work do. His expensive get-up, bohemian chitchat and touchy-feely ways beguiled her. He was so different from the men she was used to. Fast-forward several years and here she was in her well-located, detached home, mortgaged to the hilt, with David and their two boys – Oriel and Miles – who were as verbose as their father. Parminder knew she was terribly lucky to live as she did, but had begun to wake up feeling numb, with a longing for silence.

Gurpreet didn't like to admit it but he had a type: anything but Asian. To be more specific, anything but South Asian. Absolutely no Indian, Pakistani or Bengali women. No. Brown didn't do it for him. Never had and never would. He'd had enough from his desi childhood: Mum and sisters and numerous female relatives – Auntie This and Massi That. No. He didn't want any more of it.

He'd met Aisling after uni. Her red hair, green eyes and soft Irish accent were exotic. Five years later they had children named Sophie and Hannah. He wasn't quite sure how he had got here.

At university, Parminder and Aisling had a competitive friend-ship; Parminder had never felt entirely at ease in Aisling's com-pany. She always had the feeling of being quietly judged. Yet they'd been drawn towards one another. Meeting on Facebook gave an opportunity to show how well they had done; how far they had travelled. There was the fact that they had both married partners from other cultures.

Parminder was surprised how nervous she felt before their reunion. She made a hair appointment, had a manicure, agonised over what to wear and bought a new dress. She picked out David's clothes. She even vetted the photographs of the boys on her mobile phone so that she would share the best ones.

The highlights of Gurpreet's family evenings involved investigations of the works of Jamie Oliver, Hugh Fearnley-Whittingstall, and Nigella Lawson: each recipe a performance, each meal serving up just the right sustenance for the life they deserved to live. How quietly discerning they were. How absolutely, as the advert said, they were *worth it*. And so weekends were spent shopping at John Lewis and lunching at Café Rouge or Carluccios. Weekly grocery shops at Waitrose, or Ocado delivery with top-ups from Sainsbury. The children's clothes were from Boden, Joules – with little bits from Next and H&M; the furniture from House of Fraser, John Lewis and, only occasionally, Ikea.

It took Gurpreet a while to wonder if they really needed to change the decor and furniture every other year and did the kids really need a seasonal wardrobe?

Parminder couldn't believe how little her mother knew her. From time to time food parcels were delivered, all based on the fact that she had loved Indian sweets as a child. One parcel leaked sugar syrup onto David's favourite Paul Smith trousers. The drycleaner was unable to remove the stain and David sulked for the whole week. Parminder called her mum and scolded her thoughtlessness. She didn't notice when the parcels stopped arriving.

When they got together Gurpreet took charge at the restaurant, made sure they were taken to the table Aisling had booked – the one with a view of the river that, on their arrival, they had been told was unavailable. He ordered the wine, caught the waiter's attention when required and paid the bill. At first, Parminder found this presumptuous and irritating, but, as the evening progressed, she enjoyed his decisiveness. It was refreshing after the sensitive, linguistic negotiations she was used to with David, in which everything from the colour of the children's rooms to the electricity bill had to be discussed.

Presents from their Indian grandparents used to arrive twice a year: on the children's birthdays, and for Diwali. Bright silks paired in odd colour combinations, trimmed with gold and sequins. They came folded carefully and wrapped in a plastic bag with the back of an old envelope as a label. The children would usually rip open parcels as soon as they arrived, but these were left unopened for weeks.

When they were younger and still opened their grandparents' parcels, they would hold up the shalwar kameez and kurta pyjamas and look at them with suspicion. One year Aisling was convinced the clothes had a strange odour and threw them in the bin.

For a girl raised on Dairylea triangle sandwiches, mutter paneer sabji and Coca Cola, Parminder had developed quite a taste for the regular soirees she and David threw for their friends. The evenings featured large quantities of wine, cheese from the deli and crackers, grapes, and an assortment of nuts.

These evenings made Parminder feel sophisticated and she delighted in the Orrefors wine glasses and decanter, the little Radford cheese knives, the Sagaford cheese dome, platter and the subtle porcelain plates. Delicate little things, a world away from her mother's steel thalis and the heavily floral dinnerware that appeared on the rare occasions her parents invited someone to dine with them. Even then it wasn't a dinner party as such, but the feeding of men by a kitchen full of women and children, who would eat only after the men's appetites had been sated. It had been her job as the eldest girl to serve the fresh-off-the-tuva rotis to the men – the buttered steam aroma from the roti quickening her hunger as she circled the table.

Parminder hadn't expected to see Gurpreet again. After their reunion meal, her relationship with Aisling had lapsed into irregular social media contact, and despite telling each other that they should definitely meet up again, neither had followed this up. She was surprised she recognised him when, almost a year later in Birmingham on business, she spotted him as she was checking in at her hotel. She felt strangely flustered that he hadn't seen her. That evening she ate in the hotel restaurant and chose a table facing the entrance. Dessert had finally arrived when she admitted to herself that she was waiting for him and then, as if on cue, he came through the door, immediately recognised her, and smiled.

Gurpreet had seen her at the hotel reception desk but had looked away. He found himself distracted during the day's meetings. When he saw her in the restaurant he recognised straight away that she had been waiting for him all along.

They chose Leicester for their next weekend together – a city neither of them knew. They hadn't remembered that it was Diwali until the sound of fireworks roused them from their hotel bed. From the window they could see the mela in full swing. They shared childhood memories of Diwali as they hurriedly dressed. Down on the streets they felt a rush of recklessness and ran, hand in hand, through the streets towards the bright lights.

On Melton Road the sound of bhangra filled the air as they mingled with the Indian families dressed in their finest. The women and girls shimmered and sparkled, their bindis and red kum-kum punctuating the night. Gurpreet and Parminder felt underdressed. But here they belonged, here they were comfortable.

They became aware of conversations in Punjabi, tuned into like a radio. Playfully, they followed a large Sikh in a red turban with his family, dipping in and out of the Indian restaurants with them. They copied his order, eating a starter in one, a main course in another and having chai and taking away dessert from a third.

Later, in bed, they spoke only in Punjabi and fed each other gulab jaman, jelebis and ladoo, licking the sweetness from each other's lips.

Aisling noted that something was different. She concluded that Gurpreet was distinctly more ethnic than he used to be.

Parminder started to play bhangra in the car when she took the kids to school. When they complained, she turned up the volume.

It was easy for them: their usual travel for work provided perfect cover. They became bolder and began to choose places closer to home.

One weekend they headed to Southall. The buzz of the Punjabi bazaar, the rhythmic uplift of the bhangra, the paan stalls, Indian sweet shops and the skies seared by the flights heading to and from Heathrow, took them both back to long summers with London cousins. They spent Saturday wandering around, drinking in the sights, smells and sounds of Little India.

Before they knew it they had accumulated a trousseau of shalwar kameez, traditional jewellery sets, bindis and kurta pyjamas. They discovered that one of the local dhabbas cooked food exactly like their Mummyjis. During lunch Parminder pointed out that the things Gurpreet had bought for her were those that, traditionally, her mother would have given her had she married a Sikh man, as had been expected of her. The thought made them fall silent and look away from one another.

The next morning Parminder woke with the taste of prashad in her mouth. She couldn't believe it when she found herself suggesting that they visit a gurdwara. Neither of them had been to a gurdwara for years. They associated it with hours of Sunday morning tedium. Now they were filled with anticipation. The prospect felt thrilling and strangely taboo. They dressed themselves carefully. Parminder wore one of her new shalwar kameez and fixed her hair to look modest and pious.

There was a wedding going on at the gurdwara. The bride sat head bent, sparkling in red and gold. As they entered the prayer hall both wondered if people could tell they weren't husband and wife. They sat opposite one another in the male and female sections and let the prayers wash over them. When it came time for langar they sat together, their legs touching, feeling a sense of calm and completeness, as if they had arrived home after a long, arduous and confusing journey.

Gurpreet decided that his kids should learn Punjabi and signed them up for lessons at the nearest gurdwara. They reluctantly attended their first lesson and came away discombobulated, telling their mother it was boring and the place smelled funny.

On parents' evening, Parminder surprised David and the boys by meeting them in shalwar kameez. After he put the boys to bed David told Parminder that her behaviour was confusing them.

Gurpreet started to grow his hair and beard in the traditional Sikh way. One night the kids walked in on him attempting to tie a pugri. They ran away screaming and Aisling told Gurpreet to stop scaring her children.

David was concerned. The boys had told him that "Mum was acting all weird". Parminder hardly spoke to him at all and when she did it all seemed foreign to him.

Gurpreet overheard Aisling telling the girls about their proud Irish heritage; that they came from a long line of well-to-do, middle-class Irish stock. He began to see clearly how things would go: when his girls married and had children, he would be a blip in their family tree, an exotic anomaly, soon to be forgotten.

David wanted to go to couple-counselling and when Parminder refused, he broke down and sobbed that he had no idea who she was anymore.

The days and weekends were no longer enough. Gurpreet and Parminder knew they didn't want to be tourists – day trippers into their own cultures – anymore.

Parminder found herself feeling sick at the thought of eating cheese. She craved aloo paratha and churee – things her Mummyji used to make. The English and European food she usually ate failed to satisfy her – the dishes felt thin and insubstantial. She wanted to be nourished, filled with substance, but she couldn't quite work out what.

Aisling told Gurpreet that he was no longer the man she married.

David was at work and the children at school when Parminder did the test and confirmed that she was pregnant. She sat still for a few moments and felt a quiet lightness overcome her. She found herself smiling as she got up and wandered through the house opening every window.

STREAMLINING

"So, like, nobody gets buried these days, yeah. We gotta look after the earth's resources, innit?"

"Oh, so you mean that cremation is better because it only releases toxins into the air and around the ozone layer and that's good for the earth?"

Jocie hated it when her brother started going on like this. As if he actually knew things that mattered, when the truth was that he'd half-listened to a conversation with some white girl into hippy shit he wanted to shag. Besides, they hadn't been talking about burying anyone. Nobody had died. It was just the kind of discussion they had when they were on the way to visit Mother – even thinking the word "mother" filled Jocie with dread. It was ridiculous. She'd left home when she was seventeen for God's sake. Fifteen years ago.

At the next traffic lights, near Belle Vue, or what used to be Belle Vue, she twisted the mirror round and checked her hair. It was braided neatly, not too big, not too small. Her scalp was well oiled and looked healthy. She ran her finger over her eyebrows and rubbed at the dark shadows under her eyes. She should have used her Touche Éclat but it was her summer shade and it was too dark for her paler winter face. There hadn't been time to go shopping.

"C'mon, Sis, lights won't get any greener."

"Why do you always say that? It's a ridiculous saying."

"You mean it's what Dad used to say?"

She didn't mean that. At least she didn't think she did. Besides, it was funny when Dad had said it. His accent made it fuller, coloured it in somehow.

But her brother had put his Dr Dre's back on his ears and was strumming his long fingers on the dash. He looked out of place in her Tigra. Like he'd squashed himself into a child's pedal car, his knees nearly touching his ears. Brandon never seemed to worry about visiting Mother. Took it all in his stride. That was because Mother doted on him. He couldn't do anything wrong. If he turned up in a creased shirt, it was his girlfriend's fault. If his hair wasn't neat, it was the barber's fault. If he had a hangover, it was his mates' fault. Jocie could only imagine what it would be like not to be responsible for herself and others. Her brother wasn't a bad person. He just didn't know he was irresponsible; the word wasn't in his vocabulary.

Her earliest memories were about being responsible: for waking up Brandon with her crying; for giving Mummy a headache with all her chatter; for making Daddy leave because she was always naughty. Jocie knew about responsibility. Maybe she should resent her brother, but she couldn't. It wasn't his fault he'd been born with a penis.

The traffic was really heavy. She hated coming to Reddish. It was a nightmare on match days now that Man City had moved from Maine Road. And of course today was a match day. The place had become scruffy. There were closed-down shops along the main road. The furniture stores still had the same old shit outside, covered in layers of dust. She couldn't understand why her mum wouldn't move over to somewhere in South Manchester. It wasn't like she couldn't afford it. Her house was massive, the mortgage paid off ten years before. She could easily get a small flat out in West Didsbury or somewhere like that.

The feeling of dread was working its way through her system. It started in her bladder area – her root chakra according to Anna – then clomped through her innards in wooden clogs until it reached her solar plexus. It was a little bit like when her cat padded on her lap, only this was inside and the cat was a lion wearing steel toecaps.

"What ya grinning at, Sis?"

"I was thinking about cats. In workmen's boots."

"Yeah, whatever. What's with the traffic? I've gotta get back. TJ's coming over. We wanna lay down some beats."

Seriously, he just said that – like he's a teenager from the

144

ghetto! For God's sake, he's thirty-one and has a job in insurance. It was all Mother's fault. Jocie pulled herself upright. She'd thought it. Now she had to deal with that word. Fault. Oh, and she could add blame to the mix. All the taboo words that were so easy not to use when you sat in a pale green office with the smell of lavender and old people surrounding you – tissues placed discreetly within reach and an understanding counsellor who's on your side anyway because you're paying her. It all made sense at that point. Life was just life. People ended up where they ended up. Nobody's fault; no one to blame. It was slightly different when she was on her way to see Mother.

"I forgot there was a match on."

Jocie didn't mind that they were delayed and she was pleased that, annoying as he was, Brandon was with her. She usually had to cajole and come up with something to get him to go along with her. It was not usually as easy as it had been today.

"What do you want, Bran?"

"Eh, what do you mean? I just said I've got to get back."

"Yeah, but why are you coming? Do you want money from her?"

She pulled up at the next set of lights, outside the new Tesco superstore, shifted in her seat and stared at him. He had his bottom lip pushed out, just like when he was a kid and he'd been caught out and thought he was going to get into trouble. Except it was always her fault because she hadn't watched out for him, told him, or told on him. He was looking straight out of the windscreen, his earphones back in place. He wasn't tapping any more but his head was jerking to some kind of rhythm. Typical.

Jocie swivelled back in her seat. The car behind beeped its horn and she gave him the finger in her mirror before pulling away. So Brandon wasn't doing her a favour after all. When was she going to stop being such a sucker? After Dad left, she would daydream about him still being there. About having someone who laughed at the same things as her, who understood what she meant when she made some profound statement about life. Someone who was on her side. Of course, it wouldn't have been like that. Dad had been quiet for years before he left. He'd even stopped arguing. Just upped and left one day. You'd think that would have made

Mother happy, the way she went on at him. But it made her worse. For Jocie and Brandon it was like he ceased to exist, had never been there. Mother said he'd gone back home, had a woman waiting for him. But that was rubbish. He hadn't been back to Africa in all of Jocie's twelve years, so how could somebody have been waiting for him.

God, she was in a stinker of a mood, and she shouldn't be. She'd had a good week at work. The contract they'd been chasing had come in; she'd closed the deal and was due a bonus at the end of the month. Her team was performing above par, too. All of them. No sickness, no resistance to new ideas. She was good at her job. She'd worked her way up to manage the creative team. The ones who coined the magic words for clients and made them all money. She'd made so many cutting-edge changes. Weeded out the slackers and off-loaded them onto other teams. Nicely, of course. Streamlining she called it. Saving the company money. In reality, she dumped anyone who challenged her with attitude. She didn't mind being challenged on a decision if another, better idea was offered. But some people criticised and bitched for the sake of it.

"Sis, we're moving. Are you asleep or what?"

She slotted the gear stick into first and rolled forward, turning right into Reddish Lane. Work soothed her. It's what she did, who she was. If she was being eulogised at her funeral, they would say, "There goes Jocelle Owako, a brilliant mind. Such a loss to the business world, but what a legacy she left behind."

"You're grinning again."

"I was thinking about my funeral."

"You're so weird. Who thinks about that? You've always been weird."

The grin left Jocie's face and the familiar tension returned to her solar plexus. It sat like there like a lump. Breathe into your feelings, her yoga tutor said. Bring yourself into the centre and breathe deeply. Concentrate on each breath fully. Let go.

In a room full of middle-class women and the odd right-on-man, all with serene, shiny faces and bodies that could contort in any direction, it was easy to do that. Thrusting a warrior pose or stretching into the downward dog, gazing at the ridges on her

146

extra thick yoga mat brought her easily into the zone of Zen. But sitting next to an overgrown teenager on the way to visit a mother who could slice through lead with one look was a different matter.

Jocie took a deep breath. She turned left into the cul-de-sac that housed Mother. Brandon undid his seat belt and without looking at her, bounced from the car and slammed the door. Too hard. She watched over the privets as the front door opened and he was enveloped in a bear hug. Reaching behind her seat she pulled out her handbag and slowly climbed from the car. The shopping she'd bought was in the boot and she shouted after Brandon to help her. Instead, he walked into the house. Mother stood on the step, a fixed smile on her face, scanning as much of Jocie as she could see.

"Well, are you just going to stand there? What are you gawping at? Did you get a fresh mango? I want to make some jam. Come on, hurry up I don't want to heat the street."

Jocie dragged the two bags from the boot and one of them snagged on the catch. Oranges and mangoes spilled into the gutter. The melon rolled towards the step where mother was standing. There was a subtle change in the air. Brandon appeared behind mother and pulled childish faces, wagging his finger in a ludicrous manner. Jocie wanted to scream. The volcano in her solar plexus was reaching critical mass and expanding into her chest.

"Well, don't just stand there like a lemon. Pick up my fruit. It'll be full of germs. Honestly, you'd think I'd taught you nothing. You were always like this. Gormless. I'm going to have to soak it in vinegar water to get the rubbish off it. You make my life so difficult. You're supposed to be helping me."

Jocie stood and stared. She stared at her mother's bitter, twisted mouth spewing things that didn't make any sense; at her brother who was doing monkey impressions. She started to laugh. Bending down she picked up the fruit from the gutter and placed it in the other bag. She picked up the melon. All the while she was laughing, tears were beginning to streak down her face. She laughed so hard, she thought she might pee herself, but she couldn't stop. Placing the bag on the step she stayed bent over, clutching her sides. Her mother slapped her on the back and still she laughed. She got to the point where she could hardly catch her breath.

Eventually the feeling subsided and she straightened up, wiping her cheeks with her sleeve. Looking Mother in the eye, she gave her a quick hug and a peck on the cheek. She gave her brother two fingers behind Mother's back, turned and walked back down the path. It was only when she opened the car door that Brandon suddenly came alive.

"Oi, where you going? I need to get back. What you doing?"

Jocie pretended not to hear, calmly put the key in the ignition and switched the engine on. She executed a neat three-point turn and, without glancing back at them, she drove away. Breathe. She told herself. Be in the present.

SYLVIA DICKINSON

AMBER LIGHT

Misha shows so much flesh there's a hush as she rustles across the blue-lit room. Guys sheathed in pre-shrunk jeans gangle against walls, listening to Queen. Switched on. Trying to appear indifferent, sniggering about girls who have spent hours curling lashes, glossing lips.

Thing is, Misha's not a girly girl. Five-ten at least and high-waisted. Bust almost bopping from a balcony bra. Body the colour of hay. Makes guys think of unbuttoning shirts in simmering summer fields. Grey eyes half-hidden by a bang. Auburn hair teased into a beehive, waxed by Wella extra-firm mousse. Not exactly hip. But flaunts it. The word from guys is that she's all show and no go. Ball-basher. That's what they say anyway.

Misha saunters to the stereo. She's looking for soul. Turns her back on the party, flips through a clutch of CDs. Her right winkle-picker scratches a left ankle, looped in gold filigree. Some girls admire her chic; others conspire because she whiffs the oomph of sex. Misha never togs a bloke around. She's got only one friend. Ellie.

Likeable, matchstick Ellie. Brainy – makes up for what she lacks in other departments. Come on, she's latched on to Misha, who gets guys eyeballing. Then again, she's good at listening, a frown over those big brown eyes. Doesn't gossip. But she does make Misha look the business.

A trestle-table's spread with a higgle-piggle of chicken legs and cheese squares sweating on limp lettuce. The bar's in the kitchen. Someone's tumbled a bottle of Rioja and a bunch of marjoram into the copper skillet of *coq au vin*. The sticky aroma mixes with sweet joss-scent. Misha teeters sea-green to the loo, but doesn't enter because of the sour ooze of pork puke. Doesn't drink strong stuff. Ever. Can't cope with the morning-after. On the drinks table, amongst the dregs of vodka and gin, there's lemonade. She sips, wedged against the doorjamb by this bloke breathing down her chest. Where the hell's Ellie? Misha's eyes flip round the room. He grabs her wrist. "Dance." It's not a question.

She tolerates him stroking her bottom, even a slight nibble of earlobes weighted in gold hoops. But she shoves when he wants to clutch cleavage. Then Ellie appears in a corner, listening, head bent. Smiles and gives the pert blonde a light pat. Misha can't make out if it's a touch of commiseration or appreciation. If only she could be like that. Wink-winks what she gets.

"I've had enough," she says, but only meant to think. Drunk, he's gobsmacked. She says, "Sorry," moving away. Thinks bitchily, "Bloody Ellie".

Hot. Misha slips out front. Extra-long cig dangling. She scrambles for her Ronson. Keys jingle. Diary, pens, make-up, wallet jumble out. Firm footsteps approach.

Ellie flickers under the streetlamp. "Light?"

"Ta." Misha checks the luminous dial. "Damn near one. What happened to ten?"

"You look great in red." Puppy-brown eyes smiling.

"Christ Ellie, do you have to dress like a bag? Shit, shapeless skirts. Bloody sunflowers. Again! I've had bullshitty blondes and claptrap chaps up to here! You've got some bloody nerve. Were you really trying to pull…? I don't expect you to behave… Like a typical man."

Ellie flushes then pales, making her freckles stand out. Minutes tick.

Misha relents, "You got great legs. I'll bag you something tomorrow." A cab lets rowdy passengers out. "Come on let's grab it."

Misha croons, "Summertime and the livin' is easy." A husky voice. They cruise Upper Street. Flares sputter from French flambés or from Chinese woks of giant stirfries for Islington hips. Ellie melts into remembering.

They'd met on the Internet, trawling *Women wanting Women* and finding the message: *Mate wanted for cheap last-minute package to Majorca. Straights only. For sun, fun and frolics.*

They got together at The Lamb. Anonymous, safe, central. Near to Ellie's programming job on Russell Square. Ellie got blinded on dry white. Misha manoeuvred them outside, so she could chain-smoke, her cough hacking. She talked of using blokes. Hot dinners, free rides. Ellie went on about chauvinists in offices.

"Sometimes it's better to be a man. All boys together."

"Oh, I've played at being a boy, Ellie."

"What?"

"Grew up with four bigger bothers. Played cops 'n robbers, football and trains. Then at ten, I wanted dolls. At fourteen, I chucked my brothers' cast-offs. My parents joked about having a new girl around. I took to smoking. Only a joint or two. Didn't worry them. Part of the scene, a typical teen."

"Mine would've cracked. Didn't yours want a girl?"

"Expect having a tomboy suited their pockets. Couldn't last. Buying dresses knocked them. At eighteen, I moved out. Selfish, just when I started to earn."

"You make it sound simple. Growing up, leaving and that."

"Oh yeah. Me, Misha, late-starter. Show-off, wanting to be different. Maybe why I like the old sexy garb I sell in my vintage boutique."

"My dad's a director in banking," admits Ellie, "and Mum's always been home. Knits, organises church bazaars, does committees. We don't speak much. When we do, it's not personal. Doubt you'll like them."

"Will they like me, Ellie?"

They laugh. Agree that a holiday at one hundred fifty quid's a breeze. Palma Nova third-class, cheap booze and anoraks. No matter. Chuck a bag together and fly.

Ellie can't swim. Dressed in baggy Bermudas, she dangles spindly legs over the edge at the deep end, while Misha strokes five lengths, holding her head above water. Her bouffant must last the week; karaoke in the bar, discos till dawn, wacky waiters.

Then on the third night. Stuffy June zoomed into the thirties. Misha fell into the room, flipping off her size eight stilettos. They laugh about that, taking the same size shoe. But why does Ellie always change in the bathroom? Misha thinks it's to do with being an only kid. A ma and da in Basingstoke. Grim. Not like her rappin, laughin Leytonstone home.

Later that evening, sitting in front of the mirror, Misha sucks in a whispered breath. Lifts green fingernails. There's a scrape of untaping. Pulls it off. Pops the wig on her vanity case. Ellie stops gawping. Picks up the sparkly afro-comb. Taps it in a perspiring palm. Tenderly, she strokes Misha's scalp, hair sparse like black peppercorns.

Steady grey meets Ellie's wet, brown eyes in the mirror. The hush expands in the night heat. Ellie moves close to her back, leans forward to get a brush. Misha feels a knot. In the small of her back. She tenses. Is it? Could it be? Flat eyes hide the tremor. The mirror's baiting, watching, waiting.

Misha stands, dropping the shoestring sheath. Steps from the silk puddle. Smooth. Practised. Unsnaps her bra. Freed.

Ellie unzips her dress. Its skirt of cotton sunflowers flops to the floor. Bares shy, pink-nippled peaks. Stands pigeon-toed, like a gawky teenager.

Slowly, they tuck thumbs into briefs. Stripping pretence. Face the mirror, jolt through its crack. Plunge to the carpet. Blot out the looking. Spiralling toward the fluorescent. Fumbling. Falling. Floating, caressing each other toward bed.

Funny, they never chat about that night.

Now in the cab, the lullaby shushes. Misha noses into the nook of Ellie's armpit, sprayed in gardenia perfume, fingering Ellie's stringy hair.

"We going to that do down Camden next week? You think…" Ellie says

They peck.

"What, Poppet?"

"What I think is, your auburn's better than the blonde," Ellie says.

"Uh-hah? What about Camden?"

"Ok... if we leave your wig at home."

"Uh-huh?" Misha hoots. "Why look at you, Poppet. Wearing the pants."

"We can start with the wig," Ellie says.

"My-my. That's not a start," Misha says.

"I would hope it's not the end." Ellie says to the driver, "Here's fine. Thanks."

The cab tootles to a halt and they tumble out. Ellie digs for cash in the sulphurous streetlight. They climb the steps to the murky Victorian building. Ellie's about to stick the key in the lock. Misha clutches her hand. Murmurs, "Been thinking awhile. High time we go see your parents. It's six months. Tell them. We're an item. Course, I won't need no damn wig."

Ellie doesn't answer as they enter the dark, narrow passage into the flat. Fumbles for the bedroom switch. Amber light pervades, mirrors reflecting from every wall. Dresses, shoes, stockings trail the floor. They collapse onto the unmade bed, tremble and sigh.

Misha leans on an elbow, kisses Ellie's lips, neck, breast. "You need me to move in here, Poppet. I'll take care of you."

"Uh-huh?" Ellie leans up, spreads the duvet over them. Slips under the covers, pulls Misha down, "Shush now. Crucial I get sleep, I have a project meeting early tomorrow."

Ellie curls away, feels the flip of the duvet. "Misha, lie still. Leave the lamp, you know I like sleeping in amber light."

NANA-ESSI CASELY-HAYFORD

FROM WHERE I COME

I had not expected to be contacted by *them* again, not here, so far from home, in my Aunt Zorani's place, buried in a row of decrepit Georgian houses in Leeds. But then, why shouldn't they contact me here? My grandmamma always reminded us that everything has a spirit and if we looked and listened hard enough, we could communicate with them, wherever in the world we found ourselves.

Aunt Zorani was downstairs watching *Black Girls Rock!* on the Sky BET channel. I was upstairs getting ready for bed, and missing home. A soft rain was misting the window. Outside was the growl of traffic and the raised voices of late-night revellers. For a while the carefree laughter of young women distracted me. I imagined myself with them, out there having a happy time. Then I heard my name. I'd heard that voice many times before – distant, yet present, as familiar to me as a member of my family – calling me to the front door.

I left the bedroom, went downstairs and opened the door.

Aunt Zorani must have heard me, or felt the draught. She was suddenly at my shoulder.

"What are you doing?"

"The spirits," I said, "they are calling, and I…"

"What spirits! At this hour, in England! What heathen nonsense is this." She spat the words at me. "We're all aware you miss back home, but that's no reason to make up stories and act them out! You stupid girl. How dare you!"

Aunt Zorani shouldered me aside, slammed the door and turned the lock.

It was a Friday night. The sound of the revellers in the streets outside took me back to Okampi Village. It would be the coming-of-age ceremonies this week. I visualised the outfits: slits, kabbas and *abotre* cut and sewn from wax prints with exotic birds against a patterned sky. I saw the rich, brocade-like materials worn by the wealthier folks – the yellows, the blues, the terracottas and oranges shimmering in the late-evening sunlight. Then, of course, the girls and boys arrived in the village square, dressed like colourful birds with decorative patterns stamped all over their skins. Like real birds they would be thrown high in the air, perform somersaults and pirouettes, before being caught by the laughing crowd.

I missed the tables laden with jollof rice, fish, meats and vegetables.

I wanted to remind my aunt that we were all guardians of the spirit world, regardless of where we lived or worshipped, but I knew it would only end in insults and put-downs.

"Zenobia! Why do you have to carry on with such backward rituals?" she asked next morning, as she shoved a small plate of beans on toast in front of me.

"Backward?" I said.

"Yes, backward," she snapped, pointing at the morsel of food I'd placed beside my plate. "All this nonsense about giving to ancestors before you eat. I'd prefer it if you kept these things to yourself. In fact, I don't want any of this in my house."

By the way my auntie's Christian friends looked at me I guessed that she'd told them about my "backward" habits. I refused to go to their church gatherings. I became cautious of the people around me. I desperately wanted to return home and take my chances there.

I was taking advantage of the sunshine to hang out the clothes Aunt Zorani had told me to hand-wash when I heard her shout. I left the basin on the grass and hurried into the house.

She was in the guest room, banging at the walls with a broom. Flies – a thick, dark cluster of them – had settled on the ceiling and the walls. Just hearing them buzz made me itch.

"My God, Zenobia, it is an infestation."

I said nothing.

She sprayed them. They did not die. She tried smoking them out by burning incense. This only served to agitate them. In two days the walls of the room were black with flies.

Now there was a heaviness in the house that had not been there before. The smell of wet forest earth mixed with jasmine hung about the rooms. I wished I could have told my aunt that it was the ancestors announcing their presence.

At the end of the fifth day, I couldn't hold it in anymore.

"They are here to deliver a message," I said. "They will not leave until we acknowledge them… Respectfully," I added, looking her directly in the eyes.

"What lies are you fabricating now? Are you trying to embarrass me again?"

"When did I embarrass you? I am telling you the truth. They will leave once they know the message is understood. Yesterday I saw a hen harrier at the bird table in the garden." I pointed through the window. "It was there again this morning. Two omens in two days, Aunt Zorani…"

"Go! Fetch the Bible, foolish girl. Open it at Mathew 8:28-34. Contemplate what you read. Now, out of my sight! I have to prepare for Zuma!"

Zuma was my older cousin. He and his Masters Degree in Fine Arts were all Aunt Zorani talked about to anyone who did or did not care to listen. He came home at the end of every month to a houseful of his mother's friends, and a table-spread of guinea fowl soup, palava sauce, blue crab and flaked salt-fish.

On the day when Zuma was due to arrive, I laid out platters of browned kingfish, bowls of ox-tail stew and jollof rice in front of Aunt Zorani's over-indulging, overdressed friends.

I went upstairs to change my clothes. I listened to the voices down below and tried to distract myself by thinking of the food I'd soon be consuming, but I could not get the bird of prey out of my mind.

I knew when Zuma arrived because I heard the usual commotion at the front. Through the window I saw Aunt Zorani hurrying towards the gate, welcoming her son – her voice loud and boastful.

My cousin was a tall, smiling, light-skinned young man – in a shade, which my auntie reminded me at every turn, I wasn't so blessed with. Perhaps it was my Asante blood. Despite her disapproval of my colour, I liked Zuma. He was the first to welcome me when I arrived. He folded his arms around me and called me his lovely cousin. Auntie Zorani was always kinder when Zuma was around.

Auntie Zorani opened her arms to hug him, but he did not seem to see her. He swung his body sharply left, and walked along the edges of the flower garden towards the patio.

It was then that I noticed something different about him. It was his shambling loose-limbed gait, his eyes focused somewhere above our heads. His lips were moving as if he were in agitated conversation with himself.

Auntie flung her hands up to her face, as if her son had struck her. Zuma's godmother, a senior Mother of their church, rose as briskly as her size and weight allowed and stepped forward to greet him. The hostility in his eyes froze the woman. Zuma kissed his teeth and entered the house.

Murmurs of disapproval rippled through the gathering. It wasn't long before my cousin strolled back out into the garden to gasps and murmurs of consternation. He was in his underwear. Aunt Zorani held onto the patio doors to steady herself. Though my chest began to hurt and I found that I could barely breathe, I dashed towards the washing line, grabbed a sheet and wrapped it around Zuma.

Two of the women assisted Aunt Zorani indoors and guided her – weeping – to the sofa in the living room. I followed Zuma across the yard, as he pulled at invisible things in the air and flung them about him. At one moment he was stomping the earth and brushing his body as if he were covered with ants; at another, he was scrubbing at his skin, as if wanting to scrape himself clean. Then he sat on the grass staring at his hands.

I had seen something like this before. The week before I left for London – two months after my mother's passing – my eldest sister, Szoraya, who'd cared for our mother up to the end, began speaking to herself, shouting answers to questions only she was able to hear. My grandmother said it was our mother wanting to

157

take Szoraya to the spirit world with her. It was her duty to wrestle my sister back from my mother's selfish grasp – to keep her in the world of the living, where she belonged. My grandmother lost the battle; my sister left us. Then I fell ill.

"She will not have you too," she said. "You will cross wide water where she cannot follow you. I will send you to your aunt in England."

Before my grandmother sent me off, she steeped my body in sea salt. She stripped me naked and covered me with the leaves of neem, pimento, giant cow-foot and those from the plant of life. She did this on a Tuesday – the deity day on which I was born. Then the older women of the family each laid a hand on me and chanted me to sleep. When I woke, I was cured.

Maybe Zuma's illness was not all that different. I asked him once what it was like to be working at a famous university, and all he talked about was his struggle to fit in. Or perhaps it was that other thing that he could never tell his mother. The last time he visited, I'd overheard him on the phone in his room next to mine, his voice desperate and sobbing, explaining to someone why he could not tell his mother about them.

Zuma was on the phone until the sound of Aunt Zorani's Fiat Uno reached us in the house. My cousin cut short his pleading, rushed to his bedroom door and locked it. I replayed his desperation in my mind and wondered who Michael was.

Maybe I could do something at last. As my Grandmamma said, there are lots of things in life that can take us out of ourselves, leave us empty and wandering like ghosts in the world of the living. It was not madness. Madness was anything a westerner did not understand. There were ways of re-uniting us with ourselves. She had called me to her side and said she wanted to pass on her gift to someone in the family and she had chosen me.

I went into the house and knelt beside my aunt. I reminded her of the omens: the flies, the hen harrier. I asked her why it was so hard to accept these things when she had grown up with grandmamma too, and knew about my mother's passing and the way she took my sister.

Aunt Zorani looked at me. Her lips were trembling; her eyes swollen red, and raw. "Help me," she said.

"It is you who have to help me," I told her. "It won't work if you refuse to help."

She shook her head impatiently and became my old quick-tempered aunt again. "Don't speak to me in in parables, girl. I do not understand you. What do I have to do!"

"You have to put love first, Auntie," I said.

AKILA RICHARDS

SECRET CHAMBER

Tina sits up in bed, gulps down a glass of water with two fizzing Alka Seltzers. Her next gig is in two and a half days. She'll rip the roof off the sky. But first she's got to set things right.

In two hours, yeah; exactly at 9.45 a.m. things will be back to normal.

She slides her feet onto the red shag-rug and feels a cashew nut between her toes.

She dislodges it in disgust and starts to feel queasy.

Last night's gig was off the hinge before it turned to shit. Her smoky voice was fuck-off enough for blue-haired boys and girls to chant, "Tina, Run! Tina, Run, Run!" Then, mid-break, Cosmos had trashed his guitar and stormed off, sulking like soggy bread because he caught her kissing his younger sister, Sherbet. He called them sluts. She called him a wannabe pimp.

"You can't have both of us," he said.

"I don't," she said. "You were a mistake; I was outta my head. Drunk! Besides, that was months ago."

In fact, it was eleven weeks ago. Exactly. She remembers because, right now, look at the shit it's got her into. Last night she was puking after only one vodka shot. Then she got emotional. Unheard of!

Tina shudders. *Cosmos a dad? Never!*

She would jog to the clinic. She loves running; the best songs, the coolest riffs come to her when sprinting through graffiti-lined back roads and grimy unlit streets.

She attacks the hill, is sweating when she arrives. Only the top letters of Priory Clinic are visible above the white surrounding wall.

A large glass panel slides open in front of her. She bends down, hands resting on her thighs, breathing noisily. *Fucking awesome run.*

On top of the double-decker, Ornella shifts uneasily. The top should be reserved for the young and their secrets. At forty-seven she was too old for this.

She breathes in deeply, counts to ten, then lets out a long airstream through her nose. She looks around self-consciously. Two boys with big earphones lounge at the back. They nod rhythmically. For a moment her heart stumbles; a small current of panic spirals up her throat. *Is it, is it?* She squints at the familiar red cap. *No, it's not my son.* Sweat beads trickle down her nose.

She takes out the Rescue Remedy and empties a full tube on her tongue. Instead of calming her, it makes her want to cry. She suppresses a sob. She does not want to get there bleary-eyed.

She'd told Alton that she'd be staying with her best friend, Shannon, for a spa weekend in Sussex Manor. "About time, Ornella," he'd said. "Stop worrying about me." But she saw him pushing the food away with emaciated hands. In the last seven months her husband had lost four stones. They'd hugged delicately before she left for Priory Clinic.

Ornella takes out her round hand-mirror from her bag, re-draws her lids with a touch of eyeliner. "Lying eyes," she mutters at her reflection. She stuffs the mirror back into her bag and squirts another tube of Rescue Remedy under her tongue.

Padma's designer shades almost eclipse her immaculately made-up face as she cruises her Saab up the hill. She plays her favourite song, "Wishing On A Star". This place with its market stalls along the pavement is worlds apart from Docklands where her apartment overlooks the Thames, offering a breathtaking nighttime view of lit-up London. She's a stockbroker, made a million or two but is bored with it. She grew up on a road like this. She still likes to visit the little shops in Neasden, close to the Hindu temple, breathe in spices that remind her of Mamiji and home.

Padma nudges her sunglasses onto her forehead as she approaches the clinic.

It irks her – letting her standards slip. She and Toby have been slipping for a while now. In nine months and sixteen days she will be thirty-four. She will drop the job, drop Toby too; go some-where else; do something more rewarding. She's had enough of the city smugness, the arrogance and the ugliness underneath. She knows she's part of it, has been for the past fifteen years… the screwing around, the coking up…

But maybe today is just a bad day. On Monday morning she'll be kicking ass again.

Alternating light-blue and cream walls. Two large windows. A marl-blue, three-seater settee. Two matching armchairs. Three sterilised pastel-green blankets on the day beds, one against each wall. Each cubicle has a door leading to the operation room. A polished coffee table displays women's health leaflets, helpline cards, antibacterial gel and a used-up tube of pink lip-gloss. New-smelling blue carpet. The long landscape photograph of the Peak District echoes the cloudy sky through the windows at the back of the clinic. Tea bags, sachets of instant coffee, stacked plastic cups and a silver kettle sit on a small table in the far right corner of the room. Tina, Ornella and Padma avoid each other's eyes.

Tina's legs swing over the armrest of the wooden armchair. She is staring out of the window. Her black earphones sit on her blue high-fringed hair. She opens her coke, guzzles half the bottle.

Ornella sits upright on the settee, a pillow at her back, reading glasses resting on a thick blue book with gold lettering on the spine. She is mouthing words, looking up occasionally.

Padma leafs through a *Hello* magazine, then dumps it on the table. She leans back in the cushioned armchair and crosses one Kurt Geiger boot over the other. She really could do with a line.

She stares at Ornella with assessing eyes, then swings around to face her. "What are you reading?"

Ornella ignores her.

Padma prods again. "You're praying, aren't you?"

Ornella's lips stop moving.

"Don't you think it's a little late? You can't un-pregnant yourself, you know."

Ornella rests her gaze on Padma. Says in a deep unhurried voice, "My name is Ornella Philips."

Padma sits back. Ornella holds her gaze, unsmiling.

"I'm er, Padma. Padma Desai."

"My praying bothers you?"

Padma twists her silver ring, pulls down the corners of her mouth. "Reminds me of my mother. Probably still prays every morning."

"I see." Ornella shrugs. "It's strengthening. Especially in times like these."

"Well, I prefer being practical. I…"

"You are made of stone, I guess?" Ornella raises her eyebrows.

"Well, people get all gushy in situations like these, I mean irrational, you know?"

Padma pushes herself off the chair, a rush of heat simmering under her skin. She walks over to the table by the window. "Would you like some tea?"

"White, four sugars. Thanks. I have five children and can't afford another."

It's a lie that slips out too easily for Ornella's liking.

Padma pours hot water into the cups. "You do it and it's done. That's all there is to it. That's the way I see it."

Ornella says nothing. Padma hands her the sweetened tea. "I don't let guilt control me like these religious escapists who…"

"Were you raised religious?" Ornella enquires quietly.

"Me? Uhm. Kind of. I don't practice any more. My mother, I mean… we are Hindu… she probably still prays for me everyday. Me, the lost one." Padma pushes her ring down into the soft web between her fingers. They sip in silence. Fragments of guitar music escape Tina's earphones.

Ornella looks at her. "And so… you're here."

"I really ought to have known better. I was…"

"Drunk?"

"I don't drink."

"Drugs?" Ornella's directness unnerves Padma.

"A little." Padma finds she lies too easily. "It wasn't safe to drive and it was late. So we went back to his. And you know how it is."

"No, I don't."

"Mm! I forgot you're holy."

"Adventist, actually. Seventh Day."

"Amounts to the same thing, doesn't it? We are getting rid of what's inside us. Isn't that it? Abort and go. Wonder what your adventurer friends would call you?"

"Stop it."

But Padma is unrelenting. "I see sluts everyday: the bosses, the little worker bees, me; we all sell ourselves to Mammon. We do." Padma gets up suddenly and walks to the toilet. She is there for a while, then returns smiling.

Tina's mobile vibrates. She yanks it out of her yellow skinnies and grins at Sherbet's face. Sherbert's sticking out her studded tongue.

"Hey, Sherby. Yeah, was just thinking about you too. Alright. No, not nervous. Anytime now. I wish they'd hurry up. It's past the hour. I was just listening to my songs for the next gig. It will be mega. You gonna pick me up? What now? But I haven't had it yet… Sherby. Sherby. Sherbs! I am not listening to this again. Just get off my tits, will ya… What! Scared? You're scared! Of what? I don't need more drama in my life." Tina makes a mental note to keep this as a song title.

"Sherby, Babes, I will be fine. Don't fizz, ok? What? It's got nothing to do with Cosmos! Hang on a minute. Hang on, hang on! What you mean you think he knows? What's he been saying? What? Sherbet! YOU DIDN'T! Hello? You're breaking up. I can't hear you. Hello? Shit."

Tina's tries to call back but gets an engaged tone.

Then her phone rings again – the film music from *Jaws*. Tina stares at the screen for a while, swipes it.

"Yeaaahh, Cosmos, what you want? 'Course, I'm fine." She drums her fingers on her thigh.

"Well that didn't bother you when you fucked off during the interval… So what if I threw up; it's not the first time, is it? One vodka too many… I'm with Sherby. Alright with you?… What you mean I'm lying… So what. You're watching me now? Stalker! … None of yours where I am, who I'm with, what and how I do it. GET IT?… 'Course I'll do the gig. And you better not fuck off again, otherwise you can stay fucked off… 'Course I mean it. I don't need more drama in my life." Tina sees this as a definite sign that she must write this song. She shuts off the phone, swearing under her breath. She thinks of calling Sherbert back, but changes her mind when a nurse walks into the room.

"Ms Tina Cohen."

"Yeah?"

"Would you please get yourself ready and sign the consent form? I'll be back in ten minutes."

"Okay."

Tina speed dials. "Sherby? Yeah I am on. In ten minutes. Yeah he's bloody stalking me. Just keep your mouth shut, OK? Your brother is a perv. Sorry. Didn't mean it like that. Thanks, Sherby babe. Course I'll be alright. Stop fizzing. Yeah in two hours. Love ya. Mega."

Tina goes to her daybed, draws the curtain and sits down. She's glad Sherbet called. Fact is she really needed it. She feels nauseous again. She takes an almighty gulp from her coke, closes it and chucks it on the bed. She takes a deep breath and changes into the hospital gown, revealing a tribal pattern around her ankles, her stage name "TinaRUN!" on her inner thigh and a scorpion with raised tail under her navel. She takes the consent form and signs it without reading.

Tina hears a soft knock, and the nurse enquires from behind the door, "Ms Cohen, are you ready?"

Tina walks from her daybed, opens the door and enters the operating room.

Padma and Ornella go still for a moment.

Ornella takes out her rescue drops, opens the bottle and downs the contents in one gulp. She feels empty and is still shaking.

"Ornella, sorry about my sarcasm. I…"

"It's not that, Padma. It's, it's…"

"What? That your husband doesn't know?"

"He doesn't."

"So? He won't be the first."

"It's… it's not that."

"What is it, Ornella. You haven't been raped, have you?"

"No-no-no! Thank goodness, not that."

165

"Come on tell me. Your God won't judge you."

Ornella is surprised by Padma's words.

"Can't you work it out with your husband? He may be delighted. You managed so far with five kids…"

"No Padma, he'll be hurt."

"Excuse my being thick, but are your children not his?"

"Of course they are. But since his illness… it's been tough. The last three years have aged us."

Ornella looks directly at Padma and Padma reads her.

"Oh sweet Lakshmi and Krishna in one! You had an affair! You got a lover! She's got a lover! A looover!" Padma softly sings and shakes her bangles Bollywood style. "You are deep. Check you, Mrs Seven Days."

"I was at the end of my strength." Ornella looks away.

"And needed a really good shag. So you DO know."

"I don't know how I can face him. I betrayed…"

"No, Ornella," Padma breaks in. "You were exhausted and needed support. Who would punish you for that?"

Padma gets up and sits beside Ornella. She places her arms around Ornella's big shoulders.

"You are kind…"

Ornella and Padma are still leaning into each other when they hear a door open.

"Mrs Ornella Philips?" The nurse stands in front her. Ornella looks up fearfully and sighs.

"Please get yourself ready and sign…"

"Sorry I can't. I just can't."

"Mrs Philips, no one is forcing you. You can change your mind."

"Of course, I didn't mean to… I need… I'll just…"

"Mrs Philips you have plenty of time to think it over… Ms Padma Desai?"

"Here." Padma responds promptly.

The nurse looks at her. "In ten minutes?"

"I'll be ready." As Padma gets up, the ring she'd loosened earlier drops onto the floor. She picks it up and slips it on her finger. She draws the curtain and undresses. She reads the consent form, signs and dates it. For some unexpected reason she thinks of her mother. They've not spoken for almost three years.

Padma is greeted by two masked faces in surgical gear.

"Please make yourself comfortable." A male voice points to the reclining bed. "We will give you a general anaesthetic and you'll just count backwards from twenty."

Padma lies back, her bony body settling into the moulded plastic curves. She has been here before on a chair like this, doing the practical thing. It felt right then. It doesn't now.

Padma lifts her legs and pushes her body out of the chair. "I've changed my mind," she says.

The female doctor takes off her mask. She nods at Padma. "It's alright, Ms Desai. It's alright. If you are sure?"

"Yes I am. I am. I am." Padma walks into the waiting room and says to Ornella. "I changed my mind."

Ornella lies on the same chair now, drifts off, sedated. The operation takes longer then expected. When Ornella comes round, she overhears snatches of conversation "…twins… thorough."

Padma is waiting for Ornella. She helps to ease her onto the daybed. Padma hands her a small square of paper. "Call me," she says. "Please do."

Ornella takes the paper between two fingers, looks up at Padma, then slumps into a deep sleep.

Tina is still in bed. Panda eyes. Glazed over. Hot and sweaty. There are complications. Sherbet's arrived. She's holding Tina's hand. "We'll give them a good reason why you had to cancel. You'll pack out the gig even more next time. You'll rip the roof of the sky."

Sherbet cools Tina's forehead with a cold, wet cloth.

Ornella sits in Shannon's car. They speed past miles of glued-together houses; dusk is settling over them. Ornella is staring out the car window, into herself. Next Saturday she'll be back at church.

Padma is in the park. She slides out her phone. Her heart bangs in her ears as she dials. A noisy pause. Music and voices in the background.

"Hailo… kauna hai…" a voice hesitant – her mother's.

"Mamiji?"

"Padma? Apa vastava mem yaha kya hai?" Padma's mother's voice is shaky.

"YES, it's me, Mummji. Your Padma."

"Oha, maim tumhem yada kiyah ki kaise!"

"Yes me too. I missed you endlessly."

LOUISA ADJOA PARKER

BREAKING GLASS

So here he is again, like a damn lost puppy with its tail between its legs, his fingers closed around his keys, psyching himself up.

The green door's been battered by the sea air and the paint's peeling off, exposing the faded wood underneath. He's been meaning to paint the place for ages; give everything a new coat; fresh start.

Akeem is shaking like an alcoholic. It's a *door* – what's the matter with him? All he has to do is open it and step through.

She'd thrown him out again last week; rang yesterday saying, *I miss you, baby, come home.* Yeah, it hasn't been a full week but it's still a kind of homecoming.

He can't wait to see Josh's face light up with his wide, toothy smile, or for Danni to throw herself into his arms. These are the things that tear at his heart.

He opens the door and steps inside. Zoe isn't in. The house is filthy: takeaway boxes all over the kitchen table, with pizza crusts like badly lipsticked smiles. The overflowing bin stinks of dirty nappies, cigarettes and beer. The ceilings and light fittings are mustard yellow, like the stains on her fingers. He wonders why he's never noticed this before.

Akeem runs his hand through his hair; it's getting too long; practically a full Afro. For years it's been Zoe who's cut his hair. Maybe it would be better to ask his mum.

He runs hot water into the sink over the crusted plates. He pours in too much washing up liquid; bubbles stick to his elbows and he shakes them off irritably. He leaves the plates to soak, empties the bin and fills more black bags with rubbish, tying the tops to stop the seagulls and foxes getting in, although he knows it's futile. Then he opens all the windows as wide as they can go.

What is it that brings me back to her every time? It's not just her pixie face or the way she looks up at him with those wide-spaced green eyes. It isn't even her tiny waist, so small he can fit his hands around it, and often does. Nor is it the way she rocks against him, hipbones banging against his in the bitter-sweetness of the night, or the way she sucks on his lips, his tongue, his fingers.

If only he could figure it out, isolate the single thing that binds him to her; smash it to pieces, he'd know how to leave her for good.

Of course, he still loves the kids to bits. Always will. He could still be a father to the children – her daughter and his son – if he left. He never thought he would be the sort of chap to put up with crap from a bird. Before he met Zoe, he didn't think he was the type to settle down.

His mum had always said that a woman should stay thin if she wanted to get a man and keep him. Went on and on about it as though it was a religion. Some of this must have seeped into his brain because when he'd started hunting round his seaside town for a girl he wanted to sleep with more than once, his checklist had been:

1. Pretty.
2. Thin.
3. Good in bed.
4. A Good Laugh.

Zoe was all of those, with blonde hair that shone like gold threads in the sunlight and almost reached her waist when she wore it loose. Her skin was a shock of semi-translucent white against his gold-brown.

Before he met her, there was nothing he liked better than a night out with the lads, bundling into someone's car and caning it down winding roads to a nightclub, or walking in a pack along the seafront. Those nights had stretched out in front of him like a motorway, full of possibilities and danger.

The night he'd met Zoe, the sea was glittering like a sheet of black glass with the white moon hanging over it. She was stumbling along the beach on her own, wearing a cropped T-shirt and jeans, her hair in a high, swinging ponytail.

When she saw the group of lads she stuck her fingers in her mouth and let out a long wolf-whistle. They'd gathered round her like wasps around a bin. But she went home with him, and it was him she chose to stay with. For a while, he felt truly blessed.

Later, his mates joked about pussies and how hers whipped him. They'd laugh over a pint whenever he managed to get out for a night, "You've changed since you met her, mate; come party with us."

But he could never stay out long, worrying about what chaos she'd be causing without him. Zoe blew through her days, and his, like a cold, strong wind.

Josh – the baby she'd somehow managed to carry in her tiny pelvis – was the reason she'd stopped polluting her body with drugs and drink for two whole years. He'd worried every day that something would tip her over the edge and she'd be off again, wanting to drink and sniff and fuck her sorrows away. But the baby was born in one piece, not addicted to anything other than the breast-milk she fed him. Zoe looked beautiful in those moments, their child in her arms, his hands opening and closing like a sea-creature. Akeem's heart would flip over when he saw his son's spiky lashes, jet-black like his own, resting on the perfect curve of his cheek.

In the first few months he'd watch over the boy for hours, making sure his little rounded belly was rising and falling.

"The baby's fine, Akeem," she'd say. "It isn't going nowhere. Come downstairs and roll a spliff."

"Why do you do it, Zo?" he often asked. "Don't you want something better? Something more?"

"More than what? What else is there to do in this shitty town apart from cleaning the car every Sunday or watching soaps?"

In their bedroom he finds three condom wrappers squeezed into a bog roll in the bin. He imagines her tearing at them with her tiny teeth. Imagines her in their bed, rocking her hips against someone else and the bile rises to his throat.

He strips the sheets from the bed, then looks in the cupboard for clean ones. Typical, he thinks, the only time the bloody bed gets made is when she fucks someone else.

Akeem hears the front door bang as he smooths the sheet across the mattress. He's still trying not to think of what happened here.

"Keemy, you back, then?" Zoe shouts up the stairs.

"I'll be down in a minute," he calls. His heart is thudding.

The dirty sheets are in a crumpled pile on the floor. He hopes the sight of them will shock her.

Zoe is drunk. She wobbles towards him, swaying her hips from side to side. Her hair is wild and unbrushed. Her sea-green eyes are framed with thick black lashes that are not her own.

"Where are the kids?" he asks, imagining the two children forgotten somewhere by the side of a main road.

"Where are the kids?" she mimics. "They're with your mum; she's giving them their tea. Stop being such a boring old woman and come and give me a kiss."

She sways into his arms, stands on tiptoe. Akeem feels her mouth sliding across his. Her breath, the whole of her, stinks of alcohol. It is seeping through her pores. Her fingers stroke the back of his head. He can feel the thinness of her shoulders under his hands. She's getting too thin, even for him. He wonders when she last ate anything. He doesn't want to want her.

"Who's been in my bed?" he says.

Zoe laughs, then curls her lips and for a split second she's ugly.

"Well, you weren't fucking here, were you? I was drunk anyway. You shouldn't have left me!"

"You told me to go," he says.

"Well, you shouldn't have listened to me. I didn't mean it. I need you here; the kids need you."

"Were they here when you…"

"They were fast asleep. What do you think I am?" She looks at him indignantly.

She breaks away from him, dances across the sitting room and trips. Laughing, she gets up, goes to the drinks cabinet and sloshes vodka into a cracked pint glass. She sloshes some down her throat.

Akeem thinks of his dad, drinking for days on end. He would take him and his brother down to the pub and they'd play on the beach late at night while their old man sat spilling pints in the beer garden. Then he'd stumble out and find them. They'd walk home, one on either side, holding him up.

He remembers his mum crying and telling his dad to leave. Their angry voices waking them at night. The sound of his dad hitting her. He wants better for his kids.

"This has got to stop," he says. "This has *got* to stop!"

Zoe laughs as if it's the funniest thing he's ever said to her.

"What? What's got to stop? What the fuck you on about, mate? Chill *out*, will ya?"

"Will you fucking listen to me! You need help. You've got to stop drinking and getting mashed up. If you don't stop, I'll leave, and take the kids with me."

Zoe freezes. "Don't fucking shout at me, Keem! You going to raise your fists next, yeah? Think you're the man, do ya? Fuck you!" The glass she is holding makes its way towards his face. Akeem can't move. He feels it hit him, feels skin and glass breaking together.

When he opens his eyes her face is china-white and still.

He touches the wetness on his face, stares at the bright red on his fingers. He still can't move.

"Oh for fuck's sake, you asked for it," she slurs, "winding me up about taking the fucking kids. You'll never leave us. You haven't got the balls."

Reaching up, she wipes the blood away with her sleeve. Her voice is soft now. "Do you want me to clean it up for you, baby?" Without waiting for an answer, she goes to the kitchen.

He hears the tap running; she comes back with a piece of wet kitchen roll and wipes gently at his face.

Akeem stares at the broken glass on the floor, its jagged pieces splashed with blood, the way it reflects the light, like sun-dappled water. Something inside him switches off. The hair-like thread that bound him to her snaps. He thinks of the drinking, the other men, the late nights and knows now that he can leave her.

"I'm done here," he says. He clears up the glass. Hunts for his wallet and keys.

He opens the green front door with its peeling paint and steps out into the night.

DESIREE REYNOLDS

WORKS

She cried dry. The tears did not come but bubbled and boiled inside her, making her belch loudly; they did not drip down her chin and fall onto the empty floor; they did not streak her face and make her eyes red. She cried dry. She was hunched over, low, as if she was carrying the world on her back. People bumped into her in the market.

"Moderfuckers," she muttered wandering from stall to stall, looking at the roundness of tomatoes, feeling the joy in the colour of carrots, squeezing homesick mangoes, letting her fingers remember the taste of them, staring at the sheer beauty of cabbages. "My works, wonders to perform."

She looked at the arguing men, the laughing women, the beggars, the lost and soon to be lost, the undecided lovers holed up in doorways, letting bus after bus pass them by.

"Boomboclart dem."

No one paid any attention to her. The body she inhabited appeared old, and age had rendered her dead to them.

She remembered everything. Her own cross – the cry of lonely children, the moan of grief-stricken fathers, the eyes of women who would never feel their bodies whole again. She remembered the smell and look of undiluted terror and absolute power, and he that came in her like a snake, vomiting eggs so that the world could be born. She shuddered – glad she didn't have to do *that* again.

Her left armpit was itching. That usually meant someone was going to challenge her existence, seriously. Something was going to be discovered that would tell the world she had forgotten them – that she was nothing but a small, cold flame kept alive by people's desperation.

"Fuckin Jesus pan di cross."

Some people stopped what they were doing and looked up, not seeing her but recognising the word "fuck" in the wind that passed over them.

She didn't know who to listen to. Voices fought for attention – all wanting the same thing. Then she saw him. The smell of sweat and new desperation caught her. Yes. She'd listen to him, as he walked through the market, his phone to his ear. She would listen for the millisecond it would take that would stretch across thousands of years, adding to her age, adding to the age of the world.

"Yes, Lester, you fuckin dick-head, where the shit have you been?"

"Sorry, fam. I looked for you before I left the club. You know me, catch gyal innit."

A man wanting to be a boy was working his lies hard.

"You're joking, right? Hold up! You ditched me for di white gyal dem. C'mon man, I told you bout dem!"

What did he mean about di white gyal dem?

Aaahhh, she saw them – the ones that would tear the skin off her bones with a beautiful little silver-handled whip; who would have her drown in her own milk, never destined for her own babies; who would shout, "Black bitch" or "Nigger" as she wiped their diseased backsides in the care homes; who demanded she rescue them, yet treated her as a child needing guidance and instruction – all those who expected the past to be forgotten because *they* weren't there, and yet relished the rewards; those that would be her friend, beg her to forget herself, for them. They would turn her body into a house in which they felt entitled to reside.

She really didn't know why she had created them.

"Uno gweh! Need to backside move from me!" She said this out loud and the sound rushed around time and space. Somewhere a volcano erupted and the sky met the sky.

Her big toes rubbed on the edges of the slippers she had forced her feet into. She felt corns coming.

"Just not rarse right."

She relaxed into looking around. A black woman was walking,

looking in shock at the dying shops where christening gowns could no longer be bought, where once Auntie had got her second wedding dress. These were shops crammed with old materials forced into new styles, wigs and hair, and make-up that never washed off.

This woman sat at a table by herself outside a café, trying to remember when the market had once been filled with black noise. What she was looking for had already gone and she was not yet aware of what she needed. She was like the rest of them – those black women always needing something they can fix, something outside themselves that they can pour into, onto or over. They didn't want whole men; they preferred broken ones so they could delude themselves that they could fix them with love or sex or soup. There was nothing more attractive than a broken man.

Dem mek ah woman feel powerful, hoping dat di teeth widdin dem could fool a man, trap him, bine him wid her legs to keep him in her forever. They were the ones who save up all dere tenderness for their men but could not give it to their children, feeding themselves on longing and fear, fighting their sisters tooth and nail with words and hips, all for men they didn't really want – men who lied about who they were, where they came from and where they were going. These were women who could carry shopping, children, men, family, in a tight, tight, bundle on their backs but forget all their names. Sad bitches. They were her and She had made them in Her own image.

"Hidiats, dyam fools!"

She did not know why she had created them.

"Fuckin rarse!"

A plague of ladybirds suddenly settled on the market. Delighted by their smallness and their brightness, squealing children gathered them up and stuffed them in their pockets, bags and socks. Stallholders shouted, waved their arms and scraped them off the fruits and vegetables. Walking sticks and prams crushed them. She blinked them out of her eyes. In another universe, a crack appeared under the sea, sending a wave the size of Earth to wash away whole cities. A woman, clinging high in a tree, gave birth to a child who would never put his feet on land.

She shuffled across the street. The market had cleaved into two distinct parts. The white side – high ceilinged, with room to pass – was filled with expectation and entitlement; the black side, a dark rabbit warren of shops selling plastic flowers, battered tins of nostalgic fruit and vegetables, a sense of loss. Bodies recognised each other, trying not to touch. Didn't they know, didn't they all know what it would come to: catching their own piss in a bag they'd have to walk with?

"You will see, you will know thyself, wooiiiisah!"

Her gaze found a man so pretty it crossed her mind that creating a world with him could be joyful. She laughed at herself. The sound stopped a scream from mouths already hopeless. It started another somewhere else.

"So you girls from here?" He was tall and dark-dark, his locks in a pony at the back. She always did like a locks man.

"Oh yeh. It's shit innit?"

"Is OK."

"What's your name?"

"Mightier."

"Ooo!"

"Haha! That's a silly name!"

"Ha! Yes, it is."

"Where you from?"

"Angola."

She watched him standing by the Iceland store, talking to two giggling blonde girls, laughing too hard.

"You talk lovely."

Mightier smiled. They wouldn't see that his hair needed oiling or his teeth needed brushing or his skin needed creaming or hear the noise of his hungry belly. They would see what they wanted to see. Now she was no longer sure.

She curled her lip, used her tongue to dig something out of her teeth, where excuses lived. She didn't like men like this one was revealing himself. Pretty and deadly; wanted but not liked. She shook her head and wondered at this type of man – one who had a mouth but refused to use it. A sulker, slammer of doors and puncher of walls; a crier who with snot and noise and hot baby tears would divert a woman's attention from herself, would possess rather than let be. He was one of those who swore love but boxed a woman in the mouth; who claimed to understand but all he really understood was what he wasn't getting. Who watched her grow weaker, as he got stronger. The white ones, the black ones – the liars and cheaters, the lazy ones, the ones who would revert to childhood before her very eyes. A woman with him would find herself nursing a grown man.

"What ah waste ah fuckin time!"

A memory of the smell of blood and bleach came up from the market floor. A man strode through it, pushing past people, shouting the football scores of 1958. The sun was turning to rest by her feet. The middle-aged white Rasta, on Electric Avenue, hair wound round and round his head, danced and leapt and danced and danced to the music from the chicken shop. His shirt was off and his pale, thin body moved like water. He had been there so long, had danced so much that his soul had spread out from him, attached itself to the pavement and walls and only this dancing thing was left.

She looked skywards. The day-hovering moon bowed to her. As she had always done and always would. On and on, in and in, the cracks only showing when she looked hard. Another annoyance. Another strain to bear, another lamentation to hear. Hunchback sister moon was always in need and her emptiness was her burden.

So what had she created? What was this that had come out of her? Where were the upfull sounds? Where were the thanks? In the minds of people who took the words and changed their meanings?

"You ah go neva overstand."

She wanted the praise, the songs and the sacrifice. But where was the fear?

"Yuh are bline to youselves…"

That man, weh him name? Who wrote that song? He was right. But they lived like ants on a hill, only seeing the path beneath them, the light lost.

An old man with a turban on his head and a beard that touched his chest was talking to a group of black women. He sidled up to them and pointed into their faces.

"You are lucky, your husbands is not lucky. Every time you try to do something, you fail because another woman has put a spell on you! I know the names, come, let us drink tea. We can go to McDonalds."

Ha! Ah weh di arse? Dis man can see? Beyond himself? Or this man is a clever trickster, waiting to ask for money? He could be both. It was he that had the spell on him. Or could it be Him? But He went, unable to fix what he had broken, taking it with him, in the heat of his mouth. He would come again, so would She, but She was tired of his falsehood.

Bullets were fired in her name, guns held, holding. The urge to stretch her jaw was too much and she yawned and another creature died, the last of its kind, that no one had ever seen. Noise and song, scream and laugh, collected forever under a nail.

"But what di rarse 'ave dey done, eeeee? Cho!"

As with her other children, she had to find a way to loosen her grip and watch, watch as the *that*, that was Her and Him move away from her sight, for another to take its place. Naming dem names.

She felt a small, bright, pin hole, widening in the bone at the bottom of her spine. That meant movement and soon her sight would change, space would heave itself away from her. She looked up at the quiet sky and let the hole spread, the swelling openness that would change her. It was time to go. She was tired. This constant listening. It sometimes drowned out her own feelings and thoughts. She resented it. Nothing should take you away from yourself. She just wanted to put down the world for a moment. The need to feel empty rocked her backwards.

She let the openness close her in.

AYESHA SIDDIQI

THE TYPEWRITER

The room had been empty for five years. It had grown dark and dusty in spite of the occasional half-hearted attempts at airing it out. She was determined, though, to turn it into a home office. She set to work with duster and broom, bin liners and sponges. She removed layer upon layer of dirt, threw out mattresses and cushions, and carefully placed silk saris, camisoles and petticoats into a large black suitcase.

It had been her grandmother's room when they first arrived. Her Nani had cheerfully endured the goodbyes and the packing up, the long journey and the slow unpacking. Like the soldiers who survive hard years of combat only to return to the safety of their homes, then shoot themselves in the head, her grandmother had passed away in the night, three months after they had moved.

The girl cleaned, wiped, and scrubbed, not paying much attention to the trinkets or the books and photographs she found. She replaced the floral printed bedsheets, which reminded her of another home, with some more fashionable ones from the high street. The delicate glass figurines and the perfume bottles from the dressing table she enfolded between the clothes in the suitcase. She moved the two bedside tables next to each other, facing the window. She put her laptop on this makeshift desk. By the time she'd finished cleaning, the room looked little like its former state.

In the top shelf of the cupboard, behind a box of shawls and scarves, she came across an old typewriter. She hauled it out and placed it on the desk beside her laptop. It was a metallic blue – the colour of the sky in a brighter place. Instinctively, she knew how to use it. She fed a sheet of paper into the roller-shaped mouth, and turned the silver wheel on the side of the machine to make it swallow creakily. She struck a key. A metal lever rose and hit the sheet with a satisfying tap. No mark appeared, only a soft indentation that vanished after a few seconds. The ribbon needed ink. There were some letters missing too. Absences between the stained silver buttons, like gaps in an old person's smile. She searched online and found only one typewriter shop, a half-hour train journey away. Never before in this city had anything she needed been more than a few minutes' walk away. She would go there that weekend.

The narrow door was sandwiched between a halal butcher's and a mobile phone store. The sign above it was rusty and missing several letters. Inside was a cavernous, tunnel-like space. Typewriters hung from nails on the four wood-panelled walls. There were old Victorian typewriters that looked like two-storey dollhouses, the keys spread out invitingly over the front like elaborate staircases. There were newer ones with electronic display screens and modern keyboards. Others were imposing metal boxes called *Remington* or *Underwood* that seemed heavy enough to bring the wall down. They hung next to dainty, brightly-coloured things with handles, that could be carried around like briefcases. Wooden tables were scattered around the room and each held boxes with pins, wheels, levers, and letters of all shapes and sizes. Some were arranged alphabetically: As in one box and Ys in another; others were mixed up, perhaps by brand or value.

As she moved down the shop, two or three steps led down into a narrowing space, and by the time she reached the back of the shop, the typewriters were grazing her sides, announcing her presence by a series of keys tapping paperless surfaces.

The old man behind the cash register peered at her typewriter through his circular glasses.

"A popular brand back in my day," he said. It was no problem replacing the ribbon, and she should do the same with some of the keys. "The obvious ones," he said, pointing to the gaps. "But also, I think your 'H' is loose, and your 'I', yes, your 'I' is definitely at risk of falling out."

He found the letters and fitted them. He replaced the ribbon, rolled in a sheet of paper, and typed a stream of letters. The taps now met with beautiful seriffed characters on the page.

"You're all set," he said, and charged her far less than she'd imagined. She picked up the typewriter and, cradling it under her arm, made her way home.

She set it on her desk, loaded it and pressed a key. Tap. Then another. Tap. And again. Tap. Soon her fingers were moving along the keys like a pianist's and the taps of the letters hitting the sheet of paper became like the beating of her heart. As her heartbeat grew faster, so did the rhythm of the typewriter. Before she knew it she had reached the end of the page. She pulled the sheet out of the roller mouth. As if awakening from a dream, she looked at it for the first time.

Gibberish. A stream of letters that meant nothing at all.

What had she written? Where had she been, she wondered, while her hands were moving across the typewriter?

She didn't think of it again until her mother came across the typewritten paper two days later,

"Darling, this is incredible," she said, with the sheet in her hand. "I can't believe you remember so well. Why didn't you tell me, you silly?" When her mother starting reading out the text on the sheet, the girl recognised the language of her grandmother and of her childhood.

"Ma, I didn't write that."

"Who wrote it then?"

"Well, I wrote it, but in a dream. I don't even understand half the words."

"You *do* remember. You just don't remember that you remember. I always told you you remembered. You should write more. It's a beautiful story. Are you writing it for Nani?"

"Why do you say that?"

"Well, it's set in the village where she grew up."

She tried to convince her mother that it wasn't she who'd written those words, that she didn't know the name of the village that her grandmother had grown up in. She tried to describe how her fingers had moved across the keys of their own accord, spelling out words she'd never even learned. Her mother just smiled.

"That's inspiration, dear. Memory and inspiration. Nani must have told you these things when you were very young. Now, keep going. How lovely these stories you tell of her childhood, of her relationship with her sister."

That night she sat facing the typewriter. She pressed a key with some hesitation – tap. Then another. Within a few minutes she felt the same dancing of fingers as letters appeared on paper in time with the beating of her heart. Finally exhausted, she moved to her grandmother's bed and fell asleep.

In the morning, she saw that eight sheets of paper lay next to the typewriter, all covered with text. She left them on the kitchen table and went to work. When she got back, her mother was waiting by the front door,

"Publishable!" she exclaimed, before the girl had even taken off her jacket, "definitely publishable."

The girl imagined herself sitting in a bookshop signing copies for a long queue of fans, or being interviewed by journalists. She thought, why not?

"You liked it, Ma?" she said, affecting nonchalance. Her writer persona, she quickly decided, would be nonchalant.

"Liked it? I love it. It sounds so … real. Her marriage to your Nano Abbo, the early days, the magic of – how did you say it? Love and compromise? It's beautiful."

"Would you translate it for me?"

"You can translate it yourself. What is this about, child? Why do you pretend not to understand and then write so perfectly? Is it a kind of shame?"

"I've explained to you what it is. You don't want to believe me."

"Stop that nonsense now. I'll translate it for you if you like, though I think you'd do better yourself, or just write it in English, you silly. Anyway, I do have one suggestion."

"Tell."

"Add some masala. Like, say something about her marriage being arranged, or the story of Nano Abbo falling off the horse. Do you remember that one? They like reading about things like that."

"We'll see, Ma."

"And the chickens …"

"There's chickens?"

"Well there might as well not be. You make it sound as if it's perfectly normal for young girls to have pet chickens. *Describe the chickens.*"

"Describe the chickens?"

"Describe the chickens. And put cows in there. And camels? You think you can get away with a camel?"

That night, once again, fingers moved across the keys. She didn't even look at them. Instead she looked out the window at rain-coated people going into their homes. She saw them through their windows, making dinner or watching TV. She watched their lights switch off for the night. Soon, even the trees and the pavements disappeared into darkness.

She woke up the next morning with at least two dozen sheets of filled paper lying next to her. She felt like she hadn't slept better in months.

She came back from work that evening feeling an urge to once again sit at the typewriter. She was climbing the stairs towards her new study when she heard her name. She turned around. Her mother walked slowly towards her. Her hair was dishevelled and her eyes bloodshot. She opened her mouth to say something but then, it seemed, she couldn't decide what.

"Ma, what's wrong?" The girl reached for her mother's hands, and noticed that she was clutching a sheaf of papers.

"Who told you this?"

"Told me what?"

"These fucking lies."

She'd never heard her mother swear before.

"OK, Ma, listen to me. I don't know what it says."

"You and her, you were always against me. Making up these things. When did she tell you these things?" Tears fell down her mother's face. She pushed the girl out of her way and went into the study. She picked up the typewriter, and held it in the air.

"Why would you do this to me?"

"Put it down, Ma."

Her mother flung the machine across the room with a strength the girl didn't know she had. It hit the wall. The platen rolled across the floor, the silver wheel bounced onto the windowsill, and keys went in every direction. The letter D hit the girl in the chest. The metallic blue body lay dented and broken on the floor.

"Ma, what's wrong with you?" Her mother sat huddled on the floor, her face in her hands, crying like a child.

"Ma, I'm sorry."

"How did you know?"

"I don't know. I didn't know I knew."

Her mother tried to speak but choked on her words and once again burst into tears.

The girl gathered the scattered parts of the typewriter and heaped them in the middle of the room. She half-expected, when she woke up the next morning on her grandmother's bed, to find the machine magically restored. It wasn't, and her mother wasn't able to look her in the eyes as she gave her breakfast that morning.

While she sat eating her eggs, the girl wondered what had been written on those pages. She had the strange feeling that if she thought about it, she could guess, or remember that thing that nobody was supposed to know.

JACQUELINE CROOKS

SKINNING-UP

Riley stepped outside the shebeen. Steam was coming off her body. She pulled the grey rabbit-skin jacket around her. Her brown face was bloodless, leeched by the airless underground club.

Five o'clock in the morning and she'd had enough of the dub and skanking.

"Where yuh goin?" someone from a group of men called out. "The party ain't done."

The men were squinched together like quabs. Their silk shirts opened way down on their chests, like the cold was nuthn', like it wasn't biting their raas.

"My bed's waiting for me," Riley shouted back at them.

"Baby-love, *my* bed's waiting for you," one of them called out. The men laughed.

"Yeah, yeah," Riley said as she waved away their laughter. She could hear them *siss-i-sissing* behind her as she walked away, but she didn't business. If she didn't step she wouldn't get back before Tutus woke up and realised her younger sister had taken her fur.

More importantly, Riley had to get home before Mumma who was working nights at the old people's home at the back of the estate. Mumma didn't know she was bustin' out of the house at night, going to blues parties and dutty shebeens; but it was only a matter of time before she found out. Mumma was cunning like that.

Riley crossed the road to the minicab office. She didn't have any money – never did. No matter, it was just one long walk up the Cemetery Road – twenty minutes max. She walked past the minicab office – the last sign of life – and turned onto the long dark road that wound past the cemetery on one side, rundown houses and wasteland on the other. In fifteen minutes she would reach the patch of frowsy grass that tried to pass for a park.

She walked for five minutes.

The street lamps drip-fed bile-coloured light into the darkness.

She felt like a stix-gyal in the fur jacket, badn'raas. Invincible. Not like that fool-fool Barry. He'd collected her that evening, driven her to the shebeen, promised to take her home.

Inside the club he pulled her to dance, winding and grinding against her, rubbing his sweaty face against her cheek. She shook him off. Left him rubbing-up with some ugly bug-eyed gyal. Chaa! She didn't business bout his dry-arse self and his mash-up car. She just wanted to get home and climb into bed with Crimpey, her little brother. His curled-up body was always warm, sweat dotted around his scalp and down his spine.

She heard steps behind her. She stopped and turned.

It was Glendon.

Six-foot four, slit-eyed Glendon who didn't skin-up with women or men. Every now and then he pulled a gyal off the streets and into his car. If the gyal was lucky he released her within a day or two. With or without her baggy.

Every now and then he jooked-up a youth with his blade.

Riley's joints stiffened, but her brain was working hard. "Yeah, w'happen, Glendon. Yuh come to walk me home, eh?"

Glendon kept slow-skip-skanking towards her.

"Looking out for me, Glendon, thanks," Riley said. Her voice was turning speakey-spokey. *Don't lose it,* she told herself. *Play it real or you're in trouble.*

"What's up, Baby," Glendon said. "Where you goin'?" He stopped a little way behind her.

"Back to my yard," Riley replied.

"Forget *that.* Come back to my yard; mek we have a likkle drink an' t'ing. You know dem ways."

"Nah, man – gotta step before my Mumma gets up."

"Don't carry on them ways, Babe." The slitty eyes flickered in his long dark face.

187

"Know what, Glendon, I appreciate you walking me home like this. It's kinda scary walking past the cemetery this time o' night. Nevah know what's going on back there." She stopped walking.

Glendon looked over the cemetery wall. He looked back at her, and Riley could see he was unsure. *Yes*! She'd dropped the image right inna his head.

"Big-big man like you ain't scared of no duppies," Riley said. "You've come to take care of me, make sure I get home safe, ain't you. I check for that."

He stroked his chin like he was thinking about something deep.

Riley wasn't sure how long she could carry on the skank. Everybody knew that Glendon couldn't read or write. His parents left him in Jamaica when they first came over. The people he'd been left with worked him like a mule and he never went to school.

She carried on walking and he followed.

"Yuh look kinda cold," he said. "You know what I got at my yard?"

"Uh-uh."

"Come on, *guess*. Something every gyal wants."

"It could be anything. Just tell me." She was trying to keep her tone light, friendly. "Come nuh, man, what you doing walking behind me like that. How you gonna guard me if you ain't by my side?" She didn't like the way he was walking behind, like he was tracking her.

"A fur coat," he said. "That's what I got. Black mink. Know how much that thing cost? Couple grand. Gyal like you shouldn't be wearing no rabbit. You betta dan dat."

"Sounds crisp," Riley said.

"Crisp? It's more than crisp. It's hanging in my cupboard, waiting for you."

Riley didn't want to think bout no black fur coat in Glendon's cupboard. She walked faster.

"Hold up nuh, Baby. Why you stepping so quick?"

He caught up with her, pulled her wrist so that she was facing him.

"I could come over next week," Riley said. "I'm bleached, I don't wanna come to your yard like this. I ain't fresh."

188

"I don't check for freshness. I like things a likkle renk." He put his arm across her shoulder. She could smell his sex, it clung to the back of her throat. She wanted to spit. But she swallowed it down.

"You're fit, you know dat," Glendon said.

"You're fit too, like a sprinter or something."

"Not that kinda fit – gwaan like you don't know what I'm talking bout," Glendon said.

She had to try something else: "You believe in duppies?" Riley asked.

He splayed his fingers around the back of her neck like a brace. "I don't believe in dem fuckries!"

Riley knew he believed in duppies. People who said they didn't believe were just trying to protect themselves.

"My aunt Ermeldine is an obeah woman," Riley said. "Big time obeah woman. She brought all her sorcery with her when she came to this country. Everyone else brought *bangarang*. She knew what she needed in this town."

"Are you for real?" Glendon asked her.

Riley took hold of the arm that was around her shoulders and moved it away; she linked her arm through his. Wasn't that how rich people linked and walked; people who lived good, knew how to behave.

She couldn't out-run Glendon, she had to wrong-foot him. Skank him.

His arm stiffened. Her arms and legs were trembling. She looked at him from the corner of her eye. He had the same bush features as her grandfather Poppa-Landell: thick lips, wide nose, mallet-arms.

Glendon was like all the migrants from this slum town, living underground. Carving out their lives from darkness. But Poppa-Landell had used his strength to work his way up, to get to the surface. Glendon was lost, working his way deeper and deeper down.

Darkness was his territory.

Sweet him, she had to sweet him up.

"Nice scarf, Glendon. Burberry?"

"You know dat."

"You always look crisp – you must be doin' alright."

"I'm not gonna bust my raas like my Mumma, cleaning shit for shillings. *Cho!* You gotta tek it." He swiped the air, grabbed a fist of darkness and flung it into her face.

Riley flinched, steadied herself. "Your Mumma live round here?" Her voice was drying up.

"The only place you should be thinking about is my yard and that fur coat that's waiting for you." His tone was harder now. They were getting close to the turn off for Hunt Road, close to her house.

He wasn't gonna let her go much further. She blinked, hoping that she would find herself back in her paraffin-heated bedroom. Why had Mumma come to this country? Why hadn't she stayed in Roaring River, married some bush man who did nothing but dig up yams from the rusty earth.

A fur coat, to *raas*. Glendon was after *her* skin.

They came to the large wrought iron gate, the main entrance to the cemetery. The other entrance was on the northern side, close to the old people's home where Mumma worked. Riley thought of her in the old people's home, pulling sheets up to the chins of old white people with cracked, powdery faces.

She thought of Aunt Ermeldine summoning duppies, fleshless, boneless spirits.

"What the raas is that?" Glendon shouted.

Through the gates Riley saw a small figure moving through the cemetery, not walking on the path, but cutting inbetween the gravestones, the shorter route to the gate. Head down, moving quickly.

"What you done? What you done?" Glendon shouted and he stood away from her.

The figure came through the gate.

"Pickney, where yuh goin' this time a de night?" it shouted.

Glendon flexed his arms a little way from his sides.

"You t'ink I don't know you been crawlin' out at night like some dutty man?" the figure bawled.

Riley realised that Mumma had been taking the short cut home through the cemetery, even though she'd told them all never to go that way – day or night.

"I'm gonna bus' you raas when I get yuh backside home, yuh hear," her Mumma shouted.

Riley didn't answer. She could see her Mumma wasn't really vex.

Her Mumma was standing between her and Glendon as she grabbed a fistful of her rabbit fur collar and dragged her closer, without looking at Glendon.

Riley and her Mumma turned their backs on Glendon and began walking slowly towards Hunt Road.

Styling-it-out.

HANA RIAZ

A CARTOGRAPHY OF ALL THE NAMES YOU'VE EVER GIVEN ME

1.

when it ached, it ached the wrong way. i did not go home and set myself alight with the burning of your things; i did not misplace my name in another lover's mouth; i did not let my body hunger into rot; i did not cut off my hair or change my skin; i did not take to drink and let it sink into everything we had; i did not collapse into a pile of bones; i did not say no to love or anything after. i did not.

i just started to lose things. it started with my train pass and then i was late for everything. even my sleep was festering, a cesspool of delayed dark. the summer became just heat and no longer desire. i could not sing any of my favourite songs without words escaping. soon i lose remembering you, how it was to love you, what it was to feel my whole body alive, how i died for you, how i died: the slow letting loose of blood that had nowhere else to go. but with the winter, you never came back.

2.

my brother has the type of light-skin that can almost pass and he spends his life trying to. it starts with a girl. his first lover is strawberry-blonde with all that frail up her skirt and each summer i count how many boys in the class try to hold her tight without breaking her.

it is the august of his thirteenth birthday, baby-blue eyes and a voice that soon echoes our father. she finally notices his height and this, he's sure, is what will make him into a man.

they use the summer making out where the park is a sea of unruly bushes, until everyone finds out. the first day of school, under the easy september sun that has left his skin a heavy golden, the boys line him up against the back wall of the gym building.

"you fuckin dirty paki, leave our women alone. my dad will make sure you go right back to where you came from if you ain't fuckin careful."

the threat swallows him in his sleep.

two weeks later she has a new boyfriend, two inches shorter than him, complexion milk-bottle white, transparent even. he spends the winter scrubbing his skin, praying the melanin out of himself.

3.
i realise i am not good for you.

on mondays you visit with a bottle of wine and an old hema malini film that plays grainy on the television screen. you fall into my lap waiting for me to succumb to the mounds of flesh i often hide beneath whatever oversized things i wear. on tuesdays we take the cab home and you are brave on the back seat, hands in hands.

by wednesday and thursday we are hiding in the dark, the rain taking all signs of laughter out of the sky. you on the kitchen counter watching the neighbours undress the gloom, me in the bathroom staring at my body.

fridays and saturdays are for letting loose, taking the entire week out of ourselves, you and the way you scrunch your face up at me when you ask me to bring you home to my parents' house and the sigh that settles deep into my guilty chest when i do not. after one too many drinks we ease up, here in soho. i lay claim to all my secrets. i can love you here publicly, openly. i can love you until early sunday morning when you are too tired to fight us anymore and surrender to your own apartment.

4.

there is a point when tired becomes more than just an exhausted body. it becomes the experiences you no longer want to have, the stories you are beyond wanting to make sense of.

my father comes home with a black eye, front tooth missing. his knuckles are swollen and he sits quietly in the chair he has sat in everyday for the last thirty years. *ammi* brings him a tea towel filled with ice and a cup of *chai*.

"*bas*, today is enough," he says, looking at nobody in particular. "i did not come here to be called *paki* this, *golliwog* that. we fought the british… we fought the british and then still left home for this."

a silence as long and as uncomfortable as this colonial history seeps from the walls of the room. looking at my brother, he continues:

"*beta*, see these people… you cannot trust them. they cheated us out of our country. see how they keep our crown jewels in that museum. they will say 'oh i am not racist, see my friend is tariq', or, 'look my neighbour is this man from nigeria'. they will all say this until like today one of them beats the *jaan* out of you and then nobody will say anything, nobody."

my brother looks up, looks at his hands, looks away, looks everywhere but into the face of the man that his body now replicates – brown dewy skin and all.

5.

and then you, beloved – the first time i saw you was the first time my body unpacked longing, how it rang right through to the core of me. i had always been devoid of desire up until that moment, awkward in my body, awkward about love, awkward about whatever those things meant.

you were standing in the common room, tattoos crawling up your thighs and your laugh was so wild i was afraid the room would catch fire. i couldn't help but watch you, how your slight fingers would wrap around the coffee cup, those thick braids running down your beautifully brown, brown back.

for weeks i saw you everywhere: in the quietest part of the library stuck into your books, in the smoking area, in the shared bathroom, in my sleep – but it wasn't until you joined the same class that you pulled up a chair right next to me. it was a gender studies class and you were vocal, ferocious in your challenges. Our white tutor looked overwhelmed, but you were unafraid and called her out knowingly. i came every week eager to hear what i might know from you, things that for once were as dauntingly familiar as my skin.

the class before christmas we were grouped to make a presentation. you asked me to go for coffee so we could work together and we ended up in a little café filled with mismatched antique furniture just behind angel station, where they played charlie parker into the brink of eve. i slowly eased into you and there was a strange shedding about the un-date that it was. my quiet turned into bold confessions, your mind peaked passionately and honestly. here and then and there, i became convinced that you, unlike everyone else, could – for once – hear all of me.

three days later, you grabbed me in a corridor and reached for my hand as you pulled out an orange-covered book from your bag titled *Zami*.

"… not like these silly white women we discuss in class," you told me. "i think you'll like her – a lot."

6.

everyone thinks it's a phase until it's not. the week before ramadan starts, my brother brings home what we discover is now his fiancée. she is not unlike the others that have come over from time to time: tall, skinny; thin lips and a slightly upturned, pointed nose. they are polite but always uncomfortable.

my father as usual is lumped in front of the tv watching the cricket when she walks in. the whole house is filled with the scent of fresh biryani, the typical feast my mum spends hours preparing when guests come over. she forgets to take off her shoes and has already made her way into the kitchen. *ammi* tries to swallow her irritation and ignore this. the rule every elder and child has abided by for decades has been broken. she refocuses her energy by choking out her best english, a careful and considered pronunciation she is sure is reminiscent of the raj. she avoids turning the 'w' into 'v'.

"*wel-come charlotte,* it is lovely to finally meeting you."

"thank you mrs mir," she pronounces mee-ur. "what a lovely home you have."

dinner is quiet and cumbersome. my father, indifferent, leaves the spoon and fork laid out for him perfectly unused and takes to his hands. i join in with him, scooping up rice with ease, and although we all notice the ring on charlotte's finger as she reaches for her first glass of *lassi*, nobody dares to worsen the discomfort.

halfway through the silence my brother breaks into the announcement we've been expecting.

"dad, mum, zara… charlotte and i came over to tell you we are getting married next spring." he smiles proudly as charlotte attempts to lift her hand to show her ring. she bites into what she doesn't know is a clove and her faces scrunches up – half smile, half sour. i smirk into my napkin.

"*mubarak ho, mubarak ho beta,*" *ammi* chimes in an attempt to cover up the confusion. "vhen will we getting to meet your family, charlotte?"

my father does not look up, he doesn't even try to.

7.

i read *Zami* in a matter of days. impatiently, i fill my notepad with everything that mattered most, quotes that manifest like secrets, and wait out what feels like an endless minefield of weeks between us.

the evening before class you text me a passage from the book:

"*i have always wanted to be both man and woman, to incorporate the strongest and richest parts of my mama and father within/into me – to share valleys and mountains upon my body the way the earth does in hills and peaks.*"

i respond, "how did you know?"

8.

after our first time making love, an ease descended into the new closeness between us. your dorm room was small. the moon made its way in through the fourth-floor window, spilling itself like exposed flesh.

police cars angrily rushed past at twenty-minute intervals but our calm remained undisturbed.

with your fingertips tracing something on my back, you asked me what made my body an enemy. for a moment i hesitated. this discomfort had consumed my barely adult body as a child and as a "woman".

there was nothing to say, nothing i was ready to say, nothing i knew how to say yet. my eyes welled up.

"my brother's marrying a white woman, you know?"

9.

the wedding is not the usual commotion. charlotte insists on wearing a white wedding dress but agrees to the *nikkah*. there is no bustle of the *mehndi* night, no preparation for the *valima* that we would have had to save up for to welcome her into the family. *ammi* insists on *baba* and i wearing traditional to showcase who and what we are.

as everyone settles into their pre-set seats, the room becomes a split down the middle. my teenage cousin umar jogs from the stage and falls into his seat.

"her family's complaining there's no alcohol apparently…"

"but they got to choose the food! so what are they even complaining about?" his older brother responds whilst picking at the white fish in some kind of cream sauce on his plate.

"it's not like it's the first in the family you know? ali got married to an english woman, so did bilal. all multicultural and shit now," umar laughs.

"you're a bit quiet, zara?"

"i don't know… just… you know. it's weird – all this. he's not even wearing a *shirvani* and we do everything their way and they're still complaining…"

"it's not so bad, it's like – whatever! these days. shows you can

197

marry whoever you want now and it don't matter, none of that arranged marriage bullshit. at least he's found someone and he's happy," umar interrupts.

an aunty, the plump and sweaty kind with lipstick between her teeth, comes and squeezes into the seat next to him.

"this food is bad, so bland. english peoples don't know about flavour."

turning to me, looking me over like hammer to nail, she carries on like it is her duty. "*beti,* you should have lost some weight for the *shaadi*. these days the boys only like the thin and fair fair girls, you know?"

staring into whatever is left on my plate, i get up to leave. i grab my *dupatta* and head out for some air.

"can't you even try to be happy for me even for one day?" my brother takes a long drag of his cigarette and i watch the smoke escape his body slowly.

"whatever. you've never needed my approval, as if you need it now…"

"oh fucking grow up, zara, it's not like i don't cover up the fact that you're a bloody dyke! who the hell do you think i did that for? you can't play the victim all the time!"

"babe, are you okay?" charlotte interrupts. "i was about to send a search party out for you. it's almost time for our first dance!"

he stubs his cigarette out, the silence broken only by the echo of his footsteps as he follows her back in.

i desperately want to lie down on the concrete and remember a time our names were just a thing we would call after one another across the house or in the playground. over time they become cartographies of everything we do not know how to inhabit.

my wrist sparkles under a streetlamp for a moment and i think only of you:

now tell me, what country can you build out of that?

10.

for two years it was almost perfect. you were a soft lullaby into morning. some days i prayed into the ether, unsure of what it meant to love a thing you could not fully understand, afraid it would leave. but it settled in so many ways and i thought my skin a new familiar under your breath, and it felt good. it felt.

what i liked about it was, there with you, i didn't have to make sense of myself or my stories in a way that said sorry, i did not have to be forgiven for being myself. you held me and held all of me.

the last time we shared a bed, plates piled with rice and peas, ackee and saltfish and some fried plantain your mama made so good it haunts me, you wondered if this was as good as it could ever get, here in a world created by us, outside of everything.

after you'd long gone, i'd drive past your flat on the nights everything in me begged to come home to you, hoping to catch a glimpse of you on the balcony. the winter let nothing out, though, the curtains holding you in, my windows fogging over when i put them back up. and just as i'd almost given up, spring came and so did your new lover and freshly painted white walls. your balcony was now filled with things in full bloom.

11.

baba believed it to be betrayal and it sure was. my brother in that god-given body was a betrayal to all of us. i mean it started with each and every one of those girls, blonde without an accent, easier to swallow whole. nothing like our mama unfurling her tongue around a third language, nothing like our mama unable to hide what is left of the language you are forced to unlearn out here, nothing like our mama brown and thick-skinned, not like our mama that kept us going, kept us.

perhaps what both my brother and i were looking for was a way out – a way out of the cursed body and i wanted to forgive him. love will either bring you closer to yourself or push you further away – the kind of further away that falls, language-less, abandoning the light. forgiveness is then only ever a choice we make for ourselves when we want to go home, when we have the courage to.

my brother almost passed till the baby came. he descended into some kind of deep sadness the moment he saw that small brown head feeding on his wife's pallid breast. for months he could not hold him, took to the drink the way he wanted to take to a knife. he was so sure this was meant to be different. all the whiteness he'd try to scoop up and stuff into whatever crevices that filled him all those years, in making love to that woman, was just a deceit he could no longer keep up. so his silence became long weekends, a house of just floors and walls.

that baby was something beautiful though: left out the blue eyes, did away with that blonde, let in the brown (nutmeg shell and all) and heavy-set brows. his skin was a testament to our history, just like my *ammi's* accent, thick in the way honey preserves. baby kept the brown, kept the sindhi to show.

we grew afraid sometimes. would the baby follow his father, confuse his shadow for his reflection? still, we knew that you can leave nothing behind for very long till it catches up with you, till you have to accept it as a whole truth, as your own. and isn't that something, when the melanin loves the man wherever he be?

HOOVER JUNIOR

Catherine's eyes flickered open as the drone of her mother's upright Hoover Junior edged into her dreams. A shaft of sunlight pierced through a gap in the layers of net and floral print at the bedroom window. It was too bright so she turned over and dug herself back into the dim haven of sleep.

The Hoover Junior followed her. Its white metal casing and rose-pink dust bag loomed large and multiplied. She was surrounded by an army of them. Their flexes coiled together, their dust-bags swaying, they advanced in time to a threatening chant: "Hoover beats, as it sweeps, as it cleans."

She crouched in a pile of dust, hoping it would hurt less when she was sucked up. The pink circles of the Hoover logos were like open mouths descending on her.

"Catherine... Catherine... are you up yet?"

Her mother's shrill voice pulled her up, onto a ledge of semi-sleep. Catherine clung on there for a while, trying to gather some energy. Eyes still closed, her limbs began to drift back over the precipice and she stretched to save herself. Her bare skin cringed as it rubbed against the brushed nylon sheets. Her mind snatched bits of information from the room. Net curtains. Nylon sheets. Single bed. She was back home.

She heard the Hoover start up again. Its relentless motor made her stomach churn. She sat up and threw her pillow across the room, "That fuckin' machine. Her damn useless cleaning rituals! Vile sheets! How did I ever cope?"

She looked around the tiny bedroom still steeped in her childhood. Dog-eared Beatles pin-ups mingled with framed school photos. They were almost lost in the gaudy wilderness of brown tulip wallpaper embossed on a background of clotted cream. Less than a child's stride away, covered in matching counterpane, was another single bed. She knew the gap was this narrow because she used to dive across it in the middle of the night, looking for the comfort of her sister's warm body.

It would be more bearable if Teresa were still at home. Teresa had been her anchor. Teresa always knew exactly what she wanted and steeled herself to get it no matter what the consequences.

"Born to be a lady, that one," their mother would say, trying to hook Catherine onto her side in one of her many arguments with Teresa. "She'll never lift a finger. Not like you, Catherine, you're my right hand. I don't know what I'd do without you."

In those days Catherine had dithered between her mother and Teresa, taking a tentative step first one way and then the other. She watched, waited, tried to work out what everyone else wanted. She walked a tightrope between the two of them. She'd be up early at weekends joining in her mother's weekly ritual of "bottoming" the house, and was always the first one up to wash the pots after meals. But every step towards her mother's smile of approval was a step away from the comfort of Teresa's sisterly love.

"You're just a muggins," Teresa would say. "She won't thank you for it. And it makes me look even worse."

So Catherine would slack off for the rest of the week until Saturday came round again and the sound of the Hoover sucked her, traitor-like, out of bed. When Teresa left to get married, their mother's view of the world took over. Helpless against its certainty, Catherine gave in and joined forces with her in the war against dust and grime.

The Hoover Junior moaned as it bumped out of the living room. With its box of cleaning tools it was her mother's one extravagance. Her school of thought valued hard graft above all else, but she had succumbed to Hoover's black and white TV adverts, then scrimped and saved to buy their latest model. Catherine was ten years old when it arrived and in those days had loved its long pink flex. Loved winding it back around its hooks at the end of the cleaning routine. But in the last few years before Catherine left home, she grew to hate its reliability and its role in her mother's mission.

Now, the hum of its motor unleashed a familiar squirm of guilt and resentment. She tried to think of something else. Someone else. Mark. She'd phone him. It was so hard making do with phone calls instead of spending days and nights with him. He'd have brought her tea in bed, woken her slowly with kisses and cosy talk. She stroked her breasts lightly with her fingertips and let her hand travel down towards her belly.

"Catherine! Catherine! Can you hear me?"

Her mother's words stomped up the stairs. Catherine imagined every tuft of carpet pile soaking up her mother's disappointments, every smudge of colour absorbing her sighs. She thought of the Virgin Mary, marble white, pious and long-suffering, looking down from the shelf above the landing, firmly in her mother's camp, piling on the guilt. "Should have dropped her long ago during one of the weekly dustings."

It was 10 o'clock on a Saturday morning and she was still in bed. She was shocked, delighted and a little afraid. But not afraid enough to be propelled out of bed.

"Are you going to lie in that bed all day?"

Her mother's voice just outside the door made her sit up and swing her legs out of the bed. But she was naked. Could she reach her dressing gown on the back of the door before her mother came in? She decided to risk it rather than face her mother's onslaught from beneath the sheets.

Her mother walked in just as Catherine was closing the shimmer of a second-hand black silk kimono around her. It felt very insubstantial and beneath it, her skin brushed against its sheen like a guilty secret. Catherine forced a weak smile and an even weaker good morning.

"Morning? It's almost afternoon. I've been on t'go for hours while you, young lady've been ligging in bed." Her mother bustled into the room with the Hoover in tow, parked it next to the bed and pushed past her to yank the curtains open.

She tugged at one of the curlers pinned to her head, "I haven't even had time to do me hair yet! I don't know what's come over you, our Catherine. Cleaning's beneath you now, I suppose. Think you're all high and mighty now you're at university? Time was when you'd be up and helping me." She bent down to straighten the creases on Teresa's counterpane, then bustled towards the door. "But look at you now. Bone idle."

Something tripped the safety catch. Catherine had learned long ago that it was useless to argue, that silence was the best response. But the words were out before she knew where they had come from. She thought she was saying them under her breath, but they travelled loud and clear across the room.

"I'm not fucking bone idle!"

Her mother spun round. "So…" and the force of the word expelled all her breath so she had to stop and take another deep one. "So… this is what they teach you down there at that university." Her face was red and she was jabbing her finger at Catherine. "Is that how your so-called la di da friends talk?" She folded her arms. "Words like that don't belong in this house, my girl."

Her mother's eyes seemed glued to the rich red embroidery on her kimono. Catherine pulled it up to cover her shoulders and tied the belt tighter. Her mother was following every line of thread as if deciphering a code. Catherine crossed her arms nervously over her breasts to cover her nipples. Her mother's mouth crinkled as if she was chewing on a ball of dust and then she placed each word slowly into the space between them.

"You… a daughter of mine and… it's come to this. Ah, now I see it! It's that boy you've met down there. You were never like this before you met him. It wouldn't surprise me if…" She paused and Catherine could see her putting the last few pieces of the jigsaw puzzle in their place. "I know what you're up to, young lady. You're living over t'brush."

Her mother's words landed like a stain on the carpet. For six months Catherine had been looking for the right words, rehearsing how and when to tell her mother that she and Mark had got a place together. Now she stood trembling and speechless, her hands still covering her breasts. Then, with a deep breath, she hauled herself up out of the abyss and anchored herself to her words. "If you mean are we living together; then yes, we are!"

Catherine's mother screamed, first at her, then at the door as she ran out, nearly tripping over the flex of the Hoover. She continued to scream as she stamped down each step. Catherine heard the click of the phone and the whirr of the dial. She grabbed yesterday's clothes from the chair and got dressed in a daze. Her legs were shaking as she pulled on her jeans, faded blue, patched with splashes of stitched colour. As she pulled the cheesecloth top over her head, she remembered Mark had bought it for her in Kensington High Street. She wished he was there with her and then just as quickly felt relieved that he wasn't.

She crept down the stairs and paused. Her mother was on the phone in the front room in a state of high alert. Catherine turned into the kitchen and switched on the kettle, wiped the surfaces down, ran the water on the washing up. She was thinking of doing the breakfast pots to redeem herself when the squeak of the back door made her turn around and Auntie Madge was through it and pulling Catherine towards her. She wriggled out of Auntie Madge's embrace and pretended to be looking for cups in the sink.

"Can I make you a cuppa?" she asked.

"You do that love." Auntie Madge disappeared into the front room.

Catherine was mashing the tea when Auntie Madge sidled back into the kitchen. She came up, too close for Catherine's comfort, and whispered, "I know how you're feeling, love. I've been there me'self. I had an affair not long after I were married. I could have run away with him. He wanted to take me to America. I could have left your uncle and gone. But I stayed and did the right thing." Auntie Madge paused then and stared out of the kitchen window. "It weren't long after that, I had my nervous breakdown."

Catherine was stirring in the sugar, losing herself in the whirlpool of tea, and wondering if she had slipped into some parallel universe. "But I'm not having an affair…" she said.

"Ay, I know what you're going through love," Auntie Madge continued and she realised Auntie Madge wasn't with her at all, but on a boat on her way to America and the life she might have had. Catherine almost felt sorry for her.

Then she heard the phone ring. What did affairs and nervous breakdowns have to do with her? She left Auntie Madge some-where in the mid-Atlantic and headed for the door.

PATRICE LAWRENCE

MY GRANDMOTHER DIED WITH PERFECT TEETH

My grandmother died with perfect teeth. I know because I saw them. When the rest of her is taken, she said – powdered, plucked and primped – from the chapel of rest to the church, to the cemetery; when her body was dust, the teeth would live on.

Teeth were the root of her success. The back of a toothpaste tube was followed more closely than scriptures. I had never seen her glance at a Bible.

Granny had a Christmas party trick, performed when the gravy turned to jelly and her brandy glass had been refilled.

"Please, Granny!"

"No, honey. You know it vexes your mother."

"Oh, come on, Mum! Please! It's Christmas!"

Mum hustled off into the kitchen. Granny closed her eyes and I slipped the tube into her hand. She'd roll it in her palms and sniff it.

"Is it blue, honey?"

"Maybe."

"Hmm." Another sniff. "Aquafresh. Water. Calcium carbonate. Sodium hydroxide. Cellulose Gum. Am I right?"

But it only worked with tubes. Granny didn't take kindly to pump action.

My very first tooth lecture came years earlier, on the night before I started full-time primary school. She appeared at our house around tea time – dress, shoes, handbag, all bright blue. She may have been wearing little matching earrings, but perhaps that's a false memory. I found studs like chips of sky in her jewellery box after she died.

I sat through the usual rumble between her and Mum about the fishfingers on my plate. Who'd want Captain Birdseye when your Granny murmured snapper and callaloo? While Mum and I glared at each other over my untouched food, Granny sailed into the sitting room for an hour of soaps.

Seven o'clock, when I was scrubbed clean and in pyjamas, Granny announced that she was reading my bedtime story. I opened my mouth, closed it. Mum and I had been working towards this evening for nearly a month – a snip of *The Lion, the Witch and the Wardrobe* every night, so the witch met her sticky end hours before my upgrade from nursery. I looked at Mum; Granny looked at Mum. Mum humphed into the kitchen to start the washing up.

Up the stairs I trotted, with Granny right behind me and Mum clanking the pans in the sink below.

In my bedroom, I pointed Granny to my bookshelf, silently slipping *The Lion* under the covers while she ran her finger across my precious spines. She pulled out a book, waved it at me.

"Your mother found a black tooth fairy?"

I nodded. *Not that one, Granny,* I wanted to yell. *I can read that by myself.*

I breathed out, happy, as she slid back the book, came and sat on the bed, her blue bottom dangerously close to squashing Aslan.

She said, "Open your mouth!"

I blinked.

"Open your mouth!"

I did.

"Not like you're yawning. Bring your teeth together. So."

She snarled at me – a show of slippery incisors, a wolf without a bonnet. My wide-eyed shock satisfied her.

"You think an old woman like me shouldn't have teeth that good?"

Not unless they eat children.

"You need to care for them, honey. Care for them well. Did I ever tell you about my first toothbrush?"

This was my bedtime story?

Her eyes sparkled. "It was green and I used it so much that soon it was bald. Then I'd take a little stick and run it around my gums."

I touched my own gums, felt the grainy residue of the hated breadcrumbs.

"These teeth lifted me out of Trinidad," she said.

Fresh from Mum's shower gel, snug inside my pirate pyjamas, I saw Granny perched on an incisor, soaring over the Caribbean Sea, waving cheerily at the circling sharks below. I flicked *The Lion* to the bottom of the bed, heeled it so it slithered beneath the duvet to the floor.

"Yes, I was the youngest. You see how light my skin is? I was going to do well. But I didn't want to do well in Trinidad; I wanted to see the world. Ma refused to talk about it and all my brothers and sisters took her side.

"But Pa... I was always his favourite. He'd come back from the oilfields, say all he wanted was my smile. This time I smiled so hard I thought I heard when the skin at the side of my mouth cracked. If the man didn't say 'yes' quick, my mouth was going to flap open like a *crapeau*. Six months later, I was on that boat."

"What's Trinidad like, Granny?"

I made her tell me about what she'd left, the distant mountains and the strange fruit, the trees that showered gold and the tiny plant by the river that furled its leaves in shyness when she touched it.

"Why did you leave, Granny?"

"Because the island was too small for a woman like me. And honey, remember, you're my only granddaughter. So this whole world is too small for you."

I nodded. Even my bed was too big for me then. I presumed I'd have a long time to wait.

She leaned into me. "I'm going to give you a present," she said. "Something for school."

Mum had already bought my bag, my shoes and my lunchbox. We'd picked them out together at Woolworths. I didn't want another bag, one that Granny insisted was even better. Everything Granny bought was always better, sneaked to me in secret. This time, there was no hidden rustle, nothing she could slip off her wrist and onto mine.

"I'm going to show you something special," she said. "School seems very big when you start. But this is something you must do when someone tries to make you feel little."

She pursed her lips like I was heading for the wettest Granny-kiss ever. *I was supposed to fight my bullies with kisses?* But then her eyes went crooked, her lips plumped into love hearts and a sound came. A hiss, a suck, a whistle. Dry and wet at the same time. I asked her to do it again, watched her face crinkle in disgust, push out that noise.

"Again, Granny!"

Louder, longer until Mum came rushing in.

"You can't teach the girl those ways!"

Next day, I walked into St Peter's reception class tasting blood. I'd followed Granny's advice to clean out the gum line with far too much enthusiasm, but the teeth themselves gleamed. I sat down in my new class, back straight like I was locked in a brace and surveyed my nervous classmates.

The teacher's name was Joan. She said she wanted us to stand up one by one, say our own name so that everyone knew it, repeat her name so that we remembered it, then tell everyone something special about ourselves. I waited my turn, preparing myself.

At last it was me. I stood up, hands folded in front.

"Nushra," I declared. "Joan, this is for you."

My teeth were as bright as ice. When I sucked the air over them, the sound was good and loud. Joan and I never quite salvaged our relationship.

When I was eight, Mum started working shifts in a customer service centre. Granny had to pick me up from school, joining the established grandmother army in the playground. They stationed themselves in cliques, casually eyeing each other's allegiances. Sade's gran was tiny and Nigerian and didn't speak any English, though she always stood next to Rosy-Lee's grandmother, who looked younger than my mum. Maurice, the autistic boy, was white, but his gran was darker than me. She once told me off for saying Maurice looked like a girl – she didn't believe me when I said it was meant to be a compliment. She was even less impressed when I kissed my teeth at her. Granny loved that story. All in red, all in turquoise, all in orange, she stood by herself. She didn't need to suck up to the other grandmas. She was the ruler of that army.

On the bus home, there'd be more stories. How Granny

perfected her smile to reel in the best-looking man on the boat coming over.

"Like so." Eyes narrowed, a twitch of the lips, a flash of brilliance. "Not so wide the man thinks you're going to eat him."

When Granny stepped on to dry land at Southampton, a young photographer was there taking pictures of the tired, wind-slapped immigrants. Granny, of course, looked perfect. All in yellow, like a poui tree. When she smiled, the camera instantly swerved towards her.

She never saw that picture, but she recreated it in a studio. She showed it to me, clamped under sticky plastic. She wasn't smiling, but it was the same outfit, she said, though I had to take her word for it that the slushy grey was really bright yellow. It was also the same photographer. He gave Granny my Uncle Sheldon before she threw him out when she found out he had a wife.

I lost Granny when I was nineteen, though she didn't die until three years later. I was at university in Liverpool and spent a month in Trinidad during my first summer holidays. I'd driven through the mountains and tasted the fruit. I'd crouched by the river and watched the small fronds flinch when I stroked them. I'd eaten roast breadfruit in the backyard and listened to tune-up in the pan-yards. I was welcomed by the surviving aunties and uncles as the stranger from England, batting away their puzzled questions. Why didn't Granny write? Why didn't she ever come back? Why didn't she bring my mother? Soon I was caught in the crossfire of their grudges, the lost land, the mislaid inheritance, the ingratitude of Pa's favourite. I saw why Granny had to escape.

Liverpool became too small for me, but I didn't run away. I planned to conquer it. The university needed the money I brought; what authority did they have over me? I thought of Granny, the sweep of colour, her heels, her smile. I used the money Mum gave me for my rent to buy clothes. The boys followed. I smiled at them and I kissed them. I clutched at them and I cussed them. When they stuck around, I blasted them with my trademark *steups*.

At the same time, Granny was escaping once again. First, she went from her house to Mum's house – it was definitely just Mum's house now, because like Granny, I never went back. Mum wrote, telling me how Granny was falling against things and losing her words. I read each letter once, then slid it away in a drawer.

Granny spent three months at Mum's before she moved to the dementia home. It's a long way from Liverpool to London and expensive unless you plan ahead. That sounds like an excuse, and I suppose it is. Every time I visited, I felt the tightness of my mother's disapproval. A shop floor was good enough for her, I reminded her, so it had to be good enough for me. I would have ended up there anyway, even if I'd finished the degree. But I wasn't going to stay down forever. I had caught Granny's spirit. When I found the right job, the right man, I'd unleash my smile.

On my last visit to Granny, she sat in her chair, silent. Her cataracts were gone, so she could see if she wanted to. I don't think she wanted to. They'd told Mum to fill her room with memories: mugs, cushions, a board full of A4 pictures, mostly me and Granny at birthdays and Christmas. Face to face, Mum said, you could see the stubbornness printed across us both. There was one picture, of Mum as a child – all thick, long plaits and shiny, red pinafore. Even then I saw the anxious look that had folded itself permanently into her face.

It was afternoon, but Granny was in her nightclothes: lilac pyjamas, lilac dressing gown, matching slippers. Her hair was coiled down into Chinee bumps, secured by purple bands.

"Granny?"

She opened her eyes and closed them again. I held her fingers and let them drop into my palm. Her nails were painted glittery rose and silver.

"Do you remember this?"

I slid the toothpaste, the biggest tube I could find, under the curve of her palm and closed her fingers around it. If I let go, she would drop it, so we sat there holding it together.

Mum asked me to deliver the eulogy at Granny's funeral. What words could I use? Maybe I could say she was incisive, had great nerve. She made my childhood shine, injected me with pride, told me secret histories that filled the cavities in my self-esteem. And thanks to Granny's advice, I'd never had a tooth filled in my life. Then I thought of Mum's dry, silent grief – words whispered when she thought I couldn't hear. Granny ground her down.

In the end, I just spoke about how much I'd loved her.

My grandmother died with perfect teeth. I know because I saw them. White and pink shiny choppers, ready to tear their path through chicken bone, pigfoot, orange skin. She had died without them and the care home carefully wrapped them in tissue for us to take away, along with her pictures and clothes.

They were, Mum said, the last of many dentures that started when the photographer knocked out her two front incisors – all her own teeth gone by the time she was thirty. She spent six months in a psychiatric hospital and sent baby Sheldon to a couple in Portsmouth. To be honest, Mum said, he'd have been better off staying there because when he came back, he and Granny could never work out how to get to know each other. He didn't come to Granny's funeral.

Perfect teeth. False tales. Mum said she'd wanted to shout, *It wasn't like that! She didn't do that!* But she knew these stories kept Granny nourished.

I asked Mum, "Did Granny report the photographer?"

Yes. When her mouth stopped bleeding, she walked into a police station. She told them a man beat her to the ground when he heard she was carrying his baby. A white man. A married man. The policeman wrote it down, or maybe just pretended to. She heard no more, until a "good friend" told her that the photographer's wife had taken him back in.

"Bastards!" Mum and I spat out the word, the same time.

It was the first time I'd heard my mother do it. A half-breath in, front teeth clenched, air drawn in sharp and quick, chirrup, chirrup, chirrup, like an angry sparrow. I joined in, almost a smile, almost a kiss. Now Granny was growing taller and taller, all orange, all red, all yellow, her smile so bright it could blind the world.

JACQUELINE CLARKE

THE DRAW

Lynden Hall dozed next to his wife, Cora. Recently she had taken to nudging him in the side whenever *Strictly Come Dancing* came on. It vexed him to have his little sleep interrupted, especially when his snoring made no difference to her reaction to the judges' comments.

He looked at her as she sat on the edge of the sofa, arguing with the panel.

"You see that," Cora glanced at him. "Stiff like I don't know what."

Lynden frowned and straightened up as the credits rolled. In a few minutes it would be his turn. He felt for the ticket in his trouser pocket, but did not take it out. He always chose the same six numbers. They carried no sentimental value, theory, or luck. He had won ten pounds twice in the eight years of marking the draw.

"You want a hot drink?" Cora got up and puffed up a cushion.

Lynden shook his head. The National Lottery had begun.

"What about some cocoa then?"

Every Saturday night she did the same – fidget around him while his programme was on. "No," he said, without looking up at her.

Cora placed the cushion back on the settee and eyed her husband. The older he got the less he spoke to her. She'd learned to interpret his frowns, grunts, and sharp looks. Still, it irked her that the only time he showed any animation was when the numbers were called out on *his* favourite show.

"I'll get some toast then."

Lynden softened in the chair when she left the room, relieved that he could now concentrate. He wanted the song to be over and for the small talk to end. He needed no delaying tactics to

213

manufacture an anticipation he had never got used to. The first number came up – eight. Then the second ball – four.

Cora came back in with a tray. "Here, take your cocoa."

Lynden glanced at her. "I told you I didn't want…"

"Take it."

Lynden took the cup and drank; it was too sweet. He glared at the screen. The third number had been picked and called. His wife offered him buttered toast from the plate balanced on her lap. He refused it and turned up the volume with the remote. The fourth and fifth numbers came and went.

Cora picked the crumbs off her skirt, putting them back on the plate. She hated wasting food. She knew that when she was nice and comfortable on the settee he would ask her where his supper was. She took out the tray, covered the toast with a clean tea-cloth, ready for later. She returned to the sitting room.

"You won again?"

Lynden looked at her, then slowly nodded.

"Ten pounds? What will that buy, eh – a pack of Guinness?" Perhaps the win might loosen his tongue. It did not. He turned back to his programme as if he hadn't heard her. Cora reached for a cushion to puff up, sucked her teeth and left the room.

Lynden slumped back in the chair. It was on his lips to tell her when she returned, but he could not find words for that amount or what it meant. If she had been fussing less, then maybe he would have said something. She was the one who jumped to conclusions, and he was in no mood to put her straight. Let her think he could only afford Guinness. Tomorrow she would know different.

Cora woke and gazed at the sunlight flickering on the wall. It was rare for her to sleep right through. Usually she found herself too hot or too cold, or the pillows full of lumps, or the bed gritty. She sank deeper into the warmth of the blankets. She heard a cough and turned over, taking in the outline of the back lying next to her, the dark-blue pyjamas stretched too tightly over the bulk of his frame, his hair thin and patchy, greying at the nape of his neck and behind his ears. He stirred and his soles touched her. She moved away a little. His feet sought her out again and rested on her skin, as if used to combat and capitulation.

She got up and went to the kitchen while he slept on. She made herself a cup of tea and drank it, then fetched four eggs from the fridge, boiled them in a pot of water and began making porridge in another pan. He came downstairs in his dressing gown and sat at the table. She gave him coffee in a mug, snatching glances at him, taking in the way he held his cup and drank, his hunched way of sitting and his gaze at nothing in particular.

All through breakfast Lynden tried to figure out how to tell Cora about his win. He had said "Morning" with a determined cheerfulness. She continued cooking with her back towards him. The one time he caught her gaze she swung away to stir the porridge, then sat down in the chair opposite and ate without looking his way. He took his cue from her and was silent.

Lynden's first thought had been to avoid Sam's corner shop in case the newsagent already knew the winning ticket had come from there. His apprehension proved unfounded. Sam sold him his cigarettes and Sunday papers without inquisition, mentioning only that Cora had left behind the bread and sugar she'd bought the previous day.

Lynden dropped the groceries back at the house, then went to the florist and ordered six yellow carnations and seven pink roses, to be sent to Cora. It was the first time he had given her flowers. He felt awkward and left for his allotment, the card unsigned.

Lynden hacked at clumps of soil until his fingers went numb. He went inside his shed and warmed his hands over the paraffin heater.

It had taken Cora until late morning to find again some of the details of her life with the man who shared her home. She knew they had children together. How many and whether they were boys or girls she could not say. They were married, of course; the ring on her finger told her so, but for how long? It had taken all her effort not to ask him his name and she had chosen silence rather than risk conversation. At lunchtime the word "Lynden" burst from her mouth and her relief surprised her. All her life there were times when she muddled or forgot names, even of those closest to her. It meant nothing.

Cora busied herself with the ironing and clung to the ease that came as she pressed a dress, then his shirt. But as she ironed a pair of his trousers something nagged at her. She stopped. The moments when she did not know her husband had begun to lengthen. Hours would pass without recollection of the things she had done.

There were times when every detail of her girlhood rose to overwhelm her and everyone she knew and loved surrounded her once more – as if death and departures had not yet come. She remembered the laughter of her four sisters dressing for church; the scent of nutmeg on her mother's fingers; Shaun, her brother, letting her smoke his cigarettes with Carver Milton, his best friend – who gave her a look that made her toes warm…

The doorbell rang. Cora unplugged the iron and went to the door. A smiling courier handed her flowers. Did he have the right address, 22 Valance Estate? She made him recheck his list of destinations. How could they be meant for her? The tag was nameless. She was used to cards on Mother's Day, and when she got ill and was in hospital that time. No one had given her flowers before… except… except… She thanked the courier and cut away the cellophane wrapper from the bouquet. There was no vase. She had never found a reason to own one until now. She sat down. He always did know her favourite colours. She closed her eyes and hummed a song from her youth. He had come back for her.

Lynden walked from the allotment, restless. He slowed down, resisting home. He had been hasty in sending Cora a gift like that. She would see right through his foolishness and become suspicious. She would want to know where the money had come from and he was not yet ready to reveal it. What would such wealth do to his family? His children would come round more often and not just settle for a Sunday evening phone call if they felt like it. He could see the four of them becoming helpful again, biding their time, hovering in wait for their share. His friends would be no better. Every pub night he would be expected to pay for their beers without hope of getting anything in return.

Cora would demand more from him too, not just a new home in Hampstead or Knightsbridge, but afternoons having cream teas in County Hall and evenings out in restaurants, serving tiny food on big plates.

He would not admit it to himself, but more than this, he feared her old liveliness would return. Even now, as he remembered it, he felt a wave of envy. It was the way she had of telling stories, drawing friends in, her ability to make even changing a bedpan sound as if you wanted to be there.

In their marriage he had succeeded in curtailing her – and then later the children's exuberance – with his own silence. He just had to walk into a room full of their laughter and noise and they would be subdued, tidying up in minutes and withdrawing to the kitchen and their bedrooms, leaving him to his chair and the television news. He enjoyed the mastery, the seclusion of it, and the pleasure of living in a family where his own powerlessness only emerged when he left home for the morning shift.

Lynden knew Cora had been an odd choice of partner. He had settled on her long before she chose him. There had been no active pursuit, proposals or fanciful promises, despite the other men who courted her. Instead he had waited, not for love to fade, but for disappointment to arise, for her to become weary of sweet but empty words. It was only then that he spoke to her. Unadorned and straightforward, he offered her the steadiness of an ordinary life and when she accepted his proposal it was quietly and without fuss.

Lynden opened the door. The sound of Sam Cooke's "Wonderful World" filled the flat. Cora was in the front room, dancing with her eyes closed, a rose in her hand. She looked radiant. *She had wanted a plain life hadn't she?* A few hours earlier he would have said, yes, but now –

Cora's eyes opened. Her smile faded and the dancing stopped. "You didn't…" Lynden faltered. The record came to an end. "You didn't hear me…" He stood in the doorway waiting for something in his wife's expression to invite him in.

Cora put down the flower on the coffee table. "I'll get dinner." She passed him by. Against his instincts, he found himself wanting to salvage that moment, for her to stay with the delight his gift had helped to make. He needed to see her more like that.

It would be easy. Every day for the next week he would send her something, secretly. Then on Saturday, before the next lottery, he would tell her everything and show her that he, too, had depths.

At dinner Cora spoke more than usual. The old ease returned and she found herself tolerating his lack of response. She felt giddy and full of an anticipation that couldn't be quelled by having Lynden near her. She wondered what Carver looked like now: grey-haired, skin lined, girth widened, a tooth missing perhaps?

Yet how could he have known where she lived? He was probably still living back home. It was foolishness to think it could be him; more than likely it had been her son or one of her daughters surprising her like that. In the morning she would call her children and get to the bottom of it.

As Cora got ready for bed, she decided she would not allow herself to be taken over by the forgetfulness that had marked her day. She wrote Lynden's and her children's names on pieces of paper. She jotted down their relationship to her, the meals they liked, and the interests they had. She screwed up each sheet, rolled it into a tight ball, placed some in her dressing-gown pocket and the others in drawers and cupboards around the house. Tomorrow, if her mind should wander, she would be ready for it.

She slept until Lynden came to bed and rested his cold feet on her warm skin. Any other night she would have put distance between them, instead she let his feet stay on her until he began to snore. Slowly, she eased herself out of bed, bothered by her own quickness to lay her marriage aside for an assumption that Carver was back. It had been more than forty years since she had seen him and couldn't someone else, including Lynden, have given her the flowers? But her husband was not a man given to trivial things, though Carver…

She left the room, avoiding her children's empty bedrooms; she wrapped herself in a blanket from the linen cupboard and slept on the settee downstairs.

Another gift came late morning whilst Lynden was out, perfume this time, blue in an oval bottle, wrapped in tissue paper, boxed with a message left unsigned. She knew the presents could not have come from her children. They would have phoned, impatient to know if she had received anything. It had to be Carver, playful again, as if the years hadn't passed. She laughed, spraying a little of the scent behind her ears.

Over the next few days Cora found herself perfectly able to remember the names and details of her husband and children. She began to suspect she was being overcautious in keeping the paper balls about the place. By Wednesday afternoon she had gathered together all but one of them, when Lynden arrived home from the barbers and asked her why she was wearing her skirt inside out and her slippers on the wrong feet. Cora joined in with the laughter. As the tears gathered in her eyes she left to change. What was remembering anyway? Sure, her recollections came and went, but wasn't that true for everyone? She doubted if there was a person alive who could say they never forgot a thing or could even bring back to mind all their thoughts from five minutes ago. No. She was fine.

Two hours later she came downstairs, having adjusted some of her clothes and put all her shoes in precise rows, as if defying anyone to tell her she didn't know left from right.

Lynden felt relieved when Saturday came round again. Choosing presents had become trickier as the week progressed. He had wanted to give her earrings but couldn't recollect whether Cora's ears were pierced or not. In the end he had sent her a bracelet and then wondered if a necklace would have been better. He had thought that having money would lead to an abundance of ideas. Instead he looked back on the week with some disappointment. Bunches of flowers, scent, and jewellery seemed a little too dull and predictable now that he was a man of wealth. Besides he wanted to do more practical things with his money. They needed a new bed, of course, then his wife could sleep without being restless, or absent from him each night.

Still, Cora seemed happier, though he was glad her good spirits had not led to an excess of talk. He enjoyed seeing Cora's face full of questions when he arrived home after the gifts came. He smiled at how often during the week he had caught her gazing at him.

Lynden flicked through the paper until his eyes steadied on the 3 o'clock race at Kempton. "We need to talk," came out of his mouth with awkward urgency. "Come sit with me a little." It threw him slightly to have Cora take a seat across from him.

"I sent you the things."

"What you talking about?"

"The presents, Cora, I sent them."

She laughed.

"I sent them."

Cora stood up. "Stop your foolishness."

"The perfume, the flowers, the bracelet, I bought them."

She shook her head. "It can't be."

"Look! Who else would spend money on you like that?"

Cora stared at him. In the silence between them she sat down.

"My win, that's where it came from."

"That Guinness money couldn't buy all of…" Cora's voice faltered.

"I can buy us a house anywhere, Cora. Any bed you like, any place you like in the country: Hampstead, or five minutes walk from Harrods. We can have anything, Cora, anything."

Lynden waited for delight to arrive on his wife's face. "Well?"

"I better finish up." Cora went back to the dishes in the sink.

Lynden gazed at her, bewildered. "I meant to…" He stumbled over the words. "I should've told you last week when it happened."

She was squeezing more washing-up liquid into the bowl.

"Cora?"

She placed a pot on the draining board.

"Cora, talk to me."

She stood still.

"I should've –"

She left the kitchen.

Lynden resisted the urge to follow her. He heard the latch on the front door. He tried not to be irritated. Of course, she needed time to take it all in. He could see that.

There was a draught and he found the front door open. He looked outside. He could not see Cora. Perhaps she was still inside and had forgotten to shut the door. He called out but there was no answer. Her coat was gone but her shoes remained in the hallway. Lynden shook his head and went to boil the kettle. His wife could not have gone far in slippers. He guessed she was at one of their neighbours. He took his tea into the sitting room and turned on the TV.

At half past seven Cora still had not returned. Lynden called at his neighbours – Iris, then Katherine. None of them had seen her. He stalled over calling his children. He did not want them prying into things he was not yet ready to concern them with. He hung on another hour before phoning them. Cora had not gone to any of their places. By ten-thirty, Lynden's son and three daughters had come round, anxious, questioning. He resisted elaboration, and left them to check their mother's phone book and ring her friends.

By midnight, Lynden's home was full. Sam, Iris, Katherine and an assortment of other neighbours, friends and relatives had turned up, looking worried and draining his house of cups of tea. Two officers arrived once Elsa, his eldest girl, had finally got Lynden to agree to contacting the police. They wanted a description, and Lynden gave them a picture of Cora from five years ago. He stumbled over her exact height, but knew she had gone out in her fawn coat and red slippers. The policeman asked if he and his wife had argued. Lynden shook his head and his face burned at having so many eyes on him. The policewoman harassed him with all sorts of questions, digging behind his answers. She wanted him to repeat every word from their last conversation; she wanted to know Cora's state of mind, and whether anything had upset her before she left. Why wouldn't they take him aside and talk to him privately? What kind of questions were these to ask in front of so many people. Why were they asking him the same thing using different words? He didn't like what they were getting at.

His wife had no reason to be miserable; she'd been happy all week, in fact, happier than he'd seen in a long while, with all those presents he had racked his brain to give her. Of course, he should've told her about the draw right from the start, but the win was his own business. Besides, he had mentioned it to her today and she should have been joyful. He had said he could buy her anything and all she did was walk out of his house in her slippers.

Lynden's ears burned. He went upstairs to his room to rest.

Elsa was the only one who stayed overnight. She was present the next morning when Lynden received the call to say Cora had been found at Heathrow and that as a precaution the police had taken her to a hospital for observation. Lynden put the phone down, troubled as to why his wife had gone so far from home.

When Cora woke the next morning she found her husband and children surrounding her hospital bed. The worry on their faces turned to smiles as her son and daughters embraced her and sat her up, adjusting her pillows. Lynden kept his distance, allowing the children's fussing to carry on.

She thought of the house in Hampstead he had promised her and all the rooms they would have and fail to live in. She sensed that he wanted to know what had happened to her in the hours since she left. In truth, she could not say how she had passed the time. All she knew was the impulse to get on a plane and find out if Carver was buried under a tombstone, or still alive, though an old man.

She wondered why the urge was not quelled by having her children and husband so near, talking around her, laughing even, making her smile. She would not go home. She knew that now, even with her faltering mind, she wanted…

The doctor came – young, tall and awkward. Glancing at her relatives without seeing them he flicked through his notes. He asked her if she knew her name.

"Cora," she said, "Mrs. Cora Carver Milton."

MAHSUDA SNAITH

CONFETTI FOR THE PIGEONS

Every Saturday I watch the rituals. On the weatherworn bench opposite the Town Hall I hold camera in one hand, sandwich in the other, studying each decorated figure filing through the large arched door. They wear fresh suits and summer dresses that flap in the breeze. Some of the women wear sunhats – big and ridiculous. When the groom arrives he shakes hands, wipes his brow then strides straight in. The bride will come later – in campervan, pink limousine or horse-drawn carriage. Once I saw a triple-decker bus. It was wondrous.

When I was eight, I attended a wedding in Bombay where the groom rode in on an elephant. I looked up at the beast and felt the breath evacuate my lungs. The elephant's head was adorned with silver coins latticed together with wire. Flowers were painted along his trunk in vibrant pinks and yellows. From this I developed my love of weddings – the colours, the food, the dancing and laughter. There is a joy at these ceremonies that cannot be matched.

Of course, in England there is not so much colour. But there is still a majesty about these ceremonies that bring me back each week. Today, I see the bride arrive in a white Rolls-Royce, hubcaps gleaming. She creeps out with bridesmaids waddling behind her like goslings. Her cheeks flush mulberry red as the photographer leaps forward. I rise to my feet, the *cckzzzp* of the shutter opening and closing on my digital SLR. It has an excellent zoom and even from this distance I can get a clear shot. Her head is angled to the side, veil fluttering behind her like a banner in the breeze.

Click. Click. Click.

I take a few more shots as the guests enter the main entrance, then I sit back on the warped wood of the bench. The ceremony will be no longer than half an hour – enough time for me to eat my sandwich and sink into thought. On days like this, when the sun is dazzling, I like to imagine what my own wedding could have been like. I have done this many times, sometimes changing the order of the service or the colour scheme. I may even make my entrance on a festooned elephant.

The details change each time, but when I look into Rekha's eyes, I always feel the same sweetness. Her pupils are dilated, kohl circling blinking lids as she looks at me. There are jewels glued above the line of her brow and a burgundy bindi on her third eye. She is not crying like other Indian brides, but smiling with a hint of mischief in her eyes.

This morning's ceremony at the Town Hall is shorter than expected; guests are flooding out before I finish my sandwich. I throw the remains into a bin and get my camera ready. I feel bolder than usual and walk amongst the guests. The crowd is too excited to notice me. I laugh as they laugh, look towards the arched entrance with the same anticipation. When the bride and groom step out, I raise my hands, clapping and cheering, "Good show! Good show!" as confetti is thrown over their heads. I pull a handful of rice from my pocket and throw it to the sky.

"Isn't that bad for the pigeons?"

A plump lady looks at me from beneath a pink hat that rises from her head like the pert petals of a water-lily.

"No, no," I tell her. "That is only a myth. Birds eat grain; they enjoy it."

She hears my accent, lifts her chin into the air.

"The rice swells in their stomach. It makes the poor things explode!"

The floppy flesh under her chin shakes from side to side as if from the aftershock of her statement; even she seems amazed by her words. I smile, but do not call her an imbecile. I do not tell her I have attended over 263 weddings in my lifetime and have not once seen the corpse of a detonated pigeon near the ceremony. I do not tell her that it is the mess that the churches and halls do not like, not the number of bird deaths in their vicinity.

Her forehead creases but she lets the matter drop, pulling out a disposable camera from her pocket and turning towards the bride and groom as they pose on the steps.

Rekha was a great lover of birds. I often found her in her courtyard scattering seeds. When she saw me, an index finger sprang to her lips, urging me to keep quiet. If her father had found us without a chaperone he'd have kicked his sandalled foot straight up my backside.

The day I asked for Rekha's hand, he said, "You must prove yourself to be a man."

I was seventeen – sitting in his living room with marble floors, teak furniture, and oil paintings hanging on the walls. The wooden ceiling fan whirled above our heads. When I looked up my eyes spun with it.

"All of this," he said, gesturing at the room, "came from nothing. I made my fortune from scratch. If you wish to take care of my daughter you will need to do the same."

I left that house with a fizzing brain. How was I, the son of a bank clerk, to make my fortune? The question had never occurred to me before. Then the answer came.

"Don't worry, my dear Rekha," I whispered. "I am certain to make my fortune in England."

She did not look up as she scattered the seeds across the cracked earth. "Why make your fortune when we could simply elope?"

Her scattering became quicker, the grains bouncing off the ground as she flung them.

"Don't worry; I shall be back soon enough."

A tear fell from her cheek, darkening the dry earth beneath her. I smiled because this meant she loved me.

"And how do *you* know the bride and groom?"

The man is leaning in so close I smell the dull stench of his cologne. He wears a tatty suit and the knot of his tie is askew.

"I don't," I say, continuing to shoot.

The bride and groom are standing with the ushers and brides-maids in front of the fountain in the middle of the square. Behind them glistening crystal droplets spurt from the jaws of bronze griffins. Occasionally a pigeon flies across the frame. The photographer knots his brow.

Pigeons are the bane of the wedding photographer's life, yet my favourite pictures are the ones with their blurred bodies in the shot. They are there and not there at the same time. In this way, I think I am like them.

I was fourteen when I saw pigeons in Madurai. I was a pilgrim, following the white and pink garland in Amma's hair, my hands filled with coconut pieces as we stepped inside Sri Meenakshi Temple. Coils of incense smoke rose to the ceilings. My eyes widened as I saw pilgrims prostrate themselves in front of the golden statues, looking up, hands clasped, lips trembling as they muttered prayers. When we left, I looked up at the pagodas that soared into the sky. They were covered with so many carvings of gods and goddesses that just gazing at them made me dizzy. I watched as the pigeons perched on ledges beside avatars with frenzied eyes who bared their teeth. I mistook them for gods and wondered why no one worshipped them.

"I think you should stop that."

A new man now, his hand on my shoulder. He is tall and thin, head as bald as a curried egg. I turn to him and smile.

"Isn't it a beautiful day?"

"Well, yes," he says. His eyes dart back and forth in their sockets. "But that's not the point. I don't want you to take any more photographs."

Again I smile. I do this because it is friendly and it infuriates people. I want to tell him that I mean no harm, that my presence here is a habit I find harder and harder to break. But there is no point in telling him. The pigeons would understand more readily than him. Instead I prepare my camera for another shot.

I'm halted by the sweet scent of lilies.

"Is there a problem, Dad?"

It is the bride, standing right beside me, a bouquet clutched in her hands. Her father begins to splutter a series of words I decide not to hear. She looks at me with curious but not cruel eyes. They are gem-green – her skin fair. I am reminded of Rekha.

It was Rekha's auntie who gave me the news. I had been working at the car plant for four years, saving whatever I could for my return home when they called me into the office. I used an old rag to hold the receiver.

"He is a very charming man," her auntie told me. "Though I suppose that won't be much comfort for you. Rekha is very taken with him, you see, and her father very eager for the two families to join. Please do not take this too badly, my boy. I am sure there are lots of suitable women in England."

I staggered out of the office. When the floor manager repri-manded me for taking personal calls I could not reply. Later, seeing how my work had slowed, he asked what was wrong. As I finished speaking I looked up at his shaking head. "I was trying to be an honourable man," I told him.

His moustache wiggled across his upper lip like a bloated caterpillar. "That's where you went wrong, me lad; honour and love are two different businesses. Best to keep them separate."

He said I could have the rest of the day off. It was the kindest a man has ever been to me.

"He doesn't know anyone!" the father cries.

I look at the bride and she gives me a small smile as though it is her father she is embarrassed by. She is beautiful, skin translu-cent, pure as the lilies in her bouquet. I find myself raising my camera, the image of her emerald eyes appearing on the screen.

"Don't you dare!" her father yells, his hand darting towards me.

There is a cry. At first I think it is because of the scene this foolish man is creating, but then my attention is drawn to the sky. Pigeons are flying towards us. There are so many it looks like a gigantic cloud moving at great speed.

"Get down!" the photographer cries.

Bodies drop to the ground, except for the woman with the water-lily hat. She screams as pigeons pummel into her. My body presses on the concrete slabs as the pigeons continue to fly. The noise of their flapping wings is like thunder above our heads. I watch the green and pink sheen of their bellies as they glide over us.

Everyone is looking at the pigeons. Everyone loves them. Everyone is worshipping them, their bodies prostrate on the floor like pilgrims.

The cloud rises and for a moment the wedding guests sigh. They rise only to drop to the ground again as the pigeons circle back in a perfect grey loop. I push my body to my feet.

"Get down, you fool!" cries the man with the bald head.

I do not look at him. Gods and goddesses come in many forms. As the pigeons approach I raise my camera, watching the screen as beaks and feathers hurtle towards the lens. I place my finger on the button.

Click. Click. Cli-

MONICA ALI

CONTRARY MOTION

Minutes ago he had crouched down, one shoulder wedged under the Bechstein, and performed what the tabloids call "a sex act", while she stood with one foot up on the piano stool, playing – remarkably steadily – the Moonlight Sonata. Now the lesson had ended, and he was saying goodbye to her at the front door. His wife, Stephanie, was coming down the stairs.

"Same time next week," he said to Julia.

"Remember," said Julia, "two octaves, contrary motion for all the major scales."

"Absolutely," said Henry. He smiled, but started closing the door before Julia could turn.

She resolved never to set foot in that house again because she saw, quite suddenly, how undignified the whole thing had become. By the time she'd taken a few steps down the garden path, she felt less certain. Henry hadn't slammed the door in her face. It was thoughtful of him, actually, to let her get away before Stephanie made it into the hallway. He assumed, no doubt, that she found encounters with Stephanie awkward.

Henry wasn't her lover, anyway. They weren't having an *affair*. She didn't expect sweet nothings at the doorway. God, no! And if she stopped Henry's lessons, she'd have to stop Amelia's too (his nine year old daughter), and she couldn't afford that. By the time she closed the gate behind her, Julia had come to her senses. Of course she would return next week!

She caught the bus back from Halting Village, the genteel ghetto where most of her pupils lived, to Tapham, a fifteen minute ride and a world away. Here Somali and Kurdish refugees clogged the tower blocks, and the artistically or socially enriched but financially challenged restored their subdivided Georgian properties and wore organic clothing. Julia got off the bus at the corner of Tapham High Street, so that she could walk past The Albert. She'd look in the window and if she saw anyone interesting she'd stop for a glass of dry white.

Tally, Stevie and Legs were playing darts. They were all dull, in their own special ways, but Julia decided to go in. At the bar, she saw Louise with another new guy, flirting with grim determination. Lust, sex, hope, doubt, boredom, panic, hate, indifference. It would all play out over the next six to eight weeks, and then Julia would walk into the pub and find Louise flirting with another victim.

"Oh, *hi*," said Louise, "this is Gareth." She touched his arm.

"Great," said Julia, moving away.

"I never knew you were engaged," said Stevie, when Julia sat down.

"Well," said Julia. "There's a lot you don't know about me."

Stevie abandoned the darts match and joined her with his pint.

"Tally said you've got a violinist fiancé who gives concerts all round the world."

Julia's fiancé was fourth chair in the second violin section of a provincial orchestra, which sometimes played in Reykjavik or Bonn, but mostly played Hooked-on-Classics style programmes at a West Country concert hall.

"You say that like it's difficult to believe," said Julia.

"How old are you?" said Stevie. "Twenty-four? Twenty-five?" He wiped the Guinness froth from his beard. A few nights ago, they'd all been in The Albert and Stevie explained the plot of the novel he was writing. Julia had been faint with boredom, but stuck it out because Stevie had got a round in. Whenever someone bought a round of drinks it entitled them to bollocks on about writing or painting, or the audition that would have been the Big Break, if only the alarm had gone off, if only they had arrived on time.

"How's the book going?" said Julia. When Oliver asked her to marry him they had just graduated, and he'd taken the job with the provincial orchestra. He obviously envisaged a perfect domestic set up: coming home every evening to eat the lasagnes and chicken kormas that she'd lovingly microwave. Julia sobbed heartily at the proposal, said yes, and moved to London. She kept the engagement ring in the box that contained her diaphragm, so that she wouldn't forget it when she went to visit her fiancé.

"You know what it is?" said Stevie. He leaned in, and Julia stared at the little acne-pits on his temples. For a moment she imagined him crumbling like a sand sculpture, running grain by grain to the floor. "You know what it is? It's this fucking place. Can't get anything done. I need to get out of here, rent a cottage. Have your parents got a cottage? I could pay. Well, not very much. Cottage in the Outer Hebrides, or somewhere… anywhere. If they're not using it, I bet they wouldn't mind me staying. I'd pay the electric and gas."

"I've written three songs this month," said Julia. She said it so convincingly she almost believed it herself. She'd hummed a couple of tunes and thought of a few lyrics, but nothing had quite coalesced yet. If she went home right now, she could probably crack out one entire song by the end of the evening, maybe two, but you had to let your subconscious do a lot of the work, otherwise the results felt strained.

Tally sat down with them. Legs was chatting up a girl with two full tattoo sleeves.

"When's the wedding, then?" said Tally. He was a photographer. He'd taken photos of all of them, in the pub or in someone's back garden at a barbecue, and he always said the same thing. *So when you're famous, I'll be able to say once I photographed you.* Julia knew he was hoping for someone to reply: when *you're* famous, I'll be able to say you once photographed *me*.

"What makes you think you're invited?" said Julia. She hadn't advertised her engagement, but now that Louise knew about it, everyone would know. Julia didn't mind. It seemed to have made her more interesting, especially as her intended had been elevated to world class soloist, although why he would jet around the globe leaving her to rot in a Tapham basement bedsit wasn't entirely clear.

"No, really," said Tally. "Are you, like, getting married this year? Because if you're moving out of your flat, I was wondering if I could move in."

"There's a lot to think about," said Julia.

She went to stay with Oliver most weekends, but they had stopped discussing things like where or when they might get married, or where they would live, or anything at all to do with a future that stretched beyond the next seven days. She wasn't in love with Oliver any more, which was horrible, but sometimes she felt that he wasn't in love with her anymore, and that was even worse.

"Oh, sure," said Tally. "You could sub-let to me so you don't lose your tenancy."

"I'll think about it," said Julia.

Louise stopped by their table, on her way out with her doomed young man. "Did you see Warren Peston in here earlier? Are you all blind, or what? He was over the other side, with all these bright young wannabes. Sad, really. He kept looking round to see if people were looking at him, but nobody was."

"He's done nothing good in the last ten years," said Stevie.

"He was always crap," said Tally.

"I hope we don't end up like that," said Louise.

"I'm going home," said Julia.

"Hang on," said Stevie, "about your parents' cottage…"

"Oh, yeah, I'll ask them," she said. Her parents didn't own a second house. The closest they had got was when they attended a whole day sales pitch for a timeshare apartment, in exchange for a week's free stay in a "holiday village" in Benidorm.

The next afternoon she rode the bus back to Halting Village. Three pupils to see, all boys; the youngest was ten and the oldest thirteen. A gouty old man was dying in the seat next to her. She turned her face away from him and his germs.

The very first lecture, on their first day at university, the professor had stood there so pleased with himself and said, "I don't wish to shatter anyone's illusions, I don't want to ruin anyone's lovely dreams, but you'll find out sooner or later so I may as well tell you now. Most of you, of course, won't pursue a career in music. You'll go into retail or leisure or catering. You know the old joke, don't you, – what do you say to a music graduate? Burger and fries, please. But for those of you who do continue with music, 95% – or more – will inevitably teach."

Julia was never going to become a piano teacher. She made that vow right then and there in the lecture hall.

This morning she had sat at her keyboard and tried to finish a song. If you sold a song to a top recording artist you could make millions. You had to know the right people, but Julia had started reading *Rolling Stone* recently, which was the first step. She kept lists of songwriters and producers. It was a start.

"I'm not looking for love," Julia sang quietly, trying out her new chorus. "I don't need understanding."

The gouty man sneezed without covering his mouth.

"Give me respect," she sang, louder. She pushed the bell so that the bus would stop. "Or you'll see what I'm planning."

Hand on heart, Julia could say that it was Henry who had made the first move. But that didn't mean anything, really. It was Julia who had made the decision. She'd made it on the day that Stephanie had asked her if she could schedule in some lessons for her husband who had played the piano as a boy and wanted to take it up again.

Two months before that, Julia had come downstairs after teaching Amelia, and overheard Stephanie on the phone. She hadn't meant to eavesdrop but she'd hesitated at the kitchen door when she'd gone to collect her cheque. Usually, Amelia ran in ahead of her, but the child had scarpered up to her bedroom to finish watching something on her laptop before her next sched-uled activity began.

"No, I do absolutely recommend her," said Stephanie, drawl-ing in that rich person's way (they never worried about taking up too much of your time). "Amelia's really coming on, she's got her playing Mozart, would you believe."

The door was slightly open and Julia should have walked through it right then. Instead she waited outside.

"She's got these *huge* eyes," said Stephanie. Julia smiled to herself. "They're buggy. Bug eyes. And she wears the most extraordinary clothes, but she *is* classically trained. I'll text you her number when I hang up. She'll amuse you. What? I don't know… but she will. There's something so… *unformed* about her. It's like she just struggled out of a shell."

So when Stephanie scheduled lessons for Henry, Julia decided straight away.

The following week Henry took her from behind while she played standing up – Chopin, Etude Op. 10, No. 3 in E Major, popularly known as "Chanson L'Adieu". As she reached the mid-section and a long sequence of diminished sevenths, a scholarly appraisal that she had read at university came to mind. Something about the "classical chasteness" and "romantic fragrance" of the piece. She tried not to laugh in case it put Henry off, but he was huffing and puffing by now, and noticed neither her giggles nor her mashing of the climax of double sixths.

She wasn't supposed to play too well, anyway, so that it would sound like Henry, continuing with his lesson.

"God Almighty," said Henry, pulling up his trousers.

Julia reached for the packet of tissues in her handbag, made some discreet adjustments beneath her skirt, and sat down on the chair, leaving the piano stool free for Henry. "Shall we finish with scales today? We seem to have skipped them at the beginning."

"Julia," whispered Henry. He leaned over and breathed heavily into her ear, and she pulled away sharply, fearing he would poke his tongue in.

"Thought I heard someone…" said Julia. The music room, as Stephanie called it, was on a kind of mezzanine level, jutting out at the back of the house. You went up three stairs from a landing that served only the music room, so nobody passed by directly. Julia and Henry always left the door slightly open to show there was nothing to hide.

"Kiss me," said Henry.

"A major," said Julia. "Two octaves, contrary motion."

Mostly, after the deed, Henry acted as though nothing had happened, as did Julia. It was a *modus operandi* that she had initiated which nevertheless irked her from time to time. Did he feel anything for her at all? But when he slobbered like this her back stiffened. If she played something now the tensions in her shoulders and hands would wring a tinny sound from the keys.

"We can't keep on like this," said Henry. When he stood up his stomach seemed quite flat, but sitting down, especially now when he'd gone all slack, you could see his paunch.

"Play it," said Julia.

Henry complied.

"Not bad," she said. "Your fourth fingers are still weak."

"I feel terrible," said Henry. "I've been taking advantage of you. I swore to myself that last week would be the last time, and now I've gone and done it again."

"What the fuck is wrong with you?" snapped Julia. A moment ago he was drooling in her ear, and now he was… what? Dumping her?

"What the fuck *is* wrong with me?" moaned Henry.

Julia stared at him. Henry was a Managing Director at an investment bank. The suit he was wearing probably cost more than all of her possessions put together, her keyboard included. He was pathetic.

She scooted across from her chair, squeezing onto the piano stool with him so that their legs were pushing against each other as tightly as if they had been bound for a three-legged race.

"It's okay," said Julia softly. Last week, on the doorstep, she had decided to stop seeing him. If anyone was going to get dumped it should be him. "I'll tell you a secret. It's me who's been taking advantage of you."

"Right," said Henry. He laughed miserably.

"Poor little innocent lamb," she said, rubbing her hand along the inside of his thigh.

Henry groaned. "God Almighty," he said.

Everyone was in The Albert, but Julia walked on by. When Stephanie had said she was "unformed", Julia hated her. It was the thing that frightened her most. Everyone else seemed so definite, and she was just a blur. Sometimes at university, when she was supposed to be studying, she'd go online and take personality tests – questionnaires that you filled in, clicking on the answer that applied most to you, or answering on a scale of 1 to 10 where one means "very" and 10 means "not at all", or vice versa. Then you got your results back, and you could read what kind of personality you were ("passionate and extrovert… you're heading for a career in the creative industries!"), which was comforting until she took the next test and got a completely different result ("rational and introvert… your strengths lie in coolly detached analysis"). There was a specific kind of personality test, a kind of psychopath test that measured empathy. The first time Julia completed it, she scored like a bereavement counsellor but when she took the same test again, a few months later, she had turned into Hannibal Lecter. Each time, with all of the tests, she had answered as honestly as possible. There was no one looking over her shoulder. And she was a different person every time!

She could be Stephanie. She could be another Stephanie – marry an investment banker and live in a big house, and hire private tutors. But she wouldn't marry someone like Henry, even though he'd stroked her hand in the front hall as he said goodbye, and despite herself she'd shivered with pleasure. She wouldn't marry Oliver either. Not now. Not ever. She'd have to give him the ring back. He wouldn't want it but he'd take it, and he'd probably be relieved.

Julia descended the steps to her basement flat. She stood in the dark, damp stairwell and looked up into the misty orange light of the street. She thought of Henry, zipping his trousers and moaning. In the morning he'd be at his desk, doing clever things with money. Julia took her key from her coat pocket. For a moment she hesitated. The flat would be cold and she would be alone. She could go to the pub first and sink a few with Stevie and Tally and Louise. When you were with other people, even if they didn't really know you, you came into focus, as though you'd stepped outside of yourself and looked back in through borrowed eyes.

She slid the key into the lock. There was work to be done, and she hadn't even started yet.

KOYE OYEDEJI

SIX SATURDAYS AND SOME VERSION OF THE TRUTH

1. The Saturday she found sanctuary.

She finds her bravery that morning and tucks it into the chest pocket of her dungarees. When she sees him she asks him to open his mouth and close his eyes. He is hesitant but does as instructed. They are in the park, sitting on the mound the slide is built on. Bricks have been set into the soil on the incline and, beneath this, their BMX bikes lie on their sides. Sunlight strikes his sealed eyelids so that all he can see is red. He worries about the state of his breath. Once he feels her mouth on his, he presses his lips together. She parts his lips with an urgent tongue; forces her wet flesh inside his mouth. He smells the anti-climbing paint that clings to her, feels her sticky fingertips on his forearms. She tastes like peppermint. He feels desirable, important, even attractive. As she pulls away, he opens his eyes and asks if it is always supposed to be like that.

"Like what?" she says.

"Wet. With the tongue."

"Wet," she repeats. She rises and lets her momentum steer her down towards the ground. She climbs back onto her bike as though she needs more time to consider a response. She kicks the pedal up and tells him that it's what her father has taught her.

They spend most weekends together. She comes over to his home to draw, read comics or play fantasy board games. He has no siblings; she is usually the only other child in the flat. His tall, brooding and short-tempered father intimidates most of his friends. But not her; she likes his dad. Each Saturday evening she sits down for dinner with them at the Formica-topped table, drinking what he drinks and eating what they eat. A white girl who balls the pounded yam and scoops the okra as well as he does: it takes him a while to get used to the picture her presence creates, the way she listens to his father's childhood memories as though each tale held some promise – like a movie trailer offering splices of what's to come.

There are times when the boy is taunted for letting a white girl take up so much of his space, especially one whose forehead is slightly larger than average and whose skin seems to pull at her skull around the cheekbones. He knows she isn't the most put-together girl in their neighbourhood. She is deathly pale, and during summer the rosacea and broken capillaries in her cheeks burst to life. But she is ten-years-old and he is ten-years-old and it feels like everyone else their age is trying to be fifteen.

They both live in council flats in South London. He, in a post-First World War structure; she, close by on the Aylesbury Estate – a collection of tower blocks and maisonettes, all linked by a network of walkways and footbridges. He knows her building but he cannot point out her door. She never invites him to her home and he knows better than to ask. When they are not in his bedroom they are in the nearby park where all the bikers and skaters assemble. They are fascinated by the teenagers who come to the park to smoke; bewitched by their casual airs, the shrug they give the world – and impressed by the size of the tongues on their Adidas.

That Saturday in the park, she wants him to ignore the green-eyes and auburn hair and focus on the nose she pushes down with her wrinkled index finger. She tells him she has been told that there is black in her family bloodline and asks if he can see it in her features.

He thinks about the weeks gone by, how he hasn't dared to call her his "girl". But they have been beside each other, roaming the neighbourhood together and he believes that has to count for something. He studies her now: her nails are broken, her nose is

Greek and her lips are thin. She is the whitest girl he knows. He thinks it is enough, for now, to paper over her troubles with the nickname "Black".

"Black. I see it," he says. "I can definitely see it."

She doesn't believe him, but his lie is enough. She looks away, breathes in, and squints in the sun. She turns back to him. "Open your mouth and close your eyes," she says and he does as instructed.

2. The Saturday without the rehearsal.

He watches her through the side windows of the Datsun he hides behind as she emerges from the entrance of her building. She is in an apricot tube dress he hasn't seen before and it makes everything else she has ever worn seem droll and conservative. He tries to keep a safe distance as she makes her way, first to the newsagents, then to the bus stop. It's here that he wants to confront her, but he waits.

He waits for her to board the bus, climbing the steps to the upper deck as he knew she would. He jumps on after her and finds a seat at the rear of the bus, on the bottom deck. He brings his cap over his face. As the bus rolls over Westminster Bridge towards the tourist crowds that move beneath the shadow of monuments, he feels a sense of vindication. For three consecutive weeks she has spoken of Saturday rehearsals at her performing arts college in Croydon. And now, for him, "circuitous" doesn't begin to explain why they are on a bus heading toward the West End.

He has felt the threads fraying at the seams for some time now. Over the years she'd dropped her tomboy airs. The worn dungarees gave way to designer outfits. And she'd bloomed – a tall girl in a woman's body, a force to be flirted with. Older guys ask her out on dates. He has to ask himself – why is she with *him?* The anxiety grew malignant when she started attending drama school. For the first time they were students in different buildings, and while there had always been moments when she appeared distant and sullen, he frets now about the frequency of her blues and how distracted she appears most of the time. They would plan to meet on weekday evenings only for her to cancel on him to stay behind at college for workshops and master classes. Then the Saturday rehearsals began.

There are several bodies between them when "Black" alights at Piccadilly Circus. He follows her through the dense crowds of Leicester Square and the Trocadero shopping mall, keeping his distance as they climb the escalators to the Arcade centre and amusement rides on the top floor. He loses her amongst a swell of teenagers, a throng of bomber jackets and baggy jeans, aerobic footwear and high-top basketball trainers. He weaves his way between the video arcade and coin pusher machines. He spots her at an arcade game, the screen light casting a velvet-blue hue on her face. He takes in the man who stands close behind her: the olive skin and dark hair, the single stud earring, the square set of his jaw and the facial hair. His clothes are south London chic – a laundry-beaten polo shirt, straight-fit jeans and Hi-Tech squash trainers. His arms caress Black's midriff.

The boy stands there, unsure of what he sees. The resemblance could be all in his mind. But he has seen this man in and around the neighbourhood and he is confident that it is Black's father. He doesn't have the presence of mind to keep himself concealed, and just one GAME OVER later, Black lifts her eyes from the screen, gazes across the floor and spots him. Her features tense. She turns from him as from an unsatisfactory reflection, breaks from her father's grasp and rushes away. Her father, startled by her abrupt departure, looks around him for an explanation.

The boy turns towards the exit, puts his Walkman headphones back on. He hesitates at the top of the escalator weighing what he thinks he has witnessed. He is embarrassed by the helplessness he feels, the tears that begin to stream down his cheeks.

3. The Saturday morning in the Kebab shop with the elephant.

She gives him "The Talk" in the takeaway area of a Turkish restaurant. It is close to 3 a.m. on a Saturday morning, after their Friday night revelries. There are a dozen or so people around them, most of them exhausted. It is a ritual – an early morning kebab before heading home. They stand sharing a bag of chips at the small table in the narrow dining area and try to talk over the din. Even though music blares over the speakers, he hears her clearly when she says she's tired of his accusations and announces that "they are done".

She has cut her hair in recent weeks, shorn on the sides but tall on the top, spray-held in a huge quiff and dyed platinum blonde. She wears fuchsia lipstick with electric-blue eyeshadow and a matching sequined dress.

"You're a bitch," he says, "a fucking bitch." Then he stops himself. "I didn't mean that, Black."

"I've told you not to call me that," she spits. For a time she'd demanded he call her by her birth name, Natalie Newton, but now she has a stage name and insists he use that. She tells him that she doesn't care what he thinks of her or what his friends have told him.

"People do that. People will talk about me, bad or good, and I'm not going to let anyone or anything stand in the way of making it."

"And I stand in the way of you 'making it'?"

She says nothing at first, but then tells him that they are different; they want different things and are heading in different directions.

"That's rubbish and you know it," he replies. "I know what you're doing. What you've been doing all these years. It's disgusting. You're no better than a dog." He calls her a bitch again as he wipes his eyes.

Her mouth hangs open but there are no words. It takes all of her will just to fling the chips in her hand back into the bag. She has sidestepped confrontation well enough over the last few years, and will not start now. She doesn't know if there is anything she could say to him even if she wanted to. She looks at him and his tears; she sees boy, she sees man, and realises that she shouldn't expect anything of either of them. She snatches her clutch bag from the table and walks out.

They'd had half-a-dozen mini break-ups since he left for Liverpool University, but he'd put them down to the difficulty of a long-distance relationship and they'd always managed to work out their differences. This, he knows, is something else. He has kicked dirt between them and roused the elephant in the room.

He wraps the chips up in their paper and tosses them in the rubbish bin. It's only then that those around him, despite their best efforts to pretend they weren't listening, return to their conversations.

She does not come to his house on Saturdays for dinner anymore. The first few weeks of summer pass by and his parents stop asking after her. He suffers her silence when he sees her in the neighbourhood. It is an excruciating silence in which she busies herself, looks past him and ignores anything he has to say to her. After a few weeks he begins to see her with the same boy – a wannabe New Jack Swing star, black with light skin and a Gumby style haircut.

He heads back to school in Liverpool during the autumn and doesn't return to London as frequently as he used to. He tells his mother, during a phone conversation, that over the break he will be doing extra hours at his job in the HMV store.

"I'm trying to save," he tells her, and only when he says it does it feel like some version of the truth.

4. The Saturday at the Theatre.

He is seated just a few rows from the stage, slightly left of centre. He tries, without success, to follow the onstage brothers as they come to terms with the suicide of their father. Natalie is playing the role of wife to one of the brothers, and he is preoccupied with her every gesture. He wonders how far she is from the person offstage. He wants her to fail at everything she does, just as much as he wants her to succeed. The only thing he is sure of is that after fifteen years, she still has the capacity to confuse him. The two tickets had arrived at his mother's address without warning, in an envelope marked with the Soho Theatre's branding. The note attached simply read:

Hope you can make it.

Best

Natalie Diamond.

He had felt compelled to go. He also felt compelled to bring his fiancée along.

After the show they mingle in the bar area, waiting to thank Natalie for the tickets. She is among the last of the performers to emerge. She's in sheer tights and red high heels, in full make-up. A black dress exposes her shoulders. She spots him, throws her arms up and screams in delight. He is thrown by how excited she is to see him. She hugs him and plants an air kiss on each cheek. He feels obliged to tell her the performance was amazing when really he found it tepid. Yetunde, his fiancée, steps forward and extends a hand.

"This is Yetunde," he says and he knows it will be a crime if he doesn't quickly add "my fiancée". He is not sure if Natalie is rattled or if he just wants to believe this is the case. They exchange brief histories, and are tortured by the silence that drops into their conversation until the actor who played the alcoholic brother steps into their circle with a group of grey-haired white men and begins introductions. Natalie comes alive again, raising her arms just as she did with him, hugging people, grasping hands, leaving traces of her red lipstick on cheeks.

When the opportune moment arrives, he thanks her for the tickets.

"Thank you for coming," she replies. Then she winks.

It stops him for a moment and, at first, he considers the thought that tonight's invitation might be part of some game she is playing with him. But then he acknowledges the truth: that wherever she is, she is always onstage and he is just a member of her audience.

5. The Saturday with the status update.

He slouches in his chair and runs his finger along the dining table's edges. His wife sits two and a half chairs away from him, sharing a seat with her girlfriend. Her laughter roars around the room, drowning out the *Bitches Brew* that dribbles from the iPod speaker system in the adjoining living room.

He has no comment to make on Miles Davis, the Iraq occupation or the 1999 bottle of port. He excuses himself, telling them he has to add some money to the parking meter, even though he knows there is credit left. He stands outside for a while and takes in the cool evening air; the road is quiet but cramped with parked cars and lit up by the streetlights. He thinks about his marriage – he always does when amongst his wife's social circle – and wonders whether love ever really exists in the way that it is supposed to, and if his parents and in-laws, as Nigerians, even believe in such an idea. He cares for Yetunde, appreciates her willingness to tolerate his fragility. He is grateful, but not content. Neither of them is content, but each is scared to give the other up. Then there is the endometriosis Yetunde has struggled with. He sympathises with her pain, but a truth he'll never admit to is that the absence of kids is a relief. He suspects that while Yetunde feels the loss of being unable to have children, she does not regret being unable to have his children.

He takes out his phone and checks his Facebook account. He browses Natalie Diamond's profile page, a habitual preoccupation. She has been his virtual "friend" for a couple of years, every now and then giving a thumbs-up to a statement or photo he has posted. Her profile photo has changed: a new professional headshot; her hair is big and bottle blonde. She has recent photos of herself in a police uniform – stills from a bit part she briefly played on TV.

He browses for a while, until a burst of laughter leaps from the house. It is his wife's unmistakable roar. He puts the phone away, knowing he has been gone too long and that they will argue later about his antisocial behaviour amongst her friends.

6. The Saturday with the clammy handshake.

He walks towards where he parked his car, making his way through the Aylesbury Estate. The playground is abandoned; teenagers race by on their long-boards; a homeless man rifles through the rubbish bags at the foot of the chute. Then there is a woman in the parking area, loading boxes into the back of a minivan.

His nerves race like he is fourteen again.

He makes his way across the forecourt towards her, rehearsing his words. Natalie is different. The changes he'd watched evolve online are amplified to the naked eye. The extensions in her hair are huge – thick sweeping curls that fall to her shoulders. She wears a tan shearling coat with a matching pair of UGG boots.

She stiffens as he nears, but then she recognises him and allows her shoulders to slump once more.

"Well, well," she says as he draws close, "all my cobwebs tumblin' out the woodwork today."

"Natalie…" he says, and as they hug he takes her in at close range: the fake tan that runs from her neck down; the hot pink cheeks, eyebrows thin and dark and pronounced. He feels the need to say something worthwhile, something significant. But nothing comes to him.

"Shit, it's been ages. What are you doing 'ere?" she asks, as they break apart.

"I was passing through – from my parents."

"Oh my word! It's been so long since I've seen 'em. How's your dad?"

"Facing retirement with dignity," he replies. "Now the two of them are talking about returning to Nigeria. How are yours doing?" He gestures towards the building's stairwell but she shakes her head and tells him her mother died four years ago and she hasn't spoken to her dad in over fifteen years.

"I didn't know they weren't together."

"They split up the year we – you – went to university."

"I'm sorry," he says.

She chuckles. "You sorry? What you sorry for?"

"I'm sorry about everything."

"We were kids."

"I'm sorry about your dad."

"My mum?"

He shakes his head. "No. Your dad."

Her smiles falls away. "What do you mean?" she says.

"It doesn't matter."

"No," she replies, "say what you mean."

"I'm sorry. I shouldn't have said anything."

"You keep saying you're sorry. Say what you mean."

"I didn't do anything about him."

"You didn't do anything about him? What was there to do? What was there to do about him?"

A middle-aged man, heavy-set and balding, waddles over towards them. He wears an oversized elderflower coloured suit over a white polo shirt. "We all set?" he enquires.

"My dad didn't do anything," she says.

"Alright?" the man asks.

"Sorry, Scott, this is Ade an old school friend. Ade, this is Scott, my husband."

"Ade," he says and shakes the man's hand. His palm feels clammy. Husband. He rolls the word around in his head. Scott is everything he would not have expected her to want.

"Ade and I grew up here, Scott," she says. "We would spend every Saturday together. He was my best friend." Her smile is tight and her words are hesitant.

He doesn't want to look at her, or to remember her like this.

"I should be going," he says and throws a thumb over his shoulder.

"Yes," she says. "I understand. It was good to run into you though."

He walks a few metres before she calls out his name. He turns to face her. "Have a great birthday," she says. "Isn't it your birthday in a couple days?"

"Yes. I'm surprised you remembered. After all these years, Natalie."

He turns again to walk away.

"Natalie?"

Scott is confused, both by her questioning her own name and the weight of her tone.

He stops. This time he makes his way back towards them. He places an index finger on her nose and presses gently. "Black," he says. "Black. Black. Black."

He'll leave it for her to explain it all to Scott.

JUDITH BRYAN

RANDALL & SONS

Randall was napping in the back of the mini-van, squashed between the window and another man's broad shoulders. The man was a Foreign. He smelled of spice and fruit, a comforting smell that infused Randall's half-dream: Janice in a big kitchen, stirring pots; the boys sitting around a table, all of them laughing. Then the man nudged him awake.

The van was pulling up outside Legacy Village. Randall peered out of the window. Tower One loomed above them – the perspex balconies and beige cladding made almost beautiful by a pink sunrise. Forty-eight storeys. His back ached in anticipation of the day's work. It would be the usual: two men per ten storeys and the toppers got whatever was left, sometimes as few as three floors. It was only fair: the electricity was off, the lifts out of order. Less fair was that the boss got to sit on his arse in the mini-van, playing *Viral Vengeance Five* or whatever the hell he did while the rest of them worked.

Randall closed his eyes again. He listened as the boss called the pairs: a lullaby of foreign names, incomprehensible, barely pronounceable.

"Randall. Biggs."

He opened his eyes with a start. From two seats ahead, he saw a young lad nod at him, jaws moving mechanically around a wad of gum. An obvious work-scheme recruit, he was all knobbly joints, not a muscle in sight. Randall groaned. He *would* get the one Englishman. Randall preferred Foreigns. They were strong and silent.

"Boss, give us a break."

But the boss said the others were needed for higher up. Randall was a fat bastard and the kid was a kid: they could do one to ten and thank him for the favour.

Randall said, "What use is he if we find Squatters or Ferals?"

Biggs's pale eyes blinked furiously under the brim of his hard hat.

The boss shrugged. "Got your tasers, ain't you? Got your phone?"

Grumbling, Randall collected a kit bag: gloves, crowbars, tasers, e-pad and some cans of spray paint. With a jerk of his head, he led the way into Tower One. Oil-sheened puddles lay in the reception area. Electrical cabling spilled like entrails across the floor.

Straight off, Biggs began to gab. About *Serial Killer Eight*, what level he'd reached and what you had to do to get there. His voice scratched and scrabbled against the concrete walls. Randall made himself count to ten. He knew the lad was spooked. The job *was* spooky the first few times, especially with the distant noise of the other pairs echoing in the stairwell, as though the building was still occupied. Which was always a possibility.

The tenants from Legacy Village had been moved to Jubilee Skyway, and the tenants from Jubilee Skyway had gone to Olympic Reach. Sometimes people clung on. Sometimes, in the weeks between emptying an estate and finishing the refurbishment, Squatters and Ferals got in. It made the job interesting, in a funny kind of way, never knowing what you'd find.

Outside the door of the first unit, Randall made Biggs shut up and listen. He showed him how to clip his taser on one side of his tool belt and the crowbar on the other. "We," he explained, "are the second wave. Police are the first wave; they clear the tenants. Second wave clears the shit the tenants leave behind."

The work had got easier over the years. People kept most of their stuff now, however ramshackle. Still, there was the odd mattress, general litter, electrical items. Bash them up, dump them down the rubbish chutes. Sign off on the unit, job done.

Biggs said, "What's the third wave, then?"

"Builders, decorators, proper skilled people. Don't worry about them. All you need to know is B.D.S: Bash, Dump, Sign-off."

Biggs nodded. "Bash, Dump, Sign-off."

"Use your crowbar and your boots." Randall rocked on his heels. He was beginning to enjoy himself, telling Biggs the ins and outs. "It's why they give us steel toecaps: good for bashing things."

He opened the door into an hexagonal kitchen-living room. Doors to the bathroom, bedrooms and balcony lay on every side of the central space. From the units above came the heavy footsteps of the other pairs, the boom and creak of other chutes.

"Welcome to contemporary, open-plan living."

He said it with a sneer but he'd wanted a place like this once – back when he and Janice lived at her mum's. They had a toddler already and Janice was pregnant again. Legacy, Jubilee, Olympic – they were all brand new. But she said the flats weren't worth the cardboard they were built with. Open-plan living? What about privacy, she said, and the cooking smells? What about the kids playing near the hot oven? We'll get a microwave, he'd told her, or eat out.

"What about Squatters?" Biggs was looking around, chewing hard enough to crack teeth.

"You understand the classifications, right? Squatters are the big ones, the little bastards are Ferals?"

Biggs nodded. Randall tapped his tool belt. "Hardly get any Squatters since the tasers. Word gets around. One shot usually does it."

"If it doesn't?"

"We call for back-up."

Biggs leaned in so close, Randall could smell the minty gum and, under that, the yoghurty taint of the boy's breakfast. "What about Ferals?"

"Tasers. One shot."

Biggs blinked. Randall could guess what he was thinking: *They're just kids.* It wasn't his fault; he was young and ignorant. When he'd been on the rough end of a Feral gang a few times, he would know better. To Randall's mind, the classification hadn't gone far enough. Ferals were vermin and people should have a right to get rid of vermin.

"My Dad says they're just kids and if people didn't abandon their kids –"

"On this job, I'm your dad, right? And I'm telling you: if my kids turned Feral, I wouldn't wait for a change in the law. I'd cull 'em myself."

They set to work reducing discarded items to manageable chunks, going back and forth to the chutes. Biggs was subdued. They worked quickly, quietly, communicating in grunts and gestures, like with the Foreigns. When the unit was clear, Randall recorded it on the e-pad. He let Biggs make the mark for the third wave – a red cross on the front door. That seemed to cheer up the lad – shaking the spray can so the ball-bearing rattled, then making a big, sweeping X with a little flourish at the end. Randall noticed how he gripped his lower lip between his teeth. He was reminded of his youngest manoeuvring a tight curve on *Junior Joy Rider*.

They cleared the first, the second, the third floor and started on the fourth. Got a nice rhythm going. Randall decided he was good at showing kids the ropes. He thought he might ask the boss to pair him with a work-schemer again. It would be practice for when he had his own little company: Randall and Sons. One of these days, when his boys were old enough…

Then, in the last unit on the fourth floor, they found a fox trapped under a fallen cupboard. Half starved, it barely lifted its snout. Biggs crouched, wondering aloud what to do. Randall nudged him aside and stamped on the creature's head. Blood and brains burst under his boot. He wiped the mess off with some newspaper.

"B.D.S.," he said.

After that, Biggs started gabbing again. Faster, louder, higher, about everything and nothing. By the eighth floor, Randall's temples throbbed. Biggs was ahead of him on the stairs because Randall had slowed right down. The relentless flights were taking their toll as much as the lad's ceaseless wittering. So he threw his crowbar out of the window. He shouted, "Oi! Hold up, I've lost me bar."

He sent Biggs after it, expecting the same fuss his sons made if asked to do the littlest thing. But Biggs went scampering down the stairs, eager as a puppy after a stick. The clang of the metal entrance doors echoed through the block as he went out. Randall rested on the stairs, then decided to keep going; work in peace, for a bit. He wasn't scared of Squatters or Ferals. He had the boots and the taser.

The next unit reeked of urine and stale alcohol – a foul, animal smell. The main room was in semi-darkness, the glass balcony doors obscured by tattered blinds. Randall crossed the floor in three strides and pulled the blinds away. They fell to the floor in a clatter of perished plastic. Something made a reactive skitter. He turned, watching and listening for rats, but the place was suddenly, heavily silent.

Stomping through the unit, he collected the rubbish. The last room, the small bedroom, was bolted. Inside he found a mattress on the floor and another door propped on its side under the window. He kicked the door over. A sudden stink rose up. Someone had gouged a hole, right through the wall. Stooping, eyes watering, Randall peered out. He could see part of the balcony that ran the width of the unit. It was piled with dog mess, mini mountain ranges of the stuff. The door had formed a kind of dog tunnel, to minimise draughts and odours. Smelled like the bloody dog had died out there. He tried to see through to the end of the balcony but to do so he'd have to stick his head out of the hole. Easier to open the double doors in the living room. He stood, shaking his head and dusting down his knees. What kind of person made a hole in their own home – in a *child's* room – because they were too lazy to take the dog for a walk?

"Raze the lot," he muttered. "Tenants and all."

That's what Janice used to say, about Olympic Reach. He had paid the deposit without telling her, certain she'd love it once they actually moved in. The flat was smart, modern; two good-sized bedrooms and a small one. They could try for a girl, if she wanted. Look out the window, he'd told her, look at those amazing views.

She said, you can't live on a view, and she'd been right. The units in the Celebration Estates shared the same cellular layout. It amplified noise. On every floor, a dozen neighbours and all the neighbours above and below. They heard every footstep, every whisper, every scream. He couldn't have known; the second wave wasn't invented yet. Eventually, the government decided to refurbish each estate on a six year cycle. That was how long it took the tenants to wreck the place. They turned on each other much sooner. It was like a virus, the violence, and he'd caught it. Bashed Janice around a few times. More than a few. She dumped him, of course.

He needed his crowbar for the door, so Randall turned to the mattress. It was too big to fit the chute in one go but, if he pulled out the wadding, he could do it in stages. With the first handful, he felt something small and hard. He opened his fist. Nestled in the fibres was a toy, the jointed kind that came with Kiddy Meals. This one was a snarling, red warrior. Pull the bits in the right way and it turned into a truck. His boys had collected them.

He bounced the little plastic figure on his palm. He remembered weekend after strained weekend, eating King Burgers while the boys chomped Kiddy Meals and fiddled with plastic tat. No wonder the stairs were a challenge these days. The boys had probably turned into lard-buckets too. He did a quick mental calculation. They'd be about Biggs's age, give or take a year. Free to come and find him, if they wanted.

He put the toy in his pocket, then dragged the mattress into the main room, away from the smell, and continued the laborious job of tearing it apart.

He was about to make his second trip to the chute – wondering what was taking Biggs so flaming long – when something jumped him from behind. Sharp teeth bit into his neck; claws scratched at his back, scrabbling for purchase. He reached round; his hand met fur. He managed to drag the thing off him, heard it yelp, saw its face: bloodied maw of a mouth, bright eyes – unnaturally bright, like a fox caught in headlamps. Tears.

With a shout of horror, Randall flung the creature away. It flew through the air, hit the wall, landed and crumpled on the floor. For a minute, he sat staring at the little brown body. Saw a shaggy mane of... not fur, hair. Not haunches and forepaws but arms, legs, hands, feet. A child. A little boy.

Randall jumped up, kicked open the balcony doors, stumbled out, his feet sliding in shit. Nauseated, he leant over the balcony, pulling in air. Far below the ground spiralled, rising and receding. He saw the mini-van, tiny as a Kiddy Meal toy. Tasted salt and iron in his mouth, knew that tears as well as blood wet his face.

He never wept. Not even when he went to collect the boys one Friday night and found another family living in the flat. Janice had wanted a divorce but he'd refused. By cutting off the maintenance, he'd thought he could force her to let him come home. Instead, he had forced them onto the streets.

Pain twisted in his gut. If… if they were Squatters… Worse, if his boys had become Ferals… He rubbed his eyes with his fists, rubbing away thoughts of his own failures. Janice threw *him* out. Whatever had happened, it was down to her.

Randall took off a glove and put his hand to his neck, where the child had bitten him. The wound was not deep. He would live. Behind him, he heard a thin complaint. He turned. The child was trying to get up, bony arms pushing against the floor and his shaggy head flopping about. He watched it, trying to understand what it was. Not a Feral, not like the ones he was used to. Which came first, he wondered, the damage or being locked in that room? He wondered how long ago its parents had left and how long it had been alone. Something had nurtured it or it would have died. Maybe a dog or a fox. Maybe the fox he'd killed downstairs.

He remembered the rest of that night after he had lost his family. He was driving back to his hostel when he hit something. Such a bang. He had stopped in a screech of brakes, heart thumping as he stared wildly into the cone of light cast by his headlamps. Eventually, he got out. He saw a fox, dragging itself towards the pavement. Multicoloured entrails stretched like electrical cabling in its wake.

Without warning, he had vomited. But then the confusion he had felt since Janice dumped him cleared. With patient steps, he had followed the fox as it made its awful, slow escape. At last it reached the kerb, lay down and gave a long exhalation. Its entire body rose and fell as it gathered itself for the next big effort.

He stood straight and stared out across the city. It was late morning. Wind whistled around the tower, rattling the balconies. Sunlight glittered off buildings and along the thin beaten silver of the river. Everything was so tiny, so innocent and bright, all the squalor invisible to the eye. He was not a curious person by nature, never had been. It was better that way. Better not to look too close. Trying to understand others brought you up against their stink. Trying to understand yourself was worse, but at least he now realised his mistake. He should have signed-off on Janice and the boys. Once a thing was ruined, it was the only way. He stamped his foot, testing the force he would need. Then, fumbling for his taser, he turned.

Biggs was in the main room, kneeling beside the child. He was stroking its hair. The little creature lay calmed under his hand, its breathing slowed and its eyes shut. Biggs looked up, his face luminous with pity.

"He was crawling out of there." He indicated the bedroom. "He's hurt. What should we do?"

Follow the drill, Randall wanted to say, what else? But the words wouldn't come. He looked at Biggs and Biggs looked back at him, and he watched Biggs' face change as the lad realised what Randall planned. The shame he felt confused him; he had just got everything straight in his head. He took a conciliatory step forward. He wanted Biggs to understand.

"Vermin," he began, then Biggs was up, red-faced, snarling. He moved between Randall and the child, fists raised. A toy warrior: *Urban Hero One*. Half laughing, half afraid, Randall backed off. His feet slipped and he reached for the balcony rail, missed, flailed, smashed against the perspex, smashed through.

Falling, he thought: Bash, Dump, Sign-off, Bash, Dump...

Eight storeys. His back ached in anticipation.

BERNARDINE EVARISTO

YORUBA MAN WALKING

When Lawani sailed up the coast of Cornwall in the *Alexandria*, a
ship laden with crude rubber, cocoa beans and sheets of copper,
it was the middle of August and for a country with an international reputation for damp and rain, he was surprised to see palm
trees.

As soon as the iron chain of the anchor grated against the rail,
he watched as revenue men in black bowlers stormed the ship,
demanding to be let down into the hold. It was all show; the ship
had stopped off at a Cornish cove the night before, swaying lamps
on the rocks guiding it in.

He had already said a discreet farewell to the seamen who
mattered: Cai Lin, Mustafa, Nicolai. Fellow nomads who spent
so long away from loved ones and home that eventually no one
was loved and nowhere was home.

This was the problem, along with the swollen oceans that had
once lured him from his village by the lagoon. Lately he'd been
having nightmares of sinking down to the seabed and being eaten
by deep-sea creatures with pincers. He'd had enough, too, of the
fleeting pleasures of the world's ports: Shanghai, Bombay, Mar-
seilles, Rio de Janeiro, Antananarivo; of women who trapped a
man inside the vice of their thighs and for a few moments ecstasy,
and a few day's pay, left him burning with the clap.

He watched the well-dressed passengers disembark first, those
whose vomit he cleared up when they got soused on highballs in
the saloon and who played Speculation with the captain in his

quarters, sometimes managing to lose a fortune in between countries. Captain Bartlett would be furious when he discovered that his most steadfast bosun had vanished.

Lawani walked down the gangplank that swayed and squeaked with every step.

Peddlers selling sausages, fresh fruit, bread, halfpenny ices and tin mugs of tea were hawking their wares in between the carts and carriages clogging up the dock.

He stocked up and, knapsack over his shoulder, slipped out of the port like a shadow.

He passed fishermen's cottages with nets strewn outside and an old woman bent double by a large basket of crabs strapped to her forehead. He walked uphill past Maddox & Sons Cobblers, Mrs Penberthy's Haberdashers, Killigrew Butchers, Vellanoweth & Andrewartha Undertakers.

He could read and write, of that he was proud. As a boy he'd learnt from officers who missed their sons.

Lawani was at least a head taller than the tallest of these people and as bald as a ball of pitch. He wore a blue pea jacket, thick calicos hoisted by braces and a wide, brown leather belt. On his head was a straw hat. On his feet were black, steel-toed boots. In his peripheral vision he registered people slowing down, stopping. To settle his gaze upon someone might invite confrontation. He scowled, even though no rifles were being levelled at him as had once happened in the Florida Keys for being in the wrong part of town, when he was too young to understand that he was not as free there as elsewhere.

Over the years he had learned to become metal, inside and out.

This too was the problem.

When three dainty young women appeared in his path, carrying cream parasols, he could not help but stare. They wore hats embellished with ostrich feathers and dresses of dazzling blues, greens and yellows that showed off waists the size of his thighs. A mirage of exotic Amazonian birds fluttering down the streets of this plain little town.

They saw him, and froze. He stood aside as they passed by in a supercilious huff that could fell a man's pride. Then the youngest one, the loveliest one, the comeliest one, looked back and proffered a sneaky, moist-lipped smile. As her little booted feet proceeded down the street, he was sure he noticed a slight sashay.

He threw his hat into the air and caught it on one finger, spinning it as a fairground juggler does plates.

Yes, in this country he would find himself a wife.

He noticed a dirt slope between two houses and beyond that, woods. He followed the encrusted footprints of donkey hooves. At the top he turned back and surveyed the red-tiled roofs of the town in the valley behind him. Beyond it lay the harbour and the *Alexandria* that had become a floating prison. He waited for the pull, the drag that always made him return to whatever seafaring vessel he was manning. He waited and waited. Perhaps the cord had finally been cut. He turned his back and walked through a small woodland and eventually came upon a wide open space that did not move beneath his feet.

The more he walked, the more he felt a new weightlessness.

Alone for miles, he took off his boots and tied them to his knapsack. He stripped down to his waist and felt his feet make contact with earth, pebble, grass. He walked until the sky began to darken and then found a spot between rocks to rest for the night. He opened his knapsack and spread out his possessions: pears, apples, bread, a wheel of Port Salut cheese, strips of dried pork, salted fish, a jar of pickled onions, Garibaldi biscuits, China tea, billycan, matches, dentifrice, a leather water bottle, a shirt, a brown woollen blanket, three guineas in promissory notes, a pouch full of shillings and crowns – and the dagger he had purchased in Aden, its horn handle studded with coins.

That night, for the first time in a long time, he slept peacefully under an open sky.

In the morning he made tea in his billycan.

Sometimes he avoided people for days – no villages, no hamlets, no farms. Only when it rained did he take refuge in barns, arriving late, leaving early. When the weather began to cool, he gathered brushwood to get a fire going before dark. He began to sleep fully-clothed and awoke to powdery grey ashes and a dew-soaked blanket. His breath became visible in the damp morning air. He drank tea. Blew rings of vapour. Setting off again, he was a caped crusader as the blanket billowed behind him, drying out.

He made a staff from a fallen limb of oak tree and etched animals onto it: pangolin, bee-eater, fish eagles, queleas, bongo, aardvark. His father had been a carver of animals and gods; he had learned at his knee. His mother had died giving birth to him. His father had died of the fever. His first job was aboard the *Madeira* when he was still a boy, a reformed Portuguese slaver that used to trade with Brazil until it was arrested by a Royal Navy blockade.

With no duties to perform, no storms to handle, no people and demands to clutter up his mind and time, he came to enjoy, for the first time in his life, a solitude, a quietude.

When he came upon remote hamlets and villages, children would sometimes chase him, throw stones, call names and scamper, as if he'd bother to chase and beat the little rascals.

When he entered smoky taverns, their earthen floors congealed with mud, sawdust and ash, the room stopped mid-sentence. He bowed low and said Good Evening, smiling broadly to disarm himself.

He ordered a tankard of porter, found a stool and waited for the locals to approach, which they always did, with the caution of bear tamers.

He had long ago learnt that he could be whomsoever he wanted in strange lands.

They gathered around and he regaled them with tall tales: how he'd made a fortune smuggling whale sperm oil into Lisbon but lost it playing Chinese Checkers in San Francisco. How he'd fought for Sitting Bull against General Custer at Little Big Horn or narrowly avoided being decapitated by head hunters in Papua New Guinea. Sometimes he was the deposed King of Tonga, other times a great African chief. He *had* seen a public beheading of a pirate in Shanghai. Afterwards the executioner swung his victim's pony-tailed head around like a ball on a chain while the crowd rushed forwards to dip their hands in the blood leaking from the headless torso. He *had* witnessed a stampede of sabre-brandishing Ottomans in the town of Chania on Crete during one of their Christian uprisings.

His audience, many of whom had never ventured more than

ten miles, north, west, south or east, found their world made larger, and for that they were grateful. He was rewarded with drinks paid for and a roof to sleep under for the night.

★

For three days it had been raining and he had been crossing the wide, empty countryside he now knew they called the moors without passing a single settlement or stream. His boots squelched as he walked because he had sunk knee-deep into a marsh. Eventually he came upon an orchard and farmstead just as the skies were clearing. Girls wearing wide-brimmed hats and dirty white smocks were collecting apples in baskets. Boys wearing cloth caps and knickerbockers were running around waving rattles to scare off the birds. A cry went up. A dog came barking towards him. A man appeared, a Mr Renfrey Kelynack, he quickly learned, who was surprised but not alarmed. As a young man he had been sent to work with his uncle as a hammer-man in an iron foundry in the town of Deptford in Kent. He had known men who looked like this one.

By evening Lawani was seated in a thatched longhouse so old it was sinking at one end.

Mrs Kelynack had washed his boots and stuffed them with oats to dry out. She looked young enough to be her whiskery husband's daughter.

A long oak table with grooves. Flagstone floor with a layer of grit brought in from outside. Lime-washed walls perspiring with condensation. Heavy iron pans hanging from metal hooks. The granite hearth was the stove.

Mr Kelynack said prayers and Lawani dropped his head out of politeness.

Potato and rabbit stew, barley bread, baked figgy plum pudding on a pewter platter sprinkled with white sugar. All washed down with ginger beer. No ship's weevils. No mould. No grey rubbery mash to digest or disgusting watery gruel. It was the finest meal he had ever eaten but when he thanked the cook her eyes slid away from his.

The children sat there mesmerised and barely spoke. The youngest, Tamsin, sat at his side and began crawling her fingers slowly towards him like a spider. He pretended not to notice. Emboldened, she stroked his hand.

Stop it, Tamsin, said her father.

Mr Kelynack told his guest that his farm was called Bos Eldon and when his father and older brothers died one harsh winter, he had been urged to come home from London.

The farm consisted of Little Lower, Middle Lower and Great Lower Fields. They kept sheep, grew corn, barley and red wheat. A tin seam in the valley was useless, its yield negligible, unlike the mines further north that were big business in these parts. See here, an acre can produce six Cornish bushels of wheat in a good year, that being equivalent to three English bushels. Red wheat weighs more than white so it makes sense to grow that. Oxen are cheaper than mules, which is why I plough with one. Mr Kelynack inhaled on his pipe when he spoke and wheezed like rusty bellows when he did not.

I could do with some help here.

His guest nodded.

And where in the Americas are you from?

His guest laughed. I come from a village called Lagos.

I see, and where is that?

Yorubaland.

Where be Yoboyobolanda? Tamsin piped up. Can we go there?

It is far, far away.

He did not want to speak of the place of his birth. As a boy at sea, it was too painful to remember his home and the father he had lost.

Instead, he described the Victoria Falls in Matabeleland. How it dropped over three hundred feet into the great Zambezi River so that when he peered over the edge he saw only hissing froth that nonetheless left him drenched.

The local people call the Falls *Mosi-oa-tunya*: Smoke that Thunders.

Mossy tinna, Tamsin repeated.

He told them about the sadhus, holy men of India – their hair and faces white with chalk. How some of them walked for so many years with an arm raised in the air that it eventually shrivelled and hung limp. How some of them lay on a bed of nails.

S'dangris, Tamsin said.

It is indeed.

Her hand was a little ball in his so long he ceased to notice it. When he finally opened his palm to release her she jumped onto his lap and squeezed her arms around his neck, almost choking him. Everyone laughed. He carefully unclasped her limbs with fingers that individually were almost as big. She looked up at him and he took in her broad forehead, freckles, stubby nose, hair tangled as a bird's nest. He put a hand on her shoulder but felt awkward. He had never held a child before. She smelt so different, fresh; this was a child's smell. She was so tiny, so light, so warm in his lap that he realised in that moment, that if anyone had dared hurt her he would have laid him out flat and stamped on his skull until he heard it crack.

Later, when he was scrubbing himself down by the well with a bucket of water, and the children were in bed and Mr Kelynack had taken the dog off to rally the sheep, he glanced up to see Mrs Kelynack had come around the side of the house.

She was devouring him.

When he hid his shame, she did not look away.

He slept in the eaves, on a boarded platform above the larder, and was, thankfully, untroubled.

He liked his host. Mr Kelynack was a kind man.

Before dawn, Lawani was crossing Middle Lower Field, his staff pounding the ground. Three days later he had climbed to the brow of a hill and saw a strange squatter encampment below. Calwatha Mine. Chimneys blackened the sky, there was a steam-driven pump, shaft openings, pulleys, awnings, giant wheels, timber scaffolding, shuttle tracks, mountains of sludge, granite slopes and a patchwork of cabins and long huts.

The manager, a Mr Yelland, looked grateful to see him enter the camp looking for work. His men had been migrating in droves to the silver mines of Mexico and the copper mines of Tasmania. He told Lawani he'd been a supervisor at a diamond mine in Kimberly in the Cape Colony until his wife insisted they raise their children in God's Own Country, not some hellhole a million miles from civilisation.

You'll start at seven and finish at seven with half an hour for lunch, Monday to Saturday. Payday is Friday. You can park yourself in the dorm for now. No point shilly-shallying, we'll get you down below tomorrow.

A jacket, a bowler hat with a clay candle holder attached, a pot of resin to harden the hat, candles, a pick, shovel, wedges, hammers – all signed for and to be deducted. These people made sure a man spent his wages before he'd even earned it.

Lawani explored the mine; after so long in the wilderness, its clangs and clunks, grinds and growls jolted his senses. He was shocked to come across women, bal maidens, buttoned up with thick skirts and white hats with long side flaps. As spallers, they were crushing rocks of tin ore with sledgehammers on the mine's dressing floors. Look at them – strong women who wouldn't be afraid of him. He was right. As he edged closer, they sized him up. Some were too old to bear children, others were too brazen, except for one of the younger ones, who refused to look up even when he stared so hard she must have felt it.

He pretended to leave and then quickly spun round to catch her – flushed, curious, excited.

The next morning, he descended five hundred fathoms down a shaft in a cage. Deep inside the earth the tunnels were propped up by forests of sliced tree trunks. It was torrid, wet, suffocating. What was he doing here? Had he lost his mind? He would soon move on.

At twenty-six, Tommy Penhaligon had already spent thirteen years underground. He showed Lawani how to chip away at rock while high up a ladder that itself was perched on a thin ledge. It's one of the most dangerous jobs in the world, Tommy warned. Yeh, really dangerous. If you slip you'll be done for, Larry.

Lunchtime they stopped for crowsts, which was dinner and dessert in one: pies stuffed with meat, turnip, potato and onion on one side; jam on the other. He was instructed to hold the pie by the crust or else get tin poisoning from his hands and then to safely discard it down the shaft for the rats.

After work, Lawani joined Tommy and the other men in the winks, the drinking hole next to the mine, where they all got plastered on porter and ribbed him.

If it weren't for those teeth of yours you'd be invisible in the dark, Larry. Down the hatch in one. Huzzah!

The men quickly slurred their speech and stumbled about. Lawani did not. This was his new self. After twenty years at sea he'd witnessed how drink was the seaman's prolonged suicide. With fresh water in short supply, he and his fellow seafarers got drunk on Sudden Death and Knock-me-Down, liquor that turned the mildest of men into monsters when the fermented stew rose to the surface in a bile of bloated emotion. Nine months earlier he himself had stabbed a man in Mogadishu. For what? For tripping over his stool.

As the men got rowdier, he looked around and saw her enter, the bal maiden, with the other young women, the unmarried ones, the available ones, he was told. Her hair was thickly curled and piled up, her scrubbed-clean face was peachy, her pale eyes mocking with good humour when he sidled up to her.

We was just saying, you're as black as night alright, Sambo.

You can call me Lawani... or Larry or... Mr... Bartlett. And you?

Miss Morwenna Warmington to those who's asking, and mine's a tankard of porter.

Every evening he escorted her to the cob cottage where she boarded in the village. She brought out a new lightness in him. For the first time in his adult life he felt playful.

Miss Warmington, allow me to accompany you home.

It seems you've already made up my mind.

Miss Warmington, allow me to carry your basket.

I can manage full well on my own, thank you.

Miss Warmington, your eyes are like glittering stars.

No, Mr Bartlett, my eyes are like dung and dust and dirt and full of weariness.

She stopped outside the front door to the lodgings she shared with the other girls. He lingered.

Go now, take my lantern for the long walk back across the fields. Give it me on the morrow.

I bid you goodnight, Miss Warmington.

I bid you too goodnight, Mr Bartlett.

Sundays he courted her around the village green. She said she didn't care what anyone said or thought. He was different to all the other men around, which is what she wanted. Her mother had died after breathing in the soot of the calciner for twelve years. Her father copped it from bronchitis after twenty-three years down the pit, and not a day too soon, she said, and then mumbled, I was his daughter, not his wife.

Her three younger brothers had escaped the pits and gone to sea.

Every Sunday Lawani accompanied her to Zion, the Methodist chapel in the village.

Later, out on the moors, he lay her down upon his brown blanket. She took his weight. She was as comfy and fleshy as he had dreamed. He could not believe his luck. Nor could she. After the life she'd had, she deserved a man so special.

Am I your first, he asked. Yes, she replied, turning away and studying the sky.

Afterwards, they were happiest lying in each others' silence.

As a spaller, Morwenna stood outside in all weathers on the cobbled dressing floor of the mine and smashed a three pound sledgehammer onto the great rocks of tin ore that were brought up from underground. Every time she raised her weary arms and brought the hammer down on rock, she imagined it was the head of her father. His brains were the wet, reddish waste that made the dressing floor so slippery and dangerous.

Lawani promised her a better life, away from this dump. Perhaps London. Let's see.

That spring they celebrated becoming man and wife with a mug of porter and a turnip pie. Lawani decided to build a temporary home on the moors, near enough to the mine but far enough away to be undisturbed. He'd had enough of overpriced lodgings crowded with fellow miners and their families all sleeping together in a poorly-ventilated, disease-breeding room. It was no better than below decks and he was already coughing up the dust of the mines.

He needed air. He was beginning to miss the sea.

Our very own makeshift castle on the moors, he told her, built out of stone.

She rolled her eyes. You're mad you are.

He slapped her cheek.

Well, it's the stupidest thing I ever heard.

He slapped her again, harder.

She refused to cry.

I am your husband.

She handed over her wages every Friday.

For a nominal sum he was allowed to build their temporary home near the remains of a granite pit. On three sides was woodland that would protect it from wind. A river ran nearby. He lugged stones from the pit and slotted them into each other. It took weeks before the construction was solid and not prone to collapse. Peat filled in the gaps. Coal sacks were further insulation. For flooring, he laid planks of wood. The finished hut was large enough to sleep two people and high enough for smoke to circulate.

They had a straw mattress on a wooden pallet, a large tin chest containing provisions such as bowls, beakers, pans, billycan, rags, blankets and a bar of Pears Translucent Soap, the one luxury Morwenna asked for and got. For fuel they dug up peat in summer and stacked it like stones to dry out for the coming winter.

In the desert kingdoms they use camel dung, he said.

What's a camel, my lovely?

In summer they stripped off their garments and washed in the river. He lathered her with her precious, expensive soap. He unclipped her thick hair so that it fell in an abundance of twirling curls to her waist. She wrapped her legs around him and leaned back in the water so that her hair spread out like the fronds of water plants. Her breasts were wet, shiny mounds. He plunged and plunged until he softened.

When she grew round, he was convinced it was a boy.

Finally, he was going to be more than himself.

She began to weep in the mornings and he didn't understand why she was so unhappy with him. She said she wasn't. He said she was. Women are strange creatures. Why be so sad when you should be overjoyed? I'm not sad, she cried.

As her stomach grew, so did his dreams. New wife, first child, new life, new beginnings, new country. As soon as my son is old enough, I will take you both back to Yorubaland. I am ready.

Where is it, she asked. Why did they have to go somewhere so far away? You promised London. *Everyone*'s heard of London.

Then she held her tongue.

Mr Yelland allowed her to do lighter duties at the mine for less pay, sweeping up the waste, a job usually reserved for old women and children.

After twelve hours in the dungeon of the worm-infested earth, he enjoyed the walk home with Morwenna through the spongy tussocks of rushes. When the wind blew he imagined he was sailing between continents.

As autumn arrived the moor became soaked in a grey mist and the tors looked like ancient burial mounds. Early morning, the ground was covered with dew. As winter arrived the tall grasses blanched, dehydrated and died. When mist thickened into fog he imagined he could see the long-necked prehistoric creatures in the Natural History Museum in London, just like the ones he'd seen in photographs in the *Gazette*. Or he imagined mountainous blocks of ice against the chilly blue sky. He had once worked a whaler called the *Svend* under Captain Johannsen. The Arctic tundra – a bleakness greater than his own.

He wanted to tell Morwenna all of this.

He awoke early and sat outside wrapped in a blanket to drink tea in the chilly air.

As she grew larger, their walk to the mine slowed down; he helped her along. She was finding it difficult and had to rest often. If she didn't work until the baby dropped, she'd have no jobs to return to. She complained and wanted to move nearer town. She wanted to live in a proper house even if it was crowded and stank. She wanted to be warm at night. She wanted to be away from the wind that howled outside their hut.

That day they arrived at work and she headed, as usual, for the dressing floor while Lawani went down the shaft with Tommy to the spot they'd left the day before.

They stood on the narrow ledge as the tunnel echoed with the sound of a hundred men and boys banging chisels into rock.

Lawani always heard it as a kind of drumming. It made him homesick for a place he could barely remember. Sweat poured down him. He dreamt of roaming the open oceans. How free he had been, changing ships at whim, seeing so much of a world most people cannot even begin to imagine. He thought of the son who would soon be born.

He would name him in honour of his father: Babatunde – Father Returns.

The next morning Morwenna gave birth prematurely in a hut at the mine. It was the shock, they said. Along with everyone else, she had been up all night. The women delivered her a son but Morwenna did not name him until three months after his birth. In hope. In desperation. In disbelief.

At the time of Frank's birth, his father was trapped five hundred fathoms under the ground. Lawani was not dead at this point. At first the men and boys charged around the tunnel hoping to find a way out. But they were sealed in. They extinguished their lamps to preserve breath until, in the blackness, one by one they slumped.

Of the two of them, Tommy went first. His congested lungs were weak anyway. Lawani sat still, conserving himself in case someone broke through and air – clean, crisp, salty, invigorating sea air – rushed in to save them.

★

Epilogue

Frankie, as he was known, grew up in the last two decades of the nineteenth century. In the village and surrounding areas everyone knew him as the son of the African who had been buried in one of the worst mine disasters of the 1880s. About his father, his mother told him little. He'd once been a seaman. He'd come from foreign. Look at this dagger, Frankie. I don't have no photographs.

When the boy was teased by the other children, his mother reassured him. Don't listen to them, Frankie. You're the same as everyone else. Nay, you're better you are. You're special.

He wanted to believe her.

Morwenna remained a bal maiden until the day she died at the age of thirty-five. She was a known drinker and brawler.

A year after her death, young Frankie went to the city of Exeter in search of a job that did not involve burying himself alive down a mine or coughing up blood all day until he died before his time. In Exeter, he was mistaken for a Neapolitan or one of the Portuguese seamen who came up the canal into town. He passed and married a grocer's daughter, Emily. They had five sons, who looked as pale as their mother.

He never spoke of the father he had never known and he died before his own children were old enough to be curious enough to ask.

His sons fought in the First World War, except the youngest, Walter, who came of age in the interwar years and was posted as an administrator in the Colony and Protectorate of Nigeria. He was stationed in the city of Lagos, as a representative of his people, the British.

He died at home in the town of Exmouth in 1979, surrounded by his children and grandchildren.

Among his possessions was the family heirloom displayed in a cabinet in his living room: a dagger with a horn handle studded with coins.

Origins unknown.

CONTRIBUTORS

Monica Ali is the author of four books, *Brick Lane, Alentejo Blue, In the Kitchen,* and *Untold Story.*

Dinesh Angelo Allirajah (6.05.1967-9.12.2014) described his writing as "narratives of the unnoticed moment", giving airplay to what happens "on the edge of the crowd", where characters have to suddenly reassess who and what they are. He worked tirelessly as a believer in the liberating and educating power of the arts. The loss of his voice humorous, witty and deeply moving leaves a silence. He is survived by his mother, Evelyn, and older brother Duleep, his fiancée Vic, two sons Bruno and Rufus, and their mother, his ex-partner Jo.

Muli Amaye teaches creative writing at Soran University. She has short stories published in *Moving Worlds Journal* (2009, 2012). Her MA novel was long listed for the SI Leeds Prize 2014. She's currently editing her PhD novel for publication.

Lynne E. Blackwood's poetry, short stories and plays are inspired by a life rich in emotions, events and stories from people around the world she has met, influenced by her Anglo-Indian heritage sensitivities.

Judith Bryan's work includes *Bernard and the Cloth Monkey* (Saga Prize 1997), and *A Cold Snap/Keeping Mum* (second, Alfred Fagon Award 2008; Brockley Jack Studio Theatre, 2011). She lectures in Creative Writing at the University of Roehampton.

Nana-Essi Casely-Hayford is a storyteller and writer who works as a part-time Visiting Lecturer at one of the Leeds City Colleges, where she facilitates Positive Wellbeing & Expressive Visualisation Through the Arts.

Jacqueline Clarke was born in Bristol to parents of Jamaican heritage. She has a short story in *Voice, Memory, Ashes* (Mango

Tree Press). She has written a novel, a play and is currently working on a film script.

Jacqueline Crooks is a Jamaican-born writer. She writes about Caribbean migration and subcultures. She has been published by *Granta, Virago* and *MsLexia*.

Fred D'Aguiar has published loads of books. His latest poetry collection is *The Rose of Toulouse* (Carcanet, 2013). His most recent novel is *Children of Paradise* (Granta, 2014).

Sylvia Dickinson's stories are influenced by her multi-cultural community of Cape Town. She lives near Chichester University, where she achieved an MA in Creative Writing. Her ambition is to publish a novel.

Bernardine Evaristo is an editor, critic, dramatist and the award-winning author of seven books of fiction and verse fiction including *Mr Loverman* (Penguin, 2013). She was awarded an MBE in 2009. www.bevaristo.com

Gaylene Gould's short stories have been published in various anthologies and she is completing her first novel which won the 2012 Commonword Diversity Prize. She is an artist coach and a broadcaster presenting regularly on BBC Radio 4.

Michelle Inniss was born in Liverpool to Trinidadian parents. She is studying for an MA in Creative Writing at Brunel University. She was a runner-up for The Decibel Prize and was shortlisted for The Fish Short Story Prize. Her first play, *She Called Me Mother*, was produced by Pitch Lake Productions.

Valda Jackson is an accomplished visual artist who writes fiction and non-fiction that expands the breadth of her narrative. Shortlisted for BBC Opening Lines 2015, Jamaican born, Jackson's public sculptures and paintings are exhibited internationally. www.valdajackson.com

Pete Kalu is a novelist. He has sung opera in German, been detained in Calabar, Nigeria, busked near Islamabad, Pakistan and felled trees in Canada. Some of this is untrue.

Patrice Lawrence is of Italian-Trinidadian heritage. She writes for adults and children and has been published by A & C Black, Scholastic, Pearsons and Hamish Hamilton. Her young adult novel, *Orangeboy*, is forthcoming (Hodder, 2016). http://patricelawrence.wordpress.com/.

Jennifer Nansubuga Makumbi is an Associate Lecturer at Lancaster University. Jennifer's novel, *Kintu,* won the Kwani Manuscript Project in 2013, published in 2014. "Let's Tell This Story Properly" won the Commonwealth Short Prize 2014.

Tariq Mehmood's novels include *Hand On The Sun*, *While There Is Light* and *You're Not Proper*. He co-directed the award-winning documentary *Injustice*. He teaches at the American University of Beirut, Lebanon.

Raman Mundair is the author of *Lovers, Liars, Conjurers and Thieves*, *A Choreographer's Cartography*, both poetry, and *The Algebra of Freedom* (a play). She edited *Incoming: Some Shetland Voices*. Raman was awarded a Leverhulme Artists Residency, a Robert Louis Stevenson award and is a nominee for the prestigious Rolex Mentor and Protégé Arts Initiative. shetlandamenity.org/the-artist

Sai Murray is a writer, spoken word artist, arts facilitator and graphic designer. His poetry collection *Ad-liberation* and the first part of his novel *Kill Myself Now* are published by Peepal Tree Press.

Chantal Oakes is a multimedia artist, an MA graduate in Fine Art, a regular contributor to academic, community and fictional publications, and is currently writing her first historical novel.

Karen Onojaife's work has been published in *Mslexia*, *Sable LitMag* and *Callaloo*. Her novel won second place and the Reader's Choice Award in the SI Leeds Literary Prize 2012. She is a VONA/Voices Fellow.

Koye Oyedeji is a writer and critic. His work has appeared in the anthologies, *IC3* and *The Fire People* and featured in *Wasafiri* and *Brand* magazines. He is a contributing editor for *SABLE Litmag*.

Louisa Adjoa Parker is of Ghanaian/English heritage. Her poetry collection, *Salt-sweat and Tears*, was published in 2007. Her work has appeared in *Wasafiri*, *The Forward Prize Collection*, *Envoi* and *Out of Bounds*.

Desiree Reynolds started her writing career as a freelance journalist for the *Jamaican Gleaner* in London. She is a broadcaster and creative writing workshop facilitator. Her debut novel is *Seduce* published by Peepal Tree Press.

Hana Riaz is the director of The Body Narratives, an organisation committed to the healing, reclamation and resilience found in Women of Colour's stories and work. She believes in the transformatory power of love.

Akila Richards is of German and Liberian heritage. Her poetry and fiction has been anthologised in *Red*, and *True Tales of Mixed Heritage Experience: The Map of Me,* and she co-edited *Ink On My Lips* by Waterloo Press.

Leone Ross is the author of critically-acclaimed novels *All The Blood Is Red* and *Orange Laughter*. Her speculative fiction and erotica has been widely anthologised. Ross is a senior lecturer in Creative Writing at Roehampton University, London. www.leoneross.com

Seni Seneviratne is a writer and creative artist of English/Sri Lankan heritage, who is widely published. Her latest collection is *The Heart of It* (Peepal Tree Press, 2012) www.seniseneviratne.com

Ayesha Siddiqi is based in London. She writes short stories and plays. She is also a PhD candidate in Comparative Literature at UCL.

Mahsuda Snaith is a writer of short stories, novels and plays. She was selected as a finalist for the *Mslexia* Novel Competition 2013 and won the Bristol Short Story Prize and the SI Leeds Literary Prize in 2014. www.mahsudasnaith.com.

ALSO FROM INSCRIBE/ PEEPAL TREE

RED
Edited by Kwame Dawes
ISBN: 9781845231293; pp. 252; pub. 2010; price: £9.99

"Perhaps the most significant thing to be said about *Red* is that the poets in this volume burst through any constraining label with writing that throbs and pulses and seeps and flows."
— Margaret Busby

Featuring:
John Agard, Patience Agbabi, Maya Chowdhry, Fred D'Aguiar, Bernardine Evaristo, Linton Kwesi Johnson, Jackie Kay, Roi Kwabena, John Lyons, Jack Mapanje, Raman Mundair, Daljit Nagra, Grace Nichols, Nii Ayikwei Parkes, Lemn Sissay, Dorothea Smartt, Gemma Weekes, Wangui Wa Goro and many more…

Red collects poems that engage "red", poems by Black British poets writing with the word "red" in mind – as a kind of leap-off point, a context, a germ – the way something small, minor, or grand might spur a poem. It offers the reader the freedom to come to whatever conclusions they want to about what writing as a poet who is also Black and British might mean.

The result is a book of poets ranging from well-established and published writers to first-time published poets. *Red* does find its usual associations with blood, violence, passion, and anger. Sometimes it is linked with sensuality and sexuality. But there are surprises, when red defines a memory or mood, the quality of light in a sky, the colour of skin, the sound of a song, and much, much more. The anthology, therefore, succeeds in producing poems that seem to be first about image, and only then about whatever else fascinates the poet.

In this sense, *Red* is a different kind of anthology of Black British writing, and the richness of the entries, the moods, the humour, the passion, the reflection, the confessional all confirm that Black British poetry is a lively and defining force in Britain today.

Find over 300 Caribbean and Black British titles on
www.peepaltreepress.com